RAVES FOR *ILLUSIONS*

"Janet Dailey's name is synonymous with romance. . . . *Illusions* . . . contains a twist at every turn."

—*Tulsa World*

"The perfect beach book."

—*Wichita Eagle*

"The perfect title for this story in which things may not be as they seem. . . . Enjoyable."

—*Knoxville News-Sentinel*

"Dailey is a smooth, experienced romance writer."

—*Arizona Daily Star*

"[Ms. Dailey] . . . has had ample practice in tugging at heart strings while creating suspense. It's a sure-fire combination."

—*Cape Codder*

"Janet Dailey's mastery of sweeping romance, divided loyalties, and searing passion has made her one of the bestselling authors of all time."

—*Lanier County* (GA) *News*

"A master storyteller of romantic tales, Dailey weaves all the 'musts' together to create the perfect love story."

—*Leisure* magazine

BOOKS BY JANET DAILEY

HarperChoice

JANET DAILEY

Illusions

HarperPaperbacks
A Division of HarperCollinsPublishers

🔥 **HarperPaperbacks**
A Division of HarperCollinsPublishers
10 East 53rd Street, New York, NY 10022-5299

This book contains an excerpt from *Calder Pride* by Janet Dailey. This excerpt has been set for this edition only and may not reflect the final content of the hardcover edition.

This is a work of fiction. The characters, incidents, and dialogues are products of the author's imagination and are not to be construed as real. Any resemblance to actual events or persons, living or dead, is entirely coincidental.

ISBN 0-06-109460-9

HarperCollins®, 🔥®, HarperChoice™, and HarperPaperbacks™ are trademarks of HarperCollins Publishers Inc.

Cover illustration © 1997 by Rick Johnson
Cover design by Gene Mydlowski

A hardcover edition of this book was published in 1997 by HarperCollins*Publishers*.

First HarperPaperbacks printing: August 1999

Printed in the United States of America

Visit HarperPaperbacks on the World Wide Web at
http://www.harpercollins.com

❖ 10 9 8 7 6 5 4 3 2 1

Illusions

PROLOGUE

*T*HAT BASTARD LUCAS WAYNE was going to pay for this, Rina Cole vowed for the hundredth time, seething with suppressed fury. Again she caressed the solid shape of the pearl-handled .38 tucked inside her purse and smiled, visualizing the look on his face when she pointed it at him.

Would he recognize it as the gun he had given her? She hoped so. She dearly hoped so. It was one of the few gifts Luke had given her and now she was going to give it back—not the gun itself, only the bullets.

With the malicious smile still curving her lushly full lips, Rina looked out the tinted passenger window as the sleek limousine glided along Madison Avenue, venturing into Manhattan's fashionable Upper East Side. All was quiet, even properly sedate, at this late time of night. Streetlights intermittently broke the darkness and traffic was light, almost nonexistent, except for a cruising cab and a rumbling garbage truck.

The limousine slowed to make its turn onto 76th Street. Rina leaned forward, tensing in a mix of rage and eagerness at the familiar sight of the Carlyle Hotel, where Lucas Wayne was staying in his usual suite.

But he wasn't alone. He had a young blonde actress-bitch with him, some no-name little slut who had a small role in the movie he was currently filming in New York. Did he really think she wouldn't find out about it, that she wouldn't be told?

She wasn't some nobody to be treated like dirt. She was Rina Cole. She'd had a wall of platinum albums before he ever made his first record. She was the one who gave him his first big break in films. The bastard owed her!

The limousine rolled to a stop. The liveried doorman stepped up and opened the passenger door. Recognition flashed instantly in his face when he saw her.

"Welcome back to the Carlyle, Miss Cole."

His greeting went unanswered as she swept past him without a glance, her fingers curled around the clasp of her purse, the gun heavy inside the bag. Intent on her mission, she walked straight to the front door, her stiletto heels clicking on the concrete.

Inside the hotel, she crossed the dimmed lobby with its antiques and tapestries and went directly to the bank of elevators. No one stopped her. She was Rina Cole.

The muted wail of a siren somewhere in the city filtered into the suite's darkened bedroom. A moment ago the sound would have mingled with panting moans. Now it joined with a long, blissful sigh that came from the naked blonde lying next to Lucas Wayne in the king-size bed. She turned toward him, rolling onto her right side and sliding a hand over his bare chest.

"Luke baby, you are incredible," she said in a purring voice. "I feel just like some deliciously naughty rag doll. You do know how to rob a girl of her inhibitions."

"It was good, wasn't it?" Lucas Wayne responded with a half-smile that masked his lack of interest in the requisite small talk afterwards.

Personally, he preferred sex to be hot, wet, and wild. But two out of three wasn't bad, especially when the blonde had made an adequate attempt to fake the third, even if it had been far from an Academy Award–winning performance.

"You meanie, how can you say that?" She gave him a playful slap in protest. "It was better than good and you know it."

He chuckled and half-lifted, half-dragged her on top of him. "For a rehearsal, it was."

"Rehearsal?" she murmured lazily. "Now, there's an idea."

"Isn't it?" Lucas smiled and ran his hands up her rib cage to cup the underswell of her heavy breasts. Even though everything else about the blonde was petite, she had big, round breasts. Implants, he suspected, but it was too dark to detect the telltale scars.

No lights burned in the bedroom, but the door stood slightly open, letting in the light from the lamp he always left burning in the suite's living room. The dim glow from it played over the white mountains of her breasts, catching the sweat-slick sheen of her skin and capturing his attention.

"Are you sure you're *up* to it?" she teased, and rubbed against him in blatant invitation.

"Keep wiggling like that and it will be lights, camera, action—take two."

"Maybe this time"—reaching back, she stroked a hand over his hardening shaft—"I should take it from the top."

"By all means," he agreed.

In the next second, the bedroom door flew the rest of the way open, flooding the room with light. Startled, Lucas pushed the blonde off him and raised up on one elbow to stare at the figure silhouetted by the light.

"Who the hell—" he began, but one look at that wild mane of hair and the length of leg visible beneath the thigh-high skirt and Lucas Wayne knew who it was even before that famous smoky voice shouted at him.

"You dirty rotten bastard! I loved you and you used me!" Light glinted on metal, revealing the gun in her hand. It was aimed at him! "Never again, Luke. Never again."

The bitch was going to shoot. Fear surged through him in a rush of adrenaline. Without thinking, he grabbed the pillow under his head and threw it. The gun went off with a loud, explosive *pop* and the blonde screamed as Lucas launched himself at Rina Cole.

Before she could bring the gun to bear again, he seized her wrist and ripped the gun from her grasp, tossing it to a far, dark corner of the room. Immediately Rina hurled herself at him, kicking and clawing and shouting obscenities.

Lucas struggled to subdue her and yelled at the still screaming blonde, "Get the phone and call for some damned help!"

Making little mewling sounds of terror, the blonde scrambled across the bed, dragging the top sheet with her and clutching it close in a vain attempt to hide her nakedness. With shaking hands she picked up the receiver and punched the operator's number.

"Help! We need help," she sobbed into the phone. "Please. She tried to kill us!"

ONE

THE RINGING OF THE TELEPHONE jarred Delaney Wescott from a sound sleep. She rolled onto her side, dragging the top sheet with her and pulling it loose from the bottom of the bed in the process. Lifting her head, she looked around the darkened bedroom of her six-room bungalow, tucked away in one of the many canyons in the Santa Monica mountains above Malibu.

A breeze spiced with sagey aromas stirred the white eyelet curtains at the window. Beyond, a full moon, silvery and bright, spilled its light through the glass panes onto the bed and the tangle of sleep-ravaged covers—not that Delaney considered herself a restless sleeper, merely an aggressive one.

The phone rang again, its shrill sound in the night's silence like an electric shock to her nerves. As she grabbed for the receiver, the ninety-pound German shepherd sleeping beside her in the queen-size bed growled a warning.

"Shut up, Ollie. I'm not even close to rolling on you," she muttered, then collapsed back against the pillow with phone in hand and scraped her long, tousled hair away from an ear. "Hello."

"Delaney? This is Arthur," came the clipped reply.

"Arthur." She instantly recognized the resonant baritone voice of former colleague and contract lawyer Arthur Golden. Like her, he had left the firm of Jennings, Wade & Minski several years earlier, forming his own management company that catered to the needs of the entertainment business. Delaney peered sideways at the digital clock on the nightstand. "Arthur, it's three in the morning."

"It's six A.M. in New York—which isn't exactly my favorite hour either, but crises seldom come at convenient times. All hell has broken loose out here, Delaney. I need you in New York as fast as you can get here."

Arthur Golden had long been known for being as dramatic as some of the actors he represented. He could turn mismatched socks into a crisis. But there was an edge to his voice, an underlying agitation that prompted Delaney to take him seriously. "What happened, Arthur?"

"What happened?!! I'll tell you what happened—that crazy, washed-up she-cat tried to kill my star client!"

To Delaney's knowledge, there was only one person in the roster of entertainers Arthur Golden represented who could currently be labeled a star and that was sexthrob—as Robin Leach loved to call him—Lucas Wayne. Five short years ago, rock singer Lucas Wayne had burst onto the music scene with a megahit called "Darlin', Do Me." Two platinum albums had followed in quick succession. Then, three years ago, the sexy, dark-haired, dark-eyed Lucas had made the rare transition from the music scene to the silver screen when he co-starred in a major theatrical release with fading pop singer and actress Rina Cole, with whom he was reputedly having an affair. His second major release had been another smash this past Christmas, putting to rest any doubts that the first had been a fluke. Delaney vaguely remembered reading in the trades that Lucas Wayne was currently in New York wrapping up filming on his third movie.

"Am I right to assume you're referring to Lucas Wayne?" she asked.

"Yes."

"Tell me what happened, Arthur." Fully awake now, Delaney sat up, automatically hauling the top sheet with her and tucking it under her arms. She slept in the buff. Not for any sybaritic reason. The habit had simpler origins—she went to bed to sleep, not to wrestle with a nightgown that bunched around her middle, or a pair of pajamas that twisted and cut off her circulation. "*Who* tried to kill him? When? Where?"

"It was Rina Cole." He spoke the name slowly, with venom. "She tricked her way into his suite at the Carlyle tonight and caught Lucas in bed with a blonde—an actress named Tory or Victoria something." He paused a split second. "Dear God, Delaney, every time I think what might have happened if Lucas hadn't seen the gun before she started blasting away—" He stopped again, a faint, incredulous laugh filling the void. "He threw a pillow at her, Delaney. A pillow!"

"Arthur, was anyone hurt?"

"Fortunately, no. Lucas has some scratches on his arm where Rina clawed him when he wrestled the gun away from her, but that's all."

"I assume the police were called in?"

"The hotel security phoned them. There wasn't any choice. She was berserk—screaming, kicking, clawing when the police took her away. In my opinion, they should have hauled her off to Bellevue in a straitjacket, but they took her to the station and booked her instead. She's charged with disturbing the peace, assault with a deadly weapon, two counts of attempted murder, and resisting arrest. But we both know that one phone call and she's out on bond. There is no way they will keep Rina Cole locked up."

Delaney silently agreed with him. "Where is Lucas now?"

"With me, at my place on Park Avenue. Both he and the blonde actress. I thought it was wiser than leaving them at the Carlyle."

"True." She rubbed the base of her left temple, feeling the tension start to build. "What's the security setup in your building, Arthur?"

"Two guards on duty at the desk downstairs. After midnight, the elevators are key-operated. There's a cop outside the apartment door, but they won't keep one there indefinitely. You know how the police are."

"I know." She nodded. "That's why I'm in business."

"And that's why I called you," he retorted. "Get out here—fast!"

"I'll be on the next plane." She made a mental list of the things she would have to do between the time she hung up the phone and the time she stepped onto the plane—and tried not to think of the night's sleep lost.

"I'm counting on that."

"In the meantime, get an injunction filed against Rina Cole and have a restraining order issued," she said. In itself, that wouldn't be much protection, but it would provide a legal basis for keeping her away from Lucas. After Arthur agreed with the plan, she told him good-bye and pushed the receiver back onto its cradle.

Delaney switched on the lamp and picked up the phone again, her fingers rapidly tapping out the memorized number. After the seventh ring, a grumpy male voice came on the line, demanding, "Yeah, what do you want?"

Delaney smiled. "Up and at 'em, tiger. We're on our way to the Big Apple."

There were two short beats of silence. "Is that you, Delaney?" came the accusation, followed by a groan. "Do you know it's twenty minutes after three?"

"Sorry to interrupt your beauty sleep, Riley—"

"I can tell you're all broken up over it." Riley Owens smothered a yawn. "So tell me, what's in the Big Apple other than a lot of worms?"

Delaney filled him in.

"Rina Cole?" The sleep was gone from his voice. "You aren't getting us hooked in on some publicity stunt, are you?"

The thought had occurred to her, but only briefly. "Arthur was scared. And he's a lawyer, not an actor, Riley. The attempt was for real."

"All lawyers are actors," he said, his tone changing as his professional side asserted itself.

"If I remember right, one of the airlines has a flight to New York leaving around five or six in the morning. Make reservations for us."

"First class?"

"In your dreams, Riley," she mocked dryly.

"It was worth a try."

"After you've made the reservations, call me back and give me the flight and time, then pull together all the facts you can on Rina Cole."

"No problem. I know everything there is to know about the lady. I even have all her albums."

"You do?" Delaney couldn't conceal her surprise. She had never guessed that Riley's taste in music ran to Rina Cole. It was easier to picture him listening to jazz, something mellow and laid-back, interspersed with unexpected riffs.

"I do. I'm one of her biggest fans."

"Really? I never knew you liked her."

"There's a lot of things about me you don't know, Delaney," Riley said. "For instance, I don't care for New York in July. How about you?"

"Don't tell me you're an old song buff, too?"

"Fred Astaire."

Delaney shook her head. "I'll meet you at the airport."

Riley chuckled over the phone. "See you there."

As she hung up, Delaney glanced at the big moon outside the bedroom window. Sighing, she turned to the black and tan German shepherd lying on the other side of the bed. "Full moons always bring out the crazies, don't they, Ollie?"

The dog opened one eye, peered at her briefly, then closed it again—playing his usual role as the strong, silent type.

Delaney threw back the top sheet, untangled a leg and climbed out of bed, all five feet nine inches of her.

She padded directly to the private bath off her bedroom.

At the sink, she turned on the faucets and loaded her toothbrush with mint-flavored toothpaste. As she lifted the brush to her mouth, she looked at the mirror in front of her and paused, momentarily distracted by the reflected image of her square face angling to the point of her chin and framed by a mass of long, curly hair the color of dark European chocolate. Her eyes were equally dark and thickly lashed. At thirty-four, Delaney was a very attractive woman, but the overall impression was one of strength and confidence rather than beauty.

Unbidden came the memory of a man quietly and astutely remarking, "I'll bet you intimidate the hell out of most men you meet."

Just for a moment the pain returned, the twisting ache of remembered love and deception.

With an effort, Delaney pushed the memory to the back of her mind and proceeded to vigorously brush her teeth. A quick shower followed. After toweling dry, Delaney donned a short terry robe and belted it before returning to the bedroom.

Once there, Delaney went straight to the closet and retrieved the overnight bag that she kept—with typical organization—prepacked with toiletries and cosmetics, a kimono-style robe, and a complete change of clothes.

Next she pushed aside the white jacket and loose-fitting trousers of her karate clothes and reached for the emergency medical kit, equipped with the usual assortment of bandages, sterile dressings, gauze, aspirins, universal poison antidotes, and surgical tape, as well as wire ladder-splints, an oropharyngeal airway set, and a refillable oxygen cylinder complete with regulator and mask.

When the German shepherd heard the familiar *thump* of the bag hitting the floor, he lifted his head, then slowly got to his feet and climbed off the bed, taking a long stretch in the process. He ambled over to the edge of the Oriental rug and sat down to watch her pack.

"It's old hat to you, isn't it, Ollie?" she said and turned back to the closet.

Her clothes were grouped in coordinating outfits of three, complete with all accessories. Neatness and order had long been the rule in her life—with heavy emphasis on order.

Delaney lifted the gray tweed overnight bag from its perch on the top shelf, unhooked the matching garment bag from the clothes rod, and spread both on the bed.

From the closet, she selected a set of coordinating outfits with their accessories attached to the hangers, arranged them in the garment bag, and added a spare pair of flat shoes. A raincoat joined them before she zipped the bag shut. To the overnight bag, she included two more sets of lingerie, then walked back to the nightstand and opened its second drawer.

There, snugly nestled in its high-ride, pancake-style hip holster, was her .38 Special with a three-inch barrel and fixed sights.

She took the pair out of the drawer, removed the small handgun from its holster, and unloaded it. Delaney was careful not to recall the one and only time duty had forced her to fire it—or the look on the face of the fatally wounded man. Seven months and the images of that moment still sprang at her from out of the night.

The incident had made her eighty times more wary, determined that never again would she find herself in a situation where circumstances demanded the use of a deadly weapon.

After placing the bullets from the gun into an opened box of shells, Delaney took the gun, holster, and shell box and laid them all on top of the folded clothes in her overnight bag, then snapped the lid shut and locked it.

Thirty minutes—and a phone call from Riley with the information on the airline and flight number—later, Delaney turned the German shepherd loose in his outdoor run and stowed her bags in the car.

In L.A., you are what you drive. Delaney slid behind the wheel of her ten-year-old silver Mercedes, a present she'd bought herself six years ago when her morale had badly needed a boost. Far in the distance glittered the lights of the Malibu beach community, and farther still the halo of the City of Angels.

Overhead the full moon reminded Delaney of a giant Klieg light in the sky, lighting up the night. She reversed the car out of the drive and headed toward the Pacific Coast Highway. From there, it was virtually a straight shot to the airport.

Forty minutes before the flight's scheduled departure time, Delaney walked into the terminal at LAX, carrying her overnight case and garment bag. Pausing, she scanned the handful of travelers lined up in front of the airline's ticket counter. Riley Owens wasn't among them.

A second later she spotted him lounging against a nearby wall. He saw her and picked up a travel-worn suitcase and a brown leather briefcase at his feet, then came to meet her.

Dressed in a dark gray suit and paisley tie, Riley Owens looked like the average business traveler—except he was better-looking. His face was strong and lean, with skin bronzed by the sun and showing the attractive creases of maturity. He had thick chestnut hair that carelessly defied order and his eyes were that deep shade of cobalt blue—eyes that could glint with laughter one moment and turn to bits of sharp steel the next. The latter was the only thing about him that remotely suggested he had spent ten years in the Secret Service before the tedium of the job got to him.

As Riley had once put it, he had grown tired of living a life of utter boredom waiting for that one instant of action. Riley Owens was definitely a man you wanted at your side in a tight situation, but he cloaked that intelligence and strength with a pose of indolence and humor.

Watching his approach, Delaney considered all the roles Riley had filled in her life—client, mentor, big brother, and best friend. But never a lover. She suddenly wondered why.

He stopped in front of her, his blue eyes nearly on the same level as her dark ones, assessing her in that same thorough way they always did—a way that was sometimes disconcerting. But not this time. "I didn't bother to pick up the tickets." His glance flicked to her overnight bag. "I assumed you'd be carrying."

"I am," she replied, confirming the existence of the handgun in her suitcase.

"Then let's get in line so we can declare our weapons and check them through to New York with our bags." He nodded his head at the queue of people at the ticket counter.

"Right." Delaney led the way.

• • •

Fifteen minutes later, they proceeded through the security check with tickets and boarding passes in hand. Riley headed straight for their gate area.

"Do you want to go over this info on Rina Cole before we board?" Riley set his briefcase on the floor.

"No, we'll do it in flight. I have to call Dad." Delaney draped her garment bag over the back of a seat. "Watch this for me," she said, and went to a nearby bank of pay phones.

On the heels of the second ring, a magnificent male voice came on the line, booming a hearty, "Good morning."

Delaney instantly smiled, visualizing her father on the other end, a tall and tanned, vigorous man of seventy-seven, his dark hair now totally silver-white—except for the sides and his thick eyebrows that his hairdresser kept dyed a dark gray. She had inherited her height and strong, square features from her father; however, on him, the angles seemed much harsher. The effect was faintly forbidding, although a kinder, more compassionate man she'd never known.

"Hello, Dad."

"Delaney," he responded with delight. "You're up and about early this morning."

"So are you."

"I have an early call at the studio. Just a small role. Six lines. I play a drug lord in another one of those forgettable blood-and-guts movies they're churning out these days. It's typecasting, of course, but I've always been an actor people love to hate," Gordon Wescott declared without a trace of regret at the fifty years he'd spent playing bad guys, most notably a nine-year stint as a villain on a daytime soap before his character was finally killed off—but not before he managed to get Delaney through law school. "I even persuaded the casting director to give Eddi a bit part, too."

"Eddi" was Edwina Taylor-Brown, the fifty-two-year-old actress he'd been—to use his phrase—keeping company with. "That's good news, Dad."

"It certainly is. That gives Eddi another eighteen months of union health insurance coverage. It's too damned hard for some of our older members to get a job acting. And too damned hard for them to get affordable coverage elsewhere."

"I know." Delaney paused as the boarding call for her flight came over the public address system.

"What was that, Delaney? Where are you?"

"At the airport on my way to New York. I called to see if you would house-sit for me until I get back."

"Be glad to, but that dog is not sleeping in bed with me."

"Why?" She smiled. "Ollie doesn't snore."

"Ollie." He snorted. "What kind of name is that to give a dog? A German shepherd should be called King or Baron, something with dignity."

"Ollie suits him just fine."

"What's taking you to New York?" he asked, then guessed, "You were called on this Lucas Wayne thing."

"That's right. How did you know?"

"I heard about it on the radio while I was shaving," he answered. "So you're going to be protecting Lucas Wayne. You know, there's a horde of women who wouldn't mind guarding his body—or jumping his bones, for that matter," he added, and chuckled. "Eddi tells me he's irresistible to the opposite sex."

"He's a client, Dad. There's no way I'm going to get

personally involved with him. I made that mistake once and look what happened." Her hand tightened its grip on the receiver, her eyes closing on the old memory resurrected by his inadvertent remark.

"Delaney, I'm sorry. I didn't mean—"

"I know you didn't."

He sighed into the phone. "I really put my foot in my mouth with that one. I guess I was just trying to sound like a father and wish you could meet Mr. Right."

"I know," Delaney replied with forced lightness. "Unfortunately, so far I've managed to meet only Mr. Rude, Mr. Cheap, and Mr. Married."

"Yes." There was something sad and thoughtful in his tone. "It was too bad about Mr. Married. I liked him."

Delaney deliberately changed the subject. "Look, Dad, if you're going to invite your cronies over for one of your infamous poker games, tell them not to put their cigars out in my houseplants. The African violets are still trying to recover from the last one."

"I promise I'll have plenty of ashtrays on the table."

The airport's public address system carried the boarding announcement again. "They're calling my flight, Dad. I have to go. Remember—if you forget your key, there's a spare one in Ollie's doghouse."

"I'll remember. Fly safe."

"I will. Love you, Dad."

"I love you too, precious."

She hung up and let her hand linger an instant longer on the phone, almost in a caress, then headed back to the gate area.

Riley saw her coming and stood up, noting a dozen details about her—everything from the cool, competent image she projected to the soft, full curve of her lips that made him think of other things. The slash of her cheek-bones was strong, reminding him of an Irish maiden.

As always, he experienced that familiar jolt of desire when he saw her. He had known Delaney for somewhere around seven years now—and had been in love with her for six of them. Problem was, she had no clue how he felt. It had been a case of bad timing. Right about when he had realized he'd fallen in love with her, Delaney had been falling for someone else.

Her affair had ended abruptly, leaving her with a broken heart and a lot of scars. Riley had been waiting ever since for them to heal.

Patience had always been one of his strong suits. He needed it in his line of work. But Delaney was testing it.

Not a sign of it showed when Delaney reached him.

"How's your dad?" he asked.

"Fine." She scooped her garment bag off the chair back. "Ready to board?"

Riley reached inside his jacket and pulled out his boarding pass and ticket. "New York here we come."

TWO

DELANEY PROCEEDED DOWN THE plane's aisle until she reached their seats. "You can have the window, Riley." She stepped out of the way to let him in first, set her purse on the aisle seat and shoved her garment bag in the overhead rack, then took off the jacket to her pin-striped jumpsuit and laid it on top.

"I like the jumpsuit," he remarked when she sat down.

She gave him a sidelong look of surprise. "A compliment from you? That's rare."

He grinned. "I know. I amaze myself sometimes."

"I'm sure you do." She opened her purse and took out her ringed notebook.

"But I still like the jumpsuit."

"With the long flight, it seemed a good choice for

traveling," Delaney said absently. She noticed one of the flight attendants coming down the aisle toward them. "Excuse me. Is there a phone up front I can use when we're airborne?"

"Yes, ma'am."

"Thanks."

Riley frowned. "Who do you have to call now?"

"Glenda. But not until she gets into the office at nine. I need to let her know where we'll be—and have her cancel any appointments for the next few days." Delaney took out her pen and started jotting reminders down in the notebook. "I need to talk to Frank, too. He'll have to handle the Margo Connors obscene phone calls."

"His wife will love you," Riley murmured.

"She already does," Delaney countered.

"Ha," he replied.

"She does. She brings homemade chocolate chip cookies for me all the time."

"She's only doing it to fatten you up. Not that I blame her," he added slyly. "You could stand a little meat on those bones."

Delaney looked up from her notebook. "I should have accepted the compliment on the jumpsuit and kept my mouth shut, shouldn't I?"

"Probably." He grinned.

"I don't know why I get myself into these conversations with you." She shook her head and closed the notebook. "Let's go over that information you brought on Rina Cole."

Still smiling, Riley opened his briefcase and handed her a folder from it. Delaney flipped it open. "A glossy?"

She stared in surprise at the publicity photo on top. "How did you get your hands on this?" When she picked it up, she noticed the barely legible handwriting in silver ink near the bottom left-hand corner. She held it closer, trying to decipher what it said. "'To Riley.'" She turned to him. "This is your photo of her."

"I went to one of her concerts a few years back. She autographed it for me." When Delaney continued to regard him with curious surprise, he reminded her, "I told you I was a fan."

"I know, but I'm having trouble picturing you asking for an autograph." She looked back at the photo and deciphered the rest of the writing. "'To Riley, *Love*, Rina Cole.'" She looked at him askance. "I hope you told her not to use the word 'love' when she signed her pictures."

It was one of the first things they told celebrity clients, to forestall the possibility that some mentally ill fan might take the message literally.

"Actually—no."

"Riley," she said in disbelief.

"Why should I? She signed the photo to me."

"That doesn't matter. She—"

"But I did tell her road manager," Riley added, then chided when she failed to smile. "Lighten up, Delaney. You're getting too serious."

"I have a feeling one of us better be." She directed her attention again to the photo.

"Have it your way," Riley said and began briefing her on Rina Cole. "There seems to be some dispute about her age. One source says thirty-eight, another that she's forty-three. My money's on the forty-three. But whatever she is, she's still one sexy, bodacious woman."

Delaney noticed he didn't say beautiful. But then,

the face in the glossy photograph wasn't beautiful. Her nose was too long and her gray-green eyes were set too close together. Her lips were wide and full, almost obscenely so, and her wild mane of frosted hair was moussed into an exaggerated wind-blown style. No, Rina Cole wasn't beautiful. She was the personification of sex. She exuded it, flaunted it—openly, outrageously.

The impact was powerful. Delaney could feel her own skin heating just looking at the photo. She remembered watching Rina Cole's performance on a television special a few years ago—the way she'd strutted across the stage, dressed in an outfit that was more bare than there, and the stance she'd assumed, her hips thrust forward and her shoulders thrown back, her legs spread in a blatant invitation, her breasts pushed out. Sweat had poured down her face, but it had only made her look hot—in the sexual sense of the word. And there'd been a knowing look in her eyes that said, Anything goes, and a taunting smile on her lips—the tip of her tongue just out of sight—that added, What are you waiting for? Let's do it.

Rina Cole wasn't like any other female star, past or present. She didn't have the voluptuousness and sly insinuation of Mae West, the mocking raunchiness of Cher, the blonde naughty-girl coolness of Madonna, or the mischievous abandon of Tina Turner. She wasn't any of those . . . or even all of those. She was only sex, in its most unadulterated form.

Yet there was no sense of something bad or evil. Delaney frowned at the discovery, realizing she'd expected to feel that. But sex was part of the natural order of things, and Nature was amoral. There was no good or bad, merely the laws of survival, and sex was essential for the survival of any species.

"Well preserved, isn't she?" Riley remarked.

She replied, without thinking, "Sex is ageless."

Before Riley could comment, a flight attendant came by and reminded them to fasten their seat belts. Delaney glanced out the window and saw that the airliner had already pushed back from the jetway. She set the folder aside long enough to buckle up, then opened it again, this time shifting the photo to the back of the bio material.

"What about her background? Her childhood?" she asked, tuning out the flight attendant's instructions on seat belts, exits, flotation cushions, and oxygen masks as the jet lumbered along the taxiway.

"Poor. St. Louis poor. And if you've never seen the poor sections of St. Louis, you can't know what I mean."

"I suppose not," Delaney agreed absently.

"She doesn't talk much about her early years, but I know she was born Irene Jackson—out of wedlock, with a welfare mother who had a succession of live-in boyfriends." Riley raised his voice to make himself heard above the whine of the jet engines as the plane began its takeoff roll. "You get the feeling there was some abuse there. Physical . . . maybe sexual, I don't know. Anyway, she ran away when she was fifteen and hooked up with a rock musician by the name of Jason Cole."

"She married him, didn't she?" Delaney frowned.

Riley nodded. "A week after she signed her first recording contract, she legally became Mrs. Rina Cole. Seven months later she had the number-one song on the rock charts."

"According to this, she's been married four times."

"That's right. And all of her exes have been in the business on one side or the other."

"No children?" She glanced at Riley for confirmation.

"None. Whether that's by choice, only she can say. Whenever she's been asked, she's always claimed that her career was her baby. I tend to believe that."

"If she's like most stage performers, she needs the adulation of an audience." Frequently the desire to be nurtured was stronger than the desire to nurture.

"She *feeds* on it," Riley agreed.

"She rode high for a long time," Delaney recalled.

"Almost ten years. Then she became a fixture in the Vegas showrooms, singing her old hits to a bunch of conventioneers from Dubuque and Omaha. That's when that Broadway producer came to her. *Saints and Sinners* played to standing-room-only crowds from the first night it opened. A year later, she was on her way to Hollywood to make the movie version of it. And she went from fading rock star to rising movie star. A whole host of films came after that. Most of them forgettable, unfortunately."

"Particularly that fiasco she wrote, produced, directed, and starred in, *Hot Rhythms.* What was it—three years it took to make it and how many millions of dollars over budget did it end up going?"

Riley was quick to come to the star's defense. "She wanted control and tried to do too much. I still think that's when she got hooked on pills."

"She has a drug problem?" Delaney frowned and quickly skimmed through the material again. "There's nothing about that in here."

"Wasn't there?" He leaned closer to read over her shoulder, the fragrance of his aftershave reaching her, an intoxicating blend of island spices with a hint of

musk. "There should be. It was about five years ago—
she was living on uppers and downers and dabbling in
coke. She checked herself into the Betty Ford clinic and
got herself cleaned up. I admit it didn't make much of a
splash at the time, but—"

"Do you think she might be back on drugs?"
Delaney wondered.

"You mean because of this shooting thing with
Lucas Wayne?" he clarified, then shook his head. "I
don't know. It does read like a Frankie-and-Johnny scenario—he was her man and he done her wrong. A crime
of passion."

"In this case, someone else's passion." Delaney
thought of the blonde who'd been in bed with Lucas
Wayne. "Anyway, that seems too pat. There's nothing
here to suggest—"

"—a history of violence," Riley offered.

"Yes."

"There's a whole string of paparazzi with broken
cameras who might disagree with you on that—along
with an agent who sported a black eye for about a week,
and an ex-husband who refused to file charges after he'd
made the mistake of hitting her and wound up with a
pair of scissors in his arm."

"None of that's in here, Riley." Delaney protested,
irritated that he'd left out such important details.

"I didn't have time to put everything down. This
was a bit of a rushed thing," he reminded her calmly.

"But information like that should have headed the
sheet. What if you'd been in an accident on your way to
the airport?"

"If I'd been hurt, you wouldn't have any of this
information. You'd be flying totally blind. But . . . you're

right. That information should have been at the top of the sheet," he admitted, and treated her to a crooked grin. "It looks like the pupil is finally instructing the teacher in procedure."

Her anger dissipated in a rush, leaving a strange awkwardness in its place. "Maybe . . . it's because I had a good teacher," Delaney replied, oddly self-conscious.

Riley cupped a hand to his ear and tipped his head closer. "A little louder please."

"I said I had a good teacher. The best. But don't let that go to your head." She smiled, comfortable with him again.

"That's what I thought you said." He smiled back. "Now—what else do you want to know about Rina Cole?"

"What else *should* I know?" Delaney countered.

"Just the obvious—Lucas Wayne is on his way up; Rina's on her way down. She's more to be pitied than feared."

She nodded in silent agreement. "There's always something sad about desperation and the things it can drive a person to do, isn't there?"

"I guess so," he said, then paused. "I have to be honest, Delaney. In my opinion, we're flying to New York to guard the barn after the horse has been stolen."

"You're probably right, although I don't think we can fairly assess the situation until we get there. But while we're being honest, let's not overlook a few basic facts: one, Lucas Wayne is the hottest name in the country right now; two, this attempt on his life will make the spotlight on him that much brighter; and three, by providing security for him—whether it's strictly needed or not—Wescott and Associates will be in the backwash of that spotlight. That's advertising you can't buy."

"The company had plenty of free advertising seven months ago when it made all the headlines after the shooting."

Aware that Riley was watching for her reaction, Delaney avoided eye contact even as images of the incident flashed through her mind. "That isn't the kind of publicity I want."

"No one does," he agreed. "How are you with it?"

"Much better." She managed a quick smile. "That counselor you recommended helped a lot. I can't say that I don't still think about it sometimes, but . . ." She let the sentence trail off unfinished.

Riley nodded. "I did my share of second-guessing about it, too. But there was no way we could have foreseen that happening and avoided it. We were as well prepared as we could have been."

"I know."

"The only mistake you made was not reacting quicker. The man got off two shots before you fired." Riley remembered well the feelings of fear and raging helplessness when he'd realized that a group of panicking bystanders blocked his field of fire. When he'd heard the second shot, he'd thought Delaney had been hit. He still had nightmares about that.

"I had to make certain I had a clear shot," Delaney said in her own defense. "Firing too quickly can be as bad as too late."

"True," Riley was forced to agree.

"Anyway, the odds are in my favor that I'll never find myself in a situation like that again. That might not be the case in Europe, maybe, or the Middle East, but here in the States, such occurrences are still very rare, thank heaven."

"You can't count on odds," Riley warned. "If there is a next time, you can't hesitate."

"I know."

A flight attendant pulled a serving cart even with Delaney's seat, providing a welcome distraction. "What would you like to drink this morning?" She passed each of them a container of orange juice and a plastic-wrapped tray containing two squashed danishes.

"Coffee." Delaney lowered her tray table. "Black, please."

"I'll take mine with cream and sugar," Riley said.

The flight attendant filled two polystyrene cups with coffee and handed the first to Delaney and the second to Riley, along with a plastic stirrer, one packet of nondairy creamer, and two packets of sugar.

"Just think"—Riley stirred the creamer and sugar into his coffee—"if we were in first class, we'd be drinking coffee from *real* cups and eating—"

"—something equally leathery."

"Ah, but think of the legroom we'd have," he added on a wistful note.

A point Delaney couldn't dispute as the man in front of her chose that moment to recline his seat, hitting her knees and nearly hitting her tray. With an effort, she ignored Riley's chuckle and opened her notebook to jot down a few more things she needed to talk to Glenda about.

Riley watched her, his attention caught by the tightened corners of her lips, the furrow of concentration that pulled her dark eyebrows together, straightening their natural arch. The first time he met her, he'd been struck by the thought that here was a woman who wouldn't be squeamish about baiting a worm on a hook, and one who saw no contradiction in lazing in a tub filled with fragrant bubbles up to her neck. He'd never found either of those out for a fact yet, much to his regret, but he had learned she drank her whiskey neat and daubed a disturbingly feminine fragrance behind her ears.

During those first years of their association—a friendship of sorts—she'd possessed a freshness and a love of life he'd envied. She'd taken her knocks, had some rough times personally, but she'd rolled with them and kept her balance. Then, six years ago, it had all changed, literally overnight, at exactly the same time her love affair had ended.

Delaney had been ambitious before, but not like this, not with this single-minded devotion to work. Maybe she could fool others into believing she had, but she couldn't fool him. He had known her too long—worked with her too long. This compulsive drive to succeed didn't come from ambition or ego the way she claimed. It was more complicated than that, tangled up with the need to prove something—maybe even to make up for the love that had gone wrong.

Most people didn't see that in her. They only saw the calm that remained with her like a shield. She'd locked herself behind it, and locked her feelings away, too, so they wouldn't betray her again.

He watched the slight changes of her face, the quickening, the loosening, the small expressions coming and going. She kept at her work, pushing herself. Always pushing herself.

"Take a break, Delaney. You look tired."

"Really?" she said without looking up. "You don't suppose it's because I've been up since three o'clock, do you?"

"Not that kind of tired. Edgy tired. You're working too hard. You need to take a vacation."

"I did." She reached for her orange juice. "I spent two weeks in Puerto Vallarta, remember?"

"Delaney. That was nearly three years ago."

"Was it?"

"It was. So while you're playing around with the schedule, fit in a vacation for yourself."

"I will. I promise." But she was already shutting her mind to where she would go, what she would do—and with whom? Instead, she busied herself with a note. For once, Riley didn't interrupt.

It was a long time before she noticed his silence. All the plastic remnants of their breakfast had been removed and the in-flight movie had started before she finally glanced over and saw him sprawled—as much as the narrow space allowed him to sprawl—in his seat. His eyes were closed, but she could tell he wasn't sleeping.

A faint smile curved her mouth. "What are you doing—fantasizing about Rina Cole?"

"No," he said without stirring. It was another face he was visualizing. But he lied and said, "I'm dreaming I'm on the deck of my boat with the sun on my face, a tangy ocean breeze playing with my hair, a glass of fresh-squeezed orange juice in my hand, and a pot of coffee brewing in the galley. That's the life for me."

"You had it—remember?—and gave it up."

"Sometimes, Delaney—just sometimes—the dream is better than the reality."

She found it impossible to reply to that quietly voiced

statement. She gathered up her purse and unbuckled her seat belt. "I think I'll go see if Glenda has made it to the office yet." She accidentally bumped his leg when she stood up.

"Careful. You're rocking the boat."

"Sorry." Smiling, she headed up the aisle to the telephone.

THREE

THE TAXI PULLED CLOSE TO THE curb and stopped in front of the Park Avenue address Delaney had given the driver. A horn blared in angry protest. The cabbie ignored it as he turned in his seat to collect the fare.

"A receipt, please." She paid him, her glance following Riley when he climbed out to retrieve their luggage from the trunk.

The cabbie, an emigrant from a Middle Eastern country, took her money and handed her the printed tape from the meter. Delaney shoved it into her purse, and stepped out of the taxi into the giant solar collector that was Manhattan in late July. Its acres of concrete absorbed the sun's radiant energy and released it to bake the city. Already she could feel beads of perspiration forming along her upper lip.

She took her overnight bag from Riley. "Remind

me to thank you for holding out for an air-conditioned cab."

"I will." He draped the matching garment bag over her arm.

She turned toward the tall, buff-colored building, automatically scanning the jam of traffic on the wide street and the steady stream of pedestrians on its sidewalks. For anyone in the security business, New York represented a nightmare of clogged streets, snarled intersections, teeming sidewalks, and perpetual reconstruction—an environment totally beyond control. She tried not to think of all the problems it would present as Riley joined her. Together, they crossed the sidewalk to the building's entrance.

"No press," Riley remarked on the absence of any reporters or photographers outside.

"A minor blessing that I suspect won't last long." Delaney nodded to the doorman as she passed. Inside the marble-walled lobby, she walked directly to the uniformed guard behind the security desk. "I'm Delaney Wescott. This is my associate, Riley Owens."

"Carl Bettinger," supplied the guard, an iron-haired man Delaney judged to be a fit and trim, no-nonsense fifty-year-old. "Mr. Golden told me to expect you. He's on the twentieth floor. The elevators are to your right."

"Thanks."

She crossed to the bank of four elevators and pushed the button. Immediately the doors to the first elevator swished open. She stepped inside and turned to face the doors, leaving ample room for Riley to join her. He punched the button for the twentieth floor and the doors slid shut.

There was a grind and a whir, a faint sensation of movement as Delaney watched the digital readout tick off the floor numbers.

On twenty the elevator slowed to a stop and the doors parted again. Delaney shifted her grip on the overnight bag and stepped out of the elevator.

As she rang the bell to Arthur Golden's pied-à-terre, Delaney instinctively took note of the layout of the floor's wide corridors and the locations of the exit signs for the fire stairs and the doors to the other apartments on the floor. A second later, the door opened and Arthur Golden stood before her, dressed in a navy silk Armani suit, a cellular phone to his ear.

Delaney had seen Arthur only a few times after he left the law firm where both had been associates. He had changed little in the interim. Always meticulously groomed, he wore his hair clipped short, never a strand out of place. His skin was tanned, not too darkly, but just enough to give his aristocratic features that California look. No traces remained of the poor Kansas farm boy he'd once been. On the contrary, he looked smooth, suave, and successful—an image he had carefully crafted and one that had served him well.

Arthur said something to the party on the phone and motioned for Delaney to come in. That was the extent of his greeting as he turned and walked with purposeful strides out of the apartment's formal entrance hall into its living room. Delaney followed with Riley right behind her.

The living room was sleekly contemporary, its walls glazed in ecru, its sofa and chairs upholstered in a soft shade of rust. Horizontal blinds instead of drapes hung at the broad windows that gave the expected yet still spectacular view of the city—a kind of Gershwin sweep that declared, "This is Manhattan!"

Arthur walked straight to a long, well-equipped bar, then glanced back at Delaney and cupped a hand over the phone's mouthpiece. "I'll be right with you," he said, then turned away and resumed his telephone conversation, speaking in low, hushed tones.

Delaney draped her garment bag over one of the armchairs and set her overnight bag on the textured carpet beside it. Riley placed his bags next to them, then said in a soft undertone, "Sounds like that phone call is very important."

"With Arthur, it's hard to be sure," Delaney murmured. "When we both worked at the same law firm, it was a standing joke that when Arthur was on the phone, it was impossible to tell if he was negotiating the deal of the century or making dinner reservations. About the time you decided it was an act, he'd bring in some contract with unbelievable terms."

"You can't trust appearances."

"Especially with Arthur. Behind all that polish and the designer clothes is an extremely intelligent man."

Riley took his own measure of Arthur. "Cunning?"

Delaney smiled. "Let's just say, he isn't the kind to stand on ethics."

"Few people do nowadays," he replied.

"Careful. Your cynicism is showing," Delaney chided.

Riley slanted her a mocking look, his eyes smiling. "And yours doesn't?"

She had no opportunity to respond as Arthur concluded his conversation and turned back to them, laying the cellular phone aside.

"Let's get right to it, Delaney," he said. "What do we have to do to protect Lucas Wayne from that madwoman?"

Before Delaney could ask whether the restraining order had been issued, a petite blonde burst into the room, clad in a blue satin slip dress with rhinestone-studded straps. "I heard the doorbell. Is my driver—" She halted at the sight of Riley and Delaney, and lifted a hand to her throat in a self-conscious and practiced gesture. "I'm intruding. I'm sorry, Arthur."

Standing no more than two inches over five feet, the woman was the delicate ingenue type that always made Delaney feel like an awkward giant. Out of nowhere came the lyrics, "Five foot two, eyes of blue, but oh! what those five feet can do." Delaney knew instantly that behind the blonde's angelic face and baby blue eyes was a mind constantly working. Even now, the blonde looked at Delaney and Riley with unabashed interest, trying to assess whether they were important.

"You see"—she wisely aimed her apologetic smile at Riley—"I've been waiting forever for a car to come pick me up. Naturally when I heard the doorbell, I thought it was the driver."

"An easy mistake," Riley agreed.

"These are the security people I called in from the Coast," Arthur stated.

"I should have guessed. I knew Mr. Golden was expecting you," she declared, walking over to extend a slim hand to Riley. "I'm Tory Evans."

"Riley Owens."

"Delaney Wescott." Delaney stood straighter, absolutely refusing to slouch. "You were with Mr. Wayne last night. Is that right?"

"Yes." There was a demure lowering of her lashes, accompanied by a rush of pink to her cheeks. At that moment Delaney decided Tory Evans's success in show business was assured; anyone who could blush on cue was bound to make it. "It was a terrifying experience. I have never been more frightened in—"

Her performance was interrupted by the strident ring of the telephone. Arthur picked it up. "Yes?" Barely four seconds later he hung up and turned to the actress. "Your car is downstairs, Miss Evans."

"Thank heaven!" she declared, then caught back her smile and sent a concerned look at Riley. "It is all right if I leave, isn't it? The police said I wasn't in any danger, that Rina wasn't after me."

Riley smiled and nodded. "I'm sure it's safe for you to leave."

"Thank you." She pressed a hand on his forearm and let it trail off as she moved past him toward the door. "I'd stay if I thought it would help Lucas, but I'm afraid it would just make everything worse." She glanced quickly at Arthur. "Tell Lucas goodbye for me. The door to his bedroom was closed and I didn't want to wake him if he was asleep. Ask him to call me later, will you?"

Arthur smiled in reply, which she took to be an affirmative. When the door closed behind her, Arthur smiled with cynical amusement.

"Last night she was desperate to keep her name out of the papers, afraid it would ruin her image of virginal innocence," Arthur told them. "This morning she sees the coverage this is getting. Now she's furious about all the publicity she's missing. She's been on the phone with her agent half the morning—that is, when she could unglue herself from the television set. She thinks she's going to be the next Lolita and get a million dollars for a nude spread in *Playboy*. A smart agent might get it for her, too." He raised his hands and formed an imaginary frame of a headline. "'The blonde who drove another woman to attempt murder.' It would work. 'Course, she'd need to have a sexier hairstyle—and drop that saccharine act."

"I have a feeling you didn't tell her that." Delaney smiled.

Arthur smiled back. "Not without a piece of the action."

"That's what I thought," she said. "Now—back to business. Was a restraining order issued?"

"It's been issued, but I don't know whether it's been served."

"I'm curious," Riley spoke up. "Did she file countercharges, claim that Wayne assaulted her? Maybe even hinted at past physical abuse?"

"Sid Bloom—the attorney I called in—he mentioned that possibility. So far, she hasn't. Personally, I don't think she will. She can get more mileage and public sympathy out of playing the wronged woman. That's the tack I would recommend, and Rina Cole has some sharp people behind her. If she didn't, her career would have gone down the tubes long ago."

"The legal maneuverings and jockeying for the most favorable press position aren't my concern," Delaney said. "Only his security."

"I will need some advice from you, Delaney. I have his own PR people coming over this afternoon so we can put our heads together and figure out how we'll combat whatever she throws at us. But the last thing I want is to antagonize her into trying again. At the same time, I can't sit by and let her smear his name."

"I wouldn't be too concerned about that," Delaney told him. "It's true Rina may get a lot of public sympathy as the wronged woman, but that won't hurt your client. If anything, it should enhance his appeal. The infidelity of men is notorious. And there's nothing that attracts—or challenges—a woman more than a Casanova with a string of broken hearts behind him. It seems to be a basic flaw in us."

"True." He nodded thoughtfully. "I like that."

"I'm glad," Delaney said and started to unfasten the flap to her shoulder bag.

At that moment, Lucas Wayne appeared in the dining room arch, a glass of orange juice in his hand. Delaney recognized him instantly. How could she not when in the last three years his face had been plastered all over Hollywood and half the country?

There was no question it was a handsome face, sculpted in strong, roguish lines with just enough character to keep it from seeming too perfect. An adoring reporter had once raved that he had Brando's bedroom eyes, Eastwood's smile, and Redford's hair, albeit a much darker and longer version. Delaney had never been able to dispute that. Now, seeing him in the flesh, she found even less reason, despite the day-old stubble that shadowed his cheeks and the tracks left by combing fingers in his rumpled hair.

All he had on were the bottoms to a pair of paisley silk pajamas. They rode low on his hips, exposing the navel in the middle of his incredibly flat stomach. He had a marvelous physique, his shoulders wide and all the muscles well defined.

"Sorry, Arthur. I didn't know you had company."

When he started to turn away, Arthur called him back, "Don't go, Lucas. Come in. I want you to meet Delaney Wescott."

Lucas Wayne swung back, his glance briefly falling on her before skipping to Riley. But she felt the impact of it and took a quick, steadying breath, realizing that his charm, his magnetism, his charisma—or whatever the current buzzword happened to be—was potent. It was something she needed to remember, especially when she knew she had all the normal urges—urges that hadn't been satisfied in some time.

As he crossed the room, Delaney made another discovery: he was tall. He wasn't one of those Hollywood larger-than-life illusions; he was actually tall, topping six feet by a good two inches. For a change, she was the one who would be eye-level with someone's mouth instead of the other way around.

He went straight to Riley and extended a hand. "It's a pleasure to meet you, Delaney, although I wish it could be under different circumstances."

Riley threw an amused look. "I'm Delaney Wescott," she corrected, not at all surprised by the mix-up. It wasn't the first time a prospective client had expected Delaney Wescott to be a man.

His head snapped toward her; a frown of disbelief claimed his expression. "You are Delaney Wescott?"

"I am," she replied evenly and gestured at Riley. "You were about to shake hands with my associate, Riley Owens."

If Lucas Wayne had heard her, he gave no sign of it as he continued to stare at her. Then, suddenly, unexpectedly, he threw his head back and laughed.

Delaney stiffened. Over the years she'd encountered varied reactions from prospective clients to her gender—anger over a perceived deception, open skepticism of her ability, even an occasional chauvinistic display of outright rejection—but she had never been laughed at. She felt anger rising icy-hot, and fought to suppress it.

With laugh lines still creasing his face, Lucas Wayne turned from her, declaring: "Arthur, you are priceless! When you told me you were importing more bodyguards from the Coast, I expected a pair of musclebound gorillas. Not a woman. What is she? The latest status symbol?" he asked, turning to again survey her.

Delaney clasped her hands behind her back, the action accenting the width of her square shoulders. Her chin lifted with a certain resoluteness that gave a cool tilt to her head.

"Forgive me, Mr. Wayne, but I fail to see the humor that you so obviously do." Her voice had a nice frost to it that matched the smooth smile she gave him.

"Maybe because you're not a man," he suggested and raised the juice glass to his mouth.

"You've lost me again, Mr. Wayne."

Lucas Wayne found himself admiring her granite poise, a poise that didn't crack despite the very human anger he sensed in her. "It's simple, Miss Wescott. You see, I wasn't exactly overjoyed at the thought of being accompanied everywhere by a pair of Vegas rejects—my male ego surfacing, I suppose. I prefer to think I can take care of myself, that I don't need a bunch of muscle to protect me." His smile widened, his gaze drifting over the womanly curves of her long body. "It never occurred to me a bodyguard came packaged like you."

"Life is full of surprises, isn't it?" A trace of acid humor crept into her voice.

"It is," he agreed lazily. "Which leads me to wonder whether you're good at your job?"

"She's good, Lucas." Arthur Golden pushed away from the bar and came toward him. "You can't hire better. I wouldn't have called her otherwise."

"Arthur is telling you the truth," Delaney inserted, careful to sound confident, but not cocky. "My company is very good at what we do, Mr. Wayne."

"Really?" he replied with heavy skepticism and turned away to leave, then swung sharply back, his glance narrowing with sudden question. "Wait a minute." He shot a look at Arthur. "Is this the same personal security firm that made all the headlines last year when they saved the life of Sanford Green, that big, high-profile executive?"

"The same." Arthur's expression was somewhat smug.

Lucas Wayne turned his attention on Delaney with new and reassessing interest. "You killed the guy who was after him."

"It was a regrettable incident." Delaney took no pride in it. "My company operates on the basis of restricting our clients' exposure to danger. We do our best to avoid situations where we have to place ourselves between you and danger. Or—to put it more succinctly—we have every intention of spotting trouble before it ever gets close to you."

"You can't know it, Mr. Wayne," Riley inserted, breaking his self-imposed silence, a faint smile lingering at the corners of his mouth. "But that's one of Delaney's many rules to live by: The best way to avoid trouble is to see it coming."

"That sounds very wise," Lucas Wayne remarked. "But you don't always succeed, do you?"

There was a hairline crack in her poise, but only Riley saw it. "Let me put it this way—all my clients, both past and present, are still alive and—without a scratch, I might add." Delaney glanced pointedly at the trio of long red marks on his forearm.

Lucas laughed softly at that, then turned the full force of his wicked smile on her. "You have me there, Miss Wescott."

"Delaney," she instructed and pretended not to notice that he was flirting with her. "If you don't mind, I prefer to dispense with such formality. Mr. Wayne can become a mouthful in an emergency."

"Delaney," he repeated as if testing the sound of it, the glint in his dark eyes a little too warm and much too intimate.

She turned crisply from it and walked over to her purse. "Speaking of formalities"—she opened it—"I have a contract for you to sign." She gave it to him to read over, explaining, "It spells out our rates, the type of expenses you'll be required to reimburse, and the weekly billing schedule."

He skimmed the document, borrowed a pen from Arthur, signed it, and handed it back to her. Delaney tucked it into her purse and took out a notebook and pen, then sat down on the sofa, moving a navy silk pillow out of the way. "Now, if you don't mind, I need to ask you a few questions. There's a great deal that has to be planned, organized, and coordinated, but first Riley and I need some information from you."

Taking their cue from her, the others found themselves seats. Riley perched himself on the arm of the sofa near an ashtray; Arthur hitched his trousers and sat on the sofa, while Lucas Wayne settled himself in an armchair positioned at right angles to the sofa.

"About the movie you're doing," Delaney began, "how many days of filming do you have left?"

"Probably four. They shot around me today."

"Are we talking soundstage or location shots?"

"Both."

Scenes shot on location invariably involved public places, and any public place represented a potential security risk. Aware of that, Delaney said, "You'll need to get together with the line producer today, Riley, and take a look at the location sites. While you're at it, you might as well check out the soundstage."

"Right." Riley jotted a note to himself in the skinny spiral pad he carried in his suit pocket. "I'll also see about coordinating our operations with the film's existing security."

"Good." She added that to the list under Riley's name, then turned again to Lucas Wayne. "In the meantime we'll need a copy of your shooting schedule and your script for the remaining scenes as well."

"I can get that for you," Arthur told her.

"The sooner the better. What about the rest of the schedule this week? Any interviews, parties, personal appearances, dinners—anything we should know about?"

"I'm supposed to have dinner this week with the producer and his wife, but I don't remember what night."

"Forget it," Arthur said. "That can be canceled. I'll handle it."

Delaney put a question mark beside that notation

and moved on. "How long will you be staying in New York after you've wrapped up the film?"

"Not any longer than I have to," Lucas replied. "With luck, I'll leave on Saturday."

"Will you be taking a commercial flight to L.A.?"

"I'm not going to L.A."

She looked up from her notes. "Then where?"

"Aspen."

"Aspen, Colorado?" The mere mention of the place awakened old memories, old hurts. Delaney had never been to Aspen in her life, but . . . he had lived there. As far as she knew, he still did. She felt Riley's gaze on her, and carefully avoided looking in his direction.

"Yes, Aspen, Colorado," Lucas confirmed. "I have a house there. When the movie's finished, I have a month free. I thought I'd go to Aspen and get away from it all for a while." He eyed her curiously. "Why? Is that a problem?"

"Not really," Riley spoke up, covering for her. She threw him a grateful look, then hesitated, surprised by the hardness in his expression. "It just means that Delaney will need to leave a couple days early to get everything organized on that end before you arrive."

"Who knows?" Delaney grabbed a desperate, half-formed hope. "By the end of the week, it may not be necessary for us to accompany you to Aspen—at least, not both of us."

"What do you mean, it won't be necessary?" Arthur frowned.

Thinking fast, she said, "As I assess the current situation, our role will consist mainly of shielding Mr. Wayne from reporters and any misguided Rina Cole fans who might turn nasty out of sympathy for her."

"What about Rina?" Arthur argued. "She tried to kill him, remember?"

"Of course. But I question whether she poses any immediate threat. Assuming she would want to make another try at him, all the media attention will effectively hamstring her."

"Maybe that's true today, even tomorrow, but what about next week? Next month?" Arthur protested. "This woman blames Lucas for everything that's gone wrong in her career the last two years. She thinks he's out to ruin her. I tell you she's gone over the top. It's become an obsession with her. Do you think those nobodies out on the street are the only ones who can go berserk? Just because she's Rina Cole, does that mean she can't go off the deep end?"

"Of course not—"

"Then I don't want to hear any more of this nonsense that you aren't going to Aspen with Lucas. I didn't fly you all the way out from L.A. to do a half-assed job of protecting him. I—"

"Arthur, I only mentioned that as a possibility for the two of you to consider," Delaney broke in. Lucas Wayne was the biggest celebrity ever to engage her services. To have him as a client meant success in a town where success was everything. She had worked too long and too hard to lose a chance like this—even if it meant going to Aspen. "If you think it's necessary for us to go to Aspen, then we'll go. But that's your decision to make, not mine."

"Then consider it made," Arthur stated. "You are going."

"Fine." Delaney reluctantly made a side note to have Glenda obtain the necessary authorization from the state of Colorado to allow them to be legally armed.

"Speaking of Rina," Riley inserted, "do we know where she is now? On our way from the airport, we heard on the radio that she'd been released on bond."

"According to my attorney, she's at a friend's apartment somewhere on Fifth Avenue across from Central Park."

"It might pay to monitor her comings and goings," Riley suggested.

Delaney nodded. "Exactly what I was thinking."

"I know a guy—a paparazzo," Arthur said. "He's probably camped outside her door right now. For a price, he'll keep me posted."

"Then let's use him." Out of the corner of her eye, she saw Lucas Wayne smile in amusement. "Is something wrong?"

He shrugged one shoulder, sending a ripple of muscle across his bare chest. "Seems to me you're making a lot of work for yourself when you don't believe there's any threat."

"Under the circumstances, there's no such thing as being too careful," Delaney replied.

"Especially when we're dealing with Rina Cole," Arthur added. "She should be locked up along with that nutcase who writes you those letters all the time."

"What nutcase?" Delaney lifted her head in sharp alertness. "What letters?"

"Lucas has this kook who writes him love letters and sends him presents. It's been going on for almost a year now. She's a—"

Delaney broke in before Arthur could say more. "What kind of presents?" She directed the question to Lucas Wayne.

"Different things," he replied with unconcern. "Once she sent a lock of her hair. Another time it was a pendant in the shape of half of a heart. You know, the kind where there are two matching halves, one for the guy to wear and one for the girl." He paused and shook his head. "There were others, but I don't remember what they were. My secretary handles all the fan mail and the gifts that come in. I never see ninety percent of it. I don't have time."

"Did you keep any of these letters from her?"

"I get hundreds, probably thousands of letters a week from fans. It's impossible to keep them—hers or anyone else's."

Arthur spoke up. "I'll bet if you had Christy go through the last few batches of mail, you'd find some from her. She writes you two and three times a week." Then to Delaney he said, "She's in love with him and writes like they're having a big affair."

Delaney didn't like the sound of that. "Call your secretary and have her fax any letters she has. I'd like to look at them as soon as possible."

"All right." Lucas nodded.

"Now do you understand why I wanted you out here, Delaney?" Arthur said. "I have Rina Cole who goes crazy and tries to kill him. And she may be crazy enough to try it again. Then there's this fan writing him love letters exactly like the guy did who killed that actress on *My Sister Sam*. Is it any wonder I'm concerned? There has been too much of this kind of thing these last few years—like the guy who showed up at the studio demanding to see Michael Landon, then shot and killed two guards when they refused to let him in . . . the stabbing of Theresa Saldana. What about that axe murderer who stalked Cher and Olivia Newton-John for three years before he was locked away? And who can forget that crazy woman who claimed she was David Letterman's wife and broke into his house in Connecticut . . . or Hinckley shooting Reagan to impress Jodie Foster . . . or the one who killed John Lennon? Talk about fatal attractions."

"You don't have to list every one, Arthur." Lucas Wayne came out of his chair, suddenly restless, impatient, irritated. "I agree this fan is sick. She needs to be stopped. But how? We don't know who she is or where she lives."

Riley picked up on that. "Are you saying these letters are anonymous?"

"They might as well be," he said. "They're all signed simply 'Laura.' No last name, no return address. Not even an initial."

"What about a postmark?" Delaney asked.

Lucas Wayne glanced at her in surprise. "I remember one had an L.A. postmark, but I couldn't swear that all of them did."

"In that case, have your secretary include the envelopes that the letters came in."

"Okay."

"Christy has my fax number here at the apartment," Arthur inserted. "We'll have copies for you this afternoon."

"Good." Delaney made a note of that under Arthur's name. "Now, back to the current situation—I assume the production company provides transportation for you back and forth to the set every day. Are they using a local limousine service?"

"Yes. Imperial Limousine."

"Do you usually have the same driver?"

Lucas Wayne nodded and linked his fingers together. "His first name's Bennie. I don't remember the last."

"I'll find out from the line producer," Riley volunteered.

"Okay." She put that under his list, then faced Lucas Wayne and automatically took a deep breath. "Now comes the hard part. We need you to tell us as much as you can about Rina Cole, your relationship with her—"

"Confession time, is that it?" he challenged harshly, resentment stiffening his expression.

"I know the question sounds like an invasion of privacy, but it's important for us to know as much as we can about Rina Cole. It will help us to anticipate what she might do, when, where, maybe even how. Obviously our knowledge of her is limited to various press stories, which mostly deal with her professional career. We are aware she has a past history of violent outbursts. Beyond that, we know little about her as a person, not even how much of the reported affair between the two of you was fact and how much was a publicist's fiction. All of it will help us to determine how dangerous a threat she is."

"She's dangerous, all right. After last night I know that for a fact." He flopped back down on the chair, his dark eyes hard and faintly defiant. "They say confession's good for the soul. Maybe it is, but this all started because I used her—from the beginning. I'm not proud of it, but everybody gets used in this business one way or the other. Anyway, I had read the script for the movie we ended up making together. The minute I read it, I knew the part of Sam Connors was my breakout role from the rock scene. Rina had control of the casting and she was determined to hire a big screen actor for the part. So I arranged to meet her at a party, convinced her I wasn't interested in the part, that the road tour schedule was too tight, then asked her out. To make a long story short, I let her talk me into taking the role."

He paused and looked away as if gathering his thoughts. "As for the affair, the chemistry was there off-screen as well as on. We slept together. I've never denied that. Why should I? Affairs happen on a set all the time. Once the film was in the can, I saw her occasionally, but not often. Definitely not as often as she made it sound to reporters when we hit the talk show circuit together to promote the film. Hell, I didn't care if she was using me. I'd used her. Besides, the chemistry was still there and she was one wild, sexy lady—"

"Lady is not the term I would use," Arthur inserted.

Riley ignored that to ask, "What was she like? Personality-wise, I mean."

"Volatile," Lucas answered. "She could blow up without warning. One time she got mad at her hairdresser on the set and started shrieking and beating on her with a hot curler wand—all because she didn't like the way she was doing her hair. She was always screaming at the director, too. At the time I thought she was simply a perfectionist. But she's really paranoid—convinced that someone's out to get her or ruin her. I understand it got worse when her last movie flopped."

"That's a gentle way of saying it was a box-office bomb," Arthur inserted. "The grosses were so bad, they yanked it from the theaters after only three weeks. She's poison in Hollywood. She blames Lucas for it. Practically every other day, she's been calling him or coming by his place, banging on the door, screaming accusations that he'd done it to destroy her—that is, when she wasn't begging him to make a sequel to their movie. When his last film turned out to be another smash, she went over the top and the threats starting coming."

"The threats. She's been threatening you?" Delaney questioned as the case began to take on a different complexion, blowing Riley's theory that last night's attempt had been an impulsive act committed in the heat of passion.

"Since around April," Lucas admitted. "I didn't really take them seriously. I didn't even mention them to Arthur. I thought sooner or later she'd give up this craziness. I didn't realize how sick she was . . . until last night."

"Do we know how she got into the suite?" Delaney directed the question to Arthur.

"She talked a chambermaid into letting her in. She said she'd just flown in from Europe—which was true. She had some concert dates there. She told the maid she wanted to surprise Luke. The poor woman thought she was helping Cupid out."

"Were you asleep?" Riley asked.

"Fortunately, no. I heard her come in—or maybe I should say, I heard 'someone' come in. A lamp had been left on in the other room. When she opened the bedroom door, I could tell it was Rina, not some cat burglar. And I could see the gun in her hand. Arthur told you the rest, so there's no need to go into it."

"No, there isn't," Delaney agreed.

"Do you know what the irony of this is?" he said with disgust. "The real irony? I gave Rina that gun. A pearl-handled .38. Special order. I even had her name engraved on the barrel. And she was going to kill me with it."

"Does she own any other guns?"

"No. At least, she didn't when I gave her that one," Lucas qualified his answer.

Delaney knew that if Rina Cole wanted another gun, she could get one without much difficulty. "What about this apartment? Has she been here?"

"No. Arthur let me use it a few times when I've been in New York. She might have the phone number written down somewhere."

"Mention that to your attorney, Arthur," Delaney suggested. "If she starts calling here and making threats, he might want them taped. I'm not familiar with the evidentiary laws in New York. I don't know whether a taped threat would be admissible or not."

"I'll speak to him about it," he confirmed.

"Good." She glanced at Riley. "Unless you can think of something, I think we have covered about everything for now."

"I agree." Riley straightened from the arm of the sofa.

Delaney closed her notebook and clicked her ballpoint pen, retracting the tip as she rose to her feet. "Arthur, could you show us the layout of the apartment? If you have a spare room that we can use for a temporary office, it would be helpful. I'd rather work from here than some other location."

"You can use the library." Arthur stood up and automatically rebuttoned his suit jacket to give it a smooth line. "If one of you wants to sleep there, the sofa converts to a bed. There's also an extra bedroom now that the Evans girl has left."

Delaney glanced at her watch, conscious of the time ticking away and the mountain of logistics yet to be handled. "Give us a quick tour of the apartment, then we'll set up in the library. We have a lot to do."

FOUR

$\mathcal{D}$ELANEY SAT AT A CONTEMPORARY rosewood desk, an elbow idly propped on its top, her back to the night-darkened window that mirrored the rest of the library. Its velvet-covered walls of deep navy created an illusion of infinite shadow and isolated the light from both the desk lamp and the floor lamp that stood next to the armchair Riley occupied.

A half-smoked cigarette dangled from his fingers. His suit jacket lay across the arm of the navy sofa. The cuffs of his light blue dress shirt were rolled halfway up his forearms and the top two buttons of his shirt were unfastened, his tie hanging askew in a loose circle. His briefcase sat open on the floor next to his chair and his feet were propped on a square footstool upholstered in cinnamon leather. On the coffee table, a flat cardboard box held wadded-up napkins and the few crusts that were left from a pizza that had been delivered over three hours ago.

Riley took a drag on his cigarette and blew out the smoke. "Want to read it again?"

"Okay." Delaney lowered her hand and began to read from the letter:

> My dearest darling Lucas—
> It has been agony not seeing you every week. That time we had together meant so much to me that now it hurts not to hear your laugh or see the way your eyes shine, to feel again your love for me.
> But I know I must be strong, that we won't always have to be apart like this.
> I know, my darling, that you miss me as much as I miss you. I see how lonely you are. But each passing day brings us closer to the moment when we can be together forever and neither of us will ever have to be lonely again.
>
> Forever yours,
> Laura

When she finished, Riley said, "The obsession is there, along with the delusion of a relationship. And that 'being together forever' phrase says to me the letter has all the earmarks of being written by the type of fan who could pose a genuine threat."

"True."

"So what's bothering you—other than the fact that we might be dealing with a faceless stalking fan?"

Delaney stared at the letter, an absent frown creasing her forehead. "I don't know. I guess it bothers me that it's typed. What kind of woman would *type* a love letter? It seems so impersonal. That's what makes it feel wrong."

"Maybe this Laura knows that an expert could identify her through her handwriting." Riley crushed his cigarette out in an ashtray already mounded with butts. "Or maybe"—he swung his feet off the footstool and pushed out of the chair to walk to the desk—"her handwriting is simply lousy. Judging from that signature, I'd say that was a good bet."

"It is." Delaney admitted the name "Laura" was barely legible. "But I question whether that would occur to her?"

"It would if somebody had drummed it into her head often enough."

"I suppose."

Riley could tell she still had some doubts. He watched as she rubbed a hand over her eyes. Reading the signs of tension and fatigue in the gesture, he said, "It's late. I think it's time we called it a night."

"You go ahead." She immediately sat a little straighter. "I want to go over these letters again and recheck our strategy for the location shoot in Central Park."

"You know what that means, don't you?"

"What?"

"That I get the bedroom and you're stuck with the sofa tonight."

"The sofa will be fine." She managed a smile, but it was a tight one.

"If you think I'm going to be a gentleman and argue with you, you're crazy."

Delaney laughed faintly and laid the letter aside, as

he'd meant her to do, then rocked her chair back to look at him. "And you are crazy if you think you're going to talk me into going to bed."

"Why not? You're as tired as I am," he reasoned.

She shook her head and sat forward, reaching for the letter again. "But I know I wouldn't be able to sleep. I'd lie awake thinking."

"About what?" Riley was certain he knew that answer, but he doubted she would tell him.

She didn't. "About all this." She waved a hand, indicating the papers, maps, and letters on the desk. "Going over all the details, trying to figure out if there's any holes in the security."

"This job isn't any different from a dozen others we've handled. It's all fairly standard procedure. Certainly nothing to lose sleep over." He paused a beat, then went on the attack. "Are you sure you aren't looking ahead to the advance trip you'll have to make to scope out things in Aspen?"

"Of course not."

There wasn't the smallest break in her composure. She showed no reaction whatsoever to his challenge, which was telling in and of itself.

"Liar," Riley taunted softly, drawing a quick glare from Delaney. "Your old flame lives in Aspen, and Aspen isn't that big. You're worried that you might run into him. Admit it, 'Laney."

"You don't know what you're talking about, Riley," she replied smoothly. "All of that's in the past. It was over long ago."

"The affair is over, but you never got over him. Seeing him again could be the best thing that could happen. Maybe you'd finally get him out of your system."

"Honestly, Riley, I don't know how you come up with this nonsense," Delaney said with a coolly amused look.

Just as doubts began to form, Riley noticed the faint glimmer of pain in her eyes. Most people would have missed it, but most people didn't know her as well as he did.

"It's a lot of things, but nonsense isn't one of them. We both know that, 'Laney." He gave serious consideration to making a long, thin slice through her control. But he was afraid that his aim might be off and he'd end up slicing through his own.

"Look, Riley, we've been friends a long time—"

"That's the problem," he muttered, well aware that she had never looked at him as anything other than a friend. He also knew this wasn't the time to change that, not with the specter from the past looming before her.

"Problem?" Delaney frowned in confusion.

Unable to explain himself, Riley swung away from the desk and headed for the door, scooping up his suit jacket as he passed the chair. "Good night, 'Laney," he said over his shoulder. "I'd wish you sweet dreams, but I know whose face you'd see when you close your eyes."

Stunned into silence by the trace of bitterness in his voice, Delaney stared after him, wondering what on earth was the matter with him. She almost called him back to demand an explanation, then thought better of it. She didn't want to get drawn into a further discussion of the past. It wasn't something she wanted to face right now.

Instead, she pulled out the site map for the scheduled location shoot and spread it across the desk. She studied it for a while, occasionally jotting more notes to herself. After a time the lines began to blur. Delaney rubbed her eyes again and tried to shake off the fatigue.

Then came the sound of footsteps in the hall. Delaney glanced up, half-expecting to see Riley appear in the doorway.

But it was Lucas Wayne who paused in the opening. In place of the silk pajama bottoms he'd worn earlier, he had on double-pleated trousers and a polo-style pullover, banded in the middle with a wide chocolate stripe.

He leaned a shoulder against the frame, unconsciously striking a pose straight out of *GQ*. "Burning the midnight oil, I see," he observed lazily. "It's eleven o'clock, you know."

"I keep telling myself it's only eight in L.A." Delaney sat straighter in her chair and automatically flexed her shoulder muscles to ease their stiffness. "You're up late yourself. Couldn't you sleep?"

"I was practicing my lines for tomorrow. What's your excuse?"

"Riley and I have been going over the letters from this Laura woman—and trying to make sure we have everything covered for your location shoot the day after tomorrow." She glanced at the map on the desk and sighed. "Believe me, I wish your director had picked a site other than Central Park for your confrontation scene with the bad guy." She leaned forward to again study the detailed map of the park that Arthur had obtained for her. "It's a security nightmare."

Especially when Rina Cole's New York apartment overlooked that end of the park, but Delaney carefully avoided mentioning that particular detail.

"It could have been worse." He wandered into the room, his hands buried in the slanted side pockets of his trousers.

"Really?" She arched him a dubious look.

"Sure. It could have been a chase scene *through* the park."

"*Touché.*"

He came around the desk and stood next to her chair, leaning a hand on the desk and bending forward to look at the map. "What's the plan?"

"The scene will be filmed here." She used the pencil to point out the actual location to him. "That won't be so bad. The police will have that area cordoned off. But it's getting you to and from the site, as well as to and from your trailer, that presents the problem. We know we'll have a gauntlet of fans and reporters to run—plus who knows how many weirdos who might feel you need to be punished for your wicked ways."

"You're very encouraging, Delaney." But the note of dry amusement in his voice told her he didn't mean to be taken seriously.

"Sorry." Briefly she smiled up at him, then turned her attention back to the map.

"Makeup and wardrobe will be done here at the apartment that morning instead of on the set. We plan to use a hired car to sneak you onto the site and let your limo be a decoy. On the set, I'll have security teams deployed here, here, and here." She marked the locations for him on the map.

"As much as possible, I'd like to keep you in this protected zone and not go back and forth to the trailer unless it's a long break." She rocked back in the swivel chair, resting her elbows on its arms and holding the pencil horizontally between her hands. "What do you think?"

He turned sideways and lounged against the desk, leaning a hip against its edge. "I think it's very thorough. I also think you're damned good at your job."

"I told you I was." Actually, after going over the plan with him, she felt more confident about it, not seeing any holes—any contingencies—that couldn't be covered.

"What about tomorrow?"

"The soundstage makes it much easier. And we'll be dealing with a closed set. Your producer was quick to agree to that. I suspect the last thing he wants at this stage is any problems that might cause a delay, especially when the filming is so close to being done."

"That's an understatement," Lucas replied, then touched one of the faxed letters lying on the desk. "What's your take on these love notes from this Laura person?"

"I think she's an ardent fan, the kind that triggers alarm bells."

"Why is that?" He leaned over to study the letter more closely. "I admit reading it gives me an uneasy feeling, but the things she writes seem harmless enough. Sad and pathetic, but basically harmless. Where's the threat?"

"I see it in the part where she talks about the two of you being 'together forever.' Truthfully, if she had said she planned to kill you next Thursday, I would be less inclined to take her seriously. The dangerous ones invariably talk in terms of shared destinies—of uniting with someone—or being together forever."

"I'm impressed," he murmured.

"You're supposed to be." She briefly smiled at him.

"What's the next step?"

"With the letters? Inform the authorities, turn over the originals of any letters you still have, and make certain any new ones go to them with the minimum of handling."

"That's it?"

"No, they'll probably ask about any women you've met named Laura."

"That will take some thinking." He grinned wickedly, then feigned deep concentration. "Let's see . . . there was a cheerleader named Laura in high school who accused me of getting her pregnant. I also knew an aerobics instructor called Laurie—she was especially fond of the slant board," he added. "And there was the wife to one of *Fortune's* Four Hundred who was into blindfolds and ice cubes. Who knows how many groupies at my rock concerts might have been—"

Delaney stopped him. "The list of your conquests is obviously legion. Maybe you'd better save them for the police."

"Why?" He gave her his trademark smile. "Don't you want to know so you can track down the right Laura?"

"I think I need to explain a few things so you'll have a better understanding of our role," she said. "Wescott and Associates is not a detective agency. We don't investigate and we don't gather evidence. That is the province of the police. Naturally we cooperate with them, and pass along any information we happen to obtain. Other than that, we are here solely and strictly to protect you. That is our job—our only job. If we find out who Laura is and where she is, we will monitor her movements—but only as a defensive tactic."

"You're all business, aren't you?" He studied her thoughtfully, curiously.

"All business." Delaney nodded.

"Too bad." He moved away from the desk, crossing to the window. "You have quite a view of the city at night from here."

"I've been too busy to notice." Idly curious, Delaney pushed out of the chair, taking advantage of the chance to stretch her muscles and take a short break. She crossed the short space to stand at the window and gaze at the bands of streetlights below, the concrete towers with their uneven patchwork of lighted windows, and the shimmering reds, greens, yellows, and whites of neon signs and traffic lights.

"That jeweled crown over there is the Chrysler Building." Lucas shifted closer to point out the structure to her. "And those ropes of diamonds are the Queensboro Bridge."

"It's beautiful." She could smell his aftershave lotion and tried to identify the fragrance, finally deciding it was Giorgio for Men.

"Do you mind if I ask you a personal question?"

"That all depends on how personal it is."

"How did you get into the bodyguard business? Were you a lady cop or—what?"

"Actually Wescott and Associates is in the *security* business, which may or may not include serving as bodyguards." It was a typical misconception, one that Delaney was used to correcting.

"My mistake." Lucas dipped his head in mock apology.

"It's a common one."

"You still haven't answered my question."

"Isn't it a bit late to be checking on my qualifications?" she asked, faintly amused.

"I hired you. I can fire you, contract or not."

"True."

"So, what are your qualifications?"

Delaney smiled briefly at his persistence. "While I was in college, I was recruited by the FBI. I suppose the idea of becoming an agent sounded romantic and daring. But by the time I graduated from the academy at Quantico, I was already having second thoughts. After two months on the job, I knew law enforcement wasn't my line of work. So I went back to school and became a lawyer."

"A lawyer?" He arched an eyebrow in surprise. "That makes me even more curious to know how you got into this?"

"I got into it by accident, I guess."

"How's that?"

"The firm I was with at the time had a wealthy client who'd been receiving death threats," Delaney said, then paused to explain. "This was almost seven years ago. One day I was on my way out of the office just as this client was about to leave." She stared into the night's blackness, recalling that she had been in a hurry that day to get some motions filed on a case that was pending. She couldn't recall the details of the case, yet she could see Sanford Green, one of the firm's most important clients, standing there in the lavishly paneled reception area—his dark hair shot with gray, his fifty-odd years fleshing up his thin frame, his head tipped to catch a murmured comment from one of the senior partners.

Then he had looked up and noticed her. The down-turned corners of his mouth had lifted in a quick smile, his blue eyes lighting up with an innocently flirtatious gleam. "Well, Miss Wescott, where have you been hiding? It's been weeks since I last saw you gliding in and out of these halls."

"It has been a while, hasn't it?" Somehow she had managed to disguise her haste and continue forward to shake hands with him. "How are you, Mr. Green?"

"Fine, fine." But the declaration had held a false ring.

Belatedly Delaney had noticed the faint pallor to his face and the lines of strain newly etched in it. In recent weeks the office rumor mill had buzzed with reports about the trashing of Sanford Green's executive offices on Wilshire and the mutilation of his beloved black Scottie dog, events that had magnified the continued death threats.

Delaney had cast a brief but curious glance at the bodyguard who now accompanied Sanford Green everywhere. Even in a sportcoat and open-collared shirt, he had looked like what he was—an ex-cop, burly-chested with a bulldog jaw and an unsmiling manner that had prompted the office to nickname him Dick Tracy.

"Tell me, Miss Wescott," Sanford Green had said in a jollying voice, "has Adams here offered you a full partnership in the firm yet?"

Robert Adams had almost cringed at the question, although his mouth curved stiffly in a forced smile. With a rush, all the feelings of dissatisfaction with her job had swept through her—feelings that she hadn't known whether she should blame on the stifling atmosphere of the firm, the lack of challenge in her chosen field of law, the tedium of whereas and wherefores, or the claustrophobia of four walls.

She had managed to laugh at Sanford Green's question, pretending that he had made a joke. "Not yet, Mr. Green. Not hardly yet."

Robert Adams had almost sighed in relief at her response, then instantly braced himself when Sanford Green had spoken again. "Better not sit on your hands too long, Adams. She has the makings of a damned fine trial lawyer. Remember how fast she spotted the inconsistency in Thorgood's testimony in that patent infringement case last year," he'd said, referring to a lawsuit in which she'd acted as an assistant to the trial lawyer.

Obeying the rules of office politics, however grudgingly, Delaney had stepped in, eliminating the need for Robert Adams to come to the defense of his partner and colleague. "You are very flattering, Mr. Green. And as much as I would like to hear more"—she had made a show of looking at her watch—"I'm afraid I have to run. It was good to see you again."

After an exchange of goodbyes, Delaney had backtracked to the receptionist's desk. "Jeannie, I'm on my way to the courthouse. With luck I'll be back in an hour. If Riley Owens calls while I'm out, tell him I've received his incorporation papers back from the state. He is officially in the fishing charter business. Have him set a time for us to meet."

"Have a good day, Miss Wescott," Sanford Green had called in final farewell as he headed out the heavy oak doors that opened directly to the street, preceded as always by his bodyguard.

Delaney had lifted her hand in an acknowledging

wave. As she turned back to the receptionist, she had caught a glimpse of the gardener through the multipaned windows that looked out to the street. She had idly wondered what he was doing, since he had finished all the clipping and pruning yesterday. With a second glance, she had realized the man outside wasn't the regular gardener—more than that, he wasn't a gardener at all. So why was he standing next to the oleander bush? And why was he glaring at the entrance to the law firm's office with an expression of pure hatred?

At that instant she'd had a sudden, sickening feeling that the object of his hatred was not the law office. At almost the same moment the man had moved out of view, heading toward the landscaped path that intersected with the main sidewalk a scant twenty feet from the building.

Certain she had just seen the man behind the threats against Sanford Green, Delaney had run for the door, intent on warning him of the danger and driven by the fear she might be too late. "Call the police. Quick," she had told a startled Robert Adams, choosing not to waste valuable seconds explaining her reason.

She had charged outside in time to see the bodyguard move ahead of Sanford Green to shield him from the slightly built man who approached them, his hand raised in the supplicating gesture of a beggar. Delaney had moved hesitantly forward, watching as the bodyguard took the man by the arm to send him on his way. But the man had slipped the hold with a suddenness that caught the bodyguard flat-footed. In the next instant, the man had stepped past him and swung his arm in an arc, striking the guard on the back of his head and sending him sprawling to the sidewalk.

In a mad dash, Delaney had managed to reach Sanford Green's side at the same instant that the man spun around and leveled a gun at him. "You didn't really think that dumb ape was going to stop me, did ya, Green?" he had taunted.

Aware she had no time to think, only to act, Delaney had taken one quick step forward, bringing the man within range. Then she had swung her foot in an arcing, straight-legged kick, the inside arch of her foot hitting the man's gun hand and driving it upward.

As the gun discharged harmlessly into the air, she had shouted to Sanford Green: "Run!" and followed through on her advantage, grabbing the man's arm and shoulder and executing a leg sweep before rotating him off balance and letting him fall to the ground. The force of the impact had knocked the gun out of his hand and sent it skittering across the sidewalk.

But Sanford Green hadn't moved. He had remained standing there in ashen-faced shock. Unwilling to press her luck, Delaney had grabbed him and hustled him inside the building.

"So you saved his life," Lucas Wayne observed.

Delaney nodded absently. "He fired his bodyguard on the spot and insisted that I go to work for him."

"I assume you did."

"To paraphrase that very famous movie line, he made me an offer I would have been a fool to refuse—twice my current salary and one full year's wages guaranteed. Luckily I'd met Riley a couple of months earlier. He was ex-Secret Service, so I turned to him for help." Delaney paused, remembering the half-frantic phone call she had made to Riley later that same day.

• • •

Hearing his voice on the other end of the line, she clasped the receiver a little tighter. "Hello, Riley. It's Delaney Wescott."

"Delaney. How's the beautiful barrister this afternoon?"

"Truthfully? Either she's lost her mind or she's having a midlife crisis a few years early," she admitted, then went on to explain about her rescue of Sanford Green and his subsequent job offer. "I accepted the job, Riley. Now I desperately need a crash course in personal protection. Could I hire you? Maybe even talk you into some on-the-job training?"

After an agonizingly long pause, Riley said, "You're right, Delaney. One of us needs their heads examined and I think it's me."

"Then you're going to do it." She breathed in relief.

"I am."

"Thank you."

"Don't thank me; thank those two couples from Iowa I took out fishing this morning. *All* of them got seasick. I've spent the last three hours trying to get the stink out of my boat. Believe me, that is not what I had in mind when I named it *The Life of Riley*."

Delaney smiled, detecting more than a trace of disillusionment in his voice.

"So that's when you hooked up with Riley." Lucas shifted positions, angling his body toward her and leaning a shoulder against the thick pane of glass.

"More or less."

"What about the guy who was after your Mr. Green? Did you ever find out why he wanted to kill him?"

"He thought he'd been cheated in a real estate deal."

"What happened to him?"

"The police arrested him three months later for the murder of his mother."

He raised his eyebrows. "Nice guy."

"A real peach of a fella," she agreed dryly. "Anyway, right after that, I formed Wescott and Associates."

Far below, an ambulance raced along a New York street, its siren wailing, its lights flashing.

"As a woman, you probably encountered resistance."

"Not as much as you might think." She let her gaze wander over the geometric shapes of the skyline. "Actually, I've probably encountered less than a handful of men whose pride wouldn't let them hide behind a woman's skirt."

"Is that why you wear pants? Because if it is, don't wear them on my account . . . unless you have ugly legs," he added teasingly.

A hint of a smile hovered around her mouth. "I wear slacks because of the unrestricted movement they give me. On occasion, that can be critical." She turned her head slightly. "Any more questions?"

Fatigue was smoothing her features and giving a heaviness to her eyes. The glow from the desk lamp slid across the dark surface of her long hair, giving it a look of luxurious softness that invited his touch.

"You look tired."

"It couldn't be because I've been up since three this morning, could it?" she joked and glanced sideways at him, catching that interested look in his eyes.

"You've had a long day."

"So have you." She kept her voice level, her tone indifferently casual.

"Not really. I managed to grab a few hours' sleep this morning."

"Lucky you."

"You've been at it nonstop since you got here. A beautiful woman shouldn't work so hard." He touched her cheek, softly tracing the curve of it with his fingertips.

Lucas Wayne was not the first client to make a pass. Only once had Delaney allowed the line between business and pleasure to be crossed. She remembered the pain of it too well. It had her reaching up in a white-hot anger that she barely managed to check before she brushed his hand away and stepped back, putting distance between them.

"Sorry," she said firmly. "Maybe I didn't make myself clear. I am here to look *out* for your safety, *not* to look after your needs."

A smile played with the corners of his mouth. "Next you'll tell me you have a rule against mixing business with pleasure."

"I do."

"Rules are made to be broken, don't you know that?"

"Not mine."

He chuckled. "You intrigue me."

Delaney didn't doubt that she probably did, although she suspected the reason for it was not as straightforward as his statement. But there was no question he was good; he was very good—he knew how to treat a woman, how to draw her out, how to make her feel special. She didn't know if it was instinctive or simply a practiced technique. Either way, it was highly effective. She might even have been taken in by it if she had-n't known that not too many hours ago he'd been in bed with the blonde starlet Tory Evans.

"Let me set the record straight. This is an issue of safety—yours and mine." But it was obvious he didn't understand, so Delaney explained, "My job is to protect. Which means I can't be *watching* you, I can't be *looking* at you, I can't be laughing and talking with you. In short, I can't be paying any attention to you. I have to be watching the people around you—who's coming, who's going, who's there, and who's not. And believe me, you won't like it, because you aren't used to being ignored by women. But I *have* to ignore you; it's my job. So don't regard it as a challenge. Don't flirt with me or try to dis-tract me—in public or in private. Understand?"

"I understand." He had known many women, but not the kind of woman this tall graceful brunette was. Whether she liked it or not, she was definitely a chal-lenge, a most interesting challenge. "One question?"

"What's that?"

"Could I distract you?"

She studied him for a long second, on guard again. "Unfortunately, I'm not Superwoman. Does that satisfy your male ego?"

"For the time being."

"Good." She pushed away from the desk. "Now—if you don't mind, it's late and the car will be here to pick you up at six in the morning."

"Point taken." He crossed to the hall door, then stopped. "If I wasn't intrigued by you before, Delaney, I definitely am now."

"Good night," she said firmly.

"Good night, Delaney."

FIVE

*A*NTICIPATING THE HORDE OF REPORTERS and photographers waiting outside the studio the next morning,
Delaney had arranged for Lucas to enter through a side
entrance. Once inside the building—unharassed by the
press—Delaney stopped to confer with the head of the
production company's security while Riley accompanied Lucas to his dressing room.

To Delaney's relief, Riley was back to his old competent, easygoing self this morning. After his somewhat cryptic remarks last night, she hadn't been sure what to expect
when she got up. But Riley had acted as if nothing unusual
had happened, and Delaney had taken her cue from him.

Lucas was in makeup, seated before a large lighted
mirror, a plastic cape covering the top of him when
Delaney finally rejoined them. Riley sat on a stool by
the door, smoking a cigarette and balancing a cup of cof-

fee on his knee. The makeup girl, a redhead with frizzed hair and garish eye shadow, stood beside Lucas, a sponge in one hand and foundation makeup in the other.

Riley lifted his styrofoam cup and pointed at the television set mounted in a corner of the room. "Take a look. Arthur had her figured right."

The television was tuned to a morning news show. There, seated next to the anchor, was none other than the blonde starlet Tory Evans. Delaney crossed to the other side of Riley to get a better angle of the screen. "What has she said so far?"

"Not much. Just an account of the shooting from her perspective. Mostly her reactions."

On television, the actress wore a look of absolute sincerity. "Luke's attorney was there and he took us over to his place. That's where the police talked to me and I told them everything that happened."

"Great job, doll," Riley grumbled through the cigarette hanging out the corner of his mouth. "Now everyone knows where he is—including the press."

Privately Delaney wondered whether this Laura person was watching. So many tended to be media addicts, hungry for an item that mentioned the object of their obsession.

"Arthur Golden is Lucas Wayne's attorney and personal manager, isn't he?" the anchor asked.

"Yes."

"Is that where Lucas Wayne is staying now? With him?"

Tory Evans cast an anxious glance into the camera. "He *was* there, but I don't know if he still is."

"Of course. Now, this movie you're filming with Lucas—"

"A Cry in the Night," Tory Evans interrupted to supply the title.

"Are you finished filming yet?"

"Almost. As you know, it's being shot on location here in Manhattan. I have one major scene left with Luke. We'll be shooting it tomorrow in Central Park."

"Damn." Riley slipped off the stool and tossed his cup—coffee and all—into the wastebasket, then muttered under his breath, "We should have gagged her before she left the apartment yesterday."

"Amen," Delaney murmured as Riley took up his station in the doorway, watching the hall outside. He was barely in position when a gofer in shirtsleeves and faded jeans trotted up and ducked his head inside the room.

"There's a phone call for you, Mr. Wayne. On line two."

Delaney interceded, "Who is it?"

"Someone named Susan," he said, then frowned. "I think her last name was Jack—or something like that."

"St. Jacque?" Lucas suggested.

"Could have been. Should I tell her you'll call back?" the gofer asked.

"No, I'll take it." Lucas smiled an apology to the makeup girl and got out of the chair to pick up the phone. "Susan, how are you?" His voice had a friendly ring to it, but his expression was definitely guarded. "I'm fine. . . . At the moment, it looks like I'll be leaving here on Saturday. It can't be soon enough as far as I'm concerned. . . . I'll call in a day or two once everything is confirmed. . . . Dinner sounds fine, and don't worry—I'll take care of myself. . . . I have to go. Monica is waiting to powder my face. I'll call you later."

The plastic cape rustled as he hung up the phone

and returned to the chair. "Susan has an art gallery in Aspen," Lucas said to Delaney, his manner offhand. "Remind me to give you her address and phone number. She keeps an eye on my place when I'm not there. She can show you around the house and the grounds when you go to Aspen to do your advance work."

For an instant, Delaney was rigid. Going to Aspen was something she had successfully avoided thinking about—until now. She mentally gave herself a hard shake. There was nothing and no one in Aspen who could hurt her. That had ended long ago. She had a job to do.

She made some reply to Lucas and excused herself to go call Arthur and alert him to Tory Evans's interview in the event he hadn't caught it.

Nearly two hours later, Delaney sat quietly in the dressing room while Riley stood guard outside its closed door. At the other end of the room, Lucas walked a hole in the floor, stopping now and then to sip at the coffee in his personal mug. The script lay open on a nearby table, but his wanderings didn't take him by it. Delaney couldn't tell if the idleness was getting to him or if this was his way of getting into the part, working up a tension, letting it build, making the adrenaline flow. Whatever it was, she took her cue from him and didn't talk.

After a long day on the set, Lucas returned to Arthur Golden's apartment without any incident. Riley made certain the door was locked, then turned to Delaney and remarked, "One day of filming down, one more to go."

"Tomorrow will be the toughest, though," she replied with a touch of grimness.

SIX

MORNING BROUGHT SMOG AND A high thin overcast to block the sun's brilliance and spread a pale sky over Manhattan. The kind of sky that film crews prayed for on an outdoor shoot, the kind that meant fewer setups to adjust for the constantly changing angles of the sun's rays, and—with luck—the kind that could mean the entire shoot would go faster.

Delaney stood at the living room's long expanse of glass and watched the stream of traffic on the street below. The morning rush that had earlier clogged the streets was over, and the traffic was back to normal—bumper to bumper, but moving steadily, stopping only for red lights. The sidewalks carried their usual flow of pedestrians moving briskly despite the gathering summer heat, intent only on their destination in that single-minded, slightly defensive way of most New Yorkers.

Twenty stories up, the shrill whistles, the horns, the distant sirens, the rumble of traffic, the sounds of the city were muted into something faint, barely distinguishable, something remembered more than heard.

"You seem to be in deep thought."

Delaney turned from the window, not startled by the idle comment from Riley. She'd known he was standing only a few feet away, waiting like the rest of them for the phone call that would tell them they were ready for Lucas on the Central Park set.

"I wasn't exactly deep in thought—just going over everything one last time in my mind," Delaney replied.

If she seemed preoccupied and on edge, Delaney knew it wasn't due to any misgivings about today. Tomorrow, maybe, and the day after that. But not today.

The phone rang and Riley picked it up. He listened to the voice on the other end of the line, his glance sliding over to her. "Right." He nodded. "We'll have him there." He hung up, then immediately picked up the receiver again, saying, "They'll be ready for him on the set in twenty minutes. Let me confirm the limo's downstairs."

"We need to make sure the car's waiting at the Plaza for us to make the switch."

Riley responded with a nod as he dialed. In less than a minute he was off the phone. "I'll go down first and wait for you outside the elevators." He headed for the door, pulling out his two-way radio and talking into it.

Delaney picked up her purse off the bar, verified that her gun was inside, and slipped the leather strap over her shoulder. In anticipation of the day's heat, she wore white slacks and a red cotton top, and plaited her long hair in a French braid to keep it off her neck. She turned to Lucas Wayne, seated in a chair, already in full makeup. "Ready?"

"I'm ready," he said, then shook his head in an amused and marveling gesture. "You are one of the few women I know, Delaney, who doesn't pull out a mirror and check her makeup before she walks out the door."

"The time for that was before the phone call came."

"That wouldn't have stopped a lot of women I know."

"They're not in my line of work." She escorted him to the front door.

The man stationed on the floor pushed the DOWN button when he saw them come out of the apartment. "Riley said to come ahead. It's clear."

A pair of elevator doors immediately sprang open. "Let him know we're coming down on two." Delaney ushered Lucas into the elevator. The man relayed the message as he followed them inside, then reached over to punch the button for the first floor. She looked at Lucas out of the corner of her eye, her glance skimming his sun-bronzed profile. "You know the routine."

He nodded, a touch of amused boredom in the smile that lifted one corner of his mouth. "One guy goes first; I stay on his heels; you and Riley flank me; and a fourth guy protects my rear."

"And once we walk out, you don't stop for pictures, autographs, or a thousand-dollar bill on the sidewalk."

"Got it," he said with a mock salute. "What about the press? Will we have to plow through a bunch of reporters again?"

Delaney looked to the other member of her team for that answer. "Do you know, Gary?"

"There were only about three or four out there."

"Which means either the rest are waiting for you at the park or this business has become old news," she suggested with a smile.

A hint of grimness tightened the line of his mouth. "I'd like it to be old news. I'd like to be old news to Rina."

The elevator stopped its descent from the twentieth floor with stomach-sinking suddenness. When the doors slid open, Riley stood on the other side. His glance briefly connected with Delaney's; then he turned sideways in a shielding manner and extended an arm, shepherding them out while he continued to scan the lobby. For now, Riley walked ahead of them to the glass doors.

Beyond them, Delaney saw the limo parked at the curb. The jockey-sized Bennie with the unconscionably long Greek name of Papagiannopoulos waited beside the open rear passenger door, his chauffeur's cap tipped slightly back on his head. Delaney skipped her glance from him to the pedestrians passing in front of the building. A man in a business suit and a briefcase stepped off the curb to flag down a taxi, then swore and banged a fist on the trunk of a cab that nearly clipped him when it swerved into the outside lane. A woman with spiked blue hair and open-toed sandals laced up to her knees hustled by, a chartreuse purse as large as a satchel banging against her legs. All looked normal.

The sandy-haired MacDonald waited outside for them. He saw them coming and pushed open one of the doors, letting Riley pull open the other. Delaney stepped into the heat. The mid-morning temperature already hovered near the ninety-degree mark without a breath of air stirring. Automatically she took up her position on Lucas's right, her left arm impersonally curved along his back to keep him moving toward the limo while she scanned her side of the walk.

A photographer who'd been lounging against the side of the building sprang into action. Delaney threw a quick look at him, then spotted a woman in a scarf and sunglasses hurrying out of an adjoining shop.

Obeying the alarm bells that rang in her head, she called out, swift and low, "Riley, the woman in the sunglasses on my right." Without waiting for his response, she pushed Lucas toward the limo. "In the car. Now!"

As both Riley and MacDonald peeled away to intercept the plain-looking woman in a shapeless sundress layered over a tank top, Lucas slowed up. Before he could turn and look, Delaney had him by the neck, forcing his head down and propelling him urgently toward the waiting limo. "I said go!" At the same time, she blanketed him from the woman with her body.

She risked one glance over her shoulder as the two men converged on the woman. Then she concentrated all of her attention on reaching the limo's open door, ignoring the beseeching call of Rina Cole's voice. "Lucas! Lucas, please, I only want to talk to you. I'm sorry. I didn't mean to do that. I never wanted to hurt you. You've got to believe that. I love you!"

Cameras clicked rapid-fire, mixing in with the sound of a scuffle. The back seat of the limo yawned before her. Delaney shoved Lucas inside, following on his heels and tossing a quick order at Bennie. "Close the door and get us out of here."

"Let me go!" Rina Cole's angry protest reached her ears. "Lucas, don't leave me! You bastard, come back!" she raged. "Don't you dare go off and leave me like this.

Lucas! You can't walk away from me. Do you hear? I won't let you!"

The door shut, blotting out the fury of her voice and enclosing them in the serene hum of the limo's air-conditioning system. Scant seconds later, Bennie clambered behind the wheel. He twisted around in the driver's seat, his glance running to Delaney, a question forming.

"Move it, Bennie. Now!" she said forcefully.

"Yes, ma'am." With a hand on the horn and tires squealing, he swung the long black car into the traffic, forcing an opening where there was none.

"What about Riley and the others?" Lucas protested.

"They'll catch up with us. Either at the Plaza or the park." She squared around in the velour-covered seat and relaxed her grip on the gun in her purse, unable to remember just when she'd slipped her hand inside. She leaned back, silently blowing out a long breath, the adrenaline rush fading, her heartbeat slowing to its normal rhythm.

"Ooooeeee!" Bennie slapped the steering wheel and rocked from side to side in the driver's seat with excited glee. "'Move it, Bennie,' she says. Just like in the movies, eh, Mr. Wayne?" He craned his head to peer in the rearview mirror. "All my life, I been waiting for somebody to say that to me. I could get to like this danger business. I could. I swear I could."

"We're out of danger now," Delaney said dryly, not entirely sure they were ever in it. "You can slow down any time, Bennie."

"How did you know, Delaney?" Puzzled, Lucas Wayne tilted his head to the side. "How did you know that was Rina? I saw her—and didn't recognize her at all. You couldn't have had more than a glimpse of her. Yet you knew. How?"

"It was the scarf and sunglasses," she replied, then explained, "In situations where there are a lot of people—busy city streets, crowded auditoriums, large parties—you have to watch body language, anything that seems out of place. Sometimes it's the only warning you have. Bulky coats on a warm day, the sullen face among smiling ones, or—sunglasses and a scarf on a cloudy day without any breeze. When that registered, I asked myself—why is that woman trying to hide what she looks like?"

"She could have had a black eye and forgot to fix her hair," Lucas pointed out. "What if that had turned out to be the case?"

"Then I'd be sitting here with egg on my face and Riley would be back there apologizing profusely," Delaney admitted with a hint of a grin.

"But that wasn't the case, was it?" he mused, his gaze never breaking its thoughtful study of her. "You may have saved my life back there."

"I don't think so." She shook her head. "From the things she said—and the things you've told me about her—she's probably on her apology cycle. But it wasn't my place to make that kind of judgment. My job is to play it safe."

"Maybe." A slight frown narrowed his eyes. "But I still can't get over how you reacted so quickly."

Recognizing that his amazement came from the fact she was a woman, Delaney experienced a flicker of irritation and answered a little curtly, "In situations like that, there's no time to think, only act. After a while, it becomes all reflex."

"Reflex, eh? A programmed response to a given set of conditions," he murmured with more than a glint of interest in his eyes. "You intrigue me, Delaney. You intrigue the hell out of me."

The limo stopped in front of the Plaza Hotel, where the hired car waited and they made the switch to the second vehicle. As they started to leave, a cab sliced in front of them, forcing the car to stop. Riley and Mac-Donald piled out of the rear of the cab and climbed into the car.

"What about Rina?" Delaney asked once they were under way again.

Riley exchanged a private look with MacDonald, then replied with exaggerated mildness, "I think it's safe to say she wasn't a happy camper when we left her."

"Are you kidding?" MacDonald expelled a stunned and laughing breath. "That woman could give a marine lessons in swearing."

"Where is she now?"

Riley smiled. "With a couple cops who offered her a ride to the station or her apartment."

Lucas chuckled. "That wasn't one she could refuse."

The rest of the day passed without incident. That night Delaney, her cotton slacks and top exchanged for a speckled shirtdress of navy crepe, went over the schedule for the next two days, detail by detail, with Riley. Finishing at last, she straightened from the library desk, sweeping the hair back away from her face with an impatient, combing rake of her fingers.

"That's it," she said, conscious of the beginning throbs that signaled a tension headache. "Do you think you can handle it while I'm gone?" Riley gave her a properly aggrieved look that drew an immediate sigh of self-disgust from her. "I don't know why I said that, Riley. You're more experienced at this than I am. Sorry."

"It's been a long day." He shrugged it off.

"It has," she agreed and tunneled a hand under her hair to rub at the knotting cords in her neck. She saw him take a cigarette from his pack and stick it in his mouth. "Give me one of those, Riley."

He arched her a surprised look. "You quit."

"I'm backsliding."

"No guts," he taunted lightly.

"No willpower," Delaney replied as he shook one from the pack and offered it to her. She took it, then bent to touch the tip of the cigarette to the flame of his lighter. Straightening, she pulled the smoke into her mouth, felt a cough tickle her throat, and blew the smoke out without inhaling.

"What has you all keyed up, Delaney?"

"This business with Rina Cole, I guess," she lied, then found it easy to let the tumble of half-formed thoughts and vague feelings roll out. "Part of me keeps thinking that episode at the hotel was an isolated incident—and rejects the notion that she would continue to stalk Lucas Wayne with murder on her mind. A deranged fan, yes. But she's Rina Cole."

"Because she's Rina Cole, does that mean she isn't capable of going off her rocker?" Riley countered.

"No, it doesn't." She toyed restlessly with the cigarette. "But it's becoming hard for me to take this threat seriously, and I have to keep fighting that."

Or maybe it was closer to the truth that she didn't want to take the threat seriously because she didn't *want* this job to drag out for any length of time.

"You're in business, Delaney. You've been hired to

do a job. And it doesn't matter whether you think it's a job that needs to be done or not."

"I know," she said on a sigh and repeated one of her own ironclad policies: "'It's not our job to determine if a threat is real or imagined; we leave that to the police.' But usually I don't have to keep reminding myself of that—and I do this time."

"Maybe it's lover boy Lucas that's bothering you instead of Rina Cole."

"Lover boy." Delaney raised an eyebrow at that dated phrase. "You're showing your age with that one, Riley."

He ignored that. "Lucas has been coming on to you, hasn't he?"

"I have a feeling he comes on to every woman. It's as natural as breathing to him."

"Maybe so, but a lot of women would find that exciting."

"I'm not like a lot of women," she stated. "Besides, I have no intention of getting involved with a client."

"Again, you mean," Riley said, reminding her of the first time she had.

"Are we back to that again?" Irritated, she took a quick, angry puff of the cigarette.

"Back to what? Aspen?"

"You're beginning to sound like a broken record, Riley."

"At least I'm not dodging the issue the way you are."

"I am not dodging anything." She impatiently stubbed the partially smoked cigarette out in the ashtray.

Riley winced visibly. "Do you have any idea how

much cigarettes cost these days, Delaney? If all you wanted was a couple of drags, you should have told me. I would have let you have a couple puffs on mine."

"Sorry." Without the distraction of the cigarette, the compulsion to keep busy returned. "If there's nothing else we should go over, I need to finish packing."

"What you really mean is that you don't want to talk about this anymore."

"Riley—" she began with impatience.

He held up a hand, half-smiling. "Not to worry—the message came through loud and clear." He strolled toward the door. "Don't forget. My sister's going to pack some clothes for me and drop the suitcase by the office tomorrow morning."

"I'll bring it with me," Delaney promised.

"Thanks," he said and disappeared into the hall.

Delaney turned to the garment bag draped over the sofa, made sure the hangers were locked on their hook, then zipped the bag shut. Only her short kimono remained to be packed in the overnight bag. As Delaney shook the robe out to fold it, Lucas Wayne walked in.

"Riley just told me you were leaving." His glance went from her to the luggage on the sofa.

"That's right. I'm catching the red-eye to L.A., taking care of some business at my office, then flying to Aspen to get everything organized there." She made sure the robe's seams were together, than folded it in half, and in half again. "Riley will handle things on this end."

"I'm sure he will." He wandered over to the desk and hooked a leg over a corner of it, that initial sharpness leaving him, letting his easy manner surface. "But I've gotten used to my shadow having curves."

"I'll tell Riley to wear some padding." She laid the folded robe on top of the rest of her things in the overnight bag, conscious of the lazy way he was watching her every move.

"Unfortunately, it won't be the same."

"Riley will be relieved to hear that." A wry smile tugged at her mouth.

He slid off the desk to stand in front of her. "I'm going to miss you, Delaney."

"You'll see me on Saturday."

"Too long," he said, then arched a dark eyebrow. "Are you going to miss me?"

She allowed a trace of amusement to show. "I promise you'll be on my mind almost constantly."

"I have the distinct feeling you don't mean that the way I want you to."

"Probably not."

When she would have turned away, he hooked a finger under her chin and guided it back to him. "I'm going to have to do something about that."

With a tilt of his head, his mouth moved onto her lips in a kiss that forced nothing and promised everything. And Delaney knew, even as she felt the faint curl of warmth low in her stomach, that Lucas Wayne knew a great deal about women—including how to make love to them.

A discreet cough came from the doorway.

Lucas pulled back from her, aided by the firm push of Delaney's hand on his chest, and fired a glance at the figure in the doorway. Delaney didn't bother to look. She had the uncomfortable feeling that she already knew who it was.

"Sorry for the interruption," Riley said with irritating cheerfulness. "But I remembered I had these pay vouchers that Delaney needs to take with her."

"No problem. We were finished here anyway, weren't we?" She directed the question to Lucas for the moment, avoiding Riley's eyes.

Reining in his anger, Lucas looked her over. A satisfied gleam came into his eyes. "We are for now," he said and winked. "See you Saturday."

As Lucas sauntered out of the room, Riley came the rest of the way in. Delaney felt the slow, thorough inspection of his gaze and turned away, heat rising in her cheeks—partly from embarrassment and partly from anger.

"Don't say it, Riley," she warned through clenched jaws.

"Say what?" He feigned innocence. "Are you referring to that rule of yours about mixing business and pleasure?"

Her glance bounced away from the taunting gleam in his eyes as she grabbed the vouchers from him. "It wasn't the way it looked, Riley."

"If you say so." He wandered over to the arm of the sofa and hooked a leg over it, folding his arms and watching while she stuffed the papers in the overnight bag. "They say a new flame is the best defense against an old love."

"There is no room in my life for a new flame—or an old one." She snapped the bag shut with unnecessary vigor.

"Really?" he said with obvious interest. "You mean you've never considered getting married in the future? Settling down, raising a family?"

Delaney threw the question back at him. "Have you?"

"Frequently."

"Really?" She swung around in surprise, certain he must be joking.

"What do you find so shocking?" He tipped his head to one side, regarding her curiously, a smile tugging dryly at his mouth. "That I've actually met someone that I want to marry—or that she might consider marrying me?"

"No, it's just . . . you've never mentioned you were dating anyone." Truthfully, Delaney knew it had never occurred to her that he might be.

"There are a lot of things I've never told you, 'Laney." He stood up, his gaze locking with hers. Only inches separated them—as had happened countless times in the past. Except this time, something felt different. Delaney couldn't put her finger on exactly what it was. It was something nebulous and vaguely unsettling. "A lot," Riley repeated in emphasis, then moved away toward the hall door. "Have a good flight. I'll see you in Aspen."

"Right," she murmured, feeling confused without knowing why.

Somewhere in the apartment, a clock chimed the hour, reminding her that she had a plane to catch. Preoccupied, Delaney gathered up her luggage and headed for the door.

SEVEN

MORNING LIGHT STREAMED THROUGH the lace curtains at the hotel room window.

A few blocks beyond the lace and glass rose Aspen Mountain, called Ajax by the locals. Wisps of clouds trailed its peak. Ski runs snaked down its slopes, appearing as wide ribbons of summer-green grass. At its foot lay the town of Aspen, which had begun as a mining camp in the late 1880s, then been transformed by silver barons into a showplace of Victorian elegance, the remnants of its past still visible in its period buildings, its tree-lined streets, its gingerbread houses, and its fanciful turreted mansions.

Today, after a long sleep, Aspen was again a town that attracted the beautiful and the powerful, the wealthy and the celebrated to its valley high in the Rocky Mountains. These things Delaney knew about Aspen.

Abruptly she pivoted from the window and its view. Her glance swept the room's Victorian furnishings. The floral paper on the walls was authentic to the period. A crocheted spread covered the antique bed of black iron and brass. Marble-topped nightstands flanked it. Staying at the Hotel Jerome had been her father's idea.

She remembered his reaction yesterday morning when she'd returned to her canyon home in Malibu to pack more clothes. Concern had leapt into his face when Delaney told him where she was going.

"But that's where—"

She cut him off before he could say more. "I know." She went back to the closet and hauled out more clothes, carrying them to the bed.

Her father stepped around the German shepherd parked at his feet. "But what if you run into him—"

"What if I do?" Delaney countered with forced indifference. "I'll survive. The same way I survived before," she said and deliberately changed subjects. "Did you know Riley has a girlfriend?"

"Riley? You're kidding?"

"That was my reaction, too." She went on with her packing. "He's actually thinking about marrying her."

"Do you know who she is?"

"He never said."

"In a way, that doesn't surprise me," her father said. "Riley is a master at poker. He never tips his hand."

"You can say that again," Delaney agreed. "By the way, try to remember to water my plants while I'm gone. But don't drown them, okay?"

"I'll have Eddi come out and do it. They might live

that way," he said, then asked, "Where are you staying?"

"I don't know. When I get to the office, I'll have Glenda make reservations for me at one of the hotels."

"I told you, didn't I, that I spent time in Aspen during my wild oats days back in the fifties," he said, then hastened to add, "Naturally that was before I met your mother. Those were the days, Delaney."

He sighed and stared into space, a reminiscing smile softening all the harsh angles of his face until he looked almost handsome. Then he started talking again, dwelling on the past, something he had begun doing more often these last few years.

"All the top stars used to go to Aspen back then— Coop, Norma Shearer, Lana Turner—she was married to Lex Barker then—and Duke Wayne. He was quite the drinker and brawler in those days. There was this bar in this old hotel that was everybody's favorite watering hole. It was a grand old place, built back in the silver mining days. It was a little worn, a little faded, but you'd like it, Delaney. I had some good times in there. The Jerome, that's what it was called," he remembered with a snap of his fingers. "Hotel Jerome. You should stay there."

"I'll have Glenda see about it," she promised.

Delaney knew he would be pleased when she told him that the Hotel Jerome was not only still standing but had also been totally and lavishly restored. Tonight she'd have a drink in the Jerome Bar, his old watering hole. But today she had a long list of things to accomplish before Lucas Wayne arrived tomorrow.

Removing her trusty notebook from her purse, Delaney flipped through it until she found the phone number that Lucas had given her for his friend Susan St. Jacque.

"Gallerie St. Jacque. Good morning," a cheery voice answered.

"Good morning," Delaney responded automatically. "Susan St. Jacque, please."

"May I say who's calling?" the girl asked, her voice retaining its chipper sound.

"Delaney Wescott." She rubbed at the ache between her eyebrows, thinking it was much too early for so much gusto.

"One moment."

In less time than that, another voice came on the line—one not quite so cheery, but equally warm and friendly. "Ms. Wescott. How are you? Lucas told me to expect your call. When will you be arriving in Aspen?"

"I'm already here."

"You are? But I understood from Lucas you wouldn't arrive until later in the day."

"I flew in late last night." And tumbled into bed, exhausted from her marathon trip. "How soon can we meet so you can show me around the house?"

"That's a bit of a problem, I'm afraid. I have an appointment in a few minutes. I may be tied up until somewhere around noon. Where are you staying?"

"The Jerome."

"Isn't it marvelous? You'll love it there," Susan St. Jacque declared, then continued with hardly a break. "Let's tentatively arrange to meet at twelve-thirty in the lobby. If I see that's going to be a problem, I'll call."

"Sounds good. I have a few other things to do, so if I'm not here, leave a message. Otherwise, I'll be back by twelve-thirty."

"Will do. See you then," she said and rang off.

Delaney hung up and checked her list. The next major item was a visit to the local police station. She picked up her notebook, collected the packet containing her credentials and the backgrounds on the key personnel with her, and tucked both in her purse, then left the room.

After obtaining directions from the concierge, Delaney proceeded outside and turned left. Pausing at the crosswalk for the traffic light to change, she lifted her gaze to the rugged mountains that walled the narrow valley, then scanned the large luxury homes scattered on the mountainsides.

Finally her attention shifted to the wide Main Street and the Victorian false fronts of the buildings along it— buildings that spoke of another era. Despite its architecture and small-town look, Aspen was neither quaint nor picturesque. That was much too trite, and Aspen was too chic to be trite.

The light changed and a cyclist on a trim racing bike whizzed through the intersection. Delaney stepped off the curb and headed for the police station two blocks away.

The visit was both an official and a courtesy call in which Delaney presented her company's credentials, explained the reason for her presence, and stressed that the role of her personnel was strictly to protect the client. The special needs—and sometimes special problems—of dignitaries, celebrities, and important personages was nothing new to the Aspen police. As expected, Delaney walked out of the building an hour later, assured of their full cooperation.

As she paused to get her bearings, a man walked

toward her with an assured gait, his arms swinging loose and easy by his sides. Dressed in faded Levis and an equally faded denim jacket, he wore a weathered Stetson hat pulled low on his head. Recognition jolted through her, and with it, a sawing mixture of intense pain and pleasure. *Turn and walk away—now!*

Before she could obey that thought, his voice reached out to her, low and swift with surprise. "Delaney."

The moment to run was lost. Now pride held her rooted to the sidewalk. Delaney tilted her chin a fraction of an inch higher.

"Jared." She acknowledged him and heard the evenness in her voice, gaining confidence from it.

He took another step toward her, then stopped and swept off his hat, running a hand through his sun-streaked hair, eliminating its flatness, an action that was automatic rather than self-conscious. Delaney stared at the hat he held in front of him, reminded of the way he'd always treated her with old-fashioned courtesies. She forced her gaze to his face that was full of crags and hard surfaces like the mountains, yet one that could be touched with humor with no warning.

"It's been a long time." His gray-blue eyes studied her with a half-haunted look.

"I guess it has." She pretended that she didn't know exactly how many years, months, and days it had been.

There was a slight turn of his head as he glanced at the entrance to the police station, then back at her. "I saw you come out. Anything wrong?"

"No," she insisted with a small, stiff shake of her head. "Just business."

"That's where I'm headed." He nodded at the door,

a grim smile edging the corners of his mouth. "To make my regular monthly visit and see that they don't stick my sister's file in the back of the drawer and forget her."

"Then Kelly is still missing? You never heard from her?"

"No." As always, he was spare with his words, never using a lot when a few would do.

"I'm sorry, Jared." There was nothing else she could say, but somehow she wasn't surprised that Jared McCallister hadn't given up the search for his younger sister.

She remembered how desperate—how determined—he'd been to find Kelly the first time she met him. Wescott and Associates had still been in its growing stages. Although clients hadn't been few and far between, the telephone hadn't exactly rung off the wall, either.

Back then, she had run the company out of a two-room office on the second floor of a stuccoed building that tried to pass for Spanish, two blocks off La Cienega. She hadn't spent a lot of money on furnishings, keeping it to the basic necessities of desks, chairs, filing cabinets, and miscellaneous office equipment. The many bare spots were filled in with plants she'd hauled in from home. Her father had affectionately teased that the decor was contemporary greenhouse and chrome. But the crisp, no-nonsense air seemed to create the right impression with clients.

She had been at her chrome and black metal desk that second day of October more than six years ago drafting a proposal she was to present when the phone rang. Initially she had ignored it, expecting Glenda to answer it.

• • •

The phone rang a second time, then a third. Delaney threw an impatient look at the connecting door to the reception area. It never ceased to irritate her the way her prematurely steel-haired secretary and receptionist, Glenda Peters, could calmly finish folding a letter, slip it into an envelope, seal it, and stamp it while the phone jangled right beside her. Personally, she couldn't stand to hear a phone ring without immediately answering.

It rang a fourth time and started on the fifth before Delaney remembered that Glenda had told her not two minutes ago she was going down the hall to get water for coffee.

Delaney picked up the phone before it finished its fifth ring. "Wescott and Associates." She used her shoulder to cradle the receiver against her ear while she continued sorting through her presentation, arranging the sheets in order.

A man's voice came on the line, its tone firm, its manner concise, and possessing the slightest trace of a Western drawl. "I'd like to speak to Delaney Wescott, please."

"This is she."

"*She?* You're a woman?" His reaction was more confused than startled.

Delaney smiled faintly. "Thankfully, yes."

"Good answer." His voice conveyed the impression of a smile on his end. "Personally I don't care if you have two heads and a tail, Miss Wescott, as long as you can help me." It was said quite seriously, with no attempt to make light of the fact he was a man with a problem.

"I hope I can." She laid her papers aside and took hold of the phone, now as serious as he was.

"So do I. If you have time, I'll come over right now."

"Unfortunately, I don't. I have a luncheon meeting at eleven-thirty. Then I have to be in Long Beach by two o'clock. Depending on the traffic, I probably won't make it back to the office until nearly five. Perhaps we could meet somewhere"—Delaney paused, realizing—"You haven't told me your name yet."

"Jared. Jared McCallister. I flew in from Colorado three days ago. Los Angeles is foreign territory to me. I'm staying at a hotel called Los Robles. It's not far from the airport. Do you know it?"

"Yes."

"Is it anywhere close to Long Beach? Maybe you could stop here."

"That would work. Say between three-thirty and four?"

"I'll be in my room. Six-twelve. Call me as soon as you get here."

"I will, Mr. McCallister."

But the rest of the day didn't go as planned. The food service at the restaurant where she lunched was infuriatingly slow, forcing her to race to Long Beach to keep her two o'clock appointment. She arrived five minutes late and had to wait another fifteen minutes until her prospective client got off the phone. Then his endless questions made her presentation take longer than expected. By the time she left, she was already half an hour behind schedule and a misty rain was falling—the kind the wipers smeared across the windshield and that made the freeways treacherously slick, inevitably snarling traffic.

It was ten minutes to five when she walked into the hotel. She found a house phone and dialed his room.

After five rings with no answer, she knew he wasn't there. She had waited through another twelve before the hotel operator came back on the line.

"I'm sorry. Mr. McCallister is not in his room."

"I guessed that," Delaney murmured away from the mouthpiece, then lifted it to ask, "This is Delaney Wescott. Did he leave word where he would be?"

There was a short pause. "Yes, he said he'd be in the lounge. Shall I connect you?"

Delaney spotted the sign for the lounge over her shoulder. "No thanks."

The lounge had the look and feel of a gentleman's study. The walls were paneled in dark wood. A deep wine rug carpeted the floor, and the heavy chairs were upholstered in forest green leather, studded with brass. The few recessed ceiling lights were turned low, the effect creating more shadows than light.

Delaney paused a few steps inside the lounge and scanned the room. Other than the piano player seated at the parlor grand, there weren't more than a dozen people there, all men. Some were in business suits and others were more casually attired; some sat alone and others paired together—whether by choice or chance conversation Delaney couldn't tell. But she didn't see anybody that made her *think* he was Jared McCallister. And not one gave her anything but the eyeing look of a man on the make.

Containing a sigh of frustration, she crossed to the bar. The baggy-eyed bartender slid a cocktail napkin onto the counter in front of her and gave her a bored look. "What'll you have, miss?"

"I'm supposed to meet a man named Jared McCallister here. Would you know which one he is?"

He pulled the napkin back and nodded at some point behind her. "That's him. The cowboy at the piano," he said and almost smiled.

Delaney turned with a start and stared at the man playing the piano. There was no light above him, and he hadn't bothered to turn on the one affixed to the piano. A pilsner glass, half-full of beer, sat on a pressed-paper coaster atop the piano and a cowboy hat was on the bench next to him. His back was to her, and his head was bent over the keys. In the dim light, there was little she could discern about him other than that he had fairly wide shoulders and a rider's narrow hips.

As she started toward the piano, she became conscious of the music he was playing. The airy, sprightly tune filled the lounge.

Delaney sighed softly in admiration, painfully aware that she'd never been able to master "Chopsticks." She crossed the last few feet to stand beside the piano's front leg, close enough now to see the caramel color of his hair and his hard, irregular features—and the strong, blunt fingers moving so sensitively over the keys. He looked up and saw her standing there. He held her gaze for barely an instant, his gray-blue eyes crinkling at the corners. He finished the chorus and held the last note, bringing the song to an end.

He stood up—and for some strange reason, she was pleased to discover he was an inch taller than she was. His glance made a quick sweep of her, not in the stripping way the other men in the lounge had looked at her, but in a measuring that noted every detail about her— from her navy and white business suit to the large white bow that secured her long hair at the nape of her neck.

"You must be Miss Wescott."

She nodded once. "I apologize for being so late, Mr. McCallister."

"Just plain Jared will do, Miss Wescott."

"Then make it just plain Delaney," she countered.

"You know," he studied her thoughtfully, "I'll bet you intimidate the hell out of most men."

But not him, she noticed. "I've never asked. And I probably wouldn't have gotten a straight answer if I had."

"You can bet on that." He reached into the brandy snifter and took out the dollar bills inside. "Tips," he explained and shoved them into his jeans pocket.

"Looks like it was a good afternoon."

"It'll buy us a couple drinks." He picked up his hat from the piano, gestured, and motioned with it to a nearby table. "Shall we sit down?"

In the next second, his hand was at her elbow, guiding her to the table. Delaney noticed a leather blazer, a tan shade of palomino gold, draped over the back of one of the chairs. She guessed it belonged to Jared as he reached around and pulled out one of the heavy leather chairs for her—as deftly and naturally as if he'd done such things all his life. When she sat down in it, he just as easily pushed it up to the table. Yet Delaney had the feeling he didn't do it to impress her.

He sat opposite her and laid his hat on the seat with the blazer. "What would you like to drink?"

"A beer's fine."

"Draft or—"

"Draft."

He turned in his chair and showed the bartender two fingers. "Draw two, Barney."

Delaney waited until the bartender strolled over to

deliver their beers and strolled back, then said, "Why don't you tell me about your problem, Jared?"

"It's simple." He leaned forward, resting his arms on the table. "I want to hire you to find my kid sister."

"I'm afraid there's been some sort of misunderstanding. Wescott and Associates isn't a private detective agency," she said regretfully. "We don't look for missing persons, or follow cheating wives. We don't do any kind of investigative work. We specialize solely in personal protection."

He turned his head away from her, one hand doubling into a tight fist. "I was told you could help me."

"I'm sorry—" she began, then sensed the uselessness of the words. "Look, I don't know what happened to your sister, but there are agencies, shelters—"

"I've been to them." He lifted his head, a coldness and an anger in his eyes that Delaney knew wasn't directed at her but rather at the helpless feeling inside himself. "I've talked to all of them. Three weeks ago I even hired a private detective to look for her. He distributed a bunch of posters and collected three thousand dollars from me." His voice never altered its level pitch, yet each word came out hard and clipped, betraying his frustration. He paused and drank in a deep breath and laced his fingers around the beer glass. Sighing, he stared at the beer's foamy head. When he spoke again, his tone was quieter, softer. "The hell of it is, Delaney, if Kelly was lost in the mountains, I'd know where to look—how to look. But here . . . I don't even know where to start. She's my sister, dammit, and I have to find her."

"You love her a lot, don't you?" As an only child herself, Delaney had often wondered what it would be like to have brothers and sisters. Looking at Jared, she felt a twinge of envy for his sister, who obviously didn't realize how lucky she was to have a brother who cared so much about her.

"She's all the family I have. It's been just Kelly and me since our parents were killed in a crash ten years ago. Kelly was only seven then—old enough to understand what death was but . . . not really old enough to cope with it."

"How old were you?" She tried to guess his age and failed. The sun-bleached streaks in his hair created a youthful look, a look destroyed by the leathering of his skin from too much exposure to the sun and the wind.

"Twenty-two. I was in my last year at the University of Colorado." Although he didn't say so, Delaney guessed he never completed his senior year.

"Then Kelly's seventeen now."

"Yes— No, she's eighteen. She had a birthday two weeks ago." He took a slow sip of beer, then set the pilsner glass back on the table and absently pushed it around on its coaster. "I always baked a cake for her—and she always used to gripe about the mess I made in the kitchen doing it."

Delaney sensed his need to talk. She glanced at the full glass of beer in front of her, aware that the traffic on the freeway would still be a mess. There was nothing she could do—nothing she was qualified to do—to help him find his sister, but she could listen.

"I'm getting the impression Kelly ran away." When he didn't deny it, she asked, "What happened? Was there a quarrel, or—"

"No. At least not any major fight. She had been hard to get along with all summer. Quiet, moody, more withdrawn than usual. But she had just graduated from high school in the spring and—hell, I thought it was another phase she was going through," he said tiredly. "Summer's our busiest time. I own a ranch outside of Aspen," he explained, then released a short, laughing breath, his mouth twisting with unexpected cynicism. Or was it contempt? "Maybe I should qualify that, considering how many Hollywood types have bought three- and four-acre parcels, built two-million-dollar homes on them, then called them ranches, even though the only thing they raise there is Cain. Mine's a working ranch— eight hundred and sixty acres, plus a cattle permit for four hundred and seventy head. And on a working ranch in the mountains, the only four seasons you know are before haying, during haying, after haying, and winter."

Delaney looked at the hands wrapped around the pilsner glass. They were working hands, sun-browned and strong, fingers toughened by calluses—the same fingers that moved so lightly over the piano keys, their touch evoking poignant sounds. A cowboy who played Beethoven. She instantly revised that thought. Jared might have all the accoutrements of a cowboy—the yoked western shirt, the bolo tie, the Stetson hat, and the cowboy boots—yet the more he talked, the more she was inclined to believe he also possessed the business savvy of a corporate executive. She found herself wanting to ask personal questions—When had he learned to play the piano? What had he studied in college? Who were his favorite authors? What was his home like?

Instead, she said, "Was it during haying that Kelly left?"

"Yes." He nodded once. "It had rained. It was going to take a couple days for the hay to dry before we could bale it. I'd gone to Cheyenne to look at some purebred stock. I wanted to cull the older stock out of my cow herd and replace them with better quality. When I got back, she was gone. She'd packed her bags and left."

"She didn't say anything to anyone? She didn't leave a note?"

"Nothing, not a word."

"Did she have a car?"

"Not of her own, no, but she had the use of the ranch's Wagoneer any time she wanted it."

"But she didn't take it?"

"No."

Delaney frowned. "Then how did she leave the ranch?"

"We don't know. She could have hitched a ride into town . . . or even in the other direction. Or somebody could have come by the ranch house and picked her up. That's the police's theory."

"A boyfriend, maybe."

"She didn't have a steady one. Or if she did, I didn't know about him." His expression turned a little grim on that last comment, which suggested to Delaney that the police had offered that possibility, too.

"What about her friends? Did she indicate to any of them that she was thinking about running away?"

He shook his head. "I've talked to all of them. And all of them said practically the same thing: they'd had very little contact with her all summer. Even Connie Sommers, Kelly's best friend, said Kelly had become cool and distant with her. Whenever she called, Kelly never wanted to go anywhere or do anything." He stopped abruptly, the corners of his mouth drawing down in a tight-lipped look as his eyes challenged her.

"You might as well know, the police think she was on drugs."

In her experience, however limited it was, the police didn't make assumptions unless they had something to base them on. "Was she?" She could tell he wanted to deny it, but he was caught between a loyalty to his sister and a loyalty to the truth.

"I don't know," he admitted heavily, and again his hand doubled into a fist. "Dammit, she knew the way I felt about drugs." He released another gusty sigh. "But I suppose at seventeen, you don't particularly care what your brother thinks, especially when the use of it is so prevalent by your so-called betters. It's no secret that Aspen has a reputation of being a place where good times can be had—in the modern sense of the phrase."

"Did the police tell you why they thought she was on drugs?"

"They claim she was seen in the company of known users. Maybe she did get mixed up in it. Maybe I should have seen it." He opened his hands, turning them palm up. "They tell me changes in behavior are a sign of drug use. The moodiness, the dropping of old friends, the occasional sullenness—I suppose I should have questioned that. Instead I just held my tongue and waited for her to grow out of it."

"What if she is on drugs, Jared?" She idly swirled the beer in her glass.

"If she is, then she's more lost than I thought. And—it's all the more reason I have to find her."

"Why are you convinced she's in L.A.? She could have gone anywhere."

"Los Angeles is the only place she ever talked about. The ocean, the palm trees, the warm winters, the

Rose Bowl Parade, Disneyland. She and Connie had planned to come out after graduation. Then summer came and everything changed. Kelly changed." He paused, then gave a shrug of his shoulders. "I know it's a shot in the dark looking here, but it's the only one I have."

"What does she look like? Do you have a picture?"

In answer, he reached into his hip pocket and took out a billfold. He opened it, then turned it around to show Delaney the photo inside. "Her senior picture."

The dim light in the lounge and the clear plastic encasing the picture obscured the girl's image. "May I?" Delaney asked as she reached to take the wallet from him.

"Sure."

Delaney held it to one side, positioning it directly beneath the recessed ceiling light above their table. The smiling girl in the photo had angular features, long, honey-blonde hair, and a faint sprinkling of freckles across her nose and cheekbones. Hardly a beauty, but not unattractive, either. Her looks were . . . average, Delaney decided. Kelly appeared to be the kind of girl you'd want for your best friend—someone who was sometimes serious and sometimes not, but always someone you could count on. A little like her brother in that respect, Delaney thought.

"Did Kelly have any secret dreams? Any secret aspirations?" She passed the billfold back to him.

"What do you mean?" Jared frowned.

"A lot of people, when they think of Los Angeles, think of Hollywood. *And,* as you pointed out earlier, a lot of Hollywood types frequent Aspen."

His frown deepened, this time with disbelief. "You

think Kelly may have wanted to get into the movies."

Delaney laughed softly. "Girls have been known to have stranger dreams than that. Was she in any of the plays in school? Take drama, maybe? Or speech?"

He seemed to think a minute before answering. "No. She played Mary once in a Christmas pageant at our church, but she was only nine years old then. And I don't remember hearing her talk about acting—even to her friends. As far as I know, she never idolized any movie star either. Rock singers, that's something altogether different."

"Can she sing?"

Jared came close to smiling with his mouth, not just his eyes. "About as well as I can."

Delaney couldn't resist asking, "How well is that?"

"Let's just say a bull bellowing in the pasture sounds better than I do."

"Considering the way you play the piano, I find that hard to believe."

"That's something you're never going to find out," he insisted.

Delaney realized that was true—although not necessarily the way he meant it. They were meeting just this one time. There wouldn't be another. Jared was here to find his sister and there wasn't anything she could do to help him in his search. Which meant there'd be no reason to see him again. She was stunned to discover she wanted to.

A second later, she heard herself ask, "How long will you be in town?"

"Three weeks. Less than that now. I can't be away from the ranch any longer than this."

"Of course not." She took another sip of her beer, its former icy coolness now merely cool. "When Kelly left, do you know how much money she had with her?"

"Three hundred dollars, maybe. She'd been wait-ressing at a restaurant in town. Three hundred dollars is roughly what she made a week in tips."

"That's all she took? She didn't have any other money?"

"She has a savings account at the bank with about a thousand dollars in it, but she didn't touch it."

"I wonder why?"

"Aspen's a small town," he reminded her. "Every-body knows everybody. She probably didn't want to answer any questions about why she was withdrawing it."

"But three hundred dollars won't last long." Not if she was on drugs, Delaney was thinking. Not unless, as the police theorized, she was traveling with someone, some-one who maybe had more money, but that person was probably on drugs, too. And drugs had a way of using up money fast. "Did she take anything else of value? Any-thing she could sell?"

"No. All she took was her clothes and a few per-sonal things like her diary and an old teddy bear."

"What about jewelry?"

"She had her class ring, a few pieces of costume stuff . . . And for her sixteenth birthday, I bought her two gold chains."

"Was that all?" Without thinking, Delaney took her notebook out of her purse and began jotting the items down.

"Kelly never wore much jewelry."

"What about a watch?"

"She had a Lady Bulova. White gold."

"Anything else?"

"No—yes. Mom's locket," he remembered. "I gave

it to Kelly after . . . I thought she should have something that belonged to our mother."

"What kind of locket was it? Small? Big? Heart-shaped? Any pictures in it?"

"It was a round gold locket—about the size of a silver dollar. It had a flower design on the front with ruby chips for centers. Inside there was a picture of Mom and one of Dad." He paused and tipped his head to one side. "Why?"

"It's possible Kelly may have sold one or more of these items to have money to live on. Unfortunately, the gold chains and wristwatch would be practically impossible to trace. But the class ring and locket, they're more distinctive."

"Kelly wouldn't sell them. Especially not the locket," he insisted.

"Probably not." But Delaney also knew that drug users frequently attached little importance to sentimental value—or else justified the sale of something by promising themselves they'd buy it back. "If you don't mind, I'll make copies of this jewelry list and send it to the pawnshops in the L.A. area. I doubt if it will turn up anything, but it might."

Jared studied her with a curious and thoughtful look. "I thought you said you couldn't help me."

"I'm not sure how much help this will prove to be. It's a long shot. Like you said, she probably won't sell them. But"—she picked up her beer glass and lifted it in his direction—"it's the least I can do to pay you back for the beer."

"Payment isn't necessary. I appreciate the willing ear," he said, then remarked, "You're easy to talk to, Delaney."

"It's usually easier to talk to strangers."

"I guess it is."

She sipped at her beer, finding the sudden silence that had fallen between them awkward. "How about if I call around and get you the names of agencies known for their solid investigative work—a company that will do more than pass around missing person posters."

"*That* would be helpful," he agreed with a touch of wryness.

"Jared . . ." Delaney hesitated, then plunged on, feeling it had to be said. "There is every possibility your sister doesn't want to be found—that she'll make it hard for you to find her."

"I've thought about that." He nodded his understanding. "But I don't see that it changes anything."

"I didn't think it would." She smiled and gave the pilsner glass a push toward the center of the small cocktail table, then slipped the notebook back into her purse. "I think it's time I was going." Smoothly, Jared was on his feet and helping her push the heavy chair back. "I'll be in touch as soon as I have something," she said and extended a hand to him. His fingers closed around it, their grip sure, their texture a little rough. "I wish you luck in your search, Jared."

"I'm afraid I'll need it." He released her hand.

There was a lightness to her step when she crossed the lounge. She had an excuse to see him again; she'd deliberately created it. Was it foolish? Perhaps. But she wouldn't know until she had explored further.

EIGHT

GLENDA PETERS PEERED DOWN at Delaney over the top of her granny glasses. The gold chain clipped to the side of them swooped forward. "You want a copy of this list sent to *all* the pawnshops in the Los Angeles area? Do you realize how many there are?"

"The exact number doesn't matter. It needs to go to all of them and I'd like to get them in the mail today." Delaney swung away from the reception desk and crossed to her door.

"And I'd like to go on a ninety-day cruise around the world." Glenda picked up one of the Yellow Pages directories for the Los Angeles area and dropped it on her desk, the mountainous volume making a resounding *plop*! "I have about as much chance of doing that as you have of accomplishing this—today."

Delaney pushed her door open and paused in the

frame of it. "Then call Zelda in and have her help type the envelope labels."

"As long as she stays to fold, stuff, lick, and stamp," she added tartly.

"And maybe answer the phone, too," Delaney mocked.

Glenda turned a cool stare on her. "I thought you could do that."

"Wait a minute." Delaney shifted her weight to her other foot. "Who's the boss here, Glenda?"

"I am, of course," she replied, her gray eyes showing a hint of a twinkle. "I thought you knew the secretary is always the boss of any office. We merely let you hold the title."

"And sign the paychecks?" Delaney challenged.

"Ah, yes, there's that, too." Glenda smiled openly.

"Ah, yes," Delaney repeated, shaking her head in amusement as she turned and went into her office.

She crossed to her desk, slipped her purse in a bottom drawer, and sat down to go through her messages from yesterday. She took care of the calls that needed to be returned and any follow-ups they required, then dialed the phone number of her old law firm.

She recognized the receptionist's voice. "Hi, Betty. It's Delaney Wescott."

"Delaney, how are you? We sane ones miss you over here."

"I'm not surprised. Is Andy in?"

"His line was busy a minute ago. Let me check—as long-winded as that man is—it's free. I'll put you through."

A second later, a male voice came somewhat absently on the line. "Grissom here."

"Andy. Delaney Wescott."

"Delaney. How's the bodyguard business? Still more guards than bodies?"

"Cute, Andy. Very cute."

"You can guard mine anytime," he murmured, his voice lowering to a deliberately suggestive pitch.

"As usual, Andy, your wit is surpassed only by your lechery."

"You're a cruel woman. Cruel."

"So you've told me before. Can we cut through all this thrust and parry—"

"Thrust and parry. God, Delaney, you do talk sexy."

"Andy," she said in a taut warning voice. "This is a business call. I need the name of reliable private investigation companies, preferably ones that had some success in locating missing persons or runaways. I know the firm has used several in the past."

"True. Mostly in divorce and criminal cases. Do you want to hold or should I call you back?"

"I'll hold."

Within five minutes he was back on the line with the names and phone numbers of three agencies. Delaney wrote them down, refused his dinner invitation—fully aware *she* would be the one on the menu—and managed to hang up with a minimum of hassle. After that, she called three more attorneys she knew at different firms and obtained their recommendations. She compared the four lists and found three agencies that had been mentioned more than twice. Those she marked on a separate sheet of paper to pass on to Jared.

As she reached for the phone to call Jared, Riley strolled in, dressed in a pair of gray canvas pants, deck shoes, and a pink, gray, and yellow plaid sportshirt.

Delaney looked at him in surprise. "I thought you had a charter this morning."

"It was a couple from Ohio. The red flag was flying. They took one look at the swells in the open water and got cold feet. I thought I'd come over here and see what was stirring. By the way"—he tipped his head in the direction of the reception office, where two computers clackety-clacked away—"what's all that about? Glenda wouldn't tell me. She just glared at me over the top of her glasses and jerked her head in the direction of your door."

Briefly Delaney told him about her meeting with Jared McCallister, concluding with, "I was about to call him with the names of three agencies when you came in."

"The pawnshops were a good idea." Riley hooked a leg over the corner of her desk and pulled out a cigarette to light it.

"I probably shouldn't have offered. It really isn't our line of work, but—"

"Think of it as your good deed for the week," he suggested.

"I suppose you could call it that." It sounded better than admitting she had gotten herself personally involved for a more selfish reason. Namely, seeing Jared again.

"He didn't happen to give you his sister's Social Security number, did he?"

"No, why?"

"If you're right and she needs money, she might have gone to work somewhere. She might even have used her own Social Security number. I've got a connection in Sacramento that could run her number through the computer and see if she's shown up on any of the employers' quarterly wage reports. It might be too soon, but it's worth a shot." He tapped his cigarette in the ashtray on her desk.

"Now *that's* a good idea. I'll call him now, give him these names, and find out her Social Security number." Delaney picked up the phone and dialed his hotel. But Jared wasn't there.

She tried again before she went to lunch and again when she returned—with the same results. At midafternoon, there was still no answer in his room. When she tried at four-thirty and he still wasn't back, she left her home phone number with the hotel operator. She slipped the list of names in her purse and walked out of her office into the reception area. Glenda was at her desk, methodically stamping a stack of envelopes.

Delaney glanced around. "Where's Zelda?"

"She went home. She cut her tongue on an envelope flap. I told her to use a damp sponge to moisten them, but she wouldn't listen to me," Glenda replied in a serves-her-right tone.

"How close are you to being finished?"

She checked the stack of sealed envelopes in front of her. "About twenty more stamps." She looked up at Delaney. "I didn't think it could be done, but it looks like they'll be mailed tonight. Maybe I will get my round-the-world cruise yet."

"Not soon, I hope. A ninety-day vacation for secretaries isn't in the cards for Wescott and Associates."

"Yet."

"See you tomorrow." Delaney walked out the door, somehow certain the day would come that Glenda would get her ninety-day vacation and a cruise around the world.

In the office building's small parking lot, she unlocked the door to her compact Ford, a bland shade of blue, and slipped behind the wheel, promising herself again she'd get a new car as soon as the business was solidly on its feet. She pulled out of the lot onto the street and headed toward the Santa Monica Freeway, then, on impulse, she changed directions and drove to Jared's hotel.

She parked under the hotel's canopy and handed the car keys to an attendant. As she turned from him, Delaney caught sight of a man in a dark cowboy hat, plaid shirt, and faded jeans coming up the sidewalk at an unhurried pace. His head was down and his hat was pulled low, his fingers tucked in the front pockets of his jeans. She couldn't see his face and had only a glimpse of pale brown hair beneath his hat, but she knew it had to be Jared. She set out to meet him.

He passed the spiked leaves and flowering stalks of a bird-of-paradise and turned into the hotel entrance. He was a scant five feet away before he looked up and saw her. His mouth twitched at the corners with a near smile. "Hello, Delaney."

"Jared. I've been trying to reach you all day."

"I've been out."

"So I gathered," she said with a small smile. "Have you had dinner yet?"

"No."

"Good. I know a great little steak and seafood place by the ocean."

The parking attendant opened the driver's door for her and returned the keys. She climbed in and waited for Jared to close his door, then turned the key in the ignition, starting the car.

• • •

It was early yet for the dinner crowd. Delaney and Jared had their pick of tables next to the oceanside windows. After he saw Delaney into her chair, Jared sat down in his own and hooked his hat onto a back corner of it.

"Some view." With a tip of his head at the window, he indicated the wide expanse of ocean beyond the tinted glass. Its deceptively smooth surface was tinted a shimmering gold by a down-traveling sun.

Delaney nodded in agreement. "I come here a lot. There's something about watching the ocean that's very soothing."

"Do you suppose it can soothe the heart of an angry beast?" he asked in jest, and Delaney knew he was referring to himself.

"I think it's 'savage breast.'"

"Maybe it is."

A waiter stopped at their table. "Good evening. What would you like from the bar this evening?"

"Chivas and water," Delaney ordered.

"The same." Jared nodded.

When the waiter had moved away, Delaney opened her purse and handed Jared a slip of paper from it. "These are the three private investigation companies that were recommended to me. Hopefully one of them will be able to help you find Kelly. I suggest, though, that you talk with all three before you make your choice."

"I will. Tomorrow." He folded the paper in half and tucked it inside the breast pocket of his shirt.

"If you know Kelly's Social Security number, I'll need it," she said, then explained Riley's connection in the state offices in Sacramento. "It may not turn up anything, of course," she concluded, "but it's worth a try."

"Anything is," he stated and gave her the numbers, one at a time, while she wrote them down in her notebook.

Delaney put her notebook away as the waiter arrived with their drinks. She picked up her glass and lifted it in a toasting gesture toward Jared. "To finding Kelly."

"Amen." He clinked his glass against hers, then each took a sip of their scotch and water mixture. "For someone who's not in the detective business, you've come up with a couple things no one else has. I'm starting to feel like a real effort is finally being made to find her."

"I'm glad."

"What is it your company does? Something about protection, wasn't it?" A trace of chagrin appeared in his expression. "I admit that once you said you couldn't help me, I didn't pay a lot of attention to the rest."

"Wescott and Associates specializes in personal protection."

Jared frowned. "In other words, you're a bodyguard."

"That's an oversimplification of what we do, but—in plain language—it's fairly accurate. However, we don't exactly stand around and flex our muscles." A hint of a smile showed around the edges of her mouth. "Our strategy is more like a game of chess. We're the knights. It's our duty to always be in a position to protect our king or queen—or to check any move that's made against them. Which means we're constantly trying to outthink our opponents and anticipate their moves, not merely block them."

"Who do you protect?" he asked. "And from whom?"

Delaney raised her eyebrows at that all-encompassing question. "Let's see . . . our clients have run the gamut of occupations. There were two doctors who operated an abortion clinic and started getting bomb threats from a radical segment of a pro-life group. A female defense attorney who won an acquittal for her client on a rape charge. She was harassed and stalked by a man who turned out to be a relative of the rape victim. There was a manufacturer who was attacked by a disgruntled ex-employee he'd fired. A few celebrities, corporate executives—especially those in companies that are international—people like that." She paused for a breath. "In short, we protect all kinds of people from all kinds of people—the wealthy from extremist groups who pick targets based solely on the amount of media attention they can get; others from those bent on avenging a wrong, whether real or imagined; celebrities from fans, adoring or deranged. Sadly, there doesn't seem to be an end for the need of our services."

"A commentary on the times, I guess," he said and took a small swig of his drink. "What about your parents? Are they both still living?"

Delaney looked down at her glass and shook her head. "My mother died three years ago. A malignant brain tumor." She sipped at her scotch, nursing the glass with both hands. "She'd never been sick a day in her life. The only time she was ever in a hospital was to have me. Then she started having headaches. Instead of going away, they got progressively worse. Finally she went to our family doctor and . . . it was inoperable. In less than three months, we lost her." She rubbed the cold, wet rim of the glass across her lower lip. "Whenever I think about it, I'm glad I had the chance to tell her how much I loved her."

"What about your father?"

"Dad's still going strong." Thinking of him, she smiled. "He had a hard time of it after Mom died. He depended on her for practically everything. But he pulled through it. He even has a lady friend now."

"What does he do?"

"He's an actor. I'd say he was semiretired, but actors never retire." She sensed his withdrawal, an almost physical pulling back from her. "I have the feeling you don't care much for actors."

"Actors. Singers—stars." He turned his drink glass in place, an arm hooked over the back of his chair. "I resent the way they regard preferential treatment as one of their rights—the way they think they can do anything they want because of who they are. And maybe . . . I just wish they'd get the hell out of Aspen." With that, he downed the rest of the scotch in his glass.

Delaney simply shrugged. "They have their faults the same as everybody. The spotlights merely make their faults more noticeable."

"It's nothing personal against your father, Delaney—"

She held up a hand to stave off the rest. "Nothing personal taken."

"Maybe I'd better ask if your father is someone I should know."

"Not hardly. Dad's a character actor—one of those faces you see a lot and hardly ever remember—and never bother to check the credits to find out his name. His biggest role was playing a villain on a soap several years ago. Unfortunately his character outlived its usefulness and the writers killed him off—to the cheers of the viewers."

"Did the acting bug ever bite you?"

"No way," Delaney replied immediately. "When I was growing up, I saw how my father sat around waiting for the phone to ring. Unless an actor is in a weekly television series or a soap, he's lucky if he works a third of the time. I couldn't stand that. And I know I couldn't handle all the rejection. They refer to auditions as cattle calls in the business, and it's true. They round the actors up, herd them into a holding area, then drive them through the chute one at a time. They pass by a guy who looks at them and says, "No good, no good, no good." And out the other end they come. I'm really not surprised actors have such fragile egos—or that when they make it, they constantly need to be reassured that they are good."

The waiter came by their table again. "Another round of drinks?"

"Not for me," Delaney said.

"Me either. Why don't we look at the menu," Jared suggested.

When Delaney agreed, the waiter produced the menus with a slight flourish, then recited the specials for the evening and left them to make their decisions.

Throughout dinner, their conversation was relaxed and pleasant as they exchanged anecdotes from their childhood years and compared notes on their college experiences. Delaney was aware that Jared was steering clear of anything recent in his life. She guessed it was too closely tied to his sister, a subject he seemed intent on avoiding tonight.

Outside, the sun had gone down and the purpling twilight sky had given way to night. The ocean was a shiny black mirror, edged by ribbons of whitecaps where the waves rolled into shore. The votive candle at their table cast a flickering light over Jared's irregular features. Delaney found herself watching him while he talked, fully aware that he wasn't handsome by any stretch of the imagination—yet he had the kind of face that made any woman look at him twice.

Jared glanced at the plain gold watch on his left wrist. "It's almost nine o'clock," he said with some surprise. "I need to get back to the hotel and see whether there's been any word from Kelly." He signaled to the waiter for the check and reached into his hip pocket for his wallet.

"Dinner was my idea. Let me have that," Delaney insisted when the waiter left the check.

Jared pulled out a credit card. "I can't. I wasn't raised that way, Delaney." His response was firm, leaving no room for argument. Delaney decided against forcing one.

Twenty minutes later, she pulled up to the entrance to his hotel. Jared climbed out the passenger side, then turned around and bent down to look at her. "Thanks for the company and the conversation tonight, Delaney. I needed it."

"So did I."

But she was very conscious of all the wistful feelings she had as she drove away.

NINE

ON FRIDAY, FOUR DAYS AFTER mailing the jewelry lists, the owner of a pawnshop near Hollywood and Vine called to say he thought he had the locket in his possession. Delaney hung up and immediately called Jared's hotel. Except for a brief conversation on the phone when he'd let her know he'd hired one of the agencies she'd recommended, she'd had no contact with him.

"I'm sorry, Mr. McCallister's line is busy," the hotel operator informed her.

Delaney hesitated, briefly wondering how long he might be tied up, then decided not to find out. "This is Delaney Wescott. Tell him to meet me outside the hotel. I'll be there in thirty minutes to pick him up. Make sure he gets the message right away. It's important. Have you got that?"

"Yes, Miss Wescott."

She hung up, grabbed her purse from the bottom

drawer, and bolted from her office. "Glenda, I'm picking up Jared and heading to that pawnshop. I'm not sure when I'll be back." She slung the long purse strap over her shoulder and headed straight for the door. "When Riley gets here, tell him the schedules, the routes, the layouts, and the special notes for the concert next week are on my desk. If I'm not back, have him go ahead and make any adjustments or changes he thinks necessary. I'll go over it with him later."

She sailed out of the office, leaving Glenda with her mouth open in the midst of forming the words, "I will."

In under twenty-five minutes, Delaney whipped her car into the hotel drive and braked to a stop beneath its canopied entrance. She saw in a glance that Jared was not outside waiting for her; nor was there any sign of him just inside the lobby. Irritated by the thought that the hotel operator hadn't given him the message, Delaney slammed out of the car, informed the parking attendant she'd be right back, and swept into the hotel.

Four steps inside the lobby, she saw Jared coming toward her with a loping stride. He looked the successful rancher in his palomino leather blazer, western-cut brown dress pants, chocolate brown Stetson, white dress shirt, and bolo tie.

"What's up?" He frowned with the question.

Delaney did her explaining on the way out the door. "I got a call from a pawnshop owner who thinks he may have the locket. We'll go over there and see if you can identify it."

Two feet from the car, he caught her arm and spun her toward him, catching her by the shoulders. "You've done it, Delaney. You've done it."

She had a startled instant to see his joyous expression, then his head tipped at an angle and his mouth slammed against hers. The contact produced a sudden, sharp kick of feeling. But she recognized the kiss for what it was. Being kissed out of gratitude was the last thing she wanted. She brought her hands up to push him away. Then—something happened. His lips went still against hers for a pulsebeat or more. They started to pull away, then came back with a warm, wanting pressure that snatched at her breath.

Before it could become more than that, his fingers tightened their hold on her arms. He set her back from him and turned his head, his hat brim shadowing his face from her. "Let's go," he said, his voice a little harsh and a lot husky before he headed around the car to the passenger side.

Delaney stood there a second longer until the ground felt solid beneath her again. Then she turned and slid behind the wheel. As she drove away from the hotel in the direction of the pawnshop, she was conscious of the tension in the air. A tension that had nothing to do with the questions that would be answered once they reached their destination. A tension that had been created by that brief kiss. She didn't pretend she understood the cause of it. It was simply there. She flexed her fingers, trying to make them relax their ridiculously fierce grip on the steering wheel.

For once, luck was on her side and Delaney found a parking space less than half a block from the store. She was out of the car before Jared could come around to open the door for her.

"There it is." She pointed to the pawnshop sign above a storefront window, then felt she had to warn him. "Don't get your hopes too high, Jared. It might not be your mother's locket."

"I know." They were the first words he'd said since they'd left the hotel.

A string of bells above the door jingled to announce their presence when they entered the shop. The place had a musty smell heavily laced with lemon oil. Its walls, shelves, and counters were filled with an odd assortment of antiques, electronics, musical instruments, televisions, small appliances, and jewelry.

An old woman with a pronounced widow's hump shuffled out from behind a drum set, a bedraggled feather duster in her gnarled hand. "May I help you?"

"We're here to see Mr. Hoffmeier. I spoke with him about an hour ago—"

"About the locket." The woman nodded and waved a staying hand at them as she clumped off in her orthopedic shoes toward the back of the shop. "Karl. Karl, those people are here about the locket. Karl?" Her querulous voice rose shrilly on his name.

"Yes, yes, yes," came the impatient and complaining response from the back room, followed by the sound of uneven footsteps. Within seconds, a balding man emerged from the rear of the store, swinging his right leg in a stiff-legged limp. He wore a pair of gold-rimmed glasses with a jeweler's eyepiece attached to the frame, ready to be flipped down. He paused when he saw Delaney and Jared, studying them both with cautious suspicion. "Yes?"

"I'm Delaney Wescott, Mr. Hoffmeier. You called me earlier this morning about the locket."

"Yes. As I told you, I cannot be certain this locket is the same one you seek."

"Yes, you told me. This is Mr. McCallister, the gentleman I spoke to you about. The locket belonged to his sister. If you wouldn't mind showing it to him, we can find out whether it's the same one."

"Of course, I have it over here." He limped to the cash register. "After I spoke with you, I removed it from the case."

He produced a Prince William cigar box from beneath the cash register counter and opened the lid. He lifted out a round gold locket suspended from a gold chain, hastily located a scrap of velvet and spread it on the counter, then laid the locket on top of it.

Jared stepped closer and touched the edges of the locket with the ends of his fingers. It was the size of a silver dollar, with a posy of flowers etched on the front with four tiny red stones marking the centers of each flower. His expression was frozen into something unreadable.

"Is that the locket?" Delaney asked.

He slowly nodded that it was. "I didn't think she would sell it."

"The girl who brought this to me—she had no wish to reclaim it. I have been in this business fifty-two years. I can tell the ones who are reluctant to part with something from the ones who care only about how much money they'll get."

"Do you remember what she looked like?" Delaney watched as Jared picked up the locket and released its catch to open it. There were no pictures inside; the round frames were blank.

"She was young, blonde. . . ." He hesitated, then shook his head. "Many people have come into our store in a month's time. The faces begin to blur."

"Jared, show him Kelly's picture," she suggested. "It might help."

He took out his billfold and removed the wallet-sized photo of his sister. The pawnshop owner took it and peered at it closely. "The hair, it is perhaps the same color. The freckles, I don't remember. But these young girls nowadays, they wear too much makeup. This could be the same girl, but I cannot swear it is." He handed it back.

"Did she give you her name or address?"

"Of course. I buy nothing if a person will not tell me who they are and where they live. I keep such records for everything in my store." He checked the numbered tag attached to the locket's chain, then pivoted stiffly around to open a card file drawer atop an old wooden desk. Almost triumphantly, he pulled out a card and laid it on the counter for Delaney to see. "There it is. Johan— no, *Joanne* Smith, and her address . . ."

When Delaney took out her notebook to write down the address, Jared leaned over to look at the card. "This handwriting isn't Kelly's."

"No, it is mine," the shop owner replied, then looked up. "I remember now. Her right hand was in bandages. She'd burned it. That was the reason she was selling the locket—to pay the doctor."

"Can you find that address?" Jared asked Delaney.

She nodded. "If I'm not mistaken, it should be near Exposition Park. I have a street map in my car. I'll check."

"Do that," Jared said and slipped Kelly's photo back into his billfold. "I'll be buying back that locket, Mr. Hoffmeier. How much is it?"

"I'll wait for you in the car." Delaney headed for the door.

• • •

For two hours they searched the general area for the address. Finally, Delaney was forced to conclude, "We have to face it, Jared. There is no such address. Kelly doesn't want to be found."

He sighed, a long and discouraged sound. "You're right. But her burned hand gives us something to go on. It's merely a matter of finding a doctor who treated a Joanne Smith."

"Assuming she used that name and not some other alias." She hated being the wet blanket, but it was necessary. "Even if you were lucky enough to contact the right doctor, you'd still have the problem of doctor-patient confidentiality. He wouldn't be able to release any information to you about Kelly—not even where she lives." She glanced sideways at Jared. "I'm afraid that's a dead end, too."

He digested her words without comment. Delaney turned the car away from the curb and accelerated into the street's traffic. The silence lengthened and she wished she had said something more encouraging, but she'd always believed in dealing squarely with the facts, and the facts dictated otherwise. They couldn't be changed; therefore, they had to be faced.

"Let me out by the park up here, Delaney."

His request took her by surprise. "Why? What for?" She spotted a turn-in just ahead and hurriedly switched lanes to take it.

"I need to walk . . . on grass instead of concrete," he replied somewhat grimly.

Delaney found a place to park the car. She switched off the engine and started to gather up her purse. Jared pushed his door open.

"You don't need to come with me, Delaney. I've taken up enough of your time today. I'll catch a cab back to the hotel." His fingers closed around the locket in his hand. "Thanks for this and for everything else you've done to try to help."

"I wish it could have been more," she said to his back as he climbed out the passenger side.

The door closed and she caught the waving flick of his hand in farewell before he moved away from the car, striking out across the grass into the park. She slipped the key back in the ignition, then hesitated. She had a last glimpse of him before he disappeared from view— his head down, his shoulders hunched forward. Not exactly a picture of dejection, more like someone lost, unsure where to go, what to do. Delaney doubted being alone was what he needed—or wanted—right now.

On impulse, she pulled the key from the ignition, got out of the car, locked it, and set out after him. She hadn't gone far when she saw him standing in the shade of an oak, his head thrown back as if he was surveying the smog-layered sky above. Slowing her steps, Delaney angled toward him. When she was about ten feet away, there was a slight movement of his head in her direction, signaling his awareness of her approach.

She stopped beside him, half-expecting him to ask what she was doing there and make some kind of protest against her presence. But she didn't expect the arm that came up and draped itself around her shoulders, drawing her closer to him. Automatically she curved her own around the back of his waist.

Jared looked down at the locket still clutched in his right hand, a glimmer of moisture in his eyes. "This locket proves Kelly's in L.A. If nothing else, it does that." His fingers closed around it as he lifted his gaze. "I'll find her. I don't know how yet, but I'll find her."

"You will," Delaney agreed, convinced somehow he would.

When she leaned into his side, intending to give him a bolstering hug, Jared swung toward her and wrapped both arms around her, something fierce and needing in the tightness of his embrace. Delaney held on just as tightly, wanting to absorb some of his ache, some of the anguish over his missing sister. She had no idea how long they stood there, her head tipped to the side to avoid bumping the brim of his hat, holding him and being held by him.

"You're good for me, Delaney," he said in a thick and husky whisper near her ear. "You're so damned good for me."

At that moment Delaney didn't care whether she was reading more into that statement than he meant. She turned her head, seeking and finding his lips. Instantly they closed on hers with a pressure that was hard and wanting, and she returned it without reservation, his arms binding her to him and her own locked around him, each straining for a greater closeness, needing it.

Others had kissed her with more finesse; others had made her feel more sexually alive; yet the simple roughness of his kiss called up feelings much more basic, much more ageless—feelings that made a woman want a man for reasons that went beyond sex and filled every corner with sparkling sunshine. She was dazzled by it, wanting to laugh and cry at the same time.

Jared drew back, his callused hands framing her face, his breathing more than a little ragged. His eyes moved over her face, a warm glow shining from their dark centers.

"You're one helluva woman, Delaney." He pulled in a deep breath, shaking his head in a reluctant way. "And I think we'd better stop now, while we can."

"You're probably right," she agreed, a little surprised to discover that despite the pounding of her heart and the almost violent ache inside, she felt remarkably calm.

"I am." He lowered his head and kissed her lips with a tenderness that was at complete odds with his earlier roughness.

He stepped back, releasing her to take hold of her hand. They started walking, an aimless stroll, and Delaney wondered how she could possibly have forgotten the pleasure to be found in merely holding hands.

"Could I interest you in a change of scenery, Jared?" she asked. "Some place with acres of sky, a place with canyons and open spaces, a place where the buildings aren't so close together and where there's even a possibility of a home-cooked meal?"

"Next you'll try to convince me such a place exists in this city," he said skeptically but curiously.

"Not far from here," she replied. "My place. I live in one of the mountain canyons above Malibu. My dad's coming over for dinner tonight and I know he wouldn't mind if you joined us." She wanted her father to meet him. She wanted Jared to meet her father; she wanted to show Jared her home—her life. "What d'you say? Are you tired of restaurant food?"

"I'm tired of restaurant food, the four walls of my hotel room, and my own company."

"Is that an acceptance?" She chided its form.

"No." He stopped. "I'm afraid it's an attempt to justify to myself why I'm going to accept."

"Don't justify it, Jared." Was that her voice speaking so softly? "Just say you'd like to come."

His eyes crinkled at the corners. "I'd like to come and have dinner tonight with you and your father."

"See how easy that was?"

He kissed her again—with satisfying thoroughness. "*That's* what's easy, Delaney. Too easy."

"I'm glad."

His smile was a little stiff and a little rueful. "Then we're a pair of fools."

Privately, Delaney knew it was true. In two short weeks, he would return to his ranch in the mountains, his home in Colorado. Her life, her family, her career, her home were here in California. Every instinct told her not to become emotionally involved with Jared. But she, who'd always been such a realist, wasn't listening to them. For the first time in her life, she was living for the moment and refusing to look ahead.

Some three hours later, Jared stood in her small but cheery white-enameled kitchen, his hat and jacket on the brass halltree in the entryway, one hip propped against the counter, a cold beer from the refrigerator in his hand, his eyes watching while she put away the groceries she'd bought at the market on their way to the house.

"It feels good to be in a kitchen again," Jared remarked.

"After living in a hotel for a week, I'm sure it does." She pushed her year-old German shepherd out of the way to open a lower cupboard door and set a five-pound bag of potatoes in its bin.

Jared touched a finger to a scallop-edged leaf of the Swedish ivy plant that trailed over its hanging basket near the window. "You like surrounding yourself with living things, don't you?"

Delaney straightened from the cupboard and glanced at the plant beside him, remembering all the others in the combination living and dining room. "Isn't that odd? I've never thought about my plants as living things, but they are, aren't they?" she mused.

"Do you talk to them?"

"Only when they need it." Smiling, she folded the empty grocery sack and put it away with the others. Finished, she took a wine cooler from the refrigerator and poured it into a tall glass. "Let's go out on the patio. It's too nice to stay inside."

Signaling his agreement with action, Jared pushed away from the counter and waited for her to precede him out of the kitchen. Delaney led the way through the bungalow's combination living and dining room, which retained much of its original Art Deco look, a look that had been popular when the house was built back in the thirties.

Crossing the room, she studied it with a critical eye, wondering whether Jared liked the mix of cool teal greens, delicate mauves, and warm pinks against the glazed dove gray walls and the scattered touches of dramatic black. Did the room look comfortable and inviting to him—or a little too sleek, a little too modern? She was forced to admit there was little about it that was masculine. Would that bother him? Did he prefer something more rustic, something with more stone and wood? It was crazy to realize how much she wanted him to like her home.

"I see you have your chess board set up." With his beer glass, Jared gestured at the chess table and flanking chairs situated along one wall.

"Always." The German shepherd bounded ahead of them to the French-style patio doors, his tail wagging in eagerness.

"How long have you lived here?" Jared reached around her to open the right-hand door. The instant a crack showed, the shepherd made it wider and charged outside.

"Off and on practically all my life." Delaney stepped through the doorway onto the flagstoned patio, shaded by a 500-year-old oak. "Permanently only the last three years. The house belonged to my mother. She left it to me in her will."

She wandered over to stand by a wind-sculpted tree and lean a shoulder against its gnarled and twisted trunk, conscious of Jared coming up to stand beside her. Beyond stretched the green and gold hills of the coastal range with its series of mountainous canyons that linked the city's western valleys with Malibu's beaches. Overhead a hawk soared lazily, riding the current of a rising thermal. In the distance, the ocean was a hazy blue shimmer that almost blended in with the blue of the smog-free sky.

"My mother inherited it from a bachelor uncle years ago—before she married my father." Delaney let her gaze follow the German shepherd as he made his rounds investigating to find out who and what had invaded his territory while he'd been locked in his kennel. "Dad would never let her sell it, no matter how lean the times got between acting jobs. It was partly pride on his part, but mostly he wanted her to have some kind of security, even if he couldn't provide it."

"He loved her."

"Yes." It was as simple as that, and Delaney was pleased Jared saw it. She turned at right angles to him, resting both shoulders against the oak's trunk and idly studying him, liking the serious and quiet man before her. "While I was growing up, we used to spend some of our weekends here. Dad called it our private canyon hideaway."

Suddenly the German shepherd started barking excitedly. A second later, Delaney heard a car coming up the drive to the house.

"My father," she said to Jared in needless explanation. Together they went to meet him.

TEN

As Delaney gave the salad a final toss, the over-sized red cotton sweater slipped off one shoulder. She tugged it back in place, then laid the large salad fork and spoon aside and set the salad on an empty shelf in the refrigerator. She pushed the door shut with her hip and reached for the hand towel on the counter. She paused in midwipe, suddenly conscious of the absolute silence coming from the living room.

What on earth was wrong in there? Not twenty minutes ago, her father and Jared had been chatting away amiably. She hadn't been surprised by that. Her father had a knack for getting along with anyone. Which was why the silence bothered her.

She moved cautiously to the door and almost laughed when she discovered the cause for the silence. There was Jared, leaning back in his chair, his arms folded in front of him, a satisfied look on his face; her father sat across the chess table from him, hunched over the board, a study of concentration. Her father considered himself a master of the game. She should have guessed he'd challenge Jared to a match when Jared mentioned in passing that he played chess.

Jared saw her and nodded. Still carrying the towel, Delaney walked out of the kitchen and crossed the dining area. "Do I dare ask who's winning?"

She suspected she already knew the answer; Jared couldn't have looked more confident if he had rocked back in his chair, folded his hands behind his head, and put his feet up.

Her father turned his silvering head and fixed an accusing look on her. "Where did you find this guy?"

"I didn't. He found me." She stopped by his chair to study the board and automatically laid a hand on her father's shoulder. "I have a suggestion, Dad."

"I'll take it."

"Concede the game and put the steaks on the grill. It's checkmate in two moves no matter what you do."

"True," he admitted on a sigh. Then, with a show of graciousness in defeat, he lifted his hands and bowed his head to Jared. "The game is yours." To Delaney, he said, "My error was in underestimating him. I was taken in by his cowboy boots. Never again."

"I should hope not." She grinned.

"I like him, though, even if he did beat me," her father stated, and sent a twinkling glance at Jared.

"Thank you. I regard that as a compliment, Mr. Wescott," Jared replied.

Her father gave an exaggerated wince. "Make that

Gordon, please. *Mr. Wescott* sounds old, and regardless of the gray in my hair, I am not old."

"It's the Peter Pan syndrome," Delaney explained. "Nearly every actor has it. It's what enables them to play 'pretend' so believably."

"Don't take away all our mystique, Delaney." Her father pushed his chair back from the chess table, his smile telling her not to take his complaint seriously. She knew better and recognized the smile was for Jared's benefit rather than hers. "Where are the steaks?"

"In the kitchen."

"Lead me to them." He stood up. "I hope you like yours medium, Jared. It's the only way I know how to cook them."

"Medium's fine." Jared set about putting away the chessmen.

All the way to the kitchen Delaney was conscious of her father's jaunty air and the speculating gleam in his eye each time he glanced her way. She knew what he was thinking and felt oddly embarrassed by it, something that hadn't happened to her since she was a teenager. She gave the hand towel a toss onto the counter and picked up the plate of strip steaks and long tongs.

Before she could turn, her father whispered near her ear, "Don't let this one get away."

"Stop it, Dad." She turned and pushed the plate and the tongs into his hands, telling him the same things she'd been telling herself. "He's from out of town and—"

"Don't try to convince me you invited him to dinner out of pity," he chided with fake sternness. "That isn't pity I see in your eyes when you look at him."

"You're my father. You're not supposed to see what's in my eyes."

His quick, low laugh drew a smile from her. With his hands full, he gave her a nudge with his elbow. "Go get him, honey." He feigned a drawl. "Rope and tie and brand him if you have to."

She grabbed the towel from the counter and threatened to snap him with it. "Out."

He left, still chuckling to himself. Delaney shook her head, in truth more pleased than exasperated. With a raking comb of her fingers, she slipped her dark hair away from her face and picked up a loaf of freshly baked Italian bread. As she slipped the loaf out of its white paper sack, she heard the heavy tread of booted feet on the hardwood floor outside the tiled kitchen. A look over her shoulder found Jared in the doorway.

"Is there something I can help with? I'm starting to feel like a fifth wheel."

"How are you at setting tables?"

"I've had some experience."

She smiled at the dry humor in his voice and took a stack of three plates from the cupboard. "Have at it." She handed them to him and went back to her own task of slicing the crusty bread into thick chunks and placing them in the electric bun warmer.

He came back for the water glasses and again for the silverware and napkins. When he returned to the kitchen a third time, Delaney had the butter dish, condiments, and steak sauces sitting out on the counter for him. He carried them off to the table, then wandered back in.

"What else?"

"I'll have the salads ready in a minute." She retrieved the spinach salad from the refrigerator and placed the wooden bowl on the counter next to the salad plates.

Jared strolled over to lean a hip against the counter and watch. "By the way, I like your father. In some ways he isn't what I expected."

Aware of his opinion of celebrities in general, Delaney didn't need an explanation of that remark. Instead, she simply nodded. "I know. My dad's warm, caring, and funny at times—as well as irresponsible and impractical."

"But you're not. Irresponsible and impractical, I mean."

"Somebody has to be the parent." She shrugged and the sweater slipped off her shoulder again.

Before she could pull it back up, his fingers were there, the back of them brushing the rounded point of her shoulder as he drew the knitted red cotton over it. "It isn't easy being the strong one all the time, is it?"

She looked at him, a little stunned by his astuteness, then realized he'd experienced the same thing with his sister. "No, it isn't. But you know that."

"Yes." He lightly stroked her cheek with the back of his fingers, tracing the angle of her jaw to her chin, then coming up to rub the side of his finger along her lower lip. He watched it, staring at her mouth. Her breathing became shallow, anticipating his kiss. Instead he drew away, curling his finger into his palm. "I think I'll go see how your father's coming with the steaks while you finish up here."

Delaney watched him go, thoroughly confused. He had wanted to kiss her; she knew she wasn't wrong about that. But he hadn't. Why?

At dinner, her father typically dominated the conversation, covering a wide range of subjects before settling on the one he loved best: acting and his early days in Hollywood. Having heard the stories before, Delaney listened with only half an ear—until he started talking about her mother, how they met, their courtship and marriage. He'd hardly talked about her mother since her death—certainly not to a stranger. She was surprised he was doing it now. Then suddenly it hit her and she wanted to kick him under the table for his subtle attempt at matchmaking.

"It's trite but true, Jared," he declared. "There is nothing like the love of a good woman to make life complete."

"Ah, but what is a good woman? That's the question," Delaney inserted.

"That's easy," Jared replied. "One who's honest and doesn't cheat."

"There's no such thing. Any woman will lie." She tore a bite of warm bread from the thick slice and put it in her mouth.

"*Some* women may lie," her father said in offended protest. "But—"

She chewed quickly to break in, the soft bread practically dissolving in her mouth. "Any woman," she repeated. "It's simply a matter of what's important to her."

"I don't accept that."

"You don't *want* to accept that. There's a difference." She was conscious of her father's frown, but she was suddenly more conscious of the weight of Jared's gaze on her. She glanced sideways at him, his look sharp with question and doubt. She knew she'd put her foot in it. Still, it was what she believed.

"Any woman will lie, cheat, or steal to get the thing she wants most. Only she won't call it lying or cheating. She'll say she had no other choice. To her, a lie isn't wrong if it gets her something she'll have for the rest of her life." Delaney could tell neither of them followed her logic, and tried again. "A woman doesn't look at things the same way a man does. If something's important to a man, he'll always believe it's important no matter what he has to give up for it. But a woman will discard something she thought was important as soon as something else comes along that's more important."

"You're talking about something else now," Jared said. "A man doesn't always stay with what's important to him. He'll stray from it, too."

"But he'll always remember it and it will bother him that he strayed," Delaney insisted. "It's all part of a man's exaggerated sense of honor. Men are always fighting that. Women don't. Once something isn't important to a woman anymore, she stops worrying about it. It's in the past and she never gives it a second thought. A man would."

Jared's frown made it obvious he didn't like what he was hearing, but he appeared to be listening closely. Her father, on the other hand, was plainly shutting her out.

"Let me give you a for-instance, Dad. Right now, my career—my business—is the most important thing in my life. But if some*thing* or some*one* came along that I thought was more important, that would change immediately. That doesn't mean my career would totally *cease* to be important, only that something else has become more important and I'll adjust my life accordingly. I wouldn't feel any regret or guilt. A man couldn't do that; it would always bother him that he wasn't devoting as much time to his work or giving it the same priority as he had before."

"That's all immaterial." Her father waved a hand,

dismissing everything she'd said. "Nothing you can say will ever convince me that your mother was the kind who would lie or cheat."

"Dad, she lied to you—she lied to *get* you," Delaney declared with humor. "Or have you forgotten the first time she met you? She lied and said she'd seen you in a half-dozen films. You were so taken with her, you asked her out to dinner, and the next day she went racing around town to all the theaters that happened to be showing a film you'd been in."

"I wouldn't exactly call that a lie—"

"She didn't either. In fact, I think she used the phrase, 'I *fibbed* a little to your father.' She was never sorry she lied, and she would have done it again if that's what had been necessary to get you to notice her."

"It was a harmless deceit," he protested.

"But a deceit just the same, Dad. And that's my point—there isn't a woman in the world who wouldn't do the same."

"You'll have to admit, Gordon, your daughter is honest about a woman's basic dishonesty." A smile accompanied Jared's statement, but it didn't come anywhere close to his eyes. Instead they seemed to mirror a kind of angry bleakness. Delaney immediately sensed that this talk about lying and cheating had turned his thoughts to his sister, Kelly, and the things she must have done to conceal her drug use from him.

An awkward silence fell, the atmosphere strained and heavy. Without the words to break it herself, Delaney glanced at her father. His stern look softened a little. "The next time I play chess with you, I'm going to be watching very closely to make sure you don't cheat."

Jared picked up on it. "You think she might cheat?"

"Five minutes ago I would have said no. Now . . . I'm not so sure."

They ganged up on her and Delaney let them, making no attempt to defend herself as the conversation took a much-needed lighter note. By the end of the meal, everything was comfortable and relaxed again.

Delaney filled Jared's coffee cup a second time. When she started to do the same for her father, he covered it with his hand.

"No more for me," he said. "It's getting late and I thought I'd swing by the Country House and visit with Fred while I was out this way." Then he added in explanation to Jared, "The Country House is a retirement home for actors. Fred Silvidge, the guy who helped me get my start in this business, lives there now. He has emphysema and isn't doing too well."

"I'm sorry to hear that," Jared said and started to rise when her father stood up.

"Stay there." Her father waved him back in his chair and came over to Delaney. "Dinner was delicious as usual, precious, but you always were a better cook than your mother." He bent down to brush a kiss on her cheek, whispering, "He's all yours." Despite the sudden heat that warmed her cheeks, Delaney found herself smiling at her incorrigibly romantic father.

"Try to behave yourself, Dad," she murmured affectionately.

"Don't ask the impossible." He tapped a finger on the end of her nose, then extended a hand in farewell to Jared. "I hope to see more of you before you leave."

"We'll see," was Jared's reply.

Hearing his noncommittal response, Delaney realized that in some respects it was typical of him; he rarely signaled his intentions in advance. Even though there were times when he'd looked at her with a man's interest, he had never flirted with her, never indulged in the usual verbal foreplay. Even when he kissed her, he hadn't gazed long and deep into her eyes beforehand; he'd simply kissed her. She liked the directness of him, yet it left her feeling off-balance, without a pattern to follow, unable to anticipate the next move—not what it would be or when it would come or how she could trigger it. It was as if she had no control, and that was a new feeling. The practical, the realistic side of her wasn't sure she liked that.

The front door closed behind her father and she was alone with Jared. For the first time since she'd met him, she felt tense and uncertain in his company.

"Fred's been like a brother to Dad. There's only a year's difference in their ages." She picked up her china cup, holding it with both hands and forcing herself to relax. "Emphysema is such a debilitating disease, it hasn't been easy for Dad to watch Fred deteriorate."

"Nobody likes to be reminded of their own mortality."

"I suppose not." She took a drink of her coffee. "I know I've tried a dozen times since Mom died to convince Dad to move in here with me, but he always refuses."

At that point, the men she'd dated in the past would have made some remark like, "I'm glad he didn't,"—implying a desire for an intimate evening alone with her. But not Jared.

"He probably wants to hold on to his independence as long as he can."

"I'm sure he does. It's funny how the roles reverse, though, isn't it? For years it's the parent worrying about the child, then the day comes when it's the child worrying about the parent."

"If you're lucky, that's the way it happens," he replied, his remark reminding her that he'd lost his parents long before that day had come.

Sensing that he hadn't said it to elicit sympathy, Delaney offered none. "True."

Idly she rubbed a finger along the gold rim of her cup, aware that it was too cool outside to suggest finishing their coffee on the patio—and not cool enough for a fire in the fireplace. Suppressing a sigh of regret, Delaney drank down the last of her coffee and noticed that Jared's cup was empty, too. "More coffee?"

"No thanks."

"In that case, I think I'll clear away the rest of the dishes."

"I'll help." Somehow, before she was fully erect, Jared was behind her, pulling her chair away from the table.

"I'm not used to that," she confessed as she gathered up her father's cup and saucer as well as her own.

"Not used to what?" Jared reached for the water goblets.

"The gentlemanly things you do for me—like pulling out my chair and opening doors."

"I've been told it's old-fashioned in these liberated times. Does it offend you?" He aimed a raised eyebrow at her.

"No." In fact, she was a little surprised to discover she liked it. Leading the way into the kitchen, she said over her shoulder, "In my line of work, it's something I can't allow."

"What do you mean?"

"At the moment, I have only men working for me. Which means when I'm part of a detail protecting a client, my sex can't be a factor to them. Their—our—primary concern has to be the safety of the client. They can't be looking out for me." She opened the dishwasher and began arranging the cups and saucers in the proper slots. "In some ways that goes against a man's instincts. Therefore, I've made a point of never letting them do anything for me, whether it's opening doors or carrying my luggage. If anything, I'll carry theirs. It's a way of setting the tone, creating work habits, reinforcing the fact that I'm more than capable of taking care of myself, that I don't need them to look out for me."

"In other words, it's back to being strong all the time."

She had an instant's pause, wondering how many people recognized—as Jared did—that strength could be a trial as well as an asset. "I guess it is, but it goes with being the boss."

"Right." His eyes were warm with understanding—and a glimmer of something else.

Before Delaney could identify it, the German shepherd pushed against her leg and whined anxiously. "Wait a couple minutes until I finish up here, Ollie."

"What does he want?" Jared asked.

"To go outside."

"I'll take him," he said and slapped the side of his leg. "Come on, Ollie. We'll go outside."

"Outside" was all the dog needed to hear. He left Delaney like a shot and raced from the kitchen straight to the patio doors. Smiling, Jared trailed after him.

In two trips, Delaney had the table cleared and wiped, and the silk flower arrangement once again adorning the center of it. Back in the kitchen, she loaded the last of the dishes in the dishwasher, added the soap, and started the cycle. She heard the click of claws on the kitchen's tiled floor as the German shepherd trotted back into the room.

"Back, are you? That was good timing." She glanced at the empty doorway. "You didn't lose Jared, did you?"

She found him in the living room, standing by the patio doors, staring beyond their night-darkened panes. There was a faraway quality in his expression, something yearning and lonely in it.

"You're thinking about Kelly, aren't you?" Delaney guessed.

He twisted around to look at her, then turned fully. "No," he said quietly. "I was thinking about you . . . about taking you to bed . . . loving you."

She caught back a breath, his words seeming to come out of nowhere. The shock of them was exquisite. With a choice between laughing and crying, Delaney laughed, striving for some lightness, "I have some say about that, don't I?"

The muscles along his jaw ridged up tight. "You have everything to say about it." The roughness in his voice jolted her.

In the next second, he was striding across the room—toward the front door.

"Where are you going?" Delaney demanded in thorough confusion.

"There's a gas station about a mile down the road." He snatched his hat from the halltree and shoved it on his head, then reached for his jacket. "I'll call a cab from there and have him take me back to the hotel."

In the split second it took her to realize he was serious—he fully intended to walk a mile to the service station convenience store and catch a cab to his hotel—Delaney was in motion, crossing the room and planting herself between him and the front door. When he faced her, his jaw rigid, his muscles tense, she saw the stark need in his eyes and felt a warmth spread all through her.

"Jared," she said softly, "take off that damned hat."

His hands came up and flattened themselves against the door on either side of her head, as if it was the only way he could keep from touching her. "Dammit, Delaney, you have to understand. In two weeks, I'll go back to Colorado. I'll go home—"

"I know." She stepped closer, sliding her hands inside his jacket and onto his slim waist. He shut his eyes, steeling himself against her touch. "I want you, Delaney, but you deserve more than I can give you."

"Let me be the judge of that," she whispered and brought a hand down, smoothing it over the long, hard bulge in his trousers, feeling him and feeling the convulsant jerk her touch produced.

A gusty sigh broke from him as his weight pressed her back against the door with a suddenness that had her grabbing at his waist for balance. His mouth drove onto hers, without control, without patience, his hands, his forearms hard against the door by her head, his hips trapping hers against it.

Delaney responded with equal force, straining to give all. She had stopped questioning the wisdom of it minutes ago; she stopped thinking of all the reasons she shouldn't become involved with him. There was a time for thinking and another for feeling, a time for caution and another for giving freely, a time to be practical and a time to love. She had convinced herself of all that and now she sought to show him the truth of it.

He drew back an inch, his heated breath fanning her lips, his body heavy against hers. His hands tunneled into her hair, caging her head. "I want you, but not here—not like this. I want you in bed, your hair spread over a white pillow making a dark frame for your face."

"Yes," she whispered.

As tall as she was, no man had ever attempted to carry her. But Jared did, effortlessly scooping her up. When she wrapped her arms around his neck, she bumped her head against his Stetson. He still had it on. She reached up and sent it sailing to some corner of the room, then ran her fingers through his coarse hair while she explored his ear, chewing at its lobe.

He carried her into the bedroom and kicked the door shut behind him. Briefly she heard the German shepherd whine and scratch at the door, then Jared was lowering her legs to the floor, letting her slide down his muscled thigh, her loose-fitting sweater bunching up under her arms, his work-roughened hands gliding onto her bare skin.

His mouth came back to claim hers. There was an urgency in his kiss and his touch that she echoed. When he stripped off her sweater, she pushed at his jacket, forcing it off his wide shoulders. He shrugged out of it, then impatiently came back to run his hands over her skin. She went to work on his shirt buttons, needing to touch him as freely as he was touching her.

In minutes they were twined together on the bed, their clothes on the floor.

When he slipped inside her, there was a low murmur. From him? From her? She didn't know. All that mattered was this joining, this heat. The race began—one without winners or losers.

ELEVEN

*T*HAT NIGHT MARKED THE START of the most idyllic ten days of her life—ten days of sharing morning coffee and kisses, of making the daily commute into the city together, of stealing occasional lunches, of talking on the phone in between, of renting horses to ride along the beach on weekend afternoons, of strolling hand in hand through the hills around her home, of tossing a Frisbee for the dog to catch, of fixing late-night meals and making love. Ten days in which Delaney discovered that until she met Jared, emotionally she had been a virgin, unaware she could love so fully or care so deeply about another person.

Ten days of dreaming, of believing a love this strong had to last. Ten days before one phone call shattered it all.

Delaney was at the chess table waiting for Jared to make the next move when the phone rang. "I'll get it," she said quietly, not wanting to break his concentration.

Rising to her feet, she picked up the glass of cognac and crossed to the extension in the living room. Lifting the receiver before the phone rang a second time, she carried it to her ear, turning her body so she could observe which chessman Jared moved.

"Wescott's."

There was an instant of silence, then a woman's voice came over the line. "I was told I could reach Jared McCallister at this number. Is he there?"

"Yes, he is," Delaney replied without hesitation, aware he'd given her number out. As Jared glanced up in silent question, she asked, "May I tell him who's calling?"

"His wife."

Gripped by a rigid numbness, Delaney woodenly lowered the phone. "It's for you." She laid the receiver on the chair arm and moved away from it without looking at Jared.

She crossed to the patio doors, closed against the evening's cool air. She stared at nothing, her fingers curled around the cognac glass in an ever-tightening circle that became a stranglehold. Everything was focused inward on the echo of those devastating words—his wife. She felt cold, unbelievably cold, and sick.

The sound of his voice registered, but not his words, not until she heard him say goodbye. She turned to confront him, wrapping both hands around the cognac glass to conceal their violent trembling.

"She said she was your wife."

His head lifted at the accusation in her voice, a slight frown pulling his eyebrows together. "Yes." The matter-of-factness in his voice cut.

Control. She had to keep control. Cling to that
doubt. Give him the benefit of it. "Are you divorced?"

"No."

Cling. Cling. "Are you considering it?"

"No," he replied, shattering the doubt, exploding it.

And with that one word, he killed the love she'd felt
for him. One-sided love was not love, but it could have
become hate. It did, in the blink of an eye. And in that
blink of an eye, Delaney understood how and why
crimes of passion were committed as the need to strike
out, to tear him apart, to destroy his life the way he had
just destroyed hers.

He took a step toward her. "I thought you knew,
Delaney. I—"

"How?" She almost bodily threw the word at him,
the liquor in her glass sloshing over the rim. "You never
said anything about a wife! There is no ring on your finger!" Pushed by the growing fury within, she moved
from the doors, charging blindly away from him. "Get
out, Jared."

"For God's sake, let me explain."

She stopped, raw with the way he'd used her—at
the fool he'd made of her, that she'd made of herself.
"Explain what?" she challenged. "That your wife doesn't
understand you?"

"No, I—"

She wouldn't let him finish. "I don't want your
explanations, Jared. I don't care if you thought I knew
you were married. If anything, it makes what you've
done worse because you believed I was the kind of
woman who would become involved with a married
man—that it wouldn't matter to me. Why should it?" she
mocked sarcastically. "Women who live in Los Ange-

les—in La-La Land—are fast and free with sex. That's what you thought, isn't it? That's what you thought of me."

"I never thought that." His quiet denial only drove the hurt and anger deeper.

"Get out, Jared." She found herself under the hall-tree. She snatched his brown Stetson off the hook and threw it at him. "Take your hat and get out."

He picked up his hat, hesitated, then walked out the front door, closing it quietly behind him.

She hadn't seen or heard from him again . . . until now, until here, outside the Aspen police headquarters, beneath the pure blue of a mountain sky, with the memories of six years ago fresh, all the feelings revived, the love as well as the hate.

It's been a long time—wasn't that what he'd said? But she knew it hadn't been long enough to make the hurt go away. As much as she hated to admit it, Riley had been right about that. Riley. She wished he was there beside her—steadying her.

In pain-choked silence, she watched Jared slowly turn his hat in his hands, the idly nervous action indicative of the tension between them.

Why was she still standing there prolonging this hell?

"Goodbye, Jared," she said abruptly and started to walk away.

"Don't go, Delaney." His hand reached out to stop her, then drew back without touching her. "Let me buy you a cup of coffee."

She refused with a stiff shake of her head. "I'm busy." Then some nasty little voice made her add,

"Besides, I doubt if your wife would approve."

"I'm divorced."

Delaney paled at his words, discovering they cut deeply. "Surely you don't think that changes anything, do you?"

"I know I hurt you, Delaney."

"Yes, you did. But that won't happen again. The woman you knew doesn't exist anymore."

This time when she turned to walk away, he didn't try to stop her.

She didn't remember any of the two blocks to the hotel. If it hadn't been for the doorman rolling a luggage cart out to a waiting BMW, she would have walked past the entrance without noticing the elegant old building faced with rich terra-cotta brick and sandstone masonry.

Immediately she checked her blind flight and pushed through the door into the lobby, her lungs straining for air.

Sternly she took herself in hand and slowed her steps. Seeing him again hadn't been easy, but she had survived it, hadn't she? This time he couldn't hurt her again unless she let him. And she wasn't about to do that.

Ignoring the lobby's comfortable period furnishings and its potted palms, Delaney swung toward the desk and picked up the messages that had come in while she was gone. One was from Riley, but there was none from Susan St. Jacque, leaving Delaney to assume their meeting was still on.

The message gave her something else to concentrate on, a distraction to keep her from thinking about Jared and reliving the meeting, the things he'd said, the way he'd looked.

Returning to her room, she focused on the job she was there to do, on the things yet to be done.

Promptly at twelve-thirty, Delaney was in the lobby to await the arrival of Susan St. Jacque. As five minutes stretched into ten, she wandered restlessly about the earth-toned lobby, glancing continuously at the large oak wall clock while steadfastly ignoring the baby parlor grand. For the fourth time, she sat down in one of the lobby's striped Victorian chairs and fought the urge to drum her fingers on its curved arm.

A smoke-blue Mercedes pulled up in front of the hotel. From her vantage point inside, Delaney saw a pale blonde step out of the driver's side and exchange an airy greeting with the doorman. She was dressed in a Ralph Lauren outfit that could only be described as campestral class—a floral blouse in a country rose print with softly shirred sleeves paired with a clove-brown skirt and riding boots.

Delaney rose from her chair, knowing intuitively that this woman breezing into the lobby was Susan St. Jacque. A second later, she spied Delaney and made straight for her, extending a hand with bold grace.

"You must be Delaney Wescott. Susan St. Jacque." Her slim, rose-tipped fingers closed around Delaney's hand for a fraction of a second, then released it.

"How do you do." Automatically Delaney took in the woman's heart-shaped face and the champagne color of her hair, styled in a windblown and carefree look that was anything but. Her cheekbones were more prominent than Delaney's and expertly tinted. Her lips, shaped like a perfect cupid's bow, were carefully glossed with a shade of deep rose. There was a smoothness to her ivory skin, a youthful glow to it, that gave no hint of her age, which

Delaney suspected was somewhere in her thirties. But nothing disguised the keenness of her almond brown eyes as they swept Delaney with an assessing look that seemed to calculate her bank balance.

"If you're ready, my car's outside."

"I'm ready." She had been for the last ten minutes, but it seemed useless to point that out.

Outside, the doorman assisted Delaney into the passenger side of the Mercedes. She settled into the seat and fastened the safety belt.

"To be honest, I don't know which I like best about summertime in Aspen," Susan St. Jacque declared. "The glorious weather or that I finally get to drive my car. The poor thing spends most of the year in the garage, forcing me to tool around in my Range Rover."

"A Range Rover and a Mercedes—the gallery business must be good."

"Darling," she said with a throaty laugh. "It's the best."

"That's very fortunate," Delaney murmured as Susan swung the car into the traffic on Main Street. "Is it far to Mr. Wayne's house?"

"It's about halfway up the mountain in front of us. Red Mountain." The woman ducked her head to peer up. "Unfortunately, you can't see it from here. Just a hint of the roofline. It's a marvelous place . . . with an absolutely spectacular view."

Delaney didn't bother to look. A second later, she felt the woman's glance on her.

"This business with Rina Cole," Susan said, her tone more serious. "How serious is it? I mean . . . I know she tried to kill him, but—you don't really think she'll try again, do you?"

"Rina Cole is the only one who can answer that." Delaney kept silent about her own reservations on the matter. "It's my company's job to make sure she doesn't have the opportunity."

Glossy lips curved in a smile. "I have the distinct feeling I just heard the standard tactful response to that question."

"You did." Delaney allowed a faint smile of her own to show.

"What else can you say—especially when you're in the business of protecting celebrities? The possibility always exists that Rina Cole could become a future client of yours." One-handed, Susan unfastened the purse tucked beside her on the seat and reached inside, then paused. "Do you object if I smoke?"

"No." Towering trees lined the street, shading the collection of charming Victorian houses on either side, the "painted ladies" adorned with gingerbread-trimmed porches and fanciful turrets.

"I should mention we're taking the roundabout way to Lucas's house." She took an enameled cigarette case out of her purse, opened it, removed a long, slim cigarette, then snapped a monogrammed gold cigarette lighter to it. She took a quick puff, then returned the case and lighter to her purse. "I was in such a rush when I left this morning, I forgot to bring the security code for his alarm system with me. We'll have to stop at my place." She turned the Mercedes onto a side street, then immediately slowed the car, maneuvering it to park in front of a gracious old house on a corner lot. Switching off the engine, she glanced at Delaney, an unspoken question in the look. "It'll only take me a minute to run in and get it."

"I'll wait in the car."

Susan didn't argue as she climbed out of the car, a ring of keys jangling in her hand. Delaney watched her cross the jewel-green lawn at a quick, running walk.

The two-story house was a treasure of Victorian architecture. Painted a delicate blue with its acres of bric-a-brac trimmed in snow white and accented with mauve, it was tastefully quaint with a definite aristocratic look, a look enhanced by the manicured lawn and shrubs that surrounded it. The upkeep on such a place couldn't be cheap. But then, Susan had said the gallery business was "the best." Obviously it was—and just as obviously, she excelled at her work.

When Susan returned to the car, Delaney remarked, "You have a beautiful home."

"It is, isn't it?" Pride of possession was in her voice. "It cost me a small fortune to fix it up the way I wanted, but my 'painted lady' is worth every penny I put into it and more. The West End is one of the more fashionable sections of Aspen and this location is prime—within easy walking distance of town and only a couple blocks from the music tent."

"The music *tent*? The summer festival in Aspen advertised is held outside?"

"In the evenings, yes. Everyone goes. Some actually get seats in the tent, but most camp in the meadow under the stars, listen to the strains of Mendelssohn and Bach, while they picnic on caviar and smoked salmon." Her tone suggested the latter was the thing to do. "I understand proximity to the music tent is at the top of Rina Cole's list for a house here in Aspen."

Delaney tensed. "Rina Cole is buying a place in Aspen?"

"A friend of mine is in real estate. Rina called him from Europe two weeks ago to have him start looking for her. She said she would be flying out soon—I assumed with Lucas. Then . . . all this happened."

"I see." The business district was left behind as they turned onto a road that curled and twisted its way up a mountain slope. "Have you known Mr. Wayne long?" Delaney asked.

"About five, maybe six years—ever since he first started coming to Aspen." She cast a sideways glance at Delaney. "Did you know that Luke made his acting debut here in Aspen?"

"No," she admitted.

"He had a small part in a play that was put on here. It was a celebrity fund-raising event to benefit some worthy cause or other. It was the first real acting he'd done, other than the stuff for his music videos. He did it as a lark. But it was obvious to everyone that he was a natural. At the time, I told him that he was destined for the big screen. But you know how men are—he didn't believe me."

"I imagine he does now." From the first moment that Lucas Wayne had mentioned Susan St. Jacque, Delaney had suspected they had once been lovers. Now, after meeting the woman, she was convinced of it. The surprise was that they had remained friends. Susan St. Jacque didn't strike her as the type to make a friend out of a former lover.

"You must learn a great deal about the clients you protect," the woman remarked idly. "All their little foibles and idiosyncrasies, their secrets and their skeletons in the closet."

"To a degree, but we try to be as unobtrusive as possible and respect a client's need for privacy."

"Still, I'll bet the tabloids would love to find out some of the things you know."

"Why? They can make up things that would definitely be juicier."

Susan responded with another throaty laugh, imbued with just the right touch of warmth and humor. There was an approving glint in her eyes when she glanced at Delaney. "Tactful and discreet. No wonder Lucas hired you. You'll do well here in Aspen."

"Have you always lived in Aspen?"

"Not always." She applied the brake and turned the smoke-blue Mercedes into a narrow lane, its entrance partially concealed by wild-growing shrubs. "Here we are."

TWELVE

*T*HE NARROW DRIVE CURVED toward a sprawling, contemporary-styled house that seemed all steep-pitched roofs and sun decks. The front lawn sloped away in an organized tangle of shrubbery splashed with bright flowerbeds.

"How much land is here?" Delaney immediately noticed the absence of a fence around the property, its perimeters protected only by a tall and dense privacy hedge.

"Approximately three and a half acres." Susan stopped the car at the foot of a winding walk that led to the front entrance. "There's a detached three-car garage tucked behind the house and a smaller building on the other side that was originally built as a guest cottage. Luke has converted it into the caretaker's quarters."

"He mentioned he had a man living on the grounds

year-round." Delaney had his name written down in her notes.

Susan nodded as she switched off the engine and removed the key from the ignition. "Yes, Harry Walker. He's retired, in his sixties. He takes care of the grounds for Luke, among other things." She gathered up her purse and reached for the door handle.

"Does he have access to the house?"

"No." Susan pushed open the door and swung her legs out. "You can only trust unsupervised hired help so far. Luke knows that."

Delaney silently conceded that point as she climbed out of the car and waited for the woman to lead the way up the winding walk.

Pink and white petunias bordered the evergreen shrubbery that lined the walk. Delaney lifted her gaze to the house with its rustic fieldstone accents and endless expanse of tinted glass, the spaces in between filled with darkly stained wood. But her attention kept straying to the deck that followed the structure's jutting angles, her mind questioning how many rooms opened onto it and how many ways into the house there were.

Distracted by that concern, she almost missed the path that intersected the main walk before it disappeared behind a flowering bush.

"Where does that go?" she asked.

The woman responded with an indifferent wave of her hand. "It wanders into a small gardened area, then runs parallel with the deck. Eventually it leads to the rear of the house and the caretaker's cottage. It's accessible from the deck in a half-dozen places."

Delaney made a mental note to explore it later along with the rest of the grounds, and followed Susan up the walk to the double entrance doors of glass framed in hammered copper.

A chandelier made of deer horns hung from the foyer's ceiling, its light shining down on the white marble floor below. A wide hallway led to more rooms in the rear, while an archway on the left opened to a formal dining room.

After showing Delaney the elaborate and sophisticated alarm system, Susan took her a tour of the sleekly modern house.

Thirty minutes later, they returned full circle to the foyer. "Any questions?" Susan paused in the center of the room, her hands clasped in front of her in a waiting gesture. "Anything I haven't covered?"

"I don't think so." Delaney skimmed the notations she'd made as they'd gone from room to room. "If you don't mind, I'd like to look around outside."

"Take your time. If you need me, I'll be in the kitchen checking to see what Luke needs in the way of groceries. I promised I'd have the place stocked with food and drink when he arrives tomorrow."

Delaney watched the woman leave, then crossed the spacious foyer to the front doors.

Outside, the air was soft and warm, the light pure and golden, inviting her to bask in it. With an effort, she ignored the invitation and set out to explore the grounds, beginning with the garage in back. Once there, she noted the rear boundaries of the property and the absence of homes beyond its back line. She located the caretaker's cottage, but if Harry Walker was around, she hadn't seen any sign of him.

Spurred by that thought, she went in search of him, unconsciously setting a brisk pace. Almost immediately, she felt the burning in her lungs. She slowed down, silently reminding herself the elevation was well over eight thousand feet.

She rounded a curve in the path and saw a man crouched on his haunches, gently and carefully plucking weeds from a bed of scarlet cockscomb. He wore a plaid shirt and a pair of jeans that looked brand new. Delaney smiled when she saw the pant cuffs rolled up. She couldn't remember the last time she'd seen anybody cuff their jeans.

"Hello," she said.

Startled, the man lumbered to his feet in alarm. Delaney felt a sense of shock when he faced her. The man before her was far from sixty years old. His hair was a thick brown; there wasn't a trace of gray in it. And his face—his small dark eyes were almost lost in the heavy roundness of his cheeks.

When he spoke, the odd thickness of his speech, the childlike quality to it, seemed to confirm the impression. "You shouldn't be here. You'd better go." He eyed her warily. "Luke don't like people to be walking in his yard."

"Luke asked me to come." She saw that he was tall, easily over six feet.

"He did?" He puzzled over that for an instant, then his face lit up. "Is Luke here? Did she bring him?"

"No." Delaney guessed that by "she," he meant Susan. "Luke won't be here until tomorrow. I'm Delaney Wescott." She stepped forward and extended her hand. "What's your name?"

He hesitated, then rubbed his hand on his jeans before grabbing hers and pumping it up and down in a vigorous shake. "Toby." He beamed. "My name is Toby Williams."

"I'm glad to meet you, Toby Williams." She studied this man-boy, wondering why Susan hadn't mentioned him.

He released her hand. "Are you a friend of Luke's?"

"Not really. I work for him."

"I get to work, too," he asserted, pushing out his chest in a way that dared her to doubt him.

"I'll bet you do good work, too."

Just for an instant, the light went out of his eyes and the corners of his mouth were pulled down. "Harry gets mad at me sometimes. He says I'm slow. But Luke says it's all right if I'm slow 'cause it means I'm careful."

"I think I agree with Luke," Delaney said. "I noticed how carefully you were pulling those weeds a minute ago."

"You have to be careful or you'll hurt the flowers. I like to take care of the flowers. I like to grow things and Luke lets me."

"I like to grow things, too."

"I don't like it when things die," he said with unexpected seriousness. "I don't want anything to die."

"Nobody does, Toby—" Before she could say more, she was cut off by the sound of Susan calling for her. "I'm over here," Delaney answered.

A second later, Susan came into view, a breezy smile on her lips. "There you are. I—" She froze when she saw Toby, her face paling. "How did you get here?"

Stunned by the harshness in the woman's voice, Delaney stared at her for an instant, then turned to Toby. His head was downcast, his glance uncertain.

"Harry came and got me," he said. "It's my vacation. Luke said I could come."

"Where's Harry?" she snapped. "He's supposed to be watching you."

There was a heaving shrug of his big shoulders. "He's around somewhere."

"Go find him. Now."

"Yes, ma'am." He hung his head a little lower and turned to leave.

Delaney couldn't let him go like that. "I'll see you around, Toby. Okay?"

He nodded once, glumly. "See ya."

She waited until she thought he was out of hearing, then turned to Susan, anger simmering just below the surface. "Was it necessary to be so sharp with him? He wasn't doing anything wrong."

"I quite agree. Luke is the one doing wrong by taking him out of that home," she retorted. "He should leave him there. That's where he belongs—with his own kind." She shuddered and rubbed at her arms. "He makes my skin crawl," she said and shot a quick look at Delaney. "I know that's a terrible thing to say and a terrible thing to feel—but I can't help it."

The anger Delaney had felt an instant ago dissipated. "What's Toby's problem? Do you know?" she asked instead.

"You mean other than having the mentality of a seven-year-old?" Susan countered with caustic flippancy. "No, I don't know the cause of his condition. I don't see that it matters. That's the way he is. Nothing can be done about it."

Delaney fell in step with her. "What's Toby's connection to Mr. Wayne?"

Her answer was a quick closed-lipped look, then, "That's something you'll have to ask Luke."

Which seemed a polite way of saying it was none of her business. Which, of course, it wasn't. Still, Delaney

couldn't help being curious. She wouldn't have guessed
that the Lucas Wayne she met in New York was the type
who befriended the mentally handicapped. Obviously
there was another side to the man she hadn't seen. She
thought she had learned not to accept surface impres-
sions after her experience with Jared.

Jared. Why had she let herself think about him?

She forced her thoughts away from him. "Why did
you come looking for me, Susan?"

The woman seemed grateful for the change of subject. "I finished my list and wondered how much longer
you were going to be."

"I think I'm finished." Was she? Delaney wasn't
sure. She was letting herself become distracted by too
many other things when she needed to concentrate on
the job at hand.

"In that case, shall we go?"

"Sure." Delaney absently rubbed her fingers along
her temple.

Susan observed the action. "Headache?"

"A pounding one," she admitted on a sigh. "I've had
it ever since I got up this morning. I took some aspirin,
but they seem to have worn off."

"Altitude sickness . . ."

"Pardon?"

"Headaches, insomnia, shortness of breath, nausea,
heart palpitations, they're all symptoms of what we call
'altitude sickness,' caused by the reduced humidity and
oxygen content in our air," Susan explained. "It will take
your body a couple days to adjust to the change in altitude. In the meantime, drink plenty of fluids, stay away
from alcohol, and don't overdo it."

"I'll keep that in mind." Delaney remembered the

drink she'd planned to have in the Jerome Bar tonight. "Sorry, Dad," she murmured.

"What did you say?"

"Nothing."

From the house on Red Mountain, Susan took Delaney back to the Hotel Jerome and dropped her off. Twenty minutes later, Delaney met with a real estate agent and toured three different condominium complexes to check out the two-bedroom units that were available for rent. Another hour was spent getting leases drawn up for two of the units.

It was the middle of the afternoon before Delaney returned to the hotel—time enough for her to pick up her messages, have her rental car brought around by the parking valet, and drive to the airport to pick up Vance Hummel and John Wyatt, the other two members of her Aspen security team.

As soon as their luggage was loaded, she took them straight to the condo they would be sharing and briefed them on the next day's schedule, then left for the hotel.

Sunset's last vermilion streaks were fading from the sky when she returned to the hotel. The checkout time had long since passed. She was grateful for that. She was too tired, too exhausted to face the thought of packing and moving into the condo that night. She much preferred the thought of taking two aspirin and falling into bed.

As she passed the front desk, she heard piano music coming from the lobby's parlor grand. Agile fingers picked out a happy ragtime tune. She sent a glaring look at the offending piano player, then stiffened to an abrupt halt. Jared was seated at the parlor grand, his eyes watching her.

She tightened her grip on the shoulder strap of her purse. It wasn't fair for him to show up now. It wasn't fair when she was so tired she couldn't think straight. It wasn't fair that she had to go through this again.

When he stood up, Delaney didn't have the strength to turn and walk away. When he walked toward her, some crazy part of her mind registered the fact that he'd exchanged his Levi's and denim jacket for a pair of tan slacks and a corduroy jacket, the same dark chocolate brown as his lizardskin boots.

"What are you doing here, Jared?" Her voice sounded as brittle as she felt.

"I had to see you again. Talk to you."

"We have nothing more to talk about." It was impossible to meet his eyes without feeling that old tug of attraction.

"I think we do," he replied quietly but insistently. "We had something, Delaney. We had something special."

"Surely you don't think we can pick up where we left off," she said, not so much in exasperation as in desperation.

"No, I don't think that. But I do think we could start fresh."

She looked at him, conscious of the sting of tears at the back of her eyes. "Don't do this, Jared."

He shook his head slowly. Under the light of the lobby's chandelier, his hair was the color of dark mountain honey mixed with sunshine. "A chance, that's all I'm asking."

"No." But she was weakening and she knew it. All her fine resolve was disappearing. She tried to blame it on her weariness—the altitude—anything but the fact

that she wanted to be vulnerable, she wanted to be convinced they could find what they had lost.

"At least hear me out."

She hesitated a moment longer, than nodded
tiredly. "All right. Talk."

"Not here. There are too many people and too
many walls." His hand was at her elbow, guiding her to
the door. Delaney started to argue, then checked the
impulse. She had agreed to talk; what did it matter if it
was inside or out?

Outside the hotel, he turned down the street. Dusk
was settling, thickening over the high valley town. The
walling mountains loomed ever darker as the translucent, milk-white globes of the old-time street lamps
came on. A high-riding four-wheel-drive pickup stood
by itself at the curb, its black sides spattered with mud.
Jared steered her to it. His hand shifted to the sensitive
small of her back as he reached in front of her and
opened the passenger door.

She hesitated briefly, long enough to meet the serious light in his eyes, then stepped onto the running
board and climbed into the truck's cab. She had no idea
where he was taking her, but she wasn't about to ask.

Nor did Jared volunteer when he swung into the
driver's seat. He simply started the engine, glanced in his
side mirror to check for traffic, then made a U-turn—an
illegal one, Delaney was sure—to head down the street
in the opposite direction.

On the outskirts of town, a highway sign listed the
number of miles to Independence Pass, Twin Lakes, and
Leadville. Then the lights of town were left behind them.
For a time, there was a scattering of houselights winking
through the trees and glittering from the dark slopes on

either side of the road. Gradually, even they disappeared.

Delaney watched the track of the beams as they picked out the road's twists and curves. They were climbing, winding ever higher. She kept her eyes on the road, never looking at Jared, but conscious of him in her peripheral vision.

He didn't say a word. There was only the rush of the wind around the truck's cab, the hum of the tires on the paved road, and the low drone of the engine to break the silence. A silence that wore on nerves already frayed by tiredness and the pounding in her head.

Finally she couldn't take it anymore. "How long before we get to wherever it is we're going?"

"Soon."

"I suppose you're taking me to your ranch."

"No." His gaze never left the road. "If I took you to the ranch, I'd want to take you to my bed. I think we both know it's too soon for that."

Delaney wished he hadn't said that. She wished he hadn't reminded her of those incredible moments they'd shared in each other's arms. It was better to remember the pain than the joy she'd felt.

Rounding a curve, Jared slowed the pickup, then pulled over onto a wide layby. The headlights tunneled into night's nothingness, then blinked off and the engine stopped, encapsulating the truck in a dark silence.

Without saying a word, Jared climbed out of the cab and came around to the passenger side. Her door swung open under his hand. Delaney hesitated, then stepped out. He met her questioning glance briefly, then moved off, his boots crunching on the mixture of gravel and hard-packed earth with each step.

He halted short of that lip of blackness, his body angled away from her, his gaze directed at the night-scape. Delaney started to follow him, then checked the action, realizing she preferred to keep her distance, even if it was symbolic.

Instead she let her gaze follow his and inspect the view. A crescent moon cast a pale light at the earth, letting the deep indigo sky sparkle with its dusting of stars—stars that looked close enough to reach out and touch. Slowly, as her eyes became adjusted to the absence of brightness, she could make out the jagged peaks of the surrounding mountains, the valley meadow far below, and the quicksilver gleam of a stream running through it.

Gradually, too, the land's vast silence came alive and she could hear the sigh of the wind, the whisper of something moving in the grasses, the *whirr* of a bird's wings, even the faint, fragmented murmurings of water tumbling over rocks . . . soft sounds, soothing sounds.

His voice came to her quietly, easily blending with the hush. "You said you weren't the same woman. But some things never change, like the mountains and the moonlight."

She heard his sigh and saw his head tip to look at the moon. "I swear I thought you knew I was married. I thought I'd told you, Delaney. Then . . . later, when you didn't mention it, I couldn't either. It didn't belong—it wasn't a part of what we shared."

He swiveled his shoulders toward her, his gaze seeking hers, the moonlight bronzing the line of his jaw. He was telling her the truth. This time she believed him. Yet she couldn't say that. She couldn't say a word.

"It was heaven and hell being with you, Delaney!"

he continued slowly. "It was hell knowing I had no right to want you, hell trying to figure out how something so wrong could feel so right. I loved you and I think you loved me, even though we never said it. I'm not sure I even admitted it to myself, not until I had to learn to live without you."

He made it sound as if he was the only one who'd gone through pain. Didn't he realize it had been worse for her? He had known he was married. She hadn't. She curled her fingers into her palms, digging nails into her flesh.

"Do you remember what you said at dinner about a man's honor and the guilt he'd feel if he violated it?" Jared paused, waiting for her response. She didn't make any, not even a short, sharp nod of her head. "It was true. When I came back here to Colorado, guilt made me try twice as hard to make my marriage work. It didn't. It couldn't. Whether I'd met you or not, it would have failed."

She didn't want to hear about his marriage. She didn't want to hear any of this. Dear God, why had she come with him? She caught back a pained breath, conscious of the burning in her lungs and her throat.

He turned fully around. "After the divorce was final, I wanted to tell you. I don't know how many letters I wrote to you—and never mailed. Once, when I was in Los Angeles to meet with the detectives looking for Kelly, I even called, but I hung up before anyone answered."

Delaney listened and tried not to think, not to feel, not to notice he was moving closer.

"But there wasn't a day or night that I didn't think about you." His voice was still pitched low, but with a huskiness to it that was like a caress. He was close enough that she could see the leashed hunger in his eyes.

"And not a day or night went by, Delaney, that I didn't fantasize about how you'd react when you found out I wasn't married anymore. Sometimes I imagined that you wouldn't say a word, but there would be tears in your eyes, tears of happiness as you hurtled into my arms. Other times you'd be angry because I hadn't come to tell you before—angry over the days and nights we wasted. I even imagined that you'd slap me, call me names. But always, you wound up in my arms. Then today, this morning on the street . . . I never imagined the coolness you showed me, I never imagined you'd tell me goodbye and walk away. Why, Delaney? Didn't I mean as much to you as you meant to me? Or were you afraid I'd hurt you again?"

She couldn't answer him, finding it equally impossible to lie or admit the truth. His questions hung in the air between them, the moment and the tension stretching until he broke under it, the words exploding from him in a violent rush.

"Dammit, say something, Delaney. Hit me or kiss me or tell me to go to hell, but don't just stand there!"

Before it was over, she did all three as she raised her balled hands and brought them down on his chest, intending to pound at him, but the instant she touched him, her fingers curled into the corduroy of his jacket. She bowed her head and swore at him, pushing the words through clenched teeth. "Damn you, Jared. Damn you to hell!" Then her hands were around his neck and her mouth rising up to claim his, angrily, fiercely, and soon . . . desperately.

Confused, uncertain, she dragged her lips from his

and lowered her forehead against his shoulder, drawing her arms to wedge a space between them. She felt the raggedness of his breath against her, the heavy pounding of his heart beneath her hands.

"I'm not sure about this, Jared," she whispered tightly.

His arms loosened as he pressed a kiss against her hair, then pulled back. "I'm sure." He slowly rubbed his palms up and down her arms, keeping his fingers spread, while his warm gaze moved over the face she finally raised to him. "I'm sure that I want to discover all the ways you've changed and grown—and all the ways you haven't. I'm sure that I want this chance to know you again."

He made it sound so easy, so safe. She closed her eyes, trying to fight the pull of his words. "I'm in Aspen on a job, Jared. I'll be tied up a lot. Busy."

"I'll take whatever time you'll give me," he said. "Not many people get a second chance, Delaney. I can't make you give us that chance, but I can ask. And I'm asking, Delaney—will you?"

"I need time, Jared. The last time I leaped without looking. I won't do that again. It hurt too much when I crashed."

"I know," he said.

"Will you take me back to the hotel?"

Nodding agreement, he turned her toward the black pickup.

The ride back to the Jerome was made in silence. This time Delaney welcomed it as she leaned her head back, resting it against the seat, and closed her eyes to sort through the tumble of feelings, old and new. By the time they reached the hotel, she had been only moderately successful.

In typical gentlemanly fashion, Jared walked her to her room. "Will you be staying at the Jerome while you're here?" He took the room key from her and unlocked the door.

"No. I've rented a condo. I'll be moving in tomorrow."

He pushed the door open, then turned to give back the key. Suddenly she felt awkward and on edge again. The lines around his eyes fanned upward in a gentle smile. "Don't worry. I'm not going to invite myself in." He bent his head and brushed his mouth over her lips.

Part of her wanted more of a kiss than that, but the other part—the stronger part—said, "Good night, Jared."

"Good night," his voice echoed after her as she closed the door.

She turned the bolt, locking herself in, and slipped the safety chain into place. Moving away from the door, she gave her purse a toss onto the room's overstuffed sofa. The bed was turned down, the crocheted coverlet folded at the foot. Tiredly she ran a hand through her hair, raking the sides back from her forehead.

The telephone rang, its jangle harsh in the room's stillness. Delaney walked over to the bed and picked up the extension on the nightstand.

"Yes, hello?" she said, somewhat curtly.

"Out having a long leisurely dinner, were you?" It was Riley.

For a split second, Delaney froze, thinking that Riley had somehow found out she'd been with Jared. "Dinner?" she echoed a little stupidly, stalling for time and trying to brace herself for the questions that would come—questions she wasn't prepared to answer yet.

She wasn't even sure that she knew the answers.

"Yes, dinner. You know—the meal that people eat in the evening," Riley mocked.

"I know what dinner is, but I don't know why you're asking about it."

"Come on, 'Laney," he chided. "Dinner with Wyatt, the self-styled gourmand—he and Hummel made it in all right, didn't they?"

It hit her that Riley had no idea she'd been with Jared. Her knees buckled in relief and she sank to the bed, thankful that she wouldn't be subjected to grilling from Riley about the meeting. At least, not tonight.

"Yes, they're here. Their flight was even on time. I left them at the condo."

"Then you found us a place to stay. Good."

"The phone company promised to have the telephone installed tomorrow. Other than that, we're all set here. How are things on your end? Quiet, I hope."

"Quiet and uneventful," Riley confirmed. "They wrapped up the final scene with Lucas today, and the director has turned him loose. We'll be arriving on schedule tomorrow."

"We'll be ready for you."

"Good. I—just a sec," he said as Delaney caught the sound of voices in the background. After a short pause, Riley came back on the line. "Somebody wants to talk to you."

"Hello, Delaney." It was Lucas Wayne. "Have you missed me?"

"One way or another, you've been on my mind." The throbbing in her head had centered in the middle of her forehead. Delaney absently rubbed at it. "Riley said that you wrapped up filming today."

"That's right. I'll be flying into Aspen tomorrow. Will you be at the airport when I arrive?"

"Myself and two other members of my security team." She wanted off this subject. At the moment, she wasn't in the mood to deal with his flirting—or his man-woman word games. "By the way, I met Toby when I was out to your house today."

There was a pause that threatened to become long. "I know," he said finally. "I spoke to him earlier. He mentioned meeting you. He also said you were nice to him. Thanks."

"It was easy."

"Not many people think so," Lucas replied. "I'm glad you do, Delaney. Toby is one of the most gentle souls alive." He continued without giving her time to respond. "Your sidekick wants to talk to you again. I'll see you tomorrow—and I expect you to be waiting for me with open arms."

"I'll be waiting for you." Delaney left it at that.

Lucas chuckled softly. "You're still determined not to mix business with pleasure, aren't you?"

"It makes for fewer distractions, Lucas. It's better that way. In fact, it might save your life."

There was another pause, not nearly as long as the last one. "If you said that to knock some sense into me, you succeeded. I'll try to behave myself around you. More than that, I can't promise."

Riley came back on the line again. "Now I'm your sidekick, am I? When did I get relegated to that role?" he grumbled good-naturedly.

"I kinda like the ring of it—Riley Owens, sidekick." Delaney smiled easily and naturally for the first time since she had arrived in Aspen.

"Keep it to yourself or I'll never hear the end of it from the others."

She laughed. "I promise."

They spoke a few more minutes, then Delaney hung up, surprised at how much better she felt. She almost wished she had told Riley about seeing Jared.

He'd find out about it himself—probably sooner rather than later.

THIRTEEN

Delaney's wake-up call came precisely at six-thirty. After a night of fitful sleep, she stumbled out of bed and moved leadenly to the bathroom. For nearly fifteen minutes she stood beneath the shower spray, letting the jets beat on her. Partially revived, she stepped out of the stall into the steam-filled bathroom and made a half-hearted attempt to dry herself, then wrapped a towel around her wet hair and tugged on her silk kimono.

She absently wished she had called room service before she showered. The thought of freshly brewed coffee sounded so good she could almost smell the aroma of it in the air.

A hand rapped at her door, followed by a voice announcing, "Room Service."

Delaney frowned. Had she ordered it last night before going to bed? She finished knotting the sash around her waist on her way to the door. The peephole gave her a distorted view of a uniformed waiter with a breakfast cart—and Jared.

She fumbled with the lock and chain, then opened the door to stare in a combination of shock, question, and a guarded amount of pleasure.

"Good morning." The waiter smiled politely.

"Did I order this?" she asked cautiously.

"I took the liberty," Jared confessed without remorse.

Belatedly she became aware of the towel around her head, the lack of makeup, and the bareness of her feet. It didn't matter that Jared had seen her like this in the past. That was then, this was now; and she wasn't ready for this kind of casual intimacy with him.

But if that was the case, why had she opened the door? The answer was easy: Her heart and mind were sending conflicting messages, and her body seemed to be making its own decision on which one to obey.

Recognizing that the damage—if there was any— had been done, Delaney backed out of the doorway and moved against the wall, swinging the door wider to admit the waiter with the cart—and Jared.

"Where would you like this, Miss Wescott?" The waiter pushed the cart past her.

"Anywhere will be fine," she said, her glance sliding from him to Jared. She almost resented how fresh and vigorous he looked—how awake and fully dressed. He removed his hat and stepped inside, running a ruffling hand through his hair.

"Do you mind if I join you for a cup of coffee?" he asked with disarming sincerity.

"Of course not." Delaney was aware her answer wasn't even close to a lie.

The waiter passed them on his way out the door. "Enjoy your breakfast."

Delaney walked into the room, leaving Jared to close the door behind the departing waiter. The cart sat in the center of the room, its leaves extended, place settings for two arranged on its white damask cloth and two of the room's sitting chairs pulled up to it. Delaney turned the lid on the heavy porcelain coffee pot and proceeded to fill two cups.

"How did you know I'd be up?" she asked when Jared dropped his hat on the seat of the sofa and came over to the breakfast cart.

"I checked with the desk to see if you'd left a wake-up call." He pulled out one of the chairs for her. "I knew that no matter how full your schedule might be today, you'd take time for coffee and something to eat. I remembered you liked French toast." With a nod of his head, he indicated the covered plate on the cart. "I hope you still do."

"Yes." She sat down, noticing the glass of freshly squeezed grapefruit juice at her place setting. He had also remembered her preference for grapefruit juice over orange.

"Since the hay is still drying in the field, I thought I'd offer to help you move into the condo this morning." He went around to the opposite chair and glanced at the numerous pieces of luggage in the room, then stopped when he saw a large Samsonite suitcase standing upright next to the wall, its olive-drab sides scarred with use. "Is that yours?" He threw her a puzzled look.

"No. They're Riley's."

"Is he staying here?"

She saw Jared look sharply at the unmade bed as if

trying to determine whether it had been slept in by one person or two. "You don't really think Riley and I shared that bed last night?" she asked in a stunned voice.

Jared arched an eyebrow, his expression serious. "Is it so inconceivable?"

"As a matter of fact, it is." She was trapped somewhere between laughter and indignation. "Granted, Riley and I work closely together—but not that closely. We're friends, that's all."

"I know that's the way it used to be. But it could have changed."

"Well, it didn't," Delaney informed him, smiling at the very idea of it.

"Not by his choosing, I'd wager," Jared inserted dryly.

"Why would you say a thing like that?" She frowned in amazement.

"I remember the way he used to look at you," he replied. "It wasn't business he had on his mind."

"Riley? That's ridiculous," she declared with a trace of irritation.

"If you say so." There was a slight shrug of one shoulder. "But you have to admit, it looks a little odd seeing his luggage in your room."

"It's really none of your business, but it so happens that Riley is flying in from New York today. His sister sent some clothes along with me for him." In her near anger with Jared, she splashed more syrup on her toast than she wanted.

"Delaney, I'm not trying to start a fight with you. Merely making an observation. A slightly jealous one, if you must know the truth."

A little mollified by his explanation, she responded with less tenseness. "You have no reason to be jealous of Riley."

"Don't I? He's been with you nearly every day for the last six years. I haven't."

She remembered all the times she'd imagined Jared with his wife, the fury she'd felt—and, yes, the jealousy. She hadn't known he was divorced—any more than Jared hadn't known whether she'd turned to Riley for comfort.

"Let's change the subject, shall we?" She cut into her French toast.

"How long will you be in Aspen? Do you know yet?"

"Close to a month. At least, that's the way it looks now," she replied and forked a bite into her mouth.

"Who are you working for?"

"Lucas Wayne."

Jared lifted his head sharply. "Is he in town?"

She shook her head, quickly chewing and swallowing another bite of the maple-drenched, vanilla-flavored toast. "He arrives today with Riley. I flew in ahead to get everything ready." She laid down her fork and picked up her coffee cup. "I assume you read or heard about the attempt Rina Cole made on his life last week."

"Yes." A faint wryness pulled at one corner of his mouth. Other than that his expression was bland, almost too bland. That was all it took to remind Delaney of his prejudice toward celebrities. "Actually, I'm surprised someone hasn't taken a shot at him before now—although I always thought it would be an outraged husband instead of a jilted lover."

She took a sip of hot coffee and nearly burned her

tongue. She blew lightly on the surface to cool it, thoughtfully studying him over the rim of the cup. "Do you know Lucas Wayne?"

"Mainly by reputation." He fingered the coffee spoon on the table, studying it and avoiding her eyes. "Although I've seen him once or twice in Aspen."

"What's his reputation?"

"That he's skilled at providing an unentangled diversion for unhappy wives—or so I've heard." He paused, his glance lifting to her. "What's your opinion of him?"

"I'm not sure I've formed one yet," she admitted candidly, then shrugged. "Fortunately, my concern is for his life, not his character—questionable or otherwise."

"Be careful, Delaney, I'd hate to see you get used by him."

"I don't think that's likely to happen," she replied and dropped the subject. "So, this is haying season for you, is it?"

"Yes." He went on to talk about the ranch, the kind of year he'd had, the amount of hay he would be baling, the number of cattle he planned to winter, and his experiments in cross-breeding to come up with leaner beef. Delaney finished her toast and poured more coffee for each of them, then asked about Kelly.

"I used to think she would write or call to let me know she was all right," Jared said. "But I haven't heard a word from her. The locket was the only trace of her anybody has been able to find. It's as if she disappeared off the face of the earth."

"I'm sorry, Jared." She didn't know what else to say.

"I haven't stopped looking."

"Of course not." But the worst had to be not knowing whether he'd find her alive—or dead from an over-dose.

"How's your father?"

"Fine. He's house-sitting for me."

"Do you still have your place in the canyons?"

"Yes."

"I've often wondered whether you sold it or not."

"No. Not yet, anyway." She set her cup down with a trace of finality in the gesture. "As much as I would like to linger over another cup, it's time I got dressed."

Fluidly, Jared came to his feet. "In that case, I'll wait for you downstairs." He scooped up his hat and started for the door.

"Jared."

"Yes?" He turned, his hat in hand.

She hesitated, then said, "Thanks for breakfast."

"Any time, Delaney. Any time." He smiled and headed for the door, planting the hat squarely on his head.

Thirty minutes later the bellman loaded the suit-cases onto the luggage cart while Delaney made a last check of the room to make sure nothing had been left, then followed him to the elevators. As promised, Jared was in the lobby waiting for her.

"I'll load the bags in your car," he volunteered. "You go ahead and check out."

The clerk had her bill ready for her. It took Delaney only a few minutes to settle it, then she was outside, climbing into her rental car and driving away from the hotel. Her rearview mirror reflected the image of the black pickup truck behind her.

When they reached the condo apartments, Jared picked out the heaviest bags and carried them inside.

"You can put the gray tweed luggage in that bedroom." She pointed to a door, and continued into the living room to open the drapes and let in some light. "Leave Riley's suitcases by the door."

She immediately commandeered the dining table and turned it into an office desk, opening her briefcase and arranging stacks of forms, schedules, and expense reports on top of it, adding pencils, pens, and a calculator while leaving room for the telephone. She looked up to find Jared watching her, one shoulder propped against the wall, his hat pushed to the back of his head, and one booted foot hooked over the other.

"How do you plan to run your company when you're going to be in Aspen for a month and your offices are in L.A.?"

"With fax machines, telephones, computer linkups, and Federal Express, plus a paragon to keep things running smoothly in L.A., it won't be difficult." She unlocked her weekend case and lifted out the facsimile machine she'd brought with her. "Unfortunately, it won't be long before Wescott and Associates will be too big to allow me to work in the field anymore."

"You enjoy it, don't you?"

"Yes." She glanced at him, detecting a certain grimness in his voice, but there was nothing in his expression to suggest it. "I have to admit, I'm not looking forward to giving it up and spending most of my time behind a desk. But who knows—I may find there's just as much challenge in running two and three different teams."

From the corridor outside the condo came the heavy, slogging tread of weary footsteps. Delaney thought it sounded like more than one set. She glanced at the door she hadn't bothered to close. A second later, Vance Hummel and John Wyatt appeared in the outer hall, both dressed in jogging shorts and running shoes, sweat plastering their t-shirts to their backs and chests. The lanky, freckle-faced John Wyatt was the first to spot the open door.

"Hey, Delaney. You made it." He swung into the apartment on legs that were obviously leaden, barely managing to avoid walking into Riley's suitcases. "One question—how the hell did you manage to carry those in here?" Then he saw Jared and came to a surprised stop. "Sorry, I didn't know you had company."

But he made no attempt to retreat and neither did Vance Hummel, who had followed him inside, both eyeing Jared with undisguised curiosity.

"Come in, guys, and meet Jared McCallister," Delaney said, and introduced the two men, both formerly with the Los Angeles Police Department and both quitting for similar reasons: They'd gotten tired of the stress and the feeling they were on the losing side.

As usual, Wyatt was more lackadaisical in his greeting. "Glad to meet you, Jared. And I'm doubly glad you were here to carry those bags up. I couldn't have lifted one."

"No problem."

Then Vance Hummel stuck out a muscled arm to shake hands. "Jared," was his terse greeting.

John Wyatt came into the living room and flopped on the gold tweed sofa. "God, I'm bushed."

"You two didn't go out jogging this morning, did you? I told you last night to take it easy for a few days."

"We thought we were. Hell, all we did was walk a mile, and I usually run about ten every day."

"We thought if we walked, we'd get acclimatized

faster." Vance wandered into the room and stoically ignored the chairs.

"That was his bright idea." John wearily pointed a finger in Vance's direction.

"I don't think it works that way," Jared remarked.

"Tell me about it," John grumbled.

"A phone truck pulled up in front when we came in," Vance said. "He should be here to hook the phone up any minute."

"It looks like you'll be busy for a while," Jared said. "It's time I got out of your way."

"Thanks for the help," she said.

"I was glad to do it. I'll give you a call in a day or two after you have your schedule set. Maybe we can work in lunch or a late dinner."

Without exhibiting the least bit of awkwardness, Jared walked over and lightly, but warmly, kissed her goodbye.

The minute Jared closed the door, John Wyatt spoke up. "I didn't know you had a boyfriend here in Aspen, Delaney."

"I don't," she replied with a studied evenness. "Jared and I are old friends. Nothing more."

"Sure," he said in dubious agreement. "I kiss all my old friends goodbye, don't you, Vance?"

Fully aware that the only way to combat this ribbing was to rib back, Delaney taunted, "I wasn't aware you had any *old* friends, John. I thought all of them were nubile and nineteen."

"That's cruel," he protested.

"No, that's immature," she countered, then immediately took advantage of the moment to suggest, "Why don't you guys go take a shower before this place starts smelling like a gym?"

John Wyatt looked at his partner. "I think we've just been insulted."

Delaney smiled wickedly. "If the odor fits . . ."

"That does it." John pushed himself off the couch. "I'm outta here."

Her smile lingered as she watched them leave, then faded when she found herself staring at a closed door. With an effort, she shook off the pensive mood and focused her energies, instead, on the many things she had yet to do before Lucas Wayne arrived.

With an airport security guard at her side, Delaney was at the aircraft's door when it opened. Riley was first in line, fronting Lucas. She saw the quick look of pleasure that came to his eyes, giving them a warmth and a shine that was reserved for her and her alone. Delaney returned Riley's smiling glance. As always, his presence gave her a renewed sense of strength and confidence.

"All set?" he asked, his attention shifting beyond her to sweep the area.

"Yes."

"I'll take care of the luggage," Riley said and stepped to one side, signaling Lucas Wayne to come ahead.

Lucas stepped from the plane. Dressed in factory-faded jeans, his dark hair curling onto the collar of his pink-striped sport shirt, Lucas gave Delaney one of his patented bad-boy smiles and chided, "What? No open arms?"

It was impossible not to smile back. "In your dreams, Lucas," she murmured.

"You can bet my dreams of you have been sweet ones, Delaney," Lucas declared, his voice pitched at a low, husky level meant for her hearing alone. "Now all I have to do is figure out a way to make them come true."

Ignoring that, she took his arm and swung around to flank him. The uniformed guard copied her maneuver. "I have a car outside." She steered him from the gate area, setting a brisk pace and alertly noting the stares of recognition sent his way.

When she ignored the signs pointing to the baggage area and directed him instead to the exit doors, Lucas pulled back. "Wait a minute. What about my bags?"

"Riley has your claim checks. He'll bring your luggage when he comes."

"That's what I call service." He fell in step with her again.

"No. That's called getting you out of the airport with minimum delay." She pushed the door open and stepped ahead of him, automatically scanning the handful of cars parked along the curb. She immediately led Lucas to the rented Lincoln, parked with the motor running and John Wyatt seated behind the wheel. She opened the rear door for Lucas, then climbed in after him, offering a quick "Thanks" to the airport guard when he closed the door. In the next second, the Lincoln was accelerating away from the curb.

"As usual, that was very efficiently done, Ms. Wescott," Lucas said with mock formality. "I'm beginning to think it would be impossible for anyone to catch you off guard."

"I'm not infallible, Lucas."

"That's reassuring—at least, personally."

Within minutes, they crossed the bridge over Castle Creek and entered the town proper. Lucas continued to look out the window. The trees were in full summer leaf, shading the houses in the fashionable West End.

"I'm glad I came here. It's going to be good to be out of the fishbowl for a while." As if feeling the need to explain that statement, he glanced at Delaney, "Here, they don't sell maps showing where celebrities live. No guidebooks tell you where the stars hang out. Even I can have some privacy here."

"That's part of the Aspen allure, isn't it?" Delaney guessed.

"In addition to the mountain majesty of summer, the champagne powder of winter, and the high exclusivity year-round."

Delaney smiled, as she was meant to do, and directed her gaze out the window again.

The car turned to travel along Mill Street toward Red Mountain. The narrow road twisted its way up the slope, offering an ever-expanding view of the valley town below and the opposite range of mountains.

When the Lincoln made the turn into the driveway, Delaney recognized the Mercedes parked at the foot of the front walk. "It looks like Ms. St. Jacque is on hand to welcome you to Aspen."

"It looks that way, doesn't it?"

She caught the faintly cynical note in his voice, but she didn't have a chance to see whether his expression mirrored it as he opened the door on his side and climbed out. Irritated by his unthinking action, she scrambled after him, reaching him about the same instant John Wyatt did.

"You're to stay in the car until one of us opens the door for you, Lucas," she reminded him curtly. "This is no time to let procedures become lax."

"Sorry. I forgot."

"Please don't forget again." But she could tell his attention was already on the blonde walking toward him.

"Luke." Susan St. Jacque stepped into his outstretched arms and tilted her head back, inviting the obligatory kiss of greeting. Then she moved back to look at him, her hand resting lightly on his forearm. "It's so good to see you again, Luke—and thankfully, all in one piece."

"I'm as relieved about that as you are."

For Delaney, moments like this—when eavesdropping was unavoidable—were always slightly awkward. Like John Wyatt, she stayed in the background and directed her gaze elsewhere.

"You'll be happy to know," Susan said, "that your cupboards are no longer bare and the refrigerator is stocked with all your favorites. I've arranged for my cleaning woman to come in twice a week. If you need her more often than that, let me know."

"Twice a week should be fine."

"That's what I thought," she agreed, then paused briefly. "I'd love to stay and talk, Luke, but I know you must be exhausted after your long flight. I'll come by tomorrow afternoon around one-ish and we'll go look at the painting. Then later, we'll have dinner and talk. There's this new restaurant in town that I know you'll love. The food and the service are marvelous."

"Not tomorrow, Susan—"

"Luke, you aren't trying to stall me, are you?"

"No, of course not. I just need a few days to rest. The shooting schedule on this movie was a real grind."

"But very worthwhile, I heard. Financially speaking, of course," Susan inserted with a touch of drollness.

"Very worthwhile."

"And that's what counts, isn't it, darling."

"You're right—as always." He paused. Out of the corner of her eye Delaney saw him reach to lightly stroke Susan's cheek. "I'll call you in a few days. We'll go look at that painting you've been wanting to show me. Then we'll have dinner . . . somewhere quiet. And afterwards—" His voice dropped to a suggestive level. "Who knows how or where the evening might end?"

"You haven't changed, have you, Luke?" Susan murmured. "You still know how to make a woman feel very special. I could almost fall in love with you all over again. But that would never do."

"Why not?" he argued persuasively.

"Because I wouldn't want anything to change the relationship we now have. But I don't hold it against you for trying." She smiled with a definite smugness, something Lucas didn't seem too pleased about.

"Luke!" came the childlike squeal of delight from an adult's voice. In that same second, Delaney spotted Toby Williams running from the garage area at a lumbering gait, neither his mind nor his muscle coordination a match for his age and body. "Luke, you're here!"

Susan saw him, too, and turned on Lucas, her voice suddenly low and angry. "You should have left him in that home."

"I couldn't do that."

"More's the pity," she muttered and walked past him to her car. "I'll wait for your call, Luke. Make it soon."

But Lucas didn't have time to respond as Toby wrapped both arms around him and knocked Lucas backward a step with the force of his enthusiastic greeting.

"You came, Luke." There were tears in Toby's eyes and unabashed joy in his face. "You came just like you promised."

"I always keep my promises, sport. You know that." Luke hugged him back, then set him an arm's length away. "It's good to see you again, Tobe."

The smile on Toby's round and heavy face faded a little. "I missed you, Luke."

"I missed you too, sport." He rumpled Toby's dark hair as he would have a boy's. But Toby was a boy trapped in a man's body, a body an inch shorter and a good forty pounds heavier than Luke's.

"You and me, we're gonna have fun, aren't we, Luke?"

"You bet we will."

"Will you take me fishin'?"

"Sure."

"Can we ride horses, too, maybe?"

"If you promise not to fall off."

Toby started to giggle, but the sound was drowned out by the squeal of tires as the Mercedes accelerated out of the driveway. Toby watched it, a glumness settling over his expression. "She don't like me, Luke. I try being nice to her like you said, but—she still doesn't like me."

"It's not your fault, Tobe. You just keep on being nice." Lucas curved an arm around Toby's wide, bulky shoulders and smiled encouragingly.

Toby tried to smile back, but the attempt was a weak one. "I think she's scared of me. But I wouldn't hurt her, Luke. I promise I wouldn't."

"I know that. You'd never hurt anybody. She's just being a silly girl. A scaredy-cat."

"Yeah, a scaredy-cat." Toby nodded, his face brightening. "She's a scaredy-cat."

"Right. So you just forget about her. Okay?"

"Okay . . ."

Delaney was more than a little surprised by what she was seeing and hearing. For some reason she had expected Lucas to treat Toby with a kind of condescending patience, a pitying tolerance, something that would suggest Toby was here because it was good for Luke's image, which was a somewhat cynical view to take, but it had seemed the obvious one to Delaney . . . until she'd seen him with Toby—seen the sensitivity and warmth he showed him. It left her with the distinct impression that Toby was here because Lucas wanted to be with him— and it wasn't for any image-building purpose. She found herself curious about their relationship, wondering when and how it had begun. Maybe at some fund-raiser for the mentally handicapped? Or maybe—she didn't have time to complete that thought as Lucas guided Toby toward her, his arm still draped companionably around the man's shoulders.

"Toby, you remember Miss Wescott, don't you?" he said. "You met her the other day . . ."

"I remember." His nod had a touch of a bashful bob to it.

"Hello, Toby. It's good to see you again."

"It's good to see you," he said, self-consciously echoing her words.

"Miss Wescott's going to be spending a lot of time with us," Lucas explained. "And this is her friend—"

"John Wyatt." John stuck out a hand to Toby, a smile wreathing his bony, freckled face. "I'm glad to meet you, Toby."

"'Lo." Toby shook hands with him none too certainly, plainly reserving judgment on this stranger.

Delaney guessed this gentle man-boy hadn't been shown a lot of kindness in his life, especially by strangers. Most were probably uneasy around him—like Susan St. Jacque—or else quick to shun or laugh at him.

She heard a car slow down to make the turn into the driveway. "That should be Riley." As she swung around, the car pulled in with Riley at the wheel.

"I hope he has my luggage," Lucas remarked idly.

Toby immediately piped up, "I'll carry your suitcase in, Luke."

"It's a deal. In fact, I'll give you the heaviest one."

"That's 'cause I'm strong, huh?" he said proudly.

"That's right."

Riley parked the rental car alongside the Lincoln and popped the trunk lid. When John Wyatt walked over to help unload the bags, Toby was right on his heels, temporarily leaving Delaney alone with Lucas Wayne.

His dark eyes gave her a sidelong look. "I meant to ask—which one of the guest bedrooms did you take?"

"None. Riley will sleep here. He'll be your roommate for the duration," she replied. "A second man will be posted at the entrance to the drive. You should consider having a gate installed. It would make our job a lot easier. As it is, we'll use one of the rental cars to block the drive."

"Wait a minute. Where will you be?" There was a trace of anger in his frown that matched the demand in his voice.

"When you're here, in the house or on the grounds, I'll be at the command post, coordinating everything."

"That's not the deal, Delaney. You're supposed to be protecting me."

"I'm supposed to be *in charge* of protecting you," she reminded him patiently.

"No, dammit! You're supposed to be here—with me!" The temper she'd seen him unleash on two previous occasions was in evidence again. "I'm paying you for your services and, dammit, that's what I'm going to get. You're not going to pawn me off on your trusty sidekick!"

Delaney took a deep, calming breath and suppressed the urge to respond just as hotly. "You are paying for the services of Wescott and Associates. Mr. Owens is more than qualified—"

"I don't give a good goddamn how qualified your Mr. Owens is!" he exploded. "I want *you* with me—not him. Do I make myself clear?"

He loomed in front of her, all raging temper and ego. Delaney held her ground.

"You have made yourself very clear, Mr. Wayne." She resorted to crisp formality, and watched him recoil as if slapped by it. "However, I told you once before, my services don't extend to tucking you into bed at night. If the arrangements I have made for your protection are not satisfactory, then—"

"Hell, no, they're not satisfactory. I want you with me!" He stopped and looked away, closing his eyes for a brief moment. When he opened them again, there was no more anger. As quick as he was to temper, he was equally quick to get over it. "Delaney, how can I make you understand that I feel safe when you're around?" he said, his eyes silently pleading with her. "Can't we reach some sort of compromise on this? If you want Riley to sleep here—fine. Heaven knows, I've given you enough reason to think"—he deliberately paused for effect, a teasing smile edging his mouth—"I have designs on your virtue. But indulge me a little and be here the rest of the time."

His anger had been easy to resist, but not his smile. "There's a lot of paperwork. A lot of scheduling and advance planning involved in protecting you—work that happens to be my responsibility. But I'll be with you as much as I can otherwise. Will that do?"

"I guess it will have to. Thanks."

"We try to oblige the client when we can." But she knew that meant she would have very little free time of her own. Which also meant she would have very little time to spend with Jared. Maybe that was just as well.

Toby came back proudly carrying an oversized bag. "I got the biggest one, Luke. Do you want me to put it in your room?"

"Yeah, would ya?"

"Sure." Toby hesitated, his glance skittering around before lighting once again on Lucas. "Are you coming, too?"

"Sure." Smiling, Lucas sent Delaney a parting look and walked off with Toby.

Riley joined her. "Who's that?" He nodded at Toby.

"Someone Lucas has befriended. His name is Toby Williams. He'll be staying here." Delaney shrugged to indicate she had no more information than that. But his question drew her attention to the pair walking ahead of them, Toby jabbering away like an excited little kid while Lucas listened attentively, smiling and inserting a prompting remark now and then. "Toby isn't exactly who you would expect Lucas to invite for the month, is he?"

"As Alice would say—'Curiouser and curiouser,'" Riley replied.

FOURTEEN

*E*ARLY ON THE MORNING OF the third day in Aspen, Delaney stood on the boulder-strewn banks of the Roaring Fork River. She wore a bright green and black plaid flannel to ward off the lingering coolness and a pair of faded jeans, soft from numerous washings. A black bow gathered her long hair together at the nape of her neck and revealed the earpiece to her two-way radio.

A few yards away, Lucas Wayne and Toby fished the icy waters of the thundering river. It was a peaceful scene, with the mists raveling off the mountains and the meadow strewn with wildflowers.

"Beautiful morning, isn't it?" Riley remarked from a few feet away as he surveyed the scene, a pair of dark sunglasses shielding his eyes from the glare of a rising sun.

"It is." Delaney stole a glance at his lean face, conscious of a kind of tension rising again—one that had been building for the last two days. It made her uncomfortable with him, and she didn't like it. Deciding to do something about it, she said, "How come you haven't asked me about it?"

"About what?" He cocked his head toward her.

"You know very well what. By now, either John or Vance has told you that they saw me with Jared. So, why haven't you said anything?"

"I knew you would tell me yourself in time." There was no hint of criticism. His voice, like his expression, was bland. Too bland. Delaney wished he wasn't wearing those dark sunglasses. She hated it when she couldn't see his eyes. She looked away to make a slow scan of the area.

"I ran into him on the street—the first day," she said, trying to sound matter-of-fact.

In her peripheral vision, she saw him nod. "I see."

Delaney waited, but Riley offered no other comment than that. The silence grew, and her tension along with it. "Jared isn't married now," she said to break it. "He got a divorce."

"That makes all the difference." His remark was a dry echo of her own initial reaction.

"I suppose." But she wasn't sure about that.

"Are you going to see him again?" Riley's eyes were on her. She could feel the probe of his gaze.

"I honestly don't know." That was the truth. The old attraction was still there, but the righteous anger that had once been her armor had become hollow. "Do you think I should?"

"Don't ask me that question," he replied somewhat curtly.

"But I'd like your opinion."

"No, you wouldn't."

"I wouldn't ask otherwise," Delaney retorted, impatient with him.

"Don't kid yourself, Delaney. If I said, 'Don't see him,' you would do what you want in the end and my opinion be damned."

"What are you so angry about?" Delaney asked, puzzled by the heat in his voice.

A smile pulled crookedly at his mouth. There was no humor in it. "You figure it out," he said as a whoop of triumph came from Toby.

"I got one, Luke. I got one!" Toby battled to land the good-sized trout on his line.

"Looks like he'll be needing the stringer," Riley said and moved off to retrieve it, leaving Delaney to ponder the meaning of his previous remark.

Later, back at the house, Delaney stood at the deck railing, a cup of coffee in hand. The sun was warm on her cheeks, its heat advising her that soon it would be time to change out of her flannel shirt. She propped a booted foot on the railing and gazed at the panorama of valley and mountains, the town below and the ragged peaks above. Lucas came over to stand beside her along the rail.

"It's going to be another beautiful day." She watched the Silver Queen gondola begin its climb to the top of Ajax Mountain.

"Looks that way."

She brought her foot down and turned sideways. "You realize you're making our job incredibly easy."

He turned his head toward her, a dark eyebrow arching in silent question. "I am?"

"Yes." Delaney took a sip of her coffee. "To be honest, when you told me you were going to spend a month in Aspen, I envisioned a full slate of activities—golf, tennis, cocktail parties, dinner parties—in other words, a host of security problems. But in the last two days, the only time you've ventured from the house was to go fishing."

"The month is young." The corners of his mouth dimpled with a warning smile.

"I know." It was the only reason she hadn't done more than toy with the idea of sending Vance back to L.A. and filling his position with an off-duty policeman.

"This is probably a good time to mention that I called Susan a little while ago and asked her to get us tickets for the concert in the music tent tomorrow night. And don't forget—there's that cocktail party and reception Friday night for some environmental group."

"I haven't. In fact, I received a copy of the guest list yesterday, and I have an appointment tomorrow to look over the area to be used for the party."

She caught a movement in her side vision and turned to identify it, her glance first seeking the rental car parked crosswise to block the entrance, and the lanky John Wyatt in sunglasses lounging beside it. All was quiet there. She scanned the grounds and spotted Toby hurrying along one of the paths.

"Hey, Toby!" Lucas called. "Where are you going?"

Toby stopped and held up a stringer with two trout hooked on it. "I forgot to show Mr. Walker my fish." He immediately looked worried. "It's okay, isn't it?"

"Sure." Smiling, Lucas waved him on.

"He really enjoyed going fishing with you this morning," Delaney remarked.

"He deserves some good times."

"How long have you known Toby?" she asked curiously, then saw him stiffen, a closed-in look shuttering his face. "Sorry, you don't have to answer that. It's none of my business."

"No, it's all right." He gave a quick, curt shake of his head, then met her gaze, something almost challenging in his expression. "Toby's my brother."

Delaney tried and failed to conceal her shock. "I didn't know. I never guessed."

"I was born Lucas Wayne Williams. Toby came along two years after me. By the time he was three years old, it was obvious he wasn't—what's that ugly phrase they use?—he wasn't *normal*. My father hated him, and hated my mother for giving birth to him. He never called him by name, never accepted that he had fathered him. Damned idiot, that's what he called him. Toby thought it was his name. 'Get out of here, you damned idiot,' he'd yell. And if Toby didn't move fast enough to suit him, he'd take a belt to him. And he'd turn that belt on me if I tried to stop him."

Lucas smiled at the remembered pain, but the smile, like his voice, was cold and hard, emotions vibrating somewhere below the surface.

"My mother." His lips quivered with a mixture of disgust and revulsion. "She found refuge in illness and prayer. I can still see her holding Toby—his back, arms, and legs covered with red welts and bruises—and her rocking back and forth asking God to 'deliver us from evil.' Her deliverance from my father came in the form of death when I was eight. That same day my father took Toby and put him in a beat-up old station wagon with phony wood panels on the side. Toby was scared." His voice faded to a whisper. "He only knew one word and he kept screaming it over and over—Luke! Luke!" He stopped and dragged in a deep breath. "When my father came back, Toby wasn't with him. It was years before I found out he had left Toby in a home for mentally ill children. That's where he grew up. When he was too old for the children's home, he was transferred to a regular mental institution. That's where I finally found him."

"Thank God you looked," Delaney murmured.

"I swore when my father came back without him that I would find him and take care of him." Lucas paused again, shrugging off some of the bleakness that had held him. "Toby's come a long way—thanks to a lot of professional help. He lives in a kind of halfway house along with three others with similar handicaps. A couple lives with them. House parents, I suppose you'd call them. They look after Toby and the others. Supervise them. Help them to be independent. Toby even has a job. Did he tell you?"

"No." She watched with fascination the softness, the look of pride that stole into his eyes.

"He works at McDonald's. He keeps the tables, the floors, and the eating areas clean, and picks up the litter outside. That probably doesn't sound like much to you, but at least he isn't sitting around making potholders. He has a real job with a real paycheck. Sometimes when I think about all that Toby has accomplished, I get so proud of him, I—that sounds crazy, doesn't it?"

"Not at all. In fact, I think you have every right to be proud of him. And Toby has every right to be proud of himself."

Lucas looked at her and smiled. "Somehow I knew

you'd understand, Delaney. You're one of only a handful of people who know Toby is my brother. I'd like to keep it that way. He isn't ready to cope with the attention that goes with being the brother of Lucas Wayne. He doesn't need people staring and pointing fingers at him, or whispering behind their hands wherever he goes. And he definitely doesn't need people being kind to him just to get to me."

"No." Delaney realized that Lucas didn't keep Toby hidden away out of shame, but rather from a desire to protect him. Hollywood wasn't known for its sincerity, and she doubted Toby would understand that kind of falseness. "Actually, I'm surprised that nobody's dug into your past and found out about him. Or that Toby hasn't bragged to someone that you're his brother."

"We've made it our secret. Toby is good at keeping secrets. As for the others, it's believed my brother died when he was five. You can even find records on file to support it. But please, don't ask how I accomplished that."

"I won't." She knew it wasn't too difficult to slip a phony death certificate dated twenty-five years ago into county records—or even a notice of cremation in the files of a funeral home. The chances were slim it would be questioned—let alone disputed. If he'd done that, had Lucas arranged for the records in the institutions to be altered accordingly? And who knew the truth? Only a handful of people, he'd said. Obviously people he felt he could trust. She wondered why he'd taken her into his confidence. "Does Rina Cole know about Toby? Would she use him to get to you?" she asked, already considering whether to extend the protection screen to include Toby.

"As far as Rina knows, Toby is a retarded boy I befriended. She called him my stigma of guilt, a means to apologize for becoming so successful. Nearly everyone thinks he's my own private charity case—something I do because it's good for my image."

"To be honest, I thought along those same lines."

He lifted his coffee mug in the direction of the drive. "Looks like we have company."

Swiveling her shoulders, Delaney looked back, half-expecting to see the blunt nose of Jared's black pickup at the drive's entrance. It was almost exactly three days since she'd seen him—three days without a word or a phone call. But she saw at a glance it wasn't his truck, but a sleek and shiny car bearing the distinctive hood ornament of a Mercedes. And it wasn't Susan St. Jacque's Mercedes either; the color was gleaming copper. John Wyatt was at the driver's door, a two-way radio held close to his mouth.

The receiver in her ear crackled briefly, then John's calm voice said, "St. Louis is here." The code for Rina Cole.

"Inside, Lucas. Now." She pushed off the rail, grabbing his arm and turning him toward the glass doors as she unsnapped her radio from its holster with her other hand. "Did you copy that, One?"

"Roger." Riley's voice was in her ear. "Two seconds and I'll have this fish slime off my hands."

"What's going on?" Lucas spoke over the top of Riley's voice.

"That's Rina in the car."

"Rina."

Ignoring the shock in his voice, she opened the door. "Stay with Riley." She closed the door after him.

"The lion's inside. Three will support Two."

Riley acknowledged her transmission and verified that the "lion" was in sight. Assured that her client was out of harm's way, Delaney moved to back up her agent at the entrance. But the instant she set foot on the paved drive, she slowed to a fast walk, assuming a posture of command and control.

Any hope that John Wyatt would succeed in turning the car away without a confrontation with its occupant vanished when Delaney saw the woman planted squarely in front of him. There was no doubt it was Rina Cole—the barely tamed wildness of her frosted hair, the outlandish outfit of buckskin suede leggings with fringe running down each leg and more fringe dripping from a matching jacket—an outfit that fell somewhere between high fashion and high camp—the mixed gold and brown shadow troweled above her gray-green eyes—all unmistakable trademarks of the former pop-star-turned-actress—trademarks like the leggings that fit her so tightly that not a crack was left to the imagination, and the fringed jacket that gaped open to reveal that she wore nothing beneath it except her cleavage.

Delaney took one look at John Wyatt's reddened face and his pained attempt to focus on Rina Cole's face, and immediately interceded. "What seems to be the problem here?"

Rina Cole whirled on her. "This farm boy refuses to move his car. Tell him to get it out of the way and do it now!"

"I can't do that, Miss Cole, and you know it. Please leave without causing any more trouble."

"Just who the hell are you telling me to leave?" She vibrated with anger, the fringe on her jacket dancing crazily from it. "Luke invited me. When he finds out you're treating me like this—"

Delaney called that bluff, granting it was admirably done. "Mr. Wayne knows you're here. He doesn't want to see you."

"That's a filthy goddamned lie! We've planned this time together for months." Rina Cole played the role of outraged indignation for all it was worth.

"I repeat, Mr. Wayne doesn't want to see you. He has filed a restraining order against you. Please get back in your car—" As Delaney raised a hand to direct the woman back to the Mercedes, Rina Cole slapped it aside.

"Don't you touch me," she warned, her glossy lips curling and her hands coming up. "You're lying. Luke would never turn me away. He loves me. Somebody's putting you up to this. Who?"

"No one—"

"It's that lawyer of his, isn't it? He's always hated me because I could do so much more for Luke's career than he could!"

She didn't like the wildness she saw in Rina's eyes. She risked a quick glance at John, determining his position. "No—"

"It is him. How many times have I told Luke to get rid of him? He's got some hold over him. He must. He's making Luke do this. I know he is!"

"Miss Cole, if you don't leave, I'll have to call the police."

Her head jerked up, something feral in her look making Delaney wonder what she was on. "You're one of his sluts, aren't you? Just like the other one."

Recognizing that she couldn't persuade Rina Cole to

leave of her own volition, Delaney nodded to John. As he murmured into his radio, her earpiece picked up his message: "Call in the cavalry, One."

Riley rogered that as Rina's voice rose to a screaming pitch. "Luke is mine! You'll never have him. Do you hear?"

"I hear and you're right." Delaney tried to placate the woman before she lost all control. "Luke will always belong to you. It was foolish of me to think it could be any other way."

In her ear, Riley said, "The cavalry's rolling, Two. You should hear the bugle." At almost the same instant, Delaney heard the wail of a siren. Somehow she managed to keep Rina Cole stalled for the nerve-wracking two and a half minutes it took the local police to reach the scene. Every second she expected Rina would become wise to the ploy and erupt again.

Two uniformed officers climbed out of the Saab 9000 patrol vehicle and walked around the Mercedes. When Rina saw them, she launched into another tirade, hurling accusations and reverting to her original claim that she was here at Luke's invitation. The younger man lent a willing ear as he gently guided her back to the driver's side of the gleaming copper car. The other officer walked to Delaney and offered a commiserating smile.

"Nasty business, isn't it?" he said. "Do you want trespassing charges filed on her?"

"We'd rather not if it can be avoided." If assault charges and an injunction hadn't deterred Rina, being arrested for trespassing definitely wouldn't stop her.

Glancing over his shoulder, the officer mused, "She's something, ain't she? Talk about 'hell hath no fury . . .'" he murmured and let the rest of the quote trail off, then sauntered back to join his partner and lend the weight of his badge.

Delaney watched the proceedings from a discreet distance with John standing at her side.

"Now, Miss Cole, ma'am," the first officer said with practiced tact and respect. "You'd best accept that Mr. Wayne doesn't want to see you and leave quietly. We wouldn't want to have to take you to the station—not a star like you."

"You bastards, he paid you off, too, didn't he?" Rina spat. Then, with a lightning switch that raised the flesh on Delaney's arms, she changed the object of her hatred. "Luke thinks he's too good for me. He thinks he can treat me like this and get away with it. He's wrong. Dead wrong."

She yanked open the car door and climbed inside, shutting the door with a resounding *slam!* The engine roared to life. Rina gunned it, then threw the car into reverse, the tires spinning and finding traction to propel the car backwards. She missed the patrol vehicle by no more than a layer of chrome.

Oddly, Delaney didn't feel an ounce of relief. She walked over to the policeman. "If it's possible, find out where she goes and let me know?"

"Somehow I doubt she'll be leaving town, ma'am."

"So do I," she agreed on a sigh. "So do I."

During the long and deliberately slow walk back to the house, Delaney recognized that she'd underestimated Rina Cole. A part of her hadn't believed Rina would follow up on her previous attempt. She thought Rina would be crazy to do it, crazy to risk prison, crazy to throw away what was left of her career. But the woman was crazy.

She found Riley and Lucas in the living room. "Rina's gone," she said as she joined them. "Unfortunately, I think we can count on her being back."

Riley nodded. "Would you believe Arthur just called to warn us that Rina was on her way to Aspen?"

Delaney couldn't smile at the irony of that. "His warning came a little late."

"That's what I told him."

She turned to Lucas. "I said it before, Luke, and I'll say it again. You need a security gate installed, and it can't be done soon enough."

"I'll see about it right away," he promised. "Anything else?"

"Are you sure you want to attend that concert tomorrow night?" With Rina in town, Delaney had new concerns about the outing.

"Because of Rina."

"In a word, yes."

A sexy smile curved his mouth. "I'll be safe with you, won't I? Besides, music is good for the soul."

Delaney sighed and shook her head, smiling in spite of herself.

FIFTEEN

SCARVES OF FUCHSIA-TINTED CLOUDS trailed across the sky in the west, trapping the last rays of sunset. Lengthening shadows darkened the green of the mountain slopes, the light and heat of day slowly fading. From the music tent came the strains of Beethoven's "Violin Sonata" as deft and artful fingers coaxed evocative sounds from old wood and strings.

Delaney sat on a corner of the striped Indian blanket spread on the grassy area outside the tent. To her relief, Lucas had decided against joining the throng of people occupying seats inside the tent. Instead, he had opted to sit outside—as had many others, young and old, families with children and hand-holding couples, singles and groups. Some picnicked from baskets; others sipped wine and munched on canapés; some tossed Frisbees; others chased runaway toddlers; some stood by the entrance to the tent; some strolled aimlessly; some snoozed. Movement. Everywhere there was movement.

And Rina Cole was still in town. Susan St. Jacque had called this morning with word that Rina had taken a suite at the Little Nell.

Now, one thought kept running through Delaney's mind—the comment Susan St. Jacque had made several days ago about Rina's desire for a house near the music tent.

Lucas shifted his position on the blanket and leaned back on his elbows, hooking one leg over the other, the movement drawing Delaney's glance. Clad in sneakers, blue jeans, and a polo shirt, with dark glasses shielding his eyes, he looked like any of the many athletically built men seen all over Aspen. Almost, but not quite, as evidenced by the many glances of recognition that came his way, and the numerous greetings by longtime acquaintances. Some came over to the blanket, but most were content to wave and have their salute acknowledged by Lucas.

"Enjoying yourself?" he asked, indicating he'd noticed her glance.

"I hadn't better be. I'm supposed to be on duty." She scanned the area again, then looked at the sky.

With the sun gone, dusk would settle quickly over the valley. Delaney dreaded the moment when all these people became shadowy figures, barely distinguishable one from another except by size and lightness of their clothes or hair. Identification by sight would become difficult if not impossible, especially if someone took pains to disguise his appearance—as Rina had done once before in New York.

"Don't you like the music?" Toby sat Indian-fashion on the blanket, intermittently swaying to the tempo and sucking chocolate milk from a cardboard container through a straw.

"I like it." Actually, she wasn't sure she'd heard a single note. Her senses had tuned it out, along with the gurgling laughter of a toddler, the low murmur of conversation, and the distant hum of street traffic.

"I like it, too," he stated with an aggressive nod. "Except when it's sad. I don't like it when it's sad. It makes me feel bad. I like it best when it dances."

Delaney smiled at his phrase, finding it an apt description of the light and airy notes coming from the tent. A breeze sprang up, carrying the cool of evening on its breath—and the smoke from a cigarette. Idly she glanced in Riley's direction. He stood some thirty feet away, tall and rangy, a cigarette between his fingers. He looked straight back in silent challenge. Then he nodded toward the man standing beside him. Curious, Delaney looked to see who it was, and immediately stiffened in surprise.

"What's wrong?" Reacting to her movement, Lucas turned, balancing on one elbow.

"Nothing." She gazed at Jared with a mixture of contradictory emotions—relief, tension, pleasure, and wariness—as Jared touched the brim of his hat to her. "A friend of mine is with Riley. I'll be right back."

She crossed the grassy space between them, conscious of a rising tension. She felt the coolness of Riley's eyes on her as clearly as she felt the warmth of Jared's.

Riley dropped his cigarette and crushed it under his heel. "Want me to take your place?" he asked, showing no expression whatsoever, neither approval or disapproval.

•

"Only for a few minutes," she said.

He nodded and strolled off toward the blanket. Delaney automatically assumed his former position, her quick scan noting the expanded view it provided.

"I don't know why I'm surprised to see you here," she said to Jared. "You always enjoyed classical music."

"True, but I'm not here for the music. I came to see you."

"How—" she began, then stopped, guessing, "You stopped by the condo and Vance told you we were here."

"That's right."

She could feel his eyes on her, silently watching, silently wanting. She tried to examine her own feelings, but there was too much tension, too much uncertainty.

"The hay's in," Jared said into the silence.

"Is it?" She noticed the ruddiness beneath his dark tan, its presence confirming a recent and long exposure to the sun's burning rays. And she noticed, too, the way it weathered his face and lightened the color of his eyes, making them appear more gray than blue.

"You said you weren't ready to *leap* into anything, but I thought you might be willing to take a small step and have a late dinner with me tonight after you're through."

"I don't know how long I'll be."

"It doesn't matter. I'll wait." He wasn't giving her an out. But she didn't really want one. In that same second, Delaney realized Riley had been right—she had to find out whether anything remained of what she and Jared had shared. She didn't want to spend the rest of her life regretting that she'd thrown away her chance at love, all because of pride. There was risk involved, the risk of being hurt again. But she took risks every day.

222 ~ JANET DAILEY

"Not dinner," she said. "I doubt I'll be hungry. But I'll meet you for a drink at the Jerome Bar."

"You've got a date."

A date. The word had an innocent and old-fashioned ring to it that was somehow reassuring. Delaney smiled, no longer feeling the need to question the wisdom of her decision. The sense of ease didn't last as she encountered Riley's gaze boring into her. She glanced away from it and noticed that Lucas was watching her as well, his sunglasses off, an outstretched arm propping him upright. Instantly she made a swift, visual sweep of the area, aware that for a brief span of seconds she had been distracted by Jared and momentarily dropped her guard. A mistake that could have been costly. One she didn't intend to let happen again.

"I have to get back," she said. "Duty calls."

Jared started to protest, then apparently changed his mind. "I'll meet you at the Jerome."

"I don't know what time I'll get there. It might be late."

"I'll be waiting," he promised.

Delaney nodded absently and moved away, her attention centering once again on the protection of her client as she headed back to the blanket. She felt the brief probe of Riley's glance when she rejoined them, and ignored it.

"She's back, Luke. Can we go now?" Toby cast an anxious look at the deepening blue of the sky above. "It's getting so dark."

"The concert isn't over yet."

"I don't care. I wanna go. Please, Luke." He fidgeted on the blanket.

The smallest flicker of irritation showed in his face

as Lucas hesitated, then gave in. "All right, we'll go. Help me fold the blanket."

Toby rolled off the blanket and picked up a corner, barely giving Delaney and Lucas time to get up before he hauled the ends together.

"The car's parked about four blocks from here," she told Lucas. "I'll have John go and bring it around. It'll only take a few minutes."

"I wanna go now." Toby jiggled in place, fretting at the delay like an overgrown child. "You said we could leave."

"We'll walk to the car."

Hearing that, John Wyatt immediately moved out to take the point. Toby hurried after him at an ungainly scamper. Lucas followed, the folded blanket slung over his shoulder. He glanced sideways at Delaney when she fell in step on his right.

"Sorry." His mouth slanted in a rueful line. "Toby's afraid of the dark. I thought he'd gotten over that."

"You don't need to apologize," she replied as applause broke out in the music tent.

"Maybe not," he conceded. "Maybe apologizing for Toby's little quirks has become more of habit than I realize."

"It's understandable. Most people feel a need to protect the innocent." And there was a touching innocence about Toby, evident in the way he made no attempt to conceal either his joys or his fears.

As they left the meadow and the music tent, the melodically full notes from a harp drifted after them. The tree-lined street in the residential West End was in heavy shadow. Houselights winked on, holding dusk at bay a little longer. Somewhere a sprinkler clicked in ceaseless rhythm, throwing a hissing spray of water over a green lawn. Shying from the sound, Toby hugged the outside edge of the sidewalk and turned to walk backwards.

"Can't we go faster, Luke?"

Lucas responded by picking up the pace a little, which seemed to pacify Toby. He swung back around and hurried to catch up with John, who ranged some thirty feet in front of them while Riley lagged a few feet behind, echoing their footsteps.

"The man in the cowboy hat, he looked familiar," Lucas remarked. "Who is he?"

"Jared McCallister. He has a ranch outside of Aspen."

Lucas nodded in a remembering fashion, then gave her a curious look. "How do you happen to know him? I thought you said you'd never been to Aspen before."

"I haven't. I met him several years ago in L.A."

"L.A." He raised an eyebrow at that. "What was he doing there?"

"Trying to find his sister."

"He has a sister in L.A.?"

"He doesn't know where she is. She disappeared—ran away."

"Drugs, right?" Lucas guessed.

"That's the consensus."

"I'm not surprised. There was a time not too many years ago when they said Aspen was the 'snow capital,' they weren't referring to the white powder on the slopes. Most of that has changed. Or else, like most towns, it's gone underground. Sometimes I realize how lucky I was, that I didn't get caught up in the drug scene. But I had more important things to spend my money on." He looked at Toby when he said that.

John Wyatt made a right turn at the next corner and headed west. He slackened his pace and glanced back to make certain the change in direction had been noted. Toby waited at the corner, anxiously shifting his weight from one foot to the other.

"It's getting darker, Luke." His tone bordered on a fretful whine.

"It's only a couple more blocks to the car," Lucas assured him.

"Are you sure? I'm getting scared, Luke."

"There's no need to be afraid. We're right here with you."

But Toby didn't take much comfort from that as he hurried after Wyatt, almost running now, darting frightened glances at the deepening black shadows around him.

"Exactly how did you meet Jared?" Lucas asked, resuming their previous conversation. "Did you look for runaways and missing persons back then?"

"No, but someone told him I did. After he explained his problem, I recommended another firm to him."

"You must have seen him again after that."

"A few times." She didn't like the turn this conversation was taking.

"I suppose you gave him a call when you got into town."

"No. I ran into him quite by accident."

"You agreed to meet him later tonight, didn't you?" It was a statement, not a question, and the grimness in his voice indicated he didn't like the idea. "Don't go, Delaney." When she would have objected, he raised a hand to stop her. "I know—it's none of my business who you see. But I want it to be me. I've been interested in you from the start and you know it."

"We've been over this, Lucas," she said with forced patience.

"And we'll go over it again. You can count on it."

"You're persistent. I'll give you that."

"Why do you refuse to take me seriously?"

"Maybe you don't strike me as the serious type." She recalled too well the number of times she'd seen him use his charm and flattery on other women.

"You're wrong, Delaney. With the right woman, I could be very serious."

"Wasn't that a line in one of your movies?"

She heard the angry breath he exhaled. A second later his hand caught her arm, bringing her to a halt. She had a moment to see the flash of temper in his eyes, then Toby interrupted, his voice thin and wavering, his bulky shape backpedaling rapidly toward them. "Luke, I don't wanna go this way."

Out of patience, Lucas snapped, "Dammit, Toby—"

"There's . . . that . . . house, Luke." His voice broke with silent, frightened sobs of breath. When he turned, his face looked unnaturally pale, his chin and lower lip quivering. "Don't make me go, Luke, I don't want to."

"What the hell are you talking about Toby? It's just a house." Lucas threw a quick look at the corner dwelling.

Not a light gleamed from its windows, turning their panes into blank, sightless eyes and drenching its exterior in shadow. Its roofline was a collection of spires, turrets, and sharp peaks silhouetted against the evening sky. With a little imagination, it could seem looming and sinister.

"You don't need to be afraid, Toby. I know it looks scary, but—" She stopped, realizing that the old Victorian house belonged to Susan St. Jacque. "You know who lives there, don't—"

Too late she discovered Toby wasn't listening as he bolted past her into the street, running as fast as he could, his arms windmilling through the air, a long, drawn-out "Nooooo!" trailing behind him. Riley sprinted after him. At the same instant, Lucas muttered a curse and gave chase. She shouted at Wyatt to get the car and ran after all three.

Riley caught up with Toby more than a block away, but it took Lucas to subdue him. By the time Delaney reached them, he had Toby wrapped in a tight hug, holding him, trying to quiet him while Toby sobbed incoherent words, his whole body shaking.

"Sssh, Toby," Lucas crooned and stroked a hand down the back of his head, comforting him as he would a frightened child. "It's all right. You're safe now." Toby mumbled something Delaney couldn't understand. "Don't think about it. It's over. You're with me. I won't let anyone take you away. I promise."

Seeing Toby like that, Delaney wondered what secret monsters the sight of the darkened house had unleashed for him. The same question seemed to be on Riley's mind when he met her glance. Lucas hugged Toby tighter and gently rocked him from side to side. It was an image that stayed with her long after Wyatt arrived with the car.

"That was a curious little incident," Riley remarked after they were back at the house on Red Mountain and its occupants were settled in for the night. "What brought it on? Do you know?"

Delaney shook her head in a gesture of uncertainty. "According to Lucas, Toby is afraid of the dark. Then he saw that house . . ." She let the sentence trail off, unfinished. "It's where Susan St. Jacque lives. Maybe Toby knew that. Maybe he remembered how much she dislikes him."

"It's possible," Riley conceded. "I have to admit, there's something about that St. Jacque woman that I don't trust either."

"She seems nice enough." But Delaney knew Susan St. Jacque was not the kind of woman she would want as a friend. More than that, she suspected that the gallery owner was the type who didn't want other women for friends.

"Nice is as nice does," Riley murmured cynically. "And something tells me Miss St. Jacque is about as nice as a rogue leopard. The man-eating variety."

"Maybe." Seeking to turn the conversation away from the oddly troubling incident, Delaney glanced at her watch. "It's almost ten. Everything's quiet here. I think I'll take off and leave it in your hands."

"Got a heavy date with Jared?" Riley guessed, his eyes cool and speculating in their study of her.

"I don't know if you'd call it a date." Suddenly the word didn't sound as innocent and old-fashioned coming from Riley. "I'm meeting him for a drink at the Jerome."

"Is that wise?" he asked in a voice dry with disapproval.

"Wait a minute," Delaney protested, half-annoyed with him. "Are you saying that you don't think I should see him? *This* from the same man who, over a week ago, told me that he hoped I would run into Jared again?"

"That was four days ago."

"What changed in between?"

"Nothing," he replied evenly. "I just wouldn't like to see you get hurt again."

Unable to argue with that, Delaney managed a small smile. "Don't worry, Riley. I'm not going to fall so easily a second time."

"I hope you don't fall at all."

"If I do," her smile widened, "you can catch me like you did the last time."

Shortly after ten o'clock that night, Delaney pushed through the Gothic doors of the Jerome Bar. The evening crowd filled it and spilled over into the adjoining room. She scanned the throng of people gathered around the tables, most seated, some standing, dressed in a mixture of denim and silk.

She heard her name called and spotted Jared at the bar, an Oriental confection of the bleached wood fretwork that was popular during the Victorian period—like the pressed-tin ceiling and the brass-and-etched-glass light fixtures that hung from it. She dodged an exiting couple and walked over to join him.

"You made it." He removed his hat from the empty spindle-backed stool beside him. "Have a seat."

She shook her head. "I think I'll stand."

He shifted over, making room for her at the bar. "Did you stay for the evening concert by the string quartet?"

"No. Actually, we left shortly after I saw you. I would have been here sooner, but some minor problem cropped up at the house." She didn't explain that the problem had been Toby's agitated state or the time it had taken for Lucas to get him calmed down. "This is a busy place."

"Always."

A bartender in a white dress shirt with the cuffs rolled back, suspender and garters at the sleeves, laid a cocktail napkin in front of Delaney. "What'll you have tonight?"

Hesitating, Delaney thought of her father and said, "Cutty and Seven."

Jared indicated the empty bottle beside his pilsner glass. "Another beer." When the waiter moved off to fill their order, he glanced sideways at her. "Cutty and Seven isn't your usual drink. Or is that one of the things about you that has changed?"

"No. It isn't my usual," she admitted. "It's my dad's."

He frowned curiously. "There must be some logic there, but I'm not following it."

Delaney smiled. "This bar was a favorite hangout of his when he was here in the fifties. When he found out I was coming to Aspen, he asked me to have a drink at the Jerome Bar for him—for the sake of his old good times."

He nodded his understanding as the bartender returned with her drink and a cold bottle of beer for him. Jared pushed a twenty-dollar bill to him, then picked up the bottle and refilled his glass. "In that case— here's to your father and his old good times."

"To Dad," she echoed and touched her drink to his, their fingers briefly brushing. She took a sip of it and felt the unaccustomed burn of whiskey in her throat.

Laughter broke out around the big round table by the front window. Jared turned to look, angling his body sideways and leaning an elbow on the bar. Delaney took advantage of the diversion to absently study his burnt tan face and the play of light on his sun-streaked hair. It was disconcerting to realize that if she'd come here with Riley, she'd be regaling him with her father's tales of the Hollywood legends who had partied in the hotel bar. But she doubted Jared would be amused by them. He didn't think much of celebrity types.

Jared turned back. "I'll bet your father did enjoy it here. The fraternity-style atmosphere would suit him."

"But not you," she guessed.

There was a laconic twist to his mouth as he raised his beer glass, saying over the rim of it, "It shows, does it?"

"Slightly," she replied with a smile. "Would you like to go somewhere else?"

She could see he did, but he hesitated. "You haven't finished your drink."

"It's not mine. It's Dad's."

He reached in his shirt pocket and took out another twenty-dollar bill, then signaled to the bartender. "See this drink, Bobbie." He indicated the highball glass in front of Delaney. "Keep it here for our invisible friend when we leave."

The bartender took the folded twenty from Jared's two fingers, raised an eyebrow, and shrugged. "Whatever you say."

"Thanks, Jared," she said, moved by the gesture. She had forgotten how sensitive—how sentimental—Jared could be. "Dad would like that."

"I thought he would, too," he said with a touching hint of self-consciousness.

Outside there was a nip to the mountain night that sharpened all her senses, the stillness and quiet soothing after the steady din of voices and laughter in the bar. Jared steered her to the curb and waited for the solitary car on Main Street to pass. Then, together, they jay-walked to the other side of the street.

Delaney didn't ask where they were going, discovering she didn't care. Without thinking, she glanced northward at the gleam of light shining from the windows of the cantilevered houses on Red Mountain, easily picking out the one owned by Lucas Wayne. A car door slammed across the street, drawing her glance to the couple emerging from the Jerome to take possession of a sleek white Porsche the parking valet had brought around for them. The uniformed doorman opened the passenger door for the woman and discreetly palmed the tip her jacketed male companion slipped to him.

As the Porsche pulled away from the old and elegant hotel in a surge of race horsepower, Delaney was struck by the contrast and imagined what the scene would have been like before the turn of the century when the Jerome had been modern and new.

"What are you thinking about?" Jared asked. "You look miles away."

"Years, actually," she said and smiled. "I was thinking about Aspen, the Hotel Jerome—what it must have been like during the old days, all the grand parties and balls they must have had in it."

"With the stamp mills, the concentrators, and the sampling works constantly thumping in the background," Jared added with dry, mocking humor. "Of course, that was the purpose of the parties and the music—to drown out the clamor of a mining industry that operated twenty-four hours a day."

At the next corner, his hand guided her into a right turn that pointed them toward Ajax Mountain and the bricked walks of the mall. The moon, nearly full, drifted from behind a cloud and cast its silvery shine on the mountain's rugged slopes.

"Were there many big mines here?" Delaney searched the mountain for some trace of them.

"Quite a few. The Aspen Mine, the Durant, the Emma, the Homestake, all were major producers. There were three tramways built just to carry silver ore down the mountain."

"What happened to all of them once the mining stopped?"

"They're still there. The entrances to the shafts are boarded up or filled in now, but this whole area is riddled with abandoned tunnels—the surrounding mountains and the town."

"The town?" Delaney stopped. "If the mines were in the mountains, why would there be tunnels under the town?"

"Because when a vein of silver ore was found, the miners chased it wherever it went. If that meant tunneling under the town, they did. Typically, mining consisted of sinking a shaft—either straight down or at an angle— then tunneling off it every one hundred feet or so," Jared explained. "Those tunnels were called levels, identified by their depths. Level One would be one hundred feet, Level Two, two hundred feet, and so on. Naturally, the deeper they went into bedrock, the hotter it got. Seven and eight hundred feet below ground, it gets pretty warm. Which was why most of the miners worked stripped to the waist."

"Eight hundred feet?" She started walking again. "Do you realize that's nearly eighty stories below-ground?"

"That's right. And at each level, they'd search for ore veins by digging more tunnels called drifts. Plus, they'd need ventilation shafts."

"Interesting," she murmured. "Somehow I guess I always thought a mine was one long main tunnel with smaller ones branching off from it—but all on the same floor, not a half-dozen different ones. Are there any of these old mines you can go inside?"

Jared shook his head. "They were dangerous a hundred years ago, and they're even more dangerous today. The timbers are rotted; most have caved in or are filled with water."

"What do you mean—they were dangerous a hundred years ago? How? Why?"

"A variety of reasons," he said. "But most deaths—and they averaged one a month during the peak of the mining activity—were caused by accidents with explosives or the deep shafts."

"The shafts—you mean falling down one?"

"Right. You have to remember the miners worked underground by candlelight. Most fatal falls occurred when a miner was pushing a loaded ore cart to the shaft so it would be hauled to the surface on a platform—without knowing that the platform had been raised to another level. He'd end up pushing the cart into the shaft and getting pulled in after it, falling one hundred, two hundred feet or more."

His words conjured up an image of falling into a deep abyss, the blackness swallowing her like a descent into hell. She shuddered. "I think I just lost my interest in the subject of silver mines."

"In that case, can I interest you in a cup of coffee or hot chocolate?" He indicated the popcorn wagon on the corner, complete with an outdoor patio, scattered with wrought-iron tables and chairs.

"Hot chocolate."

"It'll probably be instant," he warned.

"I don't mind."

While Jared went to get their drinks, Delaney wandered onto the landscaped patio bordered by brick flowerbeds. She sat in one of the black iron chairs facing the dancing plumes of water that shot up from the street fountain grates in fluctuating rhythm. The cascading fall of water was a cool sound, a soothing sound.

He brought her hot chocolate to the table, and a cup of coffee for himself. They sat and drank it, talking when they felt like it, falling silent when they didn't. When she emptied her cup, Jared took it from her and threw it, along with his, into the trash.

"Want to walk a little more?"

"Why not?"

This time when they set out, Jared took her hand, linking fingers in a warm, gentle grip. They strolled along the mall with its planting of trees and flowers, the space in between paved with liver-colored brick. Ajax Mountain rose ahead of them, and the glow from the moon and the old-style iron streetlamps lit the way.

Somewhere nearby a lone instrument began to play. "Is that a harmonica?" Delaney asked, trying to identify the rich, wavering sound.

Jared nodded. "Some street musician must be working late tonight."

Delaney frowned, haunted by the familiar tune he played. "What's that song? I can't think of the name of it."

"'Stardust.'" Jared slowed to a stop and angled

toward her when she did the same. The brim of his hat shadowed all of his face except his chin and his mouth. "Would you like to dance?"

Startled, she wasn't sure she understood what he meant. "Here?"

He nodded. "Here. Now. With me. In my arms."

There was something dreamlike and slow about the way he drew her against him, his gaze holding hers, his hand and arm folding over hers and carrying it to his chest. They danced close, their clothes brushing, the rough denim of his jeans catching at the silk of her slacks with each shifting step. Her cheek was centimeters from his jaw, her nerve ends tingling with awareness of him.

Listening to the melody the harmonica played, she remembered the lyric and thought of all the lonely nights she'd spent "dreaming of a love"—of Jared. She pressed closer to him, needing to feel the warmth of his body, needing to be reminded that on this night she wasn't alone, that he was here to fill the empty ache of solitude. His encircling arm tightened to keep her close.

She rubbed her cheek against his smooth-shaven jaw, inhaling the scent of his aftershave lotion with each breath.

She closed her eyes for an instant, then smiled. "Do you realize that this is the first time we've danced together?"

"It's not going to be our last." His lips lightly grazed along her eyebrow, his breath warm against her skin. "I want to court you, Delaney. We bypassed that the last time."

"I guess we did." Did she regret that? She didn't know.

"I want to do it right this time," he insisted. "I've

never been much for candlelight dinners, roses, and soft music—"

"That isn't your style." She drew her head back to look at him. "You're more of a mountains and moon-light man."

"Do you mind?"

She gave a faint shake of her head. "I think I like it."

He said her name and took her lips in a kiss that was both tender and full of longing. She answered it, discovering how easy old patterns were to follow, how readily her body found its old alignment with his, how quickly their kisses could heat into something more.

Jared pulled away and pressed a hard kiss against her forehead, then rocked his mouth to the side. "Six years, Delaney. Six long and empty years." There was a tightness in his voice, in his body. "There were times when I wondered if I had dreamed you. Now I'm holding you and it's no dream—not you, not the way you make me feel, not the things you make me want."

She tried to smile, to say something light, but the words were locked in her throat. In the new stillness, she was conscious of a dozen things at once—the hauntingly sweet refrain of the harmonica, the distant, whispering fall of water on the bricks, and the shimmer of moonlight on the mountain behind him. As emotions funneled and merged, she felt the rawness of old memories and old desires.

"Jared." Again she tilted her head to look at him, but when she saw his eyes on her, gazing at her as if she was the only woman he'd ever seen—or ever wanted to see—she was robbed of words again.

Something like pain flickered across his face, then he dragged her close to him again and began swaying to the music, maintaining a pretense of dancing. "I have a feeling courting you is going to be hell on my nerves."

Delaney silently wondered how either of them could ignore the past intimacy they'd shared when each touch, each kiss, reminded them of the next step, the next pleasure to be rediscovered. Wasn't the thought of making love again irresistible? Wasn't it inevitable? She shied from the memory and the hurt that had followed it.

When the song ended, they separated, their glances guarded, all the old urges too close to the surface. She made a show of looking at her watch. "It's nearly eleven-thirty. I didn't realize it was so late. It's time I called it a night."

"Probably." He continued to hold her gaze. "Have dinner with me tomorrow night, Delaney."

"I don't think I can. Honest," she said, remembering tomorrow's heavy schedule. "It's going to be a long and full day—starting early. Lucas goes jogging at six."

"Lucas, is it?" His expression hardened.

"'Mr. Wayne' becomes a mouthful in an emergency."

"Sorry. I just don't like the man."

Thinking of Lucas and Toby's closeness to him, she said, "You don't know him."

Jared dipped his head briefly, conceding the point. "Then—I don't like what I know about him."

"And you only know what you've *heard* about him. Didn't some wise person once say that you should believe only a third of what you hear and half of what you read?"

"I know it's your job to protect him, but I didn't realize that included defending him."

"Defense is an integral part of protection—especially when the client is under attack. And you were attacking him."

He looked away. "Maybe I was."

She didn't want to argue with him. "I enjoyed tonight, Jared."

"So did I." He reached for her hand, fitting palms and fingers together before linking them. "Maybe I'd better take you back to your bed before I ask you to come to mine . . ."

"Maybe you'd better," she agreed.

SIXTEEN

$\mathcal{M}$ORNING SWELLED ACROSS THE mountains in warm, full waves of sunlight, its primary light blending into the green lushness of the slopes. The sky was a paintbox blue, and a piney smell lay thick and pleasant in the upland air. Birds flitted from branch to branch of the white-trunked aspens and chattered at the trio of runners traveling abreast along the old trail.

Delaney and Riley had the outside positions, with Lucas Wayne in the center setting the pace. The rhythm of his strides was steady; he didn't strain for speed, but conserved for distance. He had on a black muscle shirt and blue jogging shorts, a fine film of perspiration giving a bronze sheen to the hard tanned flesh of his arms and shoulders.

Like Riley, Delaney wore a light windbreaker over her sweatpants, fastened at the waist to conceal the holstered .38 revolver strapped to her waist. She'd left the jacket unzipped to let the air circulate against her skin, exposing her snug t-shirt already darkened with sweat between her breasts. Her long hair was skinned back in a high ponytail, the severe style accenting the wide bone structure of her face and jaw. A blue sweatband circled her head to keep the trickle of perspiration out of her eyes. There was a glow to her face that gave her skin a translucent quality.

The day was turning hot, a faint drone of the forest life disturbing this shadowy stillness. The narrow road was little more than a dirt track of red and tan clay, hard-packed and deeply rutted, worn smooth by time and weather. Eastward, the timber rose in continuous green folds.

"We haven't met anyone in more than a mile," she said, blowing easily, comfortably. "Is it usually this deserted?"

"Usually." Lucas nodded. "Another mile or so ahead, it swings back toward town. That's when we'll start meeting people again."

"Is this an old mining road?" Riley asked, his damp hair looking even darker than normal.

"Could be, for all I know," Lucas replied.

"It probably is." Delaney scanned the thickening woods ahead of them, the aspen giving way to stands of pines. "There's a lot of abandoned mines in the area."

A few yards ahead, an old trail intersected the road. It was nearly overgrown with brush and wild grasses. Erosion had gouged deep cuts into it, exposing the rock red of its soil. "I wonder where that goes." Delaney eyed it curiously as they jogged past. "Do you know?"

Lucas hardly glanced at it. "Too rough. I've never

been on it." He said nothing for two strides, then commented, "This buddy of yours on my right surprises me. He's in better condition than I thought he'd be."

"Deceiving for a smoker, isn't he?" Delaney grinned. "The guys call him Iron Legs. To him, a ten-K run is a sprint. He runs marathons purely for the fun of them."

"Didn't anybody ever tell you two that it's rude to talk about somebody as if they weren't there?" Riley chided.

"Were we doing that?" Lucas joked to Delaney.

Riley mocked, "Does a pine tree have needles?"

"That depends on what kind of needles you mean," Delaney countered. "It doesn't have sewing needles."

The conversation dissolved into a good-natured argument over semantics that lasted until the road made its swing toward town. They walked the final mile to the house on Red Mountain, cooling down hot muscles.

The telephone was ringing when they walked into the house. Lucas went to answer, but Riley was a step quicker. "Yes, hello?"

"You should always let Riley answer the phone, Lucas," Delaney said in a gentle reminder.

"I know—it's good policy."

"Right. How about some juice?" She headed for the kitchen.

"Sounds good."

"It's for you, Lucas." Riley held out the receiver, one hand covering the mouthpiece. "Susan St. Jacque."

Lucas altered his course to take the phone from Riley. "Pour me a glass, Delaney. I won't be long."

"A glass of what?" Riley fell in step behind her.

"Orange juice." She peeled off her sweatband and

blotted the lingering beads of sweat from her neck, then shoved the band in her jacket pocket.

"No thanks." He opened the refrigerator door, set out the carafe of orange juice, then reached back inside. "I'll have apple juice instead." He pulled out a bottle, uncapped it, and took a quick swig, then leaned against the counter near the carafe of orange juice. "So how did your date with Jared go? You never did say."

"Fine." Delaney took two large glasses from the cupboard.

"You obviously didn't spend much time with him. Vance said that you were back before midnight."

"What were you doing? Checking up on me?" She threw an accusing look at him, half-irritated as she carried the glasses over to the juice carafe. Riley answered with a slow, lazy smile.

"You're as bad as my father. I'm surprised you didn't have Vance turn the porch light on for me."

"Condo apartments don't have porch lights."

"Or it would have been on, right?" Delaney filled both glasses with juice.

"You've got it." His smile widened to an even lazier grin. "So—did Jared kiss you good night at the door?"

"I came home by myself." She felt a slow heat rising in her cheeks, which didn't come from her morning jog. It was painfully clear that Riley was back to his old teasing self. Instead of being relieved by that, Delaney discovered that she much preferred the cryptic comments he'd been making the last few days.

"An artful dodge of my question. Which means—he did kiss you." His gaze made a slow and much too thorough study of her.

"I never said that." She took a long drink of her juice.

"No, you didn't. But you've never been the kind to kiss and tell," Riley said. "Was the old spark there? Or only the memory of it?"

Delaney hesitated, suddenly realizing that she wasn't certain of the answer. "Keep up the questions, Riley, and I'll start asking some of my own about your love life."

He chuckled. "You won't ask."

"What makes you so sure of that?"

"Because you know if I started talking about making love to another woman, you would turn fifty shades of red. More than that, you'd never be able to look me in the eye again. Would you?" he challenged softly.

"It wouldn't be easy," she admitted with forced nonchalance, then looked him straight in the eye, surprised at how much resistance she felt about visualizing Riley in the arms of some woman.

"That's what I thought." A glint of satisfaction showed in the deep blue of his eyes before he lifted the juice bottle and took a quick swig from it, then released a gusty sigh of relish. "There's nothing better than cold apple juice after a run—except a hot shower. Which is where I'm headed now."

"Don't use all the hot water," Delaney called after him, relieved this conversation was ending.

"I'll try not to." He nodded his head in dubious promise as he walked out of the kitchen. "I'll honestly try."

Alone, Delaney drank down half the orange juice in her glass, conscious of the vague ache in her leg muscles and that peculiarly invigorating tiredness she always felt after a long run. She picked up the carafe and poured more juice into her glass, filling it to the top again.

"Not fair," Lucas said from the doorway. "You have a head start on me."

"You'll catch up soon enough." She picked up both glasses and gave him the first.

"Before I forget, Susan will be here around ten so we can go look at some painting she's been wanting me to see."

"Okay." Delaney glanced at the wall clock. It was seven-thirty; she had ample time to shower and change.

"Have dinner with me tonight, Delaney."

His invitation momentarily threw her, but she covered it well. As usual.

"Another time, maybe," she said. "I'm going to be tied up."

"With Jared, I suppose." His terseness was almost sarcastic.

"No." She picked up her glass and studied him over the rim of it. "It so happens I'm meeting with the man in charge of security for Friday night's reception."

His mouth lifted in a rueful and faintly boyish smile. "I don't suppose you'd help me get my foot out of my mouth, would you?"

"I think you can handle it," Delaney replied with more than a little amusement.

He strolled over to the counter and leaned a hip against the edge of it and an elbow on its hard surface. He filled her side vision, making it impossible for Delaney not to notice the amount of muscled flesh the skimpy top left exposed. Without question, Lucas Wayne had a physique any woman would admire—and most men would envy. That body, that face, and that sexy smile made a potent combination, on-screen or off.

"Can you blame me, Delaney, for being upset at the thought of someone beating my time?"

She wrapped both hands around her juice glass. "Inherent in that question is the assumption you have time for someone to beat. I don't think that's been established."

"Not for lack of trying on my part." His voice was low, deliberately caressing. "But you have this mental block that refuses to accept that I might be attracted to you. Why? And don't give me that worn-out excuse about mixing business with pleasure. Don't you realize you're a unique and intriguing woman?"

"And don't you realize, Lucas, that I've watched you come on to every woman you meet?"

"I come on to them because that's what they expect from me." His mouth twisted in a cynical line. "And, as P. T. Barnum once said: 'Always give the people what they want.'" Quietly he added, "It's different with you, Delaney."

For the first time, she believed he meant that. She was still trying to contemplate that when he leaned toward her. She felt his breath feather over her lips an instant before he claimed them, his mouth soft and warm, lightly nipping to coax a response.

Instinctively she pushed him back. "You're moving too fast, Lucas."

"You're too methodical."

"It's safer than being too rash." She'd learned that with Jared. "Why don't you go take a shower?"

"Why don't you come take one, too?"

"I will—as soon as Riley gets out."

He shook his head in mild exasperation. "You always have an answer ready that turns aside unwanted suggestions, don't you?"

"Most of the time," Delaney said with a faint smile.

"I guess I'll have to wait for a time when you don't."

"I guess you will."

"See? You did it to me again." Resigned and amused, Lucas pushed away from the counter bar. "I give up—this time." He gave her ponytail a playful tug and sauntered out of the kitchen.

After a short interval of absorbed reflection, Delaney took another sip of orange juice, then stepped down from the stool and unfastened the button at the gathered band of her windbreaker. As she reached to unbuckle the webbed belt that held the gun and its holster, she heard the front door close. The sound was followed by the heavy and quick clump of feet crossing the foyer, a sound made by Toby's peculiar tiptoeing run.

"Luke?" His voice came from the hall.

Delaney struggled a moment to free the buckle's hook from the belt hole. The tightly woven cloth—made damp by her body's perspiration—stuck to her skin, initially refusing to give. Finally she worked it free and felt instant relief from its chafing tightness as Toby charged into the kitchen, his face alight with eagerness.

"Luke's back, isn't he? Where is he? Have you seen him?"

"He went to take a shower." She removed the belt and its attached holster from her waist and started to lay it on the counter, then something—the silence, the lack of any movement—caused her to look up. Toby stood in the same place, transfixed by the sight of the revolver butt poking out from the leather holster.

"That's a gun, isn't it?"

"Yes." She saw his glance leap to her face, his eyes dark with mistrust and a hint of fear.

"Guns are bad." He backed away from her a step. "You shouldn't have that. Guns kill people."

"Toby—" she began.

"I'm gonna tell Luke." He turned and fled from the kitchen at a lumbering run.

Delaney started to go after him, then hesitated, reluctant to take the .38 revolver with her, and unwilling to leave it lying on the counter. She heard Toby pounding on the door to the master suite. Then there was a break—a short one before Toby started talking, his words lost to her, but not his anxious and agitated tone.

She debated an instant longer, then detached the gun and holster from the belt and slipped the pair into her right jacket pocket. The belt she rolled into a tight coil and stuffed in her other pocket before she made her way from the kitchen to the hall that led to the master suite. Toby hurried out of the room, his head down, his expression long and uncertain.

He passed her, hugging the other side of the wall and not saying a word. Delaney held her silence as well, then noticed Lucas standing in the suite's doorway, a towel wrapped around his middle. From somewhere beyond him, she could hear the shower running, although his skin was dry.

"I'm sorry. I didn't mean to upset him, Lucas."

"You didn't . . . not really. Toby is uneasy around guns, and I hope he stays that way. They're not toys; they're not something to play with—" He stopped and rubbed a hand across his forehead. Delaney considered again his amazing patience with his retarded brother, aware that at times Toby must be a trial. Lucas smiled a little tiredly. "It's all right, though. I told him you were a kind of policeman—even if you didn't wear a uniform. He knows policemen carry guns to protect people . . . and shoot the bad guys," he added, as if trying to joke his way out of an awkward situation.

"Right," Delaney knew her smile was as forced as his joke.

"He'll probably be a little nervous around you, but he'll forget about it after a while."

"I hope so." She didn't want Toby to be afraid of her.

"You have your job to do, Delaney. Toby has to accept that." A muscle worked along his jaw, flexing and relaxing, then flexing tautly again. "I can't make his world perfect. I can't make all the bad things go away. I just can't."

"I don't think Toby expects you to."

He looked at her with almost brooding intensity, then sighed. "Maybe he doesn't. Maybe it's something I expect from myself."

Delaney thought that was probably closer to the truth, but she said instead, "Your shower's running."

He glanced behind him as if realizing only at that moment what the rushing sound was. "Right." He turned away.

As she started to leave, Riley emerged from the guest room located diagonally across the hall. "Your turn," he said. "I even left some hot water for you."

"That's big of you, Riley," she replied, aware her response wasn't as lighthearted as she'd intended it to be.

"I thought so." He glanced at the closed door to the master suite. "I take it Toby finally got Lucas to open the door."

"Finally." Delaney nodded.

Catching something in her voice, Riley examined her a little more closely. "Is there a problem? Was he upset about something?"

"Toby saw I was carrying a gun—and thought I shouldn't, so he went to tell Lucas."

"Tattletale, eh?"

"Something like that. Anyway, everything is okay now."

"Good. Enjoy the shower." He moved past her and started up the hall.

Belatedly Delaney remembered, "Susan St. Jacque will be over at ten and we'll be going out again."

Riley stopped. "Where?"

"I assume to her gallery."

In the heart of Aspen's chic business district, Gallerie St. Jacque was discreetly grand and lofty, soaring two stories tall. Its elegant glass doors opened into a collection of rooms, some large and some small, interconnected by stately archways. It was to one of the more intimate rooms that Susan St. Jacque took Lucas Wayne to view the painting under consideration.

Delaney waited beyond the room's archway, keeping watch along with Riley. There were no other customers in the gallery. Shortly after they arrived, Susan St. Jacque had locked the doors and hung a sign that read CLOSED FOR PRIVATE SHOWING.

Riley idly inspected an Etruscan vase displayed on a marble pedestal, then strolled over to Delaney and stole a look into the room.

"Did you see the size of that painting?" he asked in a low undertone. "The canvas alone must be five feet tall. Add the matting and the frame to that and it has to be close to six feet."

"I don't think it will fit on your boat." She gave him a quick, mocking glance.

"No kidding."

Her gaze strayed to the blonde gallery owner standing some fifteen feet away with Lucas Wayne. Silver bracelets jingled on Susan's wrist as she gestured to the sensuous swirl of colors on the canvas, shades bleeding into shades to create twisting, sinuous shapes.

Following the direction of her gaze, Riley studied the pair. "She is determined to talk Lucas into buying it, isn't she?"

"It seems that way."

He lifted back the cuff of his shirt to look at his watch. "We've already been here thirty minutes. Maybe I should have told Arthur Golden to take a cab from the airport instead of agreeing to pick him up."

"His flight isn't scheduled to arrive for another hour and a half. You should be able to make it without a problem."

"I should, but will I?" Riley countered dryly.

"I guess we'll see." In either case, they were there for the duration—however long or short that was.

Riley sent another thought-filled glance at the pair. "I have the feeling that St. Jacque woman could turn into a piranha when she smells a sale."

"Most people in sales have a killer instinct—at least, the successful ones. That's how they earn the big commissions." And it was obvious to Delaney that Susan was eager for Lucas to buy the painting. But was Lucas eager? Susan talked and Lucas nodded. She pointed and he looked. Yet there was something perfunctory about all of his responses, as if he was going through the motions of showing an interest in the painting when he had no intention of buying it.

As Susan turned and waved a hand toward the

painting, her voice drifted across the room. "Think how stunning this will look above your fireplace, Lucas."

Lucas obviously made some suitable and noncommittal reply that Delaney didn't catch. Unfazed by his lukewarm reaction, Susan went on, "As I mentioned earlier, the current owner has found himself in an unfortunate financial situation that he would prefer to keep quiet. That's why he's reluctant to put the painting up for auction—for fear the wrong people would realize he was short of funds. I *persuaded* him to let me handle the sale of the painting for him. At auction, it would probably bring in the neighborhood of five million—"

Riley released a whistling breath. "Some neighborhood."

Judging by Lucas Wayne's expression, Delaney suspected his reaction to the price was an echo of Riley's.

"That's what it *could* bring," Susan stressed. "But the owner will take three and a half."

"Three and a half or five million, it doesn't make any difference," Lucas replied, his voice lifting with a note of finality. "I still don't have that kind of money lying around."

"But you can get it, darling."

"How?" he challenged lightly, amused—almost cynically so.

"Luke." She said his name with the indulgent patience one would show a child. "It's common knowledge that Paramount has offered you twenty million dollars to do a sequel to your last release. And if they offered you twenty, Arthur Golden should be able to get you thirty."

"An offer, Susan, that's all it is." He sounded angry, exasperated. "There is no money in the bank. Even if

Arthur came to terms with them on a deal, it would all be predicated on an acceptable script. I'm not going to jeopardize my career by making a dog of a film just to have money to buy this painting. It would be a stupid thing to do."

"I agree—it would be very stupid of you to jeopardize your career."

Lucas stiffened, his expression turning cool. "I'm glad you agree—"

"I do. But I'm also convinced you and this painting are made for each other. While you may not have the cash on hand to purchase it, you can get it. With the royalties that will roll in from your album sales, the equity you have in your home on Red Mountain, your place in Bel Air, and your potential movie contracts, a loan won't be difficult to arrange."

"I don't know. Maybe it wouldn't." He was hesitating, as if finally tempted to buy.

"Believe me, they would. I can even arrange the loan for you. You'll have the money in less than a week."

"A week?" Lucas echoed skeptically. "You can't promise that."

"Can't I?" Her low laugh was throaty and purring. "Luke, darling, do I have to remind you that it's not *who* you know that counts, but *what* you know about *whom*? It will be approved."

Riley's mouth twisted into a grim line of disgust, and Delaney knew he had heard Susan's last remark. And like Riley, she knew it meant Susan had something on some banker.

"In some circles, that's called politics," Riley murmured under his breath. "In others, blackmail."

Nodding, Delaney recalled her first meeting with

Susan and the remark she'd made that Delaney must learn a lot of secrets about her clients in the course of her work, implying that such secrets could be detrimental to the client if they became public. At the time, Delaney had shrugged off the remark as idle curiosity. Now she suspected that secrets were part of Susan's stock-in-trade.

Riley added softly, "What were you saying about a killer instinct?"

No answer was required and Delaney offered none. She wished Lucas and Susan were out of earshot. She didn't want to hear anymore. It would only make her angry—and to what purpose? There was nothing she could do. This was life—the side of it nobody liked.

Lucas spoke. "You realize you're talking about a lot of money, Susan. A lot of debt."

"I'm talking about your future, Luke. Yours and Toby's," she added. "I know how anxious you are to ensure that Toby will always be financially secure. You know how fickle Hollywood is. Your acting career could be over tomorrow. But this painting will be a tremendous investment."

Toby. The instant Susan said his name, Delaney knew that Susan was one of the handful who knew Toby was Lucas Wayne's brother. Which meant she also knew how anxious Lucas was to protect Toby from a grasping, gawking public. She knew, and she was using that knowledge—that secret—to force Lucas into buying this painting.

"You can bet she'll make a bundle of money out of the sale," Riley muttered under his breath. "Something tells me that half a million of that three and a half price tag goes to Miss St. Jacque. Maybe more."

"That's enough, Riley," Delaney murmured.

"Sorry. My disgust is showing, isn't it?"

"It's written all over your face."

"Yours, too."

Delaney tried to do something about that as Lucas and Susan wandered toward them. "Let me make an offer on the painting in your name, Luke. Just to keep him from selling it to anyone else."

"Arthur is flying in this afternoon. I want to talk to him, see what kind of tax ramifications this might have."

"But that's the beauty of it, darling. Borrowing the money, there won't be any tax ramifications to worry about."

"I need time to think about this, Susan."

"What is there to think about? There is only one smart decision and that's to buy it. Believe me, the value of the painting is easily five million. At an auction, it could even bring more. The owner wants a quick sale."

"Give me a few days. A week at the maximum."

"Very well, a week." But the delay plainly irritated her.

As they neared the archway, Riley turned to them. "Ready to leave?"

"Yes." Lucas immediately angled away from Susan to head toward the front doors.

Susan walked them outside. Riley took the ignition keys out of his pocket and walked around to the driver's side while Delaney opened the rear passenger door for Lucas.

"I'll see you at the reception on Friday," Susan said in parting. "Don't forget, you promised to introduce me to Kyle Baines."

"How could I forget? You aren't going to let me,"

Lucas replied with a rare sarcasm that his quick smile failed to disguise.

"Be sure and say hello to Toby for me, Luke," Susan added.

To Delaney, the innocent-sounding words masked a threat of exposure. Lucas didn't respond. Delaney pushed the door shut behind him, nodded curtly to Susan, and climbed in the front seat beside Riley.

Not surprisingly, Lucas had little to say during the ride back to the house. Riley turned the radio on, covering most of the silence with music and filling the rest with comments on his favorite songs, comments that required responses from Delaney.

SEVENTEEN

TWENTY MINUTES LATER, THEY walked into the air-conditioned cool of the house. Riley immediately switched off the alarm system while Delaney slipped her sunglasses to the top of her head and gave the foyer a cursory glance. The heavy stillness seemed as weighted as the silence coming from Lucas. Without a word, he took the day's mail from the table and proceeded directly into the cavernous white living room.

Riley's gaze followed him. "I've never seen him this quiet, not even on the set." He absently twirled the key ring hooked on his forefinger, the car keys rattling together. "It makes me think she might have something on him."

"It does, doesn't it?" Delaney murmured.

"I might as well head for the airport. It's early yet, but I can pick up our tuxedos for Friday's formal bash on my way."

"Good idea. It will save a trip later."

"That's what I thought." Riley headed for the door. "If Arthur's flight arrives on time, I shouldn't be gone more than an hour."

She acknowledged that with a wave of her hand and crossed to the telephone extension in the foyer as Riley went out the door. Picking up the receiver, she dialed the number for the command center, informed Vance she was back at the house with Lucas, then checked for messages—all the while conscious of faint stirrings of movement coming from the living room.

By the time she hung up, the house was silent once again. She hesitated, then crossed to the arched entrance to the living room. The mail lay unopened on a plump ivory sofa cushion. Lucas stood at the expanse of glass that soared from the floor to the peak of the thirty-foot ceiling. There was something brooding in his stance, his feet braced slightly apart, one hand buried in the side pocket of his pleated slacks, his shoulders slumped.

The stillness was broken by the sudden and distinctive rattle of ice cubes against the sides of a glass. Lucas looked down, then lifted a drink to his mouth and bolted down a hefty swallow. With more loud clinking of ice, he turned from the view and saw Delaney in the archway.

"Would you like lunch?" she asked, identifying at a glance the Bloody Mary in his hand, complete with a celery stalk in place of a swizzle stick. "There's still some fresh snow crab left in the refrigerator."

"No. This will hold me 'til Arthur gets here," he said, lifting his drink.

"Okay."

As she started to turn away, his voice stopped her. "Where are you going?"

She didn't answer immediately, her glance skimming the faint creases in his forehead and the banked anger in his eyes. "I thought you might like to be alone."

"Alone." His short laugh held no humor. "That's a good one, Delaney. Hell, I'm always alone . . . even when I'm with someone." Again she started to leave. "Don't go. Stay with me?"

She heard the faint throb in his voice that subtly turned the request into a plea. "If you want." She deliberately injected a casual note and reversed her course to join him in the living room.

For her, the situation was an awkward one. Long ago she'd learned that few clients wanted to know she'd overheard their conversations. On the contrary, they preferred to pretend she hadn't. Therefore, professionally she had to act as if she wasn't aware anything was troubling a client even when privately she knew better—as in this case, where she strongly suspected that Susan St. Jacque was threatening to expose that Toby was his brother in order to pressure him into buying the painting.

Lucas again rattled the cubes in his glass, then swung around to face the window and the mountain vista beyond it. "I used to dream about making it," he said in a grim, flat voice. "But I never imagined it like this." He paused an instant and lifted his glass in her direction. "Take it from me, Delaney, success doesn't change people. Not really. But it sure as hell changes the way other people look at you. I hate to think of the number of friends I've lost because of it."

"Why?" She frowned at that curious statement. "If they were your friends—"

"—then they should be happy for me, is that what

you think?" he mocked. "So did I. They wanted to be. Some of them even tried. But for them, my success emphasized their failure. Every time I was around them, hadn't—at least, in their eyes. The friendship becomes too painful after that and eventually dies."

"That's sad."

"Very sad," Lucas agreed. "But you can't change it, any more than you can change the attitudes of others, especially the ones who look at you and assume you must be different from them. You have to be; you're a star and they're not. It isn't that they think you're too good for them. No, it's much more subtle than that. They think they're not good enough." He hooked a finger around the celery stalk, holding it out of the way while he tossed down a swallow of the vodka-laced tomato juice. "Then there's all the rest—the users. The ones who want the money and the favors you can get for them."

Like Susan, Delaney thought, but she didn't say it.

"Then the day finally comes when you find yourself alone in your ivory tower with a drink in your hand. And you raise your glass to the emptiness and echo the words of that famous television detective: 'Who loves ya, baby?'" With bitter mockery, he acted out his scenario and drank down the rest of the Bloody Mary.

Compassion surged, and with it came the urge to soothe and comfort. But how? What could she say? Nothing would change the way things were.

"Lucas," she said softly. "It doesn't do any good to feel sorry for yourself."

"Doesn't it?" He turned on her, his hot temper surfacing in a blaze, his tight grip on the empty glass showing the white of his knuckles. "What the hell do you know about any of this? You don't know what it's like to be alone—to have a pack of vultures out there circling, waiting for the chance to pick your bones. You don't know what it's like to be hated because you're a success. Oh, the public roots for you on the way up, but once you get there, they want to tear you down. They want to see you crash and burn. The press would love to write about it. One hint of a scandal and they'd be all over it, twisting it into something ugly and sordid so they could sell more papers."

But the angry words failed to satisfy the violence within. Spinning around, Lucas hurled the empty glass at the fireplace, juice-stained cubes arcing to the floor, crystal shattering against the marble in an explosion of tinkling shards. He took two quick steps away from her, then stopped and raked his fingers through his dark hair. Delaney suspected that if there'd been a wall close by, he would have rammed a fist into it.

Without turning, he declared, "You have absolutely no idea how vindictive people can be."

"Yes, I do. It's my job."

He turned back to her, his anger dissolving in a rush. "How could I have forgotten that?"

"We tend to forget a lot of things in the pressure— the frustration—of the moment."

His mouth curved with a sudden, engaging touch of wry humor. "Do you often play mother confessor to your clients and listen while they pour out their troubles to you?"

She smiled back. "Very, very rarely."

"That's their loss." His eyes made a slow and thoughtful inspection of her face. "Instinctively I must have known you'd understand. Looking back, I think the biggest reason I was drawn to Rina was because she'd gone through it herself—old friends falling away, the users grabbing at you, the media hounding you, everybody out to get you, to use you, to take advantage of any weakness they can find—"

"Not everybody, Lucas."

He paused. "No, not everybody. Not you."

With one step, he reached out and drew her into his arms. Delaney didn't resist, recognizing that he needed the assurance of physical contact and wanting to give it to him.

He rubbed his chin against the side of her hair. "You have no idea how much it means to me to know you're here to watch out for me, not to use me. I guess that's why I feel safe with you, because I know you'll be there for me."

Listening to the low rumble of his voice, catching the quiet fervency in it, Delaney suddenly realized no one had ever been there for him—not his parents, not his friends. She was the first to attempt to protect him from harm. For an emotionally charged instant, she let her arms tighten around him, holding him closer. When she felt the brush of his lips against her hair, she drew back and attempted to reassert a professional position.

"Don't forget, Lucas, it's our job to make sure nothing happens to you."

He disputed that. "Maybe it's a job to Riley and the others. But not to you, Delaney. You care."

It was true. Somewhere along the line, she had begun to care about Lucas as a person, not just as a client. She liked him.

"I do care," she admitted in a deliberately light voice. "That's why I'm going to pick up the glass you broke before you get hurt."

"I did make a mess, didn't I?" he said with a touch of chagrin.

"Unfortunately, yes."

"Then it's only fair I help clean it up."

"If you think I'm going to turn down the offer, you're wrong," Delaney retorted with a curious light-heartedness that lasted all the way through the time it took to pick up the broken pieces and blot the puddles left by melting ice cubes.

By then Riley had returned from the airport with Arthur Golden. His glance made contact with hers. Delaney responded with a small, barely perceptible nod of her head, answering his unspoken question that all was well.

"It's good to see you again, Lucas." Arthur Golden walked over to shake his hand.

"Same here. How was your flight?"

"Turbulent," Arthur replied with a faint grimace. "That plane was like a flying earthquake. I thought I was back in L.A." His gaze narrowed on Lucas in quick scrutiny. "How are you doing?"

"Fine."

"Good. I have a stack of scripts for you to read." Arthur turned to Riley. "Bring me that black bag." Taking it for granted that he would, Arthur swung back to Lucas. "I had lunch at Morton's on Monday with Dave from Creative Artists. They are putting a movie package together and, naturally, they want you to star in it. I brought the script for you to read. They would like an answer as soon as possible on it."

"I'll take a look at it." Lucas strolled over to the mahogany bar. "Would you like something to drink? Lime and soda, maybe?"

"A cup of hot tea would be nice."

"I'll fix one for you," Delaney offered.

"There should be some Earl Grey in the kitchen," Arthur told her. "Lucas always keeps some here for me."

"I'll find it." Delaney moved toward the archway.

"Don't let the water come to a boil or—" Arthur began, then broke it off. "I'd better come with you. When it comes to tea, I'm as particular as the English."

With smooth, long strides, he hurried to join her. In the foyer, they bumped into Riley carrying a black canvas tote that bulged at the sides.

"Take that into Lucas. Tell him the script from Creative Artists should be on top." He waved Riley toward the living room, then slipped a hand on Delaney's elbow and steered her toward the kitchen. "Tell me the truth, Delaney. What's been going on here? Lucas looked a little edgy to me. Has Rina caused more problems?"

"No."

"She will," he said, much too positive.

"Have you found out something we should know?" Delaney asked as they entered the kitchen.

"I bumped into Sid Graves at LAX." He followed Delaney to the sink, watching while she filled the teakettle with water from the tap.

"Who is Sid Graves?" She frowned at the name and set the kettle on the range, then turned on the burner beneath it.

"Her manager. He was on his way to New York to meet with her attorneys there. Sid and I have known each other for years. He had some time before his flight left—I had some time. It seemed like a perfect opportunity to clear up this trouble—behind the scenes, so to speak."

"And?" Delaney prompted when Arthur paused.

"And—I cornered him. Which is why I wanted to speak to you alone." He lifted the lid to the sugar bowl, gave it a quarter turn, and set it back down, his smooth forehead puckering in a frown. "Sid told me that he met with Rina the morning after the shooting—after she had been released. According to him, she was her usual belligerent self at first, ranting and raving about what she was going to do to Lucas. Sid got mad. He told her she was in some damned serious trouble, reminded her that she was facing a felony charge—that it could mean prison."

A canister of the imported English tea blend was in the spice cupboard. Delaney set it out on the counter by the range, then automatically searched for the porcelain teapot.

"Sid said that she turned to him and said, with tears in her eyes, 'But it was an accident. I never intended to shoot him. I love him. Why would I try to kill him? It's true, I had a gun. Lucas gave it to me. I did take it to the hotel, but I only wanted to scare him with it—that's all. It went off while we were struggling. It was an accident,' she said. 'A horrible, frightening accident.' Then she broke out crying. When Sid went to comfort her, she looked up and he saw the gleam in her eyes." Arthur paused and dragged in a deep, steeling breath. "Sid described it as cold and calculating. After that she taunted him, saying, 'I have nothing to worry about, Sid. No jury will convict me once I tell my story. I can get away with it. Wait and see.'"

The kettle whistled shrilly, startling both of them. Delaney grabbed the teakettle and lifted it off the burner.

"According to Sid, everyone around her is scared

she will carry out her threat. And no one knows how to stop her. Sid has tried everything to get her out of Aspen—claiming urgent meetings, offers for new recording contracts, movie deals. But she hasn't fallen for any of them." He popped the lid off the tea canister. "If he said it to me once, he said it to me a dozen times—'Whatever you do, Arthur, don't let her get to Lucas.'" He looked at Delaney. "Now I'm telling you— don't let her get to Lucas."

"Don't worry. We won't."

"What about this party on Friday?" Arthur took a couple of pinches of loose-leaf tea from the canister and dropped them into the blue porcelain teapot. "What if Rina shows up there?"

"It's possible." With a steady show of calm, Delaney poured the water from the kettle into the pot. Steam rose in a vaporous cloud. "But the reception is by invitation only and her name isn't on the guest list."

"Don't underestimate her," Arthur warned. "She got into his suite in New York. If she needs an invitation, she'll find a way to get one."

"I have a meeting with Sam Blake tonight. He's in charge of security at the reception. I'll make certain the invitations can be used only by the guest on the list. By the way, should I have your name added?"

"I should go, but I have a couple of conference calls set for Friday night. I'll have to pass." He sighed heavily. "You know, I could cope with all of this if it was some deranged fan out there. But for it to be someone like Rina Cole . . ." He shook his head. "Why couldn't she have a normal breakdown like any other star? Why did she have to pick Lucas? It isn't fair."

"What is fair?" Delaney countered.

His mouth twisted wryly at that. "I'll tell you the truth, Delaney—I wish Lucas had never agreed to go to the party Friday. And I am going to do my damnedest to talk him out of it."

It was nearly nine o'clock by the time Delaney concluded her meeting with Sam Blake and returned to the detail's command center at the condo. Two express packets from her office waited for her. One held checks for payroll and accounts payable, requiring her signature. She relieved Vance from his watch and sent him off for a late dinner, then dealt with the checks.

The second packet was fatter and heavier, filled with correspondence to be answered, plus various billing and invoices that required her approval. Delaney fixed a pot of coffee in the small kitchen, then tackled the stack of paperwork.

Halfway through it, the phone rang. She picked up the receiver and cradled it to her ear. "Nine-two-one-one." She absently glanced at the VCR's digital clock atop the television, noting that Riley was making his check-in call five minutes early.

But it wasn't Riley's voice that came over the line. "Is that you, Delaney? It's Jared."

"Jared." She smiled without being conscious of it. "This is a coincidence. I just came across your name tonight in the most unexpected place."

"Let me guess," he said, his voice warm with amusement. "Was it the RSVP list for Friday's reception?"

"On the nose." Delaney reached for the alphabetized list of names Sam Blake had supplied to her. Jared was fourth from the top. "It never occurred to me you went to such things."

268 JANET DAILEY

"Usually I don't. But when I heard Lucas Wayne would be there, I knew you would be, too. So instead of throwing the invitation in the trash, I accepted, knowing I'd see you."

"I'll be working," she reminded him.

"No problem. I'll just stand beside you and breathe in the fragrance of your perfume." After a slight pause, he added, "I miss you."

Finding it impossible to respond directly to that, she murmured, "I wish I had more free time."

"What about Sunday? I can trailer in a couple horses from the ranch and we can ride up to Maroon Lake for a picnic."

"That sounds wonderful, but . . . I'm not sure—"

"Delaney, you can't keep working eighteen hours a day. Mentally you need to give yourself a break."

"Probably."

"Good. I'll pick you up Sunday at noon."

"We'll see."

"I'll expect a more definitive answer on Friday."

"Friday," she agreed, then remembered, "Jared, you do know it's black tie?"

"I know."

After he hung up, Delaney tried and failed to picture Jared in a tuxedo.

EIGHTEEN

OUTSIDE THE EXCLUSIVE STARWOOD estate, a string of
Mercedes, Bentleys, and Rolls-Royces vied for parking
space with Colorado-chic Jeep Wagoneers and Range
Rovers, while inside guests clad in Givenchy and Chanel
mixed and mingled. Conversation bubbled into every
corner. Delaney drifted along the fringes, her dark hair
swept up in a soft French roll, neither overdressed nor
underdressed in her midnight blue evening jumpsuit,
chosen not for its classically simple lines, but rather for
the unhampered movement it provided—like the flat
dress shoes on her feet.

She paused along the inner wall adorned with a collection of work by Twombly and Sultan. As she sipped at
the ginger ale in her fluted glass, her eyes were constantly
moving, scanning the throng of guests in the mammoth
living room of polished mahogany and marble. Beyond

the acres of glass that maximized the home's view of the Rockies, dark figures moved on its deck, silhouetted against a magenta sky that slowly gave way to the purple of twilight. She had a moment's unease, then brought her attention back inside the room, softly illuminated by indirect lighting.

Black-coated waiters—bronze hearties who could have come straight from central casting—circulated among the guests, dispensing glasses of Haut Brion from their trays or ice-cold Stolichnaya for those who preferred the more traditional accompaniment to the miniature beluga-topped potato pancakes on the hors d'oeuvre trays. A waiter stopped to offer her a sample, but she shook her head in silent refusal and moved on again.

Snatches of conversation came to her, topics ranging from acid rain and the greenhouse effect to discussions of who had the best masseuse. The guests in attendance represented a cross-section of the elite, including those from the ranks of the intellectuals and the artsy types, the social doyennes, the politically savvy, and *Forbes*'s 400, plus many who had fallen below its two-hundred-seventy-five-million-dollar cutoff point, and, of course, celebrities such as Lucas Wayne.

Delaney lost sight of him in her peripheral vision and stopped to locate him. She spotted Riley and John first. Both ranged several feet on either side of Lucas, giving him the space to mingle and chat with other guests without being obtrusive or intimidating. Even with a half a room between them, the bright green of their lapel pins stood out sharply against the black of their tuxedo jackets, the W-shaped pin identical to the one Delaney wore.

She momentarily shifted her glance back to Riley. With the soft light gleaming on his dark hair and bronzing the line of his jaw, he looked like a lethally handsome model in a men's formal wear advertisement. She tended to forget what a good-looking man Riley was. Tonight she was reminded of it.

Briefly Riley caught her eye and nodded, a small smile tugging at one corner of his mouth. Then his attention was redirected to the throng of guests.

Delaney made her own visual sweep of them before locating Lucas again. Briefly she watched as he worked his charm on the bejeweled wife of a media mogul. There was no trace of the anxiety he'd exhibited on the way to the reception, bombarding her with questions that she knew had originated from Arthur—Do you think Rina will show up? What if she does? Could she have gotten a gun? What will you do if she has? Although he had tried to sound merely curious, she had known otherwise.

Patiently she had explained the layers of protection that would be in place—the guard at the front gate, the security at the door, her own point position between Lucas and the door, Riley and John Wyatt at his side, and lastly Vance in the car parked at the rear of the house, ready to whisk him away should a threat materialize. And she had reminded Lucas again to keep to the far end of the room, close to the rear exit.

Lucas tilted his head back and laughed at something the woman said, then made a remark to her husband. Seeing that, Delaney smiled at the thought: "No matter what, the show must go on."

Turning, she skimmed the crowd again with her glance, absently noting the other bodyguards in attendance, some burly and obvious, some nondescript and not. Their presence was accepted, almost taken for granted by the guests, as if they were an ordinary accessory, like cufflinks. Whatever the case, they were definitely a sign of the times.

A man walked toward her. She started to look past him, then stopped, her attention caught by smiling gray-blue eyes, the contrast of burnished gold hair and black tuxedo. It was Jared.

He stopped before her, his gaze moving warmly over her face. "I didn't think you'd be here yet."

"Why would you think that?" She frowned in curious amusement. "The reception started forty-five minutes ago."

"I know, but usually celebrities prefer to make their entrances after their audience has arrived." The dry rustle of his voice echoed the cynical look in his eyes. "You look as elegant as the rest of them."

"Coming from you, I don't think that's a compliment," Delaney replied with humor, by now used to his thinly disguised prejudice toward so-called "important" people.

He smiled, lowering his head in silent concession. "Then let me put it another way—you look beautiful."

"Thank you." She took a sip of her ginger ale and automatically scanned the area near the room's entrance.

A waiter came by with a tray of drinks. Jared took a glass of wine, then shifted to stand beside her and idly survey the scene. "This is going to be awkward, isn't it?"

"What is?"

"Standing here—with you. I thought I'd be content just to be with you. Now I find I want your undivided attention, and I can't have that."

"No, you can't." She felt Riley's gaze on her even before she encountered it. He lifted an eyebrow, his glance flicking from Jared to her. His eyes were cool, with a hint of suppressed anger tightening the line of his mouth.

"The pin you're wearing," Jared said, "am I mistaken or does Riley have one on just like yours?"

"He does. In fact, we all do—everyone in my detail. You could call it our badge of identity," she replied. "In emergency situations, it lets the police know we're the good guys. That can be very important if weapons come into play."

"Do you think there's a chance that could happen?"

"If there wasn't a chance, we wouldn't have been called in in the first place." She gave him her standard answer while privately recalling the concerns—the fear— Rina Cole's manager had expressed to Arthur.

"I guess not."

She noticed Susan St. Jacque skillfully working the crowd, looking very smart in a white ensemble with chunky ropes of pearls draped around her neck. She spotted Delaney and sailed over.

"Delaney, have you seen—" She broke off the question when she noticed Jared. She stiffened briefly, then smiled Cheshire-cat fashion. "Jared, what a surprise to see you here."

"It is, isn't it?"

She slid a curious look at Delaney. "Do you two know each other?"

"We've met, yes." Jared seemed unusually cool and aloof with her.

"Let me offer a word of warning, Delaney," Susan murmured in a confiding tone. "Jared is terribly old-fashioned in his thinking. He doesn't like women who are aggressive and ambitious."

"It isn't a sin for a woman to be aggressive and ambitious, Susan," Jared stated. "The sin is usually in the way she goes about it."

To Susan's credit, she laughed quite convincingly, then turned to Delaney. "As you can see, Jared and I are the best of enemies."

When Jared failed to respond to her last remark, Susan glanced at him slyly. "Always the gentleman, aren't you, Jared? If you can't say anything nice about someone, don't say anything at all."

A hand touched the back of her arm. Delaney half turned, catching a glimpse of the man behind her, part of the reception's security detail. "She's here," the man said in a quick, low voice.

Delaney nodded curtly, then caught Riley's eye and held up a forefinger, advising him of the situation with the previously agreed signal. She murmured a hasty "Excuse me, I have a call" to Jared and Susan, then moved off, swift, long strides carrying her to the front entrance.

A security checkpoint to screen arriving guests had been set up outside the front door beneath a modern version of a stone-pillared and heavy-beamed porte cochere. Recessed lighting concealed within the roof timbers fully illuminated both the drive in front of the house and the entrance. The flaming torches were purely decoration.

When Delaney stepped outside, she spotted Rina Cole immediately. She was dressed somewhat tamely—for Rina—in a black strapless dress and a black bolero jacket with rose ribbon appliqués blanketing the shoulders. Her blonde hair was swept atop her head in a mass of curls à la Betty Grable's forties look. But there was no mistaking it was Rina.

The pop-star-turned-actress faced the two security men at the table with an icy hauteur that Leona Helmsley would have admired. "I demand to see the person in charge. This is an outrage, an invasion of my privacy. We are invited guests. Timothy, show them the invitation again."

She snapped her fingers at the bearded man standing beside her. Looking flushed and obviously embarrassed by the scene she was creating, the man obediently fumbled through his pockets to locate the invitation. His face was vaguely familiar to Delaney, but it wasn't until he took a pair of horn-rimmed glasses from his pocket and slipped them on that she recognized Timothy Collins-Jones, a renowned lecturer and scholar. And he was with Rina Cole? Delaney couldn't think of a more unlikely pairing.

At last, Timothy Collins-Jones produced the invitation to the impatient tap-tap-tapping of Rina's stiletto heels. "That isn't necessary, Professor Collins-Jones," one of the guards protested. "We've already seen it."

"Then let us in!" Rina snapped.

"I'm sorry, but until you let us check the contents of your purse—"

"Why should I? Timothy, do something. You can't let them treat me like this."

The philosopher nervously cleared his throat. "I must say, your actions are discriminatory. You have yet to request to inspect the contents of my pockets."

The two guards exchanged quick glances, then the second one—an off-duty officer moonlighting as part of the security detail—spoke up. "Our procedure is to check the ladies' purses, then the men's pockets. We can reverse it, if you like, and ask you to empty your pockets."

"No!" Rina protested with sudden and open anger. "Don't you do it, Timothy. They have no damned right—they have no goddamned right—" She saw Delaney and stopped, her lip, her face curling into an expression of intense loathing. "Well, if it isn't the bitch-dog Cerberus. This is your doing, isn't it?"

"I don't know what you mean, Miss Cole." Delaney calmly walked forward to make sure Rina didn't advance past the two guards. "I merely came out for some fresh air."

"I suppose you called the police first—like you did the last time," she jeered.

"Is it necessary, Miss Cole?" Delaney caught the sweep of headlight beams along the drive. Wyatt was at the wheel. Somewhere in the shadows of the rear seat was Lucas.

"You're a real smartass, aren't you? Someday you're going to find out you're not so smart after all."

Riley walked out of the evening shadows into the full light of the porte cochere. "What seems to be the problem here?" When Rina swung to face him, Riley practically beamed at her. "Miss Cole, this is an unexpected treat. I happen to be one of your biggest fans."

"Then do something about these—these people!"

"These people?" He raised an eyebrow in feigned confusion, then glanced at Delaney, the barest hint of a twinkle in his blue eyes. "What would you have me *do* about them?"

"Make them let us in!"

"Do you have an invitation?"

"Of course we have an invitation," she snapped angrily.

"Then I don't understand." Riley turned to the two security guards.

"Miss Cole has refused to show us the contents of her purse," the off-duty officer explained.

"And I have no intention of doing so." Rina glared at the pair of them.

"Why not?" Riley looked more amused than curious. "What exactly do you have in there?"

Rina didn't immediately respond. She paused as if trying to decide whether he was friend or foe. "The usual things every woman carries. Lipstick, compact, mascara . . ." One rose-weighted shoulder lifted in a dismissing shrug.

"Is that all?"

"There might be one or two other—shall we say?—intimate items that I wouldn't want to embarrass Timothy by mentioning." She deliberately looked down at Riley's crotch to make sure he understood she meant condoms.

Somehow Delaney managed to choke back a laugh. Riley turned his face and rubbed at the side of his neck. "That could be a tad awkward, couldn't it?"

"Very," Rina replied smugly.

"Under the circumstances, I think we can forego a search of your purse," he said. "The party inside could use some livening up and you're just the one who could do that, Miss Cole . . . especially now that Mr. Wayne has left."

"What?" Shock and anger warred for control.

"Mr. Wayne had to leave early," Riley repeated blandly. "Something about a previous engagement, I think."

"A previous engagement?" Rina sent an angry look in Delaney's direction. "He was probably subjected to the same rude treatment we've received." She grabbed her escort's arm. "Let's get out of here, Timothy. We don't need this."

She towed the poor confused man back to the dark-colored sedan parked beneath the porte cochere. Riley sidled over to Delaney.

"She lost interest in the party awfully quick, didn't she?" he murmured.

"Awfully quick," the off-duty policeman inserted. "I'll tell you one thing—I got a feel of that purse before she jerked it away—and if that was a tube of lipstick and a compact I felt, then Smith and Wesson have started a cosmetic line."

Delaney stiffened. "She had a gun?"

"I'd bet my badge on it."

The car was pulling away. "Get the license number, Riley." Even as she said it, he was moving.

"The license. What for?" the man asked.

"I assume it's against the law in Colorado to carry a concealed weapon, isn't it?" Delaney replied.

"Yes," the officer affirmed, still frowning.

Riley came back. "I managed to catch only two numbers—nine and six. It's a black Lincoln Town Car, a rental from Budget. It shouldn't be hard to spot."

"Got that?" Delaney asked the officer. When he nodded, she said, "Good. Call dispatch, give them the information, and let them know about the gun, then have whoever's on patrol keep an eye out for the car and pull it over for a routine traffic check. If we're lucky, they'll find the illegal weapon."

"And if we're not—" Riley began.

Delaney finished the thought for him. "—we'd better get to the house. Just in case she didn't buy your story about a previous engagement."

"I'll get the car." Moving away, he broke into a loping run.

"I'll be right there." She turned again to the off-duty officer. "Have them keep us informed of any developments."

"Will do."

Riley had the engine running when she reached the car. She climbed in and they took off. Delaney was conscious of the fine tension raveling her nerves as she scanned the road before them, searching for the red gleam of taillights.

"What do you think the chances are that a patrol car will spot the car?" Delaney wondered as Riley placed an unlit cigarette between his lips, then pushed the cigarette lighter in.

"It's a small town."

"I'm counting on that."

"Even if they catch her with that gun in her purse, you know she'll say she's carrying it for her own protection."

"What else could she say?" Delaney glanced briefly at the uniformed security guard on duty at the entrance to the exclusive Starwood subdivision. "I just want that gun taken from her. I want to know she doesn't have one in her possession."

"Temporarily."

"Temporarily will do." She regarded each delay as another victory for their side.

Riley pulled out onto the main road. "You didn't mention Jared would be at the party tonight."

"Didn't I?" Tensing, Delaney kept her gaze fixed on the road ahead of them.

"No, you didn't." His voice was drier than the Santa Ana wind. "How come?"

"It didn't seem important."

Riley muttered something under his breath, too low for her to catch. "What did you say, Riley?" she challenged out of sheer perversity. "I couldn't hear that."

"I was merely commenting on how much you two found to talk about. Too bad your little tête-à-tête was so rudely interrupted by Rina's arrival on the scene."

"It was hardly that," Delaney retorted, annoyed with him. "Or didn't you notice when Susan St. Jacque came over to join us?"

"I noticed." Again there was that note in his voice that implied he had observed a great many things, none of which he liked.

"Honestly, Riley, if I didn't know you better, I'd think you were jealous," she declared in disgust.

"There are times, Delaney," he dragged the words out with a slowness that suggested a tight hold on his temper, "when I can't decide whether to shake you or—" He clamped his mouth shut, breaking it off in midsentence.

"Or what?" she demanded, her own temper kindling.

"One of these days you'll find out." He fired her a quick look and laid a hand on the horn, advising Wyatt of their approach as they neared the driveway to Lucas Wayne's house on Red Mountain.

The house was ablaze with light when they arrived five minutes behind the others. Lucas was in the living room, his bow tie hanging loose, his pleated shirt open at the throat, the studs to it scattered atop the coffee table. His hand gripped a cognac glass, his handsome features etched in taut lines. Arthur paced the floor in front of him.

"I told you not to go. Didn't I tell you not to go? Why wouldn't you listen to me? You have to stop this macho shit, Luke. You have to stop trying to prove how brave you are before you end up dead! Do you hear? Dead!" he declared, then turned and saw Delaney. "Lucas just told me Rina showed up. What happened?"

She glanced at Lucas, conscious of the tension emanating from him. "Isn't it obvious?" She walked into the room, showing them both a calm look of unconcern. "Nothing happened."

"Nothing happened, she says." Arthur threw his hands in the air. "How in God's name can you say nothing happened? She came to the party, didn't she? You had to sneak Lucas out, didn't you?"

"He's here, isn't he? And he's safe, isn't he? Therefore, nothing happened," she reasoned.

"While you two argue this out," Riley inserted dryly, "I think I'll put some coffee on and change out of this tux."

"Good idea."

When she turned to watch Riley exit the room, Arthur started in again. "I don't care what you say, something happened. You can't convince me Rina Cole didn't make some kind of a stink. What did she do? What did she say? Where is she now?"

"I have no idea where she is," Delaney admitted. "When she found out Lucas wasn't there, she decided she didn't want to stay either and left with her date."

"Her date? She was with someone? Who?"

"Timothy Collins-Jones." She could tell the name meant nothing to Arthur. "He's a famous lecturer with a doctorate in philosophy."

"Rina Cole was with a doctor of philosophy." Arthur arched an eyebrow. "Talk about the ultimate odd couple—"

The telephone rang, interrupting him. Arthur swung toward the extension in the living room. Delaney checked the step he took toward it with, "Riley will answer it in the kitchen."

Arthur readily turned from the phone. "The woman's crazy. She should be locked up."

"Arthur, believe me, never at any time tonight was Lucas in danger." She noticed that Lucas hadn't said a single word during all this, his rigid stance never altering, his look hooded and tense.

"But what about tomorrow night? And the night after that? That's what worries me," Arthur stated, then abruptly declared, "I need a drink. Do you want another, Luke?"

"No." Lucas tossed down a swallow of the cognac and turned to wander over to a window.

For a time, the only sounds in the room were the plunk of ice cubes dropped in a glass, the splash of liquor, the spritz of soda, and the sloshing rattle of it all being stirred together.

"Sorry, Delaney, I never asked if you wanted a drink."

"No, thanks, I'll wait for the coffee Riley is fixing."

As if on cue, there was the sound of footsteps crossing the foyer's marbled floor. A second later, Riley appeared in the living room arch, still dressed in his tuxedo.

"They located the car," he told Delaney. "It's parked in Little Nell's lot. Unfortunately"—he paused and made a faint grimace—"they don't think they have sufficient probable cause to go any further. So—she still has it."

"She still has what?" Arthur jumped on that. "What's he talking about? Rina?"

"Yes." Delaney would have preferred not to tell them about this latest development. "We have reason to suspect she might have had a gun in her purse tonight."

"My God." Lucas lifted his head to stare at the ceiling. "This isn't going to go away, is it? She isn't going to let it. She's going to keep coming after me—"

"It *will* end, Lucas," she insisted against the hopelessness in his voice.

He looked at her with dark and haunted eyes. "One way or the other, I guess it will."

Something in his words raised a chill.

NINETEEN

SCUDDING CLOUDS RACED ACROSS the face of the late-afternoon sun, blocking its light, but Delaney didn't notice as she glanced at the card Riley had discarded, then picked up one from the deck. She added the ace of spades to the other cards in her hand. She tried to weigh the options it gave her, but she couldn't concentrate. Which was why she already owed Riley one dollar and twenty-seven cents.

There was too much tension charging the air, giving a sharp edge to the smallest sound, from the slip-slip of playing cards sliding together to the tap of Riley's cigarette in the ashtray, the crackle of Lucas turning a script page, and the scratching of Arthur's pen in the margins of some weighty movie contract.

"It's your play," Riley prodded.

"Right." She tossed the ace in the discard pile.

He promptly picked it up. "Do you get the feeling this is the quiet before the storm?"

"I almost wish it would erupt. Maybe then I wouldn't feel like I'm holding my breath—and maybe I wouldn't want one of your cigarettes so much." She tried to ignore the one currently balanced in the ashtray's slot, smoldering so tantalizingly near her reach.

"Nerves shot?" His smile made light of the question, but his eyes were serious in their inspection.

"No." She shook her head. Like him, she kept her voice pitched at a subdued level. "I just feel like I've been strung for two-twenty wiring all day."

"Haven't we all?"

She saw his glance slide to Lucas, sprawled on one of the room's white chairs, glowering at the script in his hand. The long sleeves of his blue knit shirt were pushed up to his elbows, his dark hair rumpled by the constant rake of his fingers. Delaney guessed Riley was remembering the way Lucas had snapped at Toby earlier in the day. The usually limitless supply of patience he had for his brother had been nowhere in evidence.

"At least Arthur has kept his mouth shut." In her opinion, Arthur Golden had contributed equally as much as Rina Cole to making her client so jumpy and uptight. She reached for the draw pile, then winced at the sudden blast of static coming from her earpiece and hurriedly reached to turn down the volume on her two-way radio receiver.

"Roger, Three. I copy that," Riley said into his, then slipped it back into the leather case at his waist. "Your radio still not working?"

"No." She rubbed near her lobe to stop the faint buzzing.

"We put new batteries in it. There must be a short somewhere. I'll take it apart when I get back, and see if I can't fix it," he said, then smiled and wagged his eyebrows. "The caterer is here with our evening repast." He got up from his chair, then leaned across the narrow game table to whisper to Delaney, "Or as the common man would say—Food!"

"You're hopeless." She smiled and shook her head, privately relieved that they were back on their old footing.

"No. My stomach is—hopelessly empty." He winked and moved away from the table.

But she had caught the flicker of concern in his eyes when they searched her face, and she knew Riley had joked about the food to try to get her to lighten up and relax. She wished she could relax and ignore the charged undercurrents that sizzled around her, wearing her own nerves thin.

Riley was halfway across the room when the phone rang. "I'll get it," he said to no one in particular.

As he picked it up, Delaney laid her cards facedown on the game table's ostrichskin top. She removed the earpiece and set it, along with her radio, on the table for Riley to repair later. That left only the familiar weight of the gun she wore clipped to the belt at her waist, making her feel strangely light.

"It's for you, Lucas." Riley held out the phone to him. "Your secretary Liz in L.A."

"Liz?" His harsh frown deepened, the impression strong that his quick temper was already on a hair trigger. "Why the hell is she calling me on a Saturday?"

"You want me to ask?"

"No, I'll talk to her." Lucas threw the script onto the

white ottoman and rolled to his feet. Delaney watched him, seeing the caged energy that colored his every movement with impatience and sharpness. He took the phone from Riley and snapped into it, "Yes, what is it, Liz?" A second later he froze in shock, the color draining from his face. "You're crazy." His voice sounded strangled, hoarse.

Delaney came out of her chair. "Who is it?"

He didn't hear her. His whole attention was focused on the voice coming over the line. "Leave me alone!" he exploded, his voice shaking with the force of it. "Dammit, I've told you before—we're through!" He stiffened at the reply, then slammed the phone down, holding the receiver on the cradle with both hands.

"It was Rina, wasn't it?" Arthur guessed, his tan fingers curling into the contract he held.

Lucas nodded, then said through tightly gritted teeth, "She said she'd never be through with me. She means it."

Arthur swore and turned away, hurling the contract onto the chair he had just vacated.

Riley cast a troubled look Delaney's way. "Sorry. I knew his secretary was named Liz. When she said that's who she was, I accepted it. My fault."

But Delaney shook off any thought that someone was to blame. Instead she concentrated on Lucas. "What else did she say? Anything?"

He made a visible attempt to collect himself, releasing his grip on the phone and straightening to take a deep, long breath, his features set in rigid lines of control. "She said she'd be seeing me"—he paused, his mouth twisting in bitterness—"soon."

"And when she sees you, she'll have that goddamned gun," Arthur declared and turned on Delaney. "Why the hell didn't you take it away from her last night? Why did you let her keep it? Don't you know she wants to kill Luke?"

She saw the apprehension that leaped into Lucas's face. Arthur's alarm was contagious. She had to stop it. "She may try, Arthur, but she won't succeed. We'll be here to stop her. Remember?" She let a smile of quiet confidence curve her mouth.

"I remember."

"In that case, why don't you fix yourself a drink and calm down? Lucas could probably use one, too." When she turned to Riley, he smiled in silent approval at the way she'd handled the situation. "I think you said the caterer was here."

"Right." He moved off again.

No further mention was made about the phone call from Rina, but the memory of it hung in the air, heightening all the previous tension. Even Delaney found herself picking at her food when they sat down to eat in the dining room. Riley was the only one who seemed to be enjoying the catered meal of black pepper-roasted duck garnished with Georgia peaches and accompanied by steamed vegetables. His plate was definitely the only one slicked clean when Delaney carried the dishes into the kitchen.

She came back with the coffee pot. "There's some double chocolate cake for dessert if anyone wants it."

"Not me." Arthur pushed his chair back from the dining table. "And no coffee, either. My nerves are jittery enough. I'll have myself a brandy in the living room instead."

"I'll pass on the coffee, too, and have a brandy with

Arthur." Lucas laid his folded napkin on the table and rose from his chair.

"You can fill my cup and I'll take it with me." Riley rose to follow Lucas into the living room.

Delaney filled his cup, then her own, and trailed after the three of them, bringing the insulated pot with her, nagged by the feeling that this was going to be a long night. Arthur headed straight for the brandy decanter atop the bar.

"For God's sake, can't somebody turn on the lights?" Lucas flipped on a lamp switch. "This place is dark as a—" He cut off the rest of the phrase, leaving the word *tomb* to dangle unspoken.

Riley immediately went over to the bank of wall switches and turned the recessed ceiling lights up to full bright, then casually announced, "I think I'll take your radio apart, Delaney. Maybe I can figure out what's wrong with it."

For a change, Arthur made an equal attempt to defuse the moment. "Here's your brandy, Luke." He handed him a snifter glass.

Lucas took it and walked stiffly away. Delaney watched him a moment, then wandered over to the game table, giving Lucas the time and the space to compose himself again. She set the coffee pot next to a stack of playing cards, well clear of the area Riley was using to take apart her radio.

"Do you know what you're doing?" she asked curiously before taking a sip of her coffee.

"I'm a wizard with electronics. Didn't you know that?"

"I think you've kept that talent hidden."

"Could be."

The telephone rang. The brandy glass in Lucas's hand crashed to the floor when he whirled to face it.

"I'll answer it." Delaney shoved her cup onto the table and went to the phone. She picked up the receiver as the phone began its second ring. "Hello."

She tensed at the initial beat of silence, then a woman's voice said questioningly, "Delaney?"

"Yes." She waited, listening closely.

There was a throaty laugh, the sound too familiar for Delaney to fail to recognize. "It's Susan St. Jacque. I'm so used to Riley answering the phone I thought I had dialed the wrong number," she declared. "Since you're there, I assume Luke is, too. Put him on the phone for me, will you?"

"Just a minute." Delaney covered the mouthpiece with her hand and lowered the receiver. "It's Susan St. Jacque." She saw his hesitation and guessed at its cause. "I recognize her voice. Do you want to talk to her or—"

"I'll talk to her." When he took a step toward Delaney, broken glass crunched under his foot. He swore softly, savagely, then sidestepped the rest of the shards to take the receiver. "Hello, Susan." He tried and failed to keep the clipped, hard edge out of his voice. Delaney walked over to help Arthur pick up the pieces of broken glass. "Yes . . . well . . . it couldn't be helped. I had to leave." Susan obviously said something and Lucas responded with a tersely impatient, "Of course I have." That was followed shortly by, "Yes, I would." Then, "All right, fine. Do that."

As Delaney dropped the last chip of glass into the ashtray, Lucas hung up the phone. She got to her feet and absently brushed at the knees of her navy slacks.

"That *was* Susan," he confirmed, then closed his

eyes tightly and released a heavy sigh. "When the phone rang, I was sure it was Rina calling back." He held out his hands and stared at the way they vibrated. "Dear God, look at me. I'm shaking. Why am I letting Rina scare me like this?" His voice began to vibrate, too, but with anger. "Why am I letting her do this to me?"

"You've been under a lot of pressure these last few days." And Delaney knew it hadn't come only from Rina; Susan had added some of her own, too. "It's natural that the strain would begin to show."

"Natural?!" Lucas shouted, his temper erupting. "Is that what you call this? Natural?! If this is natural, then tell me when the hell it's going to end!"

"I don't know," she answered quietly.

"You don't know!" He laughed harshly and swung away, running a hand through his hair, plowing dark furrows in its thickness. "And I don't know how much more of this I can take."

Aware that there was absolutely nothing she could say that would make it easier, Delaney walked back to the game table to retrieve her cup. But the coffee was cold and she set it back down. Riley gave her a lopsided smile, then glanced at Lucas and shook his head as if to say, "Poor guy."

"Any luck with the radio?" she asked.

He had it apart, the pieces arranged in an orderly semicircle. "If there's a break in the circuitry, I don't see it."

"Wyatt must be starved. I'll go relieve him."

"I'll go. You stay," Riley insisted.

"Go where?" Arthur spoke up.

"To relieve Wyatt so he can eat."

"I'll tag along with you. I've been cooped up in this house all day. I need a walk."

The two of them trooped out of the room, leaving a brittle silence behind.

Lucas broke it. "I'm sorry, Delaney. I don't know why I yelled at you a minute ago."

"Probably because I was the closest one."

"Probably." But he didn't smile when he said it. "Arthur is right. We have been cooped up in this place all day. It's starting to feel like a prison. I need some fresh air."

"Sounds good."

His mouth quirked in a stiff attempt at a smile, but all the raw tension was just below the surface, contained, controlled—for now. "Do you know I half-expected you to tell me it wouldn't be safe to go out on the deck? That's what Rina has done to me. She's made me afraid to go outside. God, I hate that woman."

"I know." Delaney sensed his need to verbalize the turmoil within, to talk it out. He wasn't seeking answers as much as he was a willing ear.

His glance moved to the gun at her waist, the butt of it visible where the front of her unstructured jacket hung apart. "It's funny, but it used to bother me to see you with that gun. I don't think I wanted to admit there was a reason for you to have it. I guess it made it easier to pretend nothing was going to happen—that this would all go away like some bad dream. But it hit me last night, when Riley whisked me out the back door of that party, that this wasn't going to go away. This was real life and no director was going to yell, 'Cut!' Now when I see you with that gun, I feel reassured." He lifted his glance, meeting her eyes. "And that's scary as hell, Delaney."

The corners of her mouth deepened in silent understanding, but she didn't bother to comment, suggesting instead, "Let's go outside." She led the way to the glass door that opened onto the deck.

A thick layer of clouds cloaked the night sky, hiding the stars and obscuring the ragged outline of the mountain peaks on the other side of the narrow valley. The town lights blazed alone against the darkness. The air was cool and still, with not a breath of a breeze to relieve it.

Delaney stood at the rail and scanned the grounds beyond the deck out of habit. Here and there, the softly diffused landscape lighting cast a pale glow on the bricked path that wound through the flowering shrubs and bushes, but it was the deep shadows beyond the soft pools of light that Delaney automatically examined.

She waited, but the curling tension didn't go away. There was nothing soothing about the cool of the night air on her face. Too much heavy stillness accompanied it. Beside her, Lucas sighed, a tense sound that echoed everything she was feeling.

"At times like this, I envy smokers," he said in a near mutter.

"True." She tried not to think about how good a cigarette would taste right now, the satisfying bite of tobacco smoke on her tongue, her lungs filling with it, the calming exhalation of it. She looked in the direction of the drive, hidden from view by a screen of shrubs. Riley was somewhere over there—with a pack of cigarettes in his pocket. She turned her back to the drive and faced Lucas. The bright lights from the living room shone onto the deck and illuminated the strong lines of his profile, revealing the compressed tightness of his lips.

His side glance ricocheted off her into the night. "I hate being scared, Delaney. I hate this feeling that I'm coming apart at the seams." It was a self-conscious admission, one he tried to joke his way out of. "Thank God you're here to hold me together, right?"

"Right." She smiled, knowing it was the response he wanted.

He turned to her, his eyes moving over her face, a trace of longing in them, a touch of wistfulness in the slant of his mouth. "A part of me wants to tell you how beautiful you are, how your hair shines, how serene and intelligent your eyes seem, how soft yet strong your lips look . . . how much I've come to rely on you." He took her hands and held them lightly between his. "I want to tease you about mixing business with pleasure, and I want to hold you close. Yet . . . it doesn't feel like the right place . . . the right time." He paused and grinned crookedly, something boyish and appealing in it. "I never thought I'd hear myself say something like that."

"Neither did I," she admitted with a twinkle in her eye.

He grew serious. "It's different with you, Delaney. I think it's always been different. I find myself turning to you. When you're not there, I feel lost . . . alone. How can I explain it?" He looked away, as if searching the darkness beyond her shoulder for the words. "I—" Alarm leaped into his expression, opening his eyes wide. "Rina," he gasped. "She has a gun."

In that blur of time when fractions of seconds expand to excruciating length, reflex took over. Even as Delaney turned to locate the attacker, her left arm was shoving Lucas down and away from the rail and her right hand was drawing her weapon. She shouted to him to get inside while she spun to plant herself in the middle.

A hoarse voice cried out: "Bastard!"

A gun flashed fire in her side vision and she heard the

sharp clap of a gunshot. A dark figure was on the path. She caught the sheen of black leather pants, the paleness of blonde hair, the gleam of something in the woman's hand as a second shot rang out. A muzzle flashed inches from the dark figure. Delaney braced her outstretched right hand with her left, took aim, and squeezed the trigger, corrected for the recoil and squeezed again, corrected and squeezed, corrected and squeezed. Adrenaline pumped through her system. The attacker jerked, jerked, jerked, and finally crumpled. Through it all, the same two questions tumbled crazily over and over through her mind: How had Rina gotten in? Where had she failed?

Even after the echo of the last shot had faded, the instinct born out of long hours of training kept her frozen in the shooting stance, her legs braced apart, her weapon trained on the prone figure, her eyes alert for any movement. Slowly she became aware of shouts, the sound of running feet, the acrid smell of powder smoke tainting the air, the faint buzzing in her ears. How much time had passed? Five seconds? Ten?

"Over here!" she yelled, not taking her eyes off the motionless figure in the shadows along the path.

The clatter of feet centered on the brick walk. A second later, Riley ran into view, his gun drawn. Wyatt was on his heels. Delaney saw Riley's stride falter when he spotted Rina.

She shouted to Wyatt, "Call the police and an ambulance, then bring the emergency kit."

He hesitated a split second, then broke from Riley and headed for the house and a telephone. Arthur came to a stop behind Riley as he halted next to the body, holstered his weapon, and knelt down. Seeing that, Delaney realized it was safe to lower her own gun. She dropped her arms to her side, stunned to discover how limp they suddenly felt—how weak her knees were. Reaction was setting in. She couldn't let it claim her . . . not yet. She returned the gun to her holster and forced her shaky legs to carry her to a break in the deck railing, then onto a side trail that connected to the main path at a point near the spot where Rina had fallen.

She halted at the juncture. Arthur's trim shape was crouched beside Riley. By his actions, she could tell Riley was checking for a pulse.

"Is she—" Her throat went shut. She couldn't say the word. She couldn't think it.

Riley came slowly to his feet and turned to look at her. Regret, sadness, and pain all chased through his gentle face. "I can't find a pulse," he said. "She's dead, 'Laney."

"No." It was a small sound.

She backed up a step and broke out into a cold sweat, nausea churning through her. She wheeled from the sight of those tiny feet and shapely leather-covered legs. As she bent over double, her stomach heaved its contents, the convulsions not stopping until there was no more.

When it was over, Riley was there, silently offering her a handkerchief. She took it from him and wiped her mouth, her hand trembling.

"I'm sorry," she murmured self-consciously.

"There's no need to apologize."

Sirens wailed in the background, racing closer. Almost reluctantly she looked behind him at the body. Suddenly she felt strangely angry—angry that it had happened, that she'd been forced to take a life.

"How, Riley? How did Rina get in here?"

"'Laney," he began, a pained look in his eyes. "That isn't Rina."

She frowned. "What are you talking about? If that's supposed to be some kind of a joke—"

"It isn't something I'd joke about," he replied in a voice too serious to doubt. "It isn't Rina. It's Susan St. Jacque."

"Susan." Delaney drew back in disbelief. "You're wrong. It can't be. I couldn't make a mistake like that." She tried to get by him and see for herself.

"Don't." Riley made a brief attempt to stop her, then let her go.

When Delaney approached the body, Arthur stepped back from it, his face a sickly white beneath his tan, his hand unsteady as he blotted the perspiration from his upper lip with a monogrammed handkerchief. Her glance skipped from him to the body lying on the side of the path.

The impulse was strong to turn away, not to look at death's face, but she had to. She forced her gaze to travel past the soft gleam of leather slacks and let it linger on the almost imperceptible wet stain that spread over the front of a charcoal-and-black-patterned sweater. Finally she focused on the blonde hair—a shade of champagne—that framed the face.

Dear God, it was Susan. Her face was frozen in a look of horror and surprise, her almond-brown eyes glossy and staring—but nobody was staring out of them. Susan St. Jacque was dead.

Nausea welled in her throat again. This time she fought it off. She felt the comforting pressure of Riley's hand on her shoulder, the steadying warmth of it. "I don't understand, Riley." Numbly, Delaney shook her head. "Why did she shoot at Lucas?"

"What?" He went still.

Puzzled by his reaction, Delaney frowned. "She had a gun, Riley. She shot at Lucas. That's when I opened fire."

"Are you sure?" He frowned back. "I didn't see a weapon when I found her and I was the first one here."

"Of course she had a gun," she protested, angry that he would doubt her.

He flicked his flashlight on and swept its bright beam over the body and the ground directly around it, then widened the search another three feet. There was no sign of a weapon.

"She had one," Delaney insisted. "She had it in her hand. I saw it. I saw the muzzle flash. I heard the shots. She fired twice. I didn't imagine it, Riley."

"'Laney."

Like him, she had caught the faint note of panic in her voice. She knew as well as Riley that this was no time to lose control. "It's okay. I'm all right." With a quick, determined toss of her head, she faced him and fought to show him the necessary calm. His eyes were warm with approval, but concern lurked at the edges.

"The police will have a lot of questions for you," he warned. "If you have any doubts about your ability to handle them, you'd better have a lawyer with you."

"I am a lawyer," she reminded him. "I know my rights and the procedure."

She also knew she didn't dare let herself become rattled by their questions. She couldn't let her own questions surface in her answers. She had to stick to the bare facts and not indulge in conjecture.

"You will need a lawyer just the same," Riley said quietly, watching her closely.

"I know." She was fully aware that there would be an investigation into the shooting, a hearing, a ruling by the judge.

Arthur spoke up. "Don't you think we should cover her—or something?"

Riley examined her expression one last time, then turned and stripped off his jacket. He covered the top half of Susan's body with it, drawing it over her face. The action lent an unnerving air of finality to the scene.

Delaney stared at the jacket-draped form, part of her mind trying to reject the sight. Then she became conscious of eyes staring at her and glanced up to see Arthur looking at her strangely, as if he'd never seen her before.

Running footsteps signaled Wyatt's return with the emergency medical kit. He stopped short at the sight of the tan fabric and swung his lanky frame toward Delaney. His eyes had that same strange look in them as Arthur's.

Riley stepped between them, quietly taking charge. "We won't need that." The sirens ceased their screaming in the background. Lights flashed nearby. Car doors slammed. "That's the police," he told Wyatt. "Go meet them and bring them here."

"Right." He pulled his gaze away from her, his forehead creasing in a worried frown as he headed for the driveway, breaking into a trot.

"What happened?" Lucas was at the deck's railing—at almost the exact same place where he'd been standing before. "Is she . . ."

Arthur provided the answer, "It's Susan—Susan St. Jacque. She's dead."

"No." The shocked denial from him sounded like an echo of the one she had made. "That's impossible! It was

Rina. I saw—my God," he whispered and leaned both hands on the rail, bowing his head. "Susan told me she was coming by when she called. I forgot. She looked like . . . I thought she was . . ."

Riley swore bitterly under his breath, then snapped at Arthur, "Get him in the house."

A flashlight threw its beam on her face. Half-blinded by the sudden glare, Delaney turned from it, holding up a hand to shield her eyes. "We thought we heard shots." The gruff voice belonged to the caretaker, Harold Walker. Delaney recognized it as he swung the light from her. It fell on Susan's body. "Sweet Jesus," he whispered.

"Is she dead?" Toby hovered behind him, the child-like inflection of his voice fearful and uncertain.

"Toby, what are you doing here?" Lucas moaned.

"Do I have to touch her, Luke?" Toby's voice turned cranky with worry. "I don't want to. I don't like to touch dead things."

"Of course you don't have to, Toby," Lucas soothed, then ordered impatiently, "Take him back to the cottage, Walker. He shouldn't be seeing this."

"Yeah, I wanna go, Mr. Walker." Toby tugged at the old man's arm. "I don't like it here."

In the next moment, the police and paramedics converged on the scene, flashlights shining, staccato voices clipping out orders, a swirl of motion and gleaming badges. An officer took Riley off to one side and Delaney found herself alone with another. When he asked for her weapon, she calmly surrendered it to him.

Yet it was all a haze, his questions, her responses, the flashbulbs going off, the body bag going on, the squawk of a police radio, the rumble of a gurney. She felt numb, detached. She welcomed the absence of emotion. For now, it was better not to feel, to keep that part of her conscious mind turned off.

"I'm going to have to ask you to come to the station with me, Ms. Wescott," the policeman said.

"Of course." She noticed the faint smile of apology he offered, but his blue eyes remained cool with professional suspicion.

As he escorted her to one of the police cars with the flashing lights, she tried to remember his name. He'd told her, but she had blocked it out, the same way she had blocked out so many other things—like the glassy stare of Susan's eyes.

TWENTY

$\mathcal{A}$LONE IN THE POLICE INTERROGATION room, Delaney pushed her empty Styrofoam plastic cup around on the heavy vinyl-topped table, absently keeping it within the perimeter of an old coffee ring. A metal ashtray sat nearby, a half-dozen stale butts in its blackened bottom.

Down some corridor, a steel door clanged shut. She tensed at the sound, then took a deep breath, catching a faint animal smell—an odor common to all jails.

She let go of the cup and flattened her hands on the table. The vinyl felt cool beneath them. Too cool. Pulling them back, she rose from the plain wooden chair and turned to scan the room and the barred window on the back wall.

There was something depressingly the same about police station interrogation rooms, no matter the size, the color of the walls, or the kind of furnishings. They all managed to be starkly impersonal and totally devoid of comfort.

Briefly she wondered if this was the room where serial killer Theodore Bundy had been questioned. But she couldn't sustain a curiosity.

How long since the sergeant had left? Five minutes? Ten? Or had it been only two? She didn't want this time alone, this privacy to think, to remember, to wonder. The protective shell of numbness was splintering. She wished Riley was with her. She longed for the steadying influence of his presence, the easy confidence and reassurance he could convey with a mere look.

She heard the rattle of the doorknob, the click of the latch releasing, and made herself turn to face it, slipping her hands into the pockets of her loose jacket, concealing the tight, tense curl of her fingers. The curly-haired sergeant gave the door a push, then stepped inside, saying to someone out of view, "She's in here."

When Riley walked in, relief soared through her—relief mixed with a kind of intense pleasure she couldn't name. Her gaze locked with his, a lump rising in her throat. Three steps—that was all she had to take to have the comfort of his strong arms around her, but she didn't take them. She felt brittle, so brittle that she might break at the slightest touch.

"You're supposed to be with Lucas, you know," she murmured, barely noticing the man with Riley. "Not here."

His mouth quirked in a smile. "There are enough police cars and uniforms at the house to protect the Pope."

"I hadn't thought of that," she admitted as a different kind of tension laced through her nerves now that Riley was here.

With a half-turn, Riley included the man accompanying him. "'Laney, I want you to meet Tom Bannon. He's a lawyer here in Pitkin County. He has agreed to act as legal counsel for you."

"With your consent, of course," Tom Bannon added in quick qualification.

At first glance, Tom Bannon reminded Delaney of a cowboy fresh off the mountain ranges. A black Stetson sat squarely on his head, a bit dusty and worn with use. Somewhere in his forties, he had the first wisps of gray showing in brown hair that was a bit on the shaggy side. His hands were buried in the pockets of his sheepskin-lined denim jacket, and the boots below his faded jeans were scarred and run-down at the heels.

"You'll have to excuse my appearance, Ms. Wescott," he said. "I have a ranch outside of town. I'd just finished up the evening chores when I got the call about you."

"You're a rancher."

"A rancher, and a damned good lawyer."

She smiled at his quiet statement of fact that held no hint of arrogance. "I believe that, Mr. Bannon."

"My friends—and my clients—call me Bannon." He paused, then extended his right hand. "Shall we make it official?"

"Yes." She shook hands with her new lawyer.

"Your associate, Mr. Owens, tells me that you are a fellow member of the bar."

"Not a practicing one, though," she replied as Riley fished a cigarette out of his pack and snapped his lighter to it. He offered the cigarette to her, filter end first. She sent him a grateful look, murmuring, "I've been needing one."

"I had a chance to talk with the boys outside," Bannon said. "You'll be glad to know they'll be releasing you shortly. Naturally, the investigation will continue."

"I expected that." She took a quick puff of the cigarette, then blew out the smoke. But the new calm she felt came from Riley's presence, not the cigarette. She drew strength from him. It had always been that way. "Do you know whether they found Susan's gun yet?"

Riley answered, "As of thirty minutes ago, they hadn't."

Delaney made no comment, aware how very crucial it was that a weapon be found. She pulled another drag of smoke into her mouth and this time made herself savor the taste of the tobacco, seeking to distract herself.

As she turned to flick the build-up of ash from its tip, Riley said, "By the way, Jared is outside. He'll be in—"

"Jared." She swung around in surprise. "How—"

"I heard what happened." Jared stood in the open doorway, his eyes shadowed by an aching gentleness.

What happened—for an instant Delaney was struck by the phrase. She knew *what* had happened; she just couldn't understand *why* it had happened.

"It wasn't necessary for you to come, Jared," she heard herself say.

"Yes, it was," he replied, then shifted his attention to the lawyer Tom Bannon. "If you want to talk privately with Delaney—"

"We've done our talking for tonight," he said. "The rest can wait until tomorrow. We should have a clearer picture of the situation by then."

The sergeant paused in the doorway. His glance

made a casual sweep of the three men before coming to light on Delaney. "You're free to leave, Ms. Wescott. But we may have some more questions for you later."

"Anytime you want to talk to my client, just contact me, Mike," Bannon said in a smooth show of cooperation.

"Right." He hesitated, then glanced at Delaney. "Please don't leave town without informing us of your intentions first."

"I won't."

The officer nodded and left without another word. Delaney turned and stabbed the cigarette out in the ashtray's blackened bottom.

"You'll need a place to stay—" Riley began.

Jared broke in, "She can stay with me."

Bannon shook his head. "That's not a good idea, Jared," he advised. "It would be better if she came out to my ranch for a few days."

"Thanks for the offer, Bannon, but—"

Riley interrupted her, "The press is swarming all over this story, Delaney. Two television crews have coptered in from Denver already. By tomorrow, they will have the condo snooped out. Your best hope is Bannon's ranch."

"Maybe you're right." She offered a wan smile of apology. "I guess I wasn't thinking."

"You've had a few other things on your mind, I believe," Riley offered.

"Are the reporters outside now?" She had run their gauntlet countless times in the past, but always as a shield for someone else, never as the target.

"Two or three." A smile ghosted across Riley's mouth. "But I wouldn't worry about them. They heard a

Delaney Wescott was brought in for questioning.
They're hanging around hoping for a glimpse of *him*.
We should be able to walk out the front door without
anyone giving you a second look."

"It might help if you created a minor diversion,
Jared," Bannon suggested, then indicated the door with
a lift of his hand. "Do you want to go first?"

Hesitating, Jared sent a quick glance at Delaney,
then headed out the door. Bannon waited until he was
down the hall, then signaled to Delaney. She needed no
second urging to leave. She walked out of the room with
both Riley and Bannon at her side.

As they approached the front entrance, she spotted
Jared surrounded by a half-dozen reporters and photographers. She caught snatches of the questions thrown at him.

"Jared, is it true they called you in—"

"When did you find out—"

"Have the police told you—"

Then she was outside in the sharpness of the mountain night, the door closing on the rush of voices from
inside. Bannon's black pickup was parked around the
corner from the police station, not far from Riley's car.
Riley walked her to the sedan. Delaney climbed into the
passenger side. When Riley slid behind the wheel, she
felt his gaze rest briefly on her, but he didn't say anything—and she didn't volunteer anything.

Within minutes they were on the highway out of
town, following the taillights of Bannon's truck. The
clock on the dash indicated it was almost one in the
morning—over four hours since the shooting. It seemed
an eternity ago—it seemed a minute ago. She rested her
head against the seat back and turned her face to the
window, staring into the encapsulating darkness.

Sounds became magnified by the stillness—the sibilant rush of the wind, the low whine of the tire on the pavement, the steady drone of the engine, the dull thudding of her heart, and the silent cry of *why* in her head.

How long or how far they drove before they turned off the highway onto a narrow dirt road, Delaney didn't notice. She merely observed the change—the slowing of speed and the roughening of the ride.

"I think we're almost there," Riley told her.

She nodded, watching the headlight beams of the vehicle in front of them as they dug a tunnel into the night, revealing the march of fenceposts on either side of the road. Soon their lights swept across a tidy collection of outbuildings, then centered on a large, sprawling house built of hand-hewn logs. Idly Delaney noted the sharp pitch of its roofline, the wraparound porch, and the light that shone above the front door.

Riley opened her door, his hand raised in a silent offer of assistance. She avoided both it and his searching gaze as she stepped out. A horse nickered and the light breeze carried the bitter, strong odors of earth and animal to her.

Bannon waited by the steps to the porch. When they joined him, he turned without a word and led the way to the door. It opened before they reached it. A woman in a blue summer robe stepped out to welcome them, a baby cradled deftly in the crook of one arm and honey-blonde hair tumbling loose about her shoulders.

"You aren't as late as I thought you might be." Her smile, like her voice, was warm as she lifted her head expectantly. Bannon dropped a kiss on her cheek and murmured something to her. To which, she replied, "Little Clint decided that he needed changing." Then to Delaney and Riley she said, "Come in."

When Delaney hesitated, Riley took her arm and guided her into the house and its brightly lit living room. Like the house itself, the room was rustic and solid, lodgelike in its vastness.

"This is my wife, Kit, and the baby in her arms is our son, Clint." Bannon completed the introductions as he shrugged out of his denim jacket and hooked it on a wall peg by the door.

"I'm sorry to be intruding on your privacy this way, Mrs. Bannon," Delaney managed to say, stiffly composed. Too stiffly.

"Call me Kit," she insisted with an engaging smile. "And the ranch is the best place for you right now. Believe me, I know how the press can be when they smell a story that smacks of the sensational. Sometimes they are worse than a flock of vultures, swooping down and picking things apart."

"They were circling when we left town," Riley said when Delaney offered no comment.

"That's what Bannon said when he called." The baby fussed sleepily in her arms. Smiling down, Kit Bannon smoothed the mass of black hair on the baby's head. "I think this little guy is ready to stretch out in his crib again. Have a seat while I put him to bed." As she moved away, she added over her shoulder, "There's fresh coffee in the kitchen if you want some."

Bannon turned a questioning glance on them. "Would you like a cup?"

"Sounds good to me," Riley answered. Delaney simply nodded.

"I'll be right back." Bannon moved off.

Riley hesitated, his glance lingering on her. "I think I'll give him a hand. Will you be okay?"

She nodded again and crossed the hard pine floor to the woven rug in front of an old fireplace of river stone. Inside, blackened andirons held a stack of split wood and kindling, ready to blaze into flame at the first touch of a match. She caught herself wishing for the cheery warmth of a fire and turned back to the room, seeking the distraction it could give. But she was more conscious of the screaming of her nerves than of the old brick-red armchair by the hearth.

She drifted over to the sofa and absently trailed a hand over the homemade afghan draped over the back of it. She fingered the thickness of its entwined brown, rust, and ochre yarns, unable to wonder who had crocheted it as she caught the sound of footsteps approaching the living room.

Riley appeared, carrying two mugs of steaming coffee. He gave one of them to her. "Bannon's on the phone. He'll be here shortly."

"Sure." She smelled the whiskey in the coffee before she took the first cautious sip. She felt the thawing burn of it all the way down, leaving not a fragment of numbness to protect her.

Suddenly she needed to sit down. The sofa was the closest. Delaney sat on the edge of it, her knees pressed tightly together, both hands wrapped around the mug.

"Do you feel like talking?" Riley asked. "I'm a good listener."

She shook her head, then pushed the hair away from her face with a rake of her fingers, simultaneously recognizing the agitation revealed by the gesture but unable to check it.

"Are you okay?" he asked quietly.

She tilted her head a little higher than necessary, pride insisting that she declare she was fine. But the lie wouldn't come, so Delaney admitted instead, "I'm . . . tired, I guess."

The shooting and the long ordeal at the police station had screwed her nerves up tight. Now, the stillness and the whiskey were loosening them. Her composure was close to cracking, and she knew it.

"Maybe if you could find out what room they want me to have . . ." She let her voice trail off, the confusion, fear, and guilt suddenly hammering at her.

Riley's glance flicked over her in quick assessment. "I'll go ask." As he set his mug down, Kit Bannon appeared at the top of the timbered staircase leading to the second floor. "Delaney's ready to call it a night—"

"Of course," she broke in before he could finish. "I have a guest room all ready for her. It's right down the hall. If you'll just follow me."

The minute Delaney stood up, everything inside recoiled from the thought of being alone. She looked at Riley. Some of her panic must have shown in her expression. His mouth quirked in a near smile, his sharp eyes turning gentle.

"How about I come along and make sure you're settled in?"

"Thanks." A small tremor shook her voice. Together they climbed the stairs to the second floor and followed Kit Bannon down the hall. She opened a door on the right, reached inside, and flipped on a wall switch, turning on the lamp by the bed. Then she stepped back to let Delaney enter.

"The bathroom is through that far door on the left,"

Kit told her. "You'll find more clean towels and washcloths under the sink if you need them. I left a nightgown and a robe on the chair for you."

"Thanks." Delaney walked over to the bedroom window and opened it to let in the night breeze.

Unable to fight off the waves of weariness anymore, she closed her eyes. This was the moment she had been dreading—when her head would become crowded with the aftermath of dark thoughts and black speculations, when her mind would start feeding her flashes of the shooting, making her relive it again and again—the muzzle flash, the weight of the gun in her hand, the vague blonde-haired figure on the path, the kick of the gun when she fired it, the aching dryness of her mouth, that instinctive bracing for a bullet to slam into her, the grotesque jerking of the body, the pounding of blood in her ears, the acrid smell of powder smoke, the stillness— and the sightless, staring eyes.

Then came the doubts and the questions—Had she fired too quickly? If she had known it was Susan instead of Rina, would it have made a difference? How could it? Susan had shot first. But why? Why would Susan want Lucas dead? What had been her motive? Had Lucas threatened to expose her blackmail attempt? Which bullet had killed her? The first? Or the fourth?

Shuddering, Delaney hugged her arms around her middle and tried to work her way through the pain and the anger, the guilt and the remorse—and the sick feeling that came from having taken a life. They were normal reactions, all of them, Delaney knew that. In time they would fade, but they would never go away. It was something she would always have to live with.

"'Laney?" Riley's questioning voice intruded.

Belatedly she realized it wasn't the first time he had called her name. She pivoted from the window and discovered he was standing before her, his eyes narrowed and searching, his expression troubled.

"Sorry, I didn't hear you." She tasted the wetness of tears on her lips and realized she was crying. Before she could wipe them from her cheeks, his hand was there, cupping the side of her face, his thumb stroking away the damp trail. She stiffened at his touch, protesting thickly, "I'm all right. Really, I—"

He pressed a thumb against her lips, cutting off her words. "Crying isn't a sign of weakness, 'Laney."

"I know that." She looked up, suddenly sick and confused, needing answers. "What did I do wrong, Riley? How could this have happened? There were shots. I swear I only returned fire."

"I know." Without another word, he gathered her to him. She resisted his offer of comfort for only an instant, then rested her head against his shoulder and rubbed her cheek against it.

"I never thought anything like this could happen." She ached so; it was an ache that the stroke of his hand couldn't soothe away. "I always thought I was too careful, too cautious. And now—?"

"Sssh." His arms tightened around her, the point of his chin burying itself in her hair.

"Every time I think about it I get confused," she murmured, conscious of his breath against her hair and the binding strength of his arms. She pressed closer, needing the warmth that came from him. "Susan is dead and I killed her. I don't see where I had a choice, but— dear God, I feel so awful."

"'Laney, don't."

"I can't help it." The instant she closed her eyes, her mind flashed images of the shooting. "I can't stop thinking about it . . . remembering." She dug her fingers into his shirt. "How could it have happened? I don't understand."

"None of it makes sense, I agree. Maybe tomorrow there will be some answers." But it was tonight Delaney was trying to get through; Riley knew that. He struggled to find a way to help her, to absorb some of her ache and uncertainty, as he pressed a kiss against her hair.

"Tomorrow." She grabbed at the thought, lifting her head slightly, bringing his mouth in contact with the salty wetness of tears on her cheek. "It seems so far away right now."

A small sound of distress slipped from her lips. Riley moved to stop it, knowing better than she did how much she hated to lose control, to let her emotions rule. When his mouth brushed over hers, she turned into it, her lips soft, seeking.

The kiss had begun as merely an attempt to comfort and reassure on his part. Her response had been little more than an acceptance of it. But the contact had his muscles tightening, his senses tingling. He had waited years to hold her in his arms like this. It was an opportunity that Riley knew might never come again now that Jared had reentered her life.

Selfishly he took it, and kissed her again, gently, experimenting in texture and taste. He encountered no resistance; on the contrary, she instinctively returned the testing pressure. He tipped her head back just enough to let the kiss deepen naturally.

Hers was a mouth to savor, he discovered. Full and generous and yielding. He dipped into it as scents from outside drifted through the open window, fresh and earthy. Her fingers uncurled their grip on his shirt and slid up to his neck. A desperate, needy sound came from her throat as he felt her skin warm, her body strain closer. He wrapped her tighter to him, conscious of the roaring in his head and the pounding of his blood.

Kissing her was like an addictive drug that only made him want more and more of her. It wasn't until the greed began to build, roughening the kiss with its crafty violence, that Riley drew back. She made a protesting sound and came at him with wild insistence and demand. As much as he wanted to believe that she wanted him and the love he could give her, Riley knew better. He knew the kinds of needs and fears that were tangled inside, directing her actions.

Fighting for some control of his own, he dragged her hands from around his neck. "We're both alive, 'Laney," he insisted, his voice thickened by the desire churning through him. "We don't have to prove we are."

Death did that sometimes. Sometimes it evoked the need to verify the existence of life. There were few ways better than the physical act of creating life.

Delaney went motionless, his words finally registering. Heat flooded through her as she pulled her hands from his grasp and stepped back, self-conscious and shaken by the needs that had been aroused, needs that left her raw and trembling, filled with a different kind of ache.

"You're right, of course." Her voice had a breathy quality, but she managed to keep it from shaking. She looked briefly away, feeling foolish, then glanced back. Riley watched her, his expression closely guarded. "I don't know what got into me."

"The same thing that got into me, I suspect." He wanted to reach out and brush the tangled hair back from her face. He lit a cigarette to occupy his hands.

"Of course," she repeated, and immediately ran a hand through her hair, releasing a nervous laugh. "I'm sorry—"

"Don't apologize." His eyes changed, darkening with a hint of temper. "In case you haven't guessed, I happened to enjoy that."

"You're joking, of course." Delaney looked at him, certain of her accuracy and wishing she wasn't.

"What do you think?" A wry smile tugged at his mouth.

Disappointed by his answer, Delaney shrugged and turned away. "It doesn't matter."

"You'd better get some rest—or try to," he told her. "Tomorrow will probably be another long day."

She nodded. A second later, she felt the touch of his hand turning her. Then he hooked a finger under her chin, lifting it. Wary, she looked into his eyes, seeing the warm, twinkling light that gleamed from their depths an instant before he dropped a quick, firm kiss on her lips.

"I was afraid of that." He smiled and shook his head, keeping it light to cut the tension. "Kissing you could become a dangerous habit. But at least now you'll have something else to think about when you go to bed tonight."

It was a prediction that proved to be very accurate. When she closed her eyes that night, the memories of the shooting came flooding back, but Riley's image always flashed in her mind before she was overwhelmed by them.

TWENTY-ONE

Delaney wakened to the vague murmur of voices. She rolled over, her body weighted, a dull and logy feeling pressing down on her. Then she remembered the shooting and sat up, hugging her knees to her chest and resting her chin on them.

The aching regret and confusion were still there, just as intense as before, but she discovered she could think about the shooting with none of last night's dark depression. That was progress of sorts, she knew.

A bird trilled outside the opened window, where sunlight streamed in. Somewhere a metal pail clanged and a barn door banged shut. Delaney sighed and wondered what time it was, then swept back the top sheet and swung her legs out of bed.

Her clothes lay in a rumpled pile on the floor. She picked up her jacket and swatted haphazardly at a wrinkle, wishing she had asked Riley to bring her some clean clothes. Out of the corner of her eye, she spotted a chenille robe of royal blue draped over the foot of the bed. She scooped it up and slipped it over her head.

A muffled giggle came from somewhere in the house. The sound was quickly followed by the clatter of feet running down the stairs. Small feet. A child's feet, Delaney suspected.

When she ventured into the hall, she spied a four-year-old boy in jeans, cowboy boots, and a black cape, his arms outstretched as he swooped through the living room like a bird—or a bat, she concluded with a smile. Kit Bannon, the lawyer's wife, walked into view, a picture of elegance in a blouse of amethyst silk, chains of gold rope, and slacks of summer white—a far cry from the attractive but rumpled housewife who had greeted Delaney last night.

The woman cast an indulgent smile at the four-year-old. "Time to come in for a landing, Batboy."

The boy came to a stop, his hands perching on his hips in a pose of indignation. "I'm not a batboy. I'm Batman."

"You are!" Kit feigned surprise, clasping her hands in front of her. "Oh, mighty Caped Crusader, will you forgive this mother for making such a terrible mistake?"

The boy giggled. "Mom, you're silly."

"You're the silly one."

"Am not."

"Are too."

"Am not." He took off again, dipping and gliding through the room as Delaney made her way to the stairs.

The baby was on a blanket in the middle of the room, waving his fists and cooing in delight at his older brother's antics. Kit Bannon walked over and picked him up. "Come on, little guy. It's time to get you ready to go. On your next swoop through the room, Batman, will you bring me Clint's cap and sweater?"

The four-year-old changed course, making a steep bank to collect the billed cap and blue and white sweater lying on the oak table. He dropped them on the baby's head as he flew past. Then he saw Delaney near the bottom of the stairs and screeched to a halt, his eyes rounding.

"Are you Catwoman?"

Delaney touched the front of her robe. "Does this look like her costume?"

"No," he replied, none too certainly.

"Then I guess I'm not." Her cheeks dimpled with the effort to hold back a smile. She glanced past the boy to his mother. "Good morning."

"Good morning," Kit Bannon returned. "I'm glad you're up. I was afraid you might not be awake before we had to leave. I'm taking the kids to Sunday school." She fastened the last button on the sweater and slipped the cap on the baby's head, eluding his attempts to grab it from her. "Did you sleep well?"

"Better than I expected," Delaney admitted, studying the woman with a sudden curiosity. There was something about her that looked familiar.

"I'm glad." She tied the cap in place and tickled the baby under his chin, laughing when he did. The sound was sunny and honest. She stood, hooking the baby on her hip with a mother's ease. "I hope Tommy didn't wake you. It can be a madhouse around here, trying to get everybody ready at once."

"Batman didn't wake me," Delaney assured her.

"Good."

"Mommy, can I carry Clint to the car?"

"I have a better idea—why don't you see if your sister is ready yet? Tell her to be sure to bring the diaper bag."

"I will." He was off, flying past Delaney to clatter up the stairs.

"I don't mean to be rude, but—how many children do you have?" Delaney wondered. "The house seemed so quiet last night."

"Blissfully so," Kit said and laughed. "I have these two little guys, Thomas and baby Clint, and a thirteen-year-old stepdaughter who's more like a little sister." The baby grabbed the gold chains of her necklace and dragged them to his mouth before she could rescue them from his clutches. "I don't know why I bother to wear jewelry," she grumbled good-naturedly.

There was something in the tilt of her head, the classic lines of Kit Bannon's profile, that struck a familiar chord. Delaney frowned, puzzling over it.

The woman looked up, noticing her expression. "Is something wrong?"

Delaney shook her head. "You remind me of someone." The minute the words were out, Kit Bannon's expression changed. It was like a mask had been slipped on, one that was cool and aloof. Suddenly it all clicked into place. "You're Kit Masters, the actress that starred in that movie with John Travis. *White Lies*, it was called. You were nominated for an Oscar."

"True." She smiled, but it was a practiced one.

"I remember now," Delaney nodded as it all came back. "You made headlines in Hollywood when you announced you were giving up your acting career to marry some rancher in Colorado."

"A rancher *and* lawyer," Kit corrected. "And before you ask—no, I have absolutely no regrets. In fact, I have never been happier in my life."

"Sorry, I didn't mean to—"

"No, I'm the one who's sorry. I have been bombarded with that question so often in the past that it's become irritating. I guess it's hard for some people to believe that a woman can be happy today—more than happy, perfectly content—to be a wife and mother."

"Don't you miss acting?"

"Oh, I haven't quit acting," Kit informed her with a breezy smile. "I merely dropped out of the race for stardom, which was never my goal. Therefore, the local theater company provides the perfect outlet for my love of acting. Actually I haven't given up anything, even if other people think I have."

"I can see that." Delaney smiled. "You're a lucky woman."

"And I know it." Kit beamed.

"Mom, can I take my Batplane with me?" Tommy, alias Batman, yelled from the top of the stairs. "Laura says I have to leave it home. I don't, do I?"

A teenage girl appeared beside him, tall and slender, dressed in white jeans and a scarlet crop top, her black hair swept back in a ponytail. "That isn't what I said, Tom-Tom. I told you that you would leave it somewhere like you always do, and wind up losing it." She gave his Batcape a teasing tug as she passed him, a blue-checked diaper bag in her hand, stuffed full.

"Can I take it, Mom?" Tommy tore after his sister as she ran skipping down the stairs. Halfway down, the girl noticed Delaney and slowed to a more adult pace.

"It would be safer if you left it home, Tommy," Kit Bannon replied. "It would be awful if Batman didn't have his Batplane. But it's your plane and your decision." Wisely, she didn't press for an answer, turning her attention instead to her stepdaughter. "Laura, I don't believe you've met our guest, Delaney Wescott. She'll be staying with us for a day or two. Delaney, this is our daughter, Laura."

"How do you do, Ms. Wescott." The girl studied her with friendly, but curious eyes.

"It's a pleasure to meet you, Laura," Delaney replied, formally shaking hands with her.

The baby gurgled happily and waved a hand at his big sister, demanding attention. Laura obliged, catching at his hand with her finger and thumb. "What are you jabbering about, half-pint? Are you being ignored?" She turned and thrust the diaper bag at the caped-crusading four-year-old. "Here, Tom-Tom, take this out to the Batmobile," she told him, then said to Kit, "I'll take little Clint and get him strapped in the car seat."

"Thanks." Kit transferred the baby to Laura's arms. "I'll get my purse and be right there."

Tommy tried to pick up the diaper bag with one hand, then realized it was too heavy and set the Batplane on the oak table. Using both hands, he picked up the bag by its straps and set after his sister, half-carrying and half-dragging the diaper bag to the front door.

Laura stopped in the open doorway. "Someone's here, Kit."

She tensed and sent a warning look at Delaney. "Let's cross our fingers that none of the press figured out Bannon had stashed you here." She grabbed up her purse and walked swiftly to the door. After one quick glance, she smiled over her shoulder. "It's one of our neighbors." With a little push, she sent Laura and Tommy on their way to the car. "This is a surprise, Jared," she said while pulling the door closed behind her. "I'm afraid Bannon isn't here and we're just on our way into town ourselves."

Before the door clicked shut, Delaney heard Jared answer, "I came to see Delaney. Bannon said last night he was bringing her here."

There was a muffled exchange outside. Then the door opened and Kit stepped back in, her curious and questioning gaze running to Delaney. "Jared McCallister is here to see you."

"Hello, Jared." She nodded to him when he followed Kit inside.

"How are you, Delaney?" His gaze searched her face.

"Fine."

Kit looked from one to the other. "I didn't realize you two knew each other."

"We met the first time I went to L.A. after my sister disappeared. Delaney helped me look for her."

"I see." Kit's expression suggested that she thought there was more to it than that. "You know where the kitchen is, Jared. There's fresh coffee—and a pan of homemade cinnamon rolls on the counter. If you're hungry for something more, you'll find eggs and bacon in the refrigerator. Just make yourself at home, Delaney. Bannon should be back around ten."

"Thanks."

Then she was gone, the door closing behind her with a click of finality. The tension in the house was suddenly electric. To Delaney's surprise, she realized that she didn't want to deal with Jared, or her feelings for him, right now.

"Which way is the kitchen?" she said to forestall any comment from him. "I don't know about you, but I dearly need a cup of coffee."

"It's that way." He pointed toward a hallway.

The instant she set foot in the hall, Delaney smelled the coffee. She followed her nose, letting it lead her to the kitchen with its heart-of-pine cabinets and cheery chintz curtains. She found a cup and filled it with steaming coffee from the pot, then poured a second cup for Jared.

"Is that for me?"

"Yes."

He hesitated a split second, then slipped his hat off and shoved it onto the counter, along with a tightly folded newspaper. "Thanks," he said, taking the cup from her. His gaze moved over her face again. "Some of the shadows are gone."

"Some of them," she admitted, her glance straying to the newspaper on the counter. "Is that today's paper?"

"Yes."

"I suppose I made the front page." Her attempt at lightness came out sour.

"Yes."

She didn't like the way he guarded his answers. "How lurid did they make it sound?" She twined her finger around her cup, a tension returning, a tension she was picking up from Jared.

"It doesn't matter. Just leave it, Delaney," he said with sudden impatience and took her arm, turning her from the counter toward the cloth-covered pine table and six ladder-backed chairs. "Come over here and sit down."

"Why?" She pulled back. "What's in there? What does it say about me?"

"I don't know. I haven't read it. What's more—I don't want to read it. Do you?"

Thrown by his challenge, Delaney shook her head. "No. Not really."

"Then let's sit down, have our coffee, and . . . talk." He walked over to the table and pulled out one of the chairs for her.

Confused, she hesitated. "I have this feeling you are trying to prepare me for something, Jared. Something I won't want to hear. What is it?"

He breathed in deeply. "It's something I should have told you before—something I don't want you to hear from someone else." When he looked at her, she instinctively braced herself. "Susan St. Jacque was my ex-wife."

Of all the possible things he might have said, that one hadn't occurred to her.

"In the past, there was never any reason to tell you. It wasn't important. After all, Susan and I were divorced. Then last night . . . last night, it didn't seem appropriate."

Dazed, she backed up and leaned against the counter. "At the reception . . . I noticed the bitterness between you, but I never guessed—I never dreamed—"

"Why should you? Dammit, Delaney, this isn't the way I wanted to tell you." In two strides, he was at her side, taking the cup from her unresisting fingers and pushing it onto the counter before drawing her into his arms. "I wanted to hold you and touch you."

She pulled back to look at him. "It's crazy, but I never let myself wonder who your ex-wife might be, whether she still lived here, whether I might see her—or meet her. I didn't want to know. And all this time it was Susan." She shut her eyes for an instant. "Her family—"

"She has an aunt in Chicago."

"Then"—she lifted her head—"last night—"

Jared nodded, guessing what she was about to say. "The police called me to get her aunt's name, address, and phone number so they could notify the next of kin. They asked me to come down and identify the body." He pushed the hair from her face. "Do you understand why I had to tell you now? Why I couldn't run the risk that you might hear it from someone else?"

"Yes."

"Delaney, I don't want you to think—"

"That's just it." She laughed soundlessly. "I don't know what to think or what to feel. Everything's so tangled. I can't change what happened. I can't change that she was your ex-wife any more than I can change that she's dead. I wish I could, but—I'm sorry, Jared."

"Don't be sorry—not because of me," he said. "There was never any love lost between us. That ended years ago. I'm not glad she's dead, but—I don't feel any grief, either. I love you, Delaney. The only reason I'm hurting now is because I know you are."

Two sharp blasts of a car's horn announced the arrival of a car at the front of the ranch house. "That must be Riley." Delaney recognized the signal they had often used in the past, conscious of a leap of gladness.

Jared's arms loosened, releasing her as he frowned in irritation. "What does he want?"

"I don't know."

The front door clattered open and Riley's voice sang

out, "Hello! Anybody home?" Then there was a *thump*, followed by a second, louder one as something was dropped on the pine floor.

"We're in the kitchen," Delaney called back.

She picked up her mug and walked out of the kitchen ahead of Jared. Two of her charcoal tweed suitcases sat on the living room floor near Riley's feet.

"Good morning." Riley tossed the greeting over his shoulder and pushed the front door shut, giving the knob a testing shake. "The lock on this door is worthless, 'Laney. I could get in with a credit card. You need to have a talk with Bannon about such things as locks and security." The suggestion was made in a lighthearted way, but Delaney knew he was serious.

"I'll do that, and good morning to you, too," she mocked his lack of a greeting.

Riley looked at her, a smile edging his mouth, but he didn't correct the omission. "I brought you some clothes." He waved a hand at the suitcases, his glance sliding past her to Jared, a coolness stealing into his eyes. "I won't guarantee how neatly they're packed, though."

"It doesn't matter, just as long as I have something clean to wear."

"You could definitely develop a case of cold feet in that outfit." Riley's glance skimmed over the robe, traveling down to her bare feet, making her conscious of her attire—something she hadn't been with Jared. "Do you want me to carry your bags up to your room?"

"I'll do it," Jared volunteered. "Which room is it?"

"The third door to the left of the stairs." Riley spoke up before Delaney could. "If that's coffee you're drinking, lead me to it." Riley nodded at her cup and moved out of

Jared's way when he walked over to collect her suitcases.

"It's in the kitchen."

Riley ranged alongside of her as they crossed the living room to the hallway. She felt odd walking beside him. Usually his presence steadied her. But she kept remembering last night—that moment when Riley had held her in his arms, when he had kissed her. There was nothing in his manner to suggest he had any memory of it all. Had she imagined that there had been more to the embrace than the casual comfort given by a close friend? Or, considering the state she was in last night, had she wanted it to be more than that, therefore convincing herself it was?

Delaney shied from the questions and their implications. "How are things at the house with Lucas?"

"Everything is under control there, thanks to the local constabulary." He leaned a hip against the kitchen counter and watched while she poured a cup of coffee for him. "They stationed a couple of their men at the house to keep the horde of reporters, photographers, and television crews at bay. They form a helluva security ring around the grounds."

"And Lucas?" She handed Riley the cup.

"He's taking it hard." He sipped at his coffee. "He still swears he thought it was Rina. And . . . Arthur is trying to figure out whether Lucas should talk to the press or merely issue some statement of profound regret and stay out of the spotlight."

"Did the police find her gun?"

"They are taking a typical closed-mouthed approach and not saying anything about what they may or may not have found."

Her shoulders sagged a little, although Delaney wasn't really surprised by his answer. It was normal procedure to withhold comment until the investigation was concluded.

"I see you have the morning paper." He picked it up and flipped it open to the front page. "Have you looked at it yet?"

She shook her head. "Jared brought it in before you came."

Jared hadn't wanted her to see that; it was his way of protecting her. Not Riley; he confronted her with it, shoving it over so she could see the photograph of Lucas Wayne and the headline above it: BODYGUARD KILLS ASPEN LOCAL.

"The story's about what you'd expect," he said. "They got the company name right and even mentioned that Wescott and Associates has a solid reputation in the security field. Publicity like that can't be all bad."

She stared at the news print. "Did you know Susan St. Jacque was Jared's ex-wife?"

"Bannon told me last night."

"How will it look with Jared, I mean."

"It shouldn't be a problem. After all, you have known Jared for several years. You assisted him in trying to locate his sister. He has a great deal of respect for you personally and professionally." Riley lined out the bare facts in a smooth and plausible way that spoke of fore-thought. "After that, the public can think what they want—and probably will."

"True." The coffee in her cup was lukewarm. She added more hot to it.

"I called your father this morning," Riley said as Jared walked into the kitchen. "I wanted to let him know what happened before he saw it in the paper or heard about it on the news."

"Dad," she murmured in a dawning voice. "I wasn't thinking. I should have called him myself."

"You've hardly had time." Jared refilled his cup. "You haven't been up that long."

"He's flying out tomorrow," Riley said. "I told him I'd pick him up at the airport."

"He doesn't need to come," she protested.

"You'll never convince a father of that," Riley replied dryly. "Especially not yours."

Delaney couldn't argue with that. Then she remembered, "Glenda. I'd better call her. There will be reporters camped outside the door when she goes to the office this morning."

"I've already talked to her," Riley said.

She looked at him. "You've been busy this morning."

He shrugged. "'No rest for the wicked,' they say."

"You haven't left much for me to do, have you?"

He smiled at her over the rim of his cup. "You could shower and get dressed before Bannon gets here. He said he'd be back around ten. It's going on that now."

"I'd better get moving." She took her cup with her when she left the kitchen.

Her suitcases stood upright at the foot of the bed. She laid the first one down on the floor and snapped the latch to open it. She glanced at the half-rumpled, half-folded clothes inside and smiled, remembering Riley's refusal to guarantee neatness. She went through the clothes and laid out a clean set, from the skin out. From the second suitcase, she added her cosmetic case, makeup bag, and hair dryer to the stack, then gathered them all up and carried them into the bathroom.

While she waited for the water to get hot in the

combination tub and shower, she finished her coffee, then adjusted the temperature and stepped beneath the spray, pulling the plastic curtain shut. She stood beneath the pulsating jets of water, letting them beat at her and massage away the tension. Steam billowed around her, an enervating heat that relaxed all her muscles and soothed her too-taut nerves.

By the time she stepped out of the shower, Delaney felt, if not exactly whole again, then at least ready to face the questions the attorney was bound to ask her—and later the press, possibly even the police. She felt confident that she could handle any unpleasant moment—and confident that eventually she would come to terms with the emotional cost of taking another life.

Wasting little time, she dried herself, wrapped her hair in a towel, and brushed her teeth. She was in the midst of drying her hair when she was interrupted by a knock at the bathroom door.

She switched off the hair dryer. "Yes?"

"Just wanted to let you know Bannon's here," Riley said from the other side of the door.

"Thanks. I'll be right out." She flipped the dryer back on.

A minute later, her long, thick hair still felt slightly damp to the touch. Delaney decided that was good enough and unplugged the dryer. Dressing hurriedly, she pulled a pair of white slacks on over her hose, slipped into a white blouse, and tucked the tails inside her slacks. She shrugged into her navy blazer, conscious all the while of the voices coming from the living room. As she fastened a navy, red, and white silk scarf ascot-fashion at her throat, she heard Jared's voice rise in anger. Frowning, she walked over to the door and opened it.

"—should have expected something like this, but I didn't. Damn them!" Jared swore while Delaney hopped on one foot, trying to slip her shoe on the other. "You and I both know what happened when some guest of Don Johnson decided to take potshots at a helicopter flying overhead. Nothing! Or when our 'esteemed' gonzo journalist decided to unload his automatic at something? Should I even mention Claudine Longet? They treat these goddamned celebrities like they have some kind of diplomatic immunity! Delaney would have been better off if Lucas Wayne had killed Susan. Hell, they probably wouldn't do more than slap his hand and scold him for being a bad boy—"

"Jared, just cool down," came the attorney's calming voice. "This isn't going to help Delaney at all."

She got the other shoe on and stepped out of the bathroom into the hall as Jared snapped, "Maybe it isn't. But what I said is still true—if Wayne had shot Susan, they'd be handling it a whole lot differently."

Delaney came down the stairs to the living room. "What do you mean, 'differently'? How are they handling it now?"

Jared turned from her without answering. Even Riley avoided her eyes. Only the attorney, Tom Bannon, met her gaze with a slow and measuring tone of his own. "I spoke to the prosecuting attorney just before I came out here. It was a courtesy call to inform me that charges have been filed against you. Rather than have an officer come out here with an arrest warrant, I said I'd bring you in."

"What are they charging me with?" The air seemed to crackle around her.

"Second degree murder."

"Murder." She breathed out the word in shock. Riley pushed off the sofa and Jared slammed a hand on the fireplace mantel. "How can they do that? It was self-defense."

"Other than your statement, there is no evidence to support that. I'm sorry, Delaney."

"They didn't find the gun?"

"The prosecuting attorney assured me every inch of the area was searched with a fine-toothed comb."

"She had one," Delaney insisted. "I saw the gun flash. I heard it. It wasn't something I imagined."

"'Laney." Riley laid a hand on her arm. "When they moved the body, the police found a small, pocket-sized flashlight lying under her. They think that's what you saw in her hand."

"A flashlight. And the muzzle flash I saw, I suppose they think that was the flashlight, too." She frowned. "Good grief, I know the difference. How do they explain the gunshots we all heard?"

"I don't know."

"Right now, it doesn't matter," Bannon stated, then paused, a touch of grimness pulling at the corners of his mouth. "Right now, we have to make a trip into town so you can turn yourself in."

"I'll go with you," Riley said.

But Delaney didn't hear him. She was still reeling from the knowledge that she was being charged with murder.

TWENTY-TWO

THE MANDATORY READING OF HER Miranda rights, the taking of her fingerprints, the posing for the official arrest photograph, a full-face shot and a profile with the number prominently displayed on both, the long wait for her bond to be posted, the jam of reporters, photographers, and television crews outside, the sight of Riley plowing a path through them for her, the close flanking by Bannon, the click of the cameras, the whir of video recorders, the thrusting of microphones in her face, the hammering of questions—

"What's your relationship to Lucas Wayne?"

"Isn't it true you're more than just his bodyguard?"

"Were you jealous of Susan St. Jacque? Is that why you killed her?"

"How does it feel to know you killed an unarmed woman?"

—the terseness of Bannon's "No comment," the sick, scared feeling in the pit of her stomach, the chin-up tap of Riley's finger and the concerned look in his eyes, the forced optimism from the attorney and the grimness behind his tight smile, Bannon's promise of a later meeting with her after he'd reviewed the prosecuting attorney's file on the case and the statements from those on the scene, and the long ride back to the ranch, her thoughts crazily distracted by the stains of fingerprint ink on the pads of her fingers and thumbs.

Delaney stood at the bathroom sink and scrubbed at her hands with a nailbrush, the stiff bristles making her flesh tingle and her skin turn pink. As she worked to scour the last traces of ink from her fingers, she caught a glimpse of her reflection in the vanity mirror above the sink—and the obsessively determined look on her face. She paused, struck by the thought that the scene was a version of Lady Macbeth's "out, damned spot" soliloquy. She wanted to laugh, but she was afraid a note of hysteria might creep into it.

Trembling a little, she laid the nailbrush aside and dried her hands on a towel. As she emerged from the bathroom, Delaney smelled the aroma of something cooking in the kitchen. But the thought of food didn't awaken any hunger pangs, only a kind of revulsion.

When she entered the kitchen, she saw Riley standing at the stove, sliding an omelet onto a plate. A stack of buttered toast and a jar of strawberry preserves sat in the middle of the table along with the salt and pepper shakers. Jared stood off to one side.

"I thought it was time you got some food in your stomach," Riley stated. "How does a fresh tomato and cheese omelet sound?"

She noticed he didn't suggest that she was hungry, or that she even should be. She wasn't, although she recognized the necessity of eating. "An omelet sounds fine."

Riley carried the plate to the table.

Delaney sat down in one of the ladder-backed chairs and unfolded a paper napkin, smoothing it over her lap. She went through the motions of shaking salt and pepper on her omelet, selecting a slice of toast, and adding a dollop of jam to it.

Riley pulled out a chair and sat down. Jared did the same. A silence stretched between them, heavy, awkward, and stiff. Finally Jared broke it. "I wish you would talk, Delaney, instead of keeping it all bottled up inside."

"I don't know what to say," she replied. "This is a horrible dream that's turned into a nightmare. None of it should be happening, but it is—and I don't understand why." For an instant, she felt close to panic again and tightened her grip on her fork. "There's so much that doesn't make sense—" Delaney stopped and started again. "You were married to Susan. You knew her."

"As well as anyone, I suppose," he agreed with a slight shrug of one shoulder.

"What do you know about her relationship with Lucas Wayne?" Riley picked up the questioning.

"If you are asking whether I knew that she had an affair with Lucas Wayne while we were still married, the answer is yes. At the time, I blamed myself for it—for leaving her alone too much. Every spare minute away from the ranch I spent looking for Kelly. Later there was the guilt I felt over you. How could I condemn her for being unfaithful when I hadn't been any better?"

"Then her affair with Lucas wasn't the reason—"

"—for our divorce? No. Our divorce was a long overdue parting of the ways."

Delaney chewed thoughtfully on a bite of toast without tasting it. "Do you think she loved him?"

A wryly lopsided smile twisted his mouth. "Love was seldom the reason Susan did anything. More than likely, she wanted the luxury of a lover. She probably saw him as a kind of status symbol. Money and position were always the most important things to her. I'm convinced she married me thinking I could give them to her. When she found out I couldn't, our marriage started going sour."

He stared off into space. "She hated the ranch, hated living here. I thought she would get used to it in time. She thought she would eventually persuade me to sell it." Pausing, he glanced at Delaney. "Do you remember the first time I had dinner at your house with you and your father? That night you said a woman would do anything—lie, cheat, and steal—to get the thing that was most important to her. I don't think I believed you then. Maybe I didn't want to, any more than I wanted to accept that I wasn't the most important thing in Susan's life."

"Would she kill if that's what it took?" Riley wondered aloud.

Jared thought about that. "I don't know. Sometimes I wonder if I ever really knew her. What made you ask that?"

"Because I think she was blackmailing Lucas," Delaney answered. "She knew something Lucas didn't want made public, and I'm positive she was using that to force him to buy a very expensive painting."

"That sounds like something Susan would do." Jared nodded, somewhat grimly. "What did she have on him? Do you know?"

"I can't answer that."

"Which means you do."

"It doesn't matter whether I do or not," Delaney insisted. "The point is—if she *was* blackmailing him and *if* Lucas had refused to give in to her threats, then it might explain why she would try to shoot him if she couldn't get him to buy the painting."

Riley cocked an eyebrow in skepticism. "That doesn't sound logical either, does it?"

"No, it doesn't," Jared agreed and reached over to cover her hand. "Delaney, you have to face the possibility that you may never know why she shot at him."

"I know." She poked at her omelet, aware she hadn't taken a single bite of it. "That doesn't bother me as much as—" Her voice broke, her throat muscles knotting up. Painfully she tried again. "I can't help thinking—what if they're right? What if she didn't have a gun? I knew she was blackmailing Lucas. I was upset about it. I even tried to think of some way to stop her. What if . . . what if subconsciously I recognized Susan? What if subconsciously I wanted to hear a shot so badly that I convinced myself I did? What if I subconsciously justified firing at her by telling myself I was protecting Lucas from a blackmailer? What if I imagined the shot?" Crazily she felt a whisper of relief at having finally voiced the fear, the questions, that had haunted her all morning.

Jared's fingers tightened on her hand. "Do you think you did?"

"No." She shook her head, then hesitated. "At least, I don't think so. But what if—"

"Stop it." Riley's voice was rough with command, his gaze hard on her. "Don't do this. You have enough grief without borrowing more."

"I know." Sighing, she pulled her hand free of Jared's fingers and gave her fork a push onto the plate.

"You're not going to eat that, are you?" Riley guessed.

Delaney looked at the omelet and the congealing cheese. "I can't."

"That's what I thought." Riley picked up her plate and carried it to the corner wastebasket, scraping the leftovers into the garbage.

"I feel as though I should be doing something," she murmured, an agitation and restlessness surfacing.

"There is nothing you can do right now." Riley wandered back to the table, snapping his lighter and holding the flame to the cigarette in his mouth.

"That's what is so frustrating. I'm not used to sitting around twiddling my thumbs."

"What you need is a change of pace, a change of scenery," Jared announced. "Something to get your mind off all this. What do you say we go riding, like we planned to do? Bannon won't mind if I saddle up a couple of his horses."

Delaney shook her head. "I know you mean well, Jared, but I'm not in the mood."

"It wouldn't be a good idea anyway," Riley put in.

"Why?" Jared turned a challenging glance on him, their eyes clashing.

"Because right now, it's better if Delaney stays close to the house, in case something new develops. However—" Riley shifted his attention to Delaney, a sparkle of devilment in his eyes, a smile deepening the corners of his mouth—both were a sharp contrast to his cool treatment of Jared—"if you are really bored, I know where there's a pile of paperwork to be done. I can easily arrange for it to be delivered to you."

Amused in spite of her situation, Delaney smiled. "Thanks a lot. Maybe tomorrow. I don't think I could concentrate on it right now."

"Now, there's a likely excuse," Riley mocked as the telephone rang in another part of the house. Startled, Delaney half-turned in her chair, her nerves tensing in instant reaction. Riley saw it and rose from his chair. "I'll get that."

He left the kitchen. Delaney listened to the sound of his footsteps, each ring of the telephone jarring her. Finally the ringing stopped, and she caught the muffled sound of Riley's voice, his words indistinct.

"Delaney." Jared reached over and covered her hand again. "It's probably just some telemarketer."

"Probably." But she didn't believe that, not when Riley was still on the phone. She clasped Jared's fingers briefly, thanking him for trying to reassure her.

Part of her attention was tuned to the phone conversation in the other room while she tried to pretend, for Jared's sake, that he had diverted her from it. "Maybe I should have Riley bring out that paperwork. It might force my mind off things."

"You've turned the operation over to Riley. Let him handle it."

Delaney smiled at that. "Riley and paperwork are like oil and water. You can put them in the same container, but they don't mix. By now there is bound to be a good-sized stack waiting for me," she said, her thoughts turning to business. "I wonder if Riley called Scotty."

"Who is Scotty?"

"Scott Cameron. He's handling things in L.A. while I'm here. We have a contract to provide security for the premiere of Tom Cruise's new movie in L.A. at the end of this month. Scotty will have to get started on the leg-work for it."

Jared frowned in apparent surprise. "I thought— Aren't you going to sell out? Get out of the security busi-ness?"

"No. Why would you think that?" Delaney stared at him, for a moment completely mystified. "You mean, because of this shooting?"

"It would be more than enough reason for a lot of people," he replied. "After all, look at the mess you're in. And for what?"

"For acting within the course and scope of my em-ployment." She cited the legal terminology that defined justifiable homicide in this case. "The shooting isn't a reason to quit. I admit none of this is pleasant—not what happened or the felony charges—but that's a risk in this profession. I knew that when I started Wescott and Associates."

She couldn't quit. Not now. It was like being thrown from a horse—she had to get back on and prove to her-self that she could do it, that she hadn't been beaten by it. But she sensed that Jared wouldn't agree with that logic.

"Some risks aren't worth it. I thought you would have figured that out after all that's happened to you."

They were a breath away from a full-blown argu-ment when Riley walked back into the kitchen. "That was Bannon on the phone," he told them, his gaze falling on Delaney. "We have permission to go over the crime scene tomorrow. Bannon has to be in court first thing in the morning to file a motion on another case. He expects to be free by no later than ten o'clock. I said we'd meet him and go over everything."

"Sounds good." At last there would be movement, action, something constructive happening. "Is there anything else new?"

"Nothing."

There seemed to be little else to say, but the silence felt thick, heavy with vague undercurrents. Right now Delaney didn't feel that she wanted to summon up the energy to dispel them—or to be sociable.

"Look, there isn't really any reason for you two to stay here. I know you probably have things to do. I'll be okay."

"I'm not going to leave you here alone." Jared settled back in his chair, a determined set to his jaw.

Riley smiled coolly. "And I'm not leaving until he does."

"We don't need a chaperon," Jared declared.

Riley's smile lengthened even as the blue of his eyes turned icy. "I think you're wrong. If some reporter comes snooping around out here, I don't want him to find Delaney alone with the victim's ex. There are enough rumors flying around town without adding that twist to the story."

Discomfort tinged with guilt flickered in Jared's expression as he darted a quick look at Delaney. "I hadn't looked at it that way."

"Then maybe now you realize," Riley pressed the advantage, "that the best thing you can do for Delaney is to make yourself scarce for the time being."

"Jared, you don't—" she began.

"No," he broke in with a shake of his head. "As much as I hate to admit it, Riley is right. My being here could come back to hurt you. I don't want to be the cause of more trouble for you." He stood up. "Will you walk me to the door?"

"Of course." She rose from her chair.

"I'll tag along with you," Riley said, earning an irritated glare from Jared. Riley smiled one of his slow smiles. "Just in case there's some photographer out there with a telephoto lens."

The kiss Jared gave her at the door was light and quick, not the kind he wanted to give her. But Riley's presence proved to be an inhibiting factor, making it all awkward and stilted.

As Jared walked off the porch, shoving his hat on, Riley closed the door and turned back to Delaney, looking very pleased with himself.

"For a wet blanket, you look very smug," Delaney observed.

An eyebrow shot up in silent challenge. "You know I'm right. Having your name tangled with his wouldn't be smart right now."

"Maybe not, but—"

"There are no *maybes* about it," he cut in. "Unfortunately, you are the kind who will stand by a friend, regardless of any negative repercussions. An admirable trait, but not very wise, under the circumstances. Which is why I took the decision out of your hands."

"I'm not about to thank you for that."

"I know. Which is another reason I admire you." He paused, looking her over, a smile lingering despite the serious light in his eyes. "Are you sure you'll be all right here by yourself?"

"I'll be fine. Besides, Kit should be back from town any time now."

"I'll only be a phone call away if you need me."

"I know." She smiled, taking great comfort from that.

"In that case . . ." His fingers tangled in her hair. He hesitated, then planted a brotherly kiss on the top of her forehead. Delaney almost tilted her head back to invite a kiss of another kind, for an instant wanting it and confused because she did. "I'll call you tonight," Riley told her. "And I'll see you tomorrow."

"Tomorrow," she confirmed.

TWENTY-THREE

MORNING SUNLIGHT SHAFTED THROUGH the cotton-wood trees that shaded the ranch buildings. It was a painter's light, Delaney decided, and leaned a shoulder against one of the porch's smooth log posts. And a painter's setting, too—the barn's weathered wood still showing dark, wet patches from the rain, the split-log fence contrasting with the emerald green of the grass, the mountain peak rising beyond the trees, showing its burnt-red face to the sun. All around were nature's sounds: the stamp of a horse in the corral beyond the barn, the chirp of a jay in the cottonwoods, the distant lowing of cattle in the pasture.

The quiet was shattered an instant later by the purring drone of a car's engine coming up the lane. Delaney straightened from the post as the rental car came into view with Riley behind the wheel. He saw her on the porch and honked. She pushed her purse strap higher on her shoulder and went down the steps. With long, quick strides, she hurried to the car.

"Good morning." She climbed in the passenger side.

"Good morning." Riley waited until she had her seatbelt fastened, then let up on the brake. "You look like you're in better spirits this morning."

"I am." Truthfully, she felt as though some massive weight had been lifted from her. "I'm not even sure why. Nothing has changed, except me—my attitude."

"Sometimes that's enough." He turned the car in a circle to head back down the lane.

"It was for me," Delaney admitted. "Yesterday—the murder charge, the fingerprinting, the arrest photographs—the whole procedure made me feel as if I had joined the ranks of the maniacs and the terrorists, the same kind of people I am supposed to protect my clients from. It disturbed me—and made me question everything. It even made me doubt myself. But I *know* what happened, Riley. I didn't imagine it, not any of it. Given the same set of circumstances, I would do it again. That sounds cold and ruthless, doesn't it?"

"A little. But knowing you the way I do, I also know that isn't the way you mean it."

"It isn't." Delaney leaned her head back and gazed at the ridge of wild mountains before them. "I keep waiting to feel grief, but all there is inside me is a hard fist of regret. Some part of it will always be there, I know. I killed someone, and I'll never be the same person again because of that."

"You shouldn't be," he told her. "If you were, then you really would have reason to worry."

"Indeed," she murmured in agreement. For a few

miles, a silence stretched comfortably between them. "What has Rina been doing all this time?"

"Who knows? There haven't been any surprise visits. No phone calls."

"Is she still in Aspen?"

"She's still here," Riley confirmed. "I spoke to one of the reporters yesterday afternoon and he told me he'd talked to a hotel maid. Supposedly she was in Rina's room while Rina was watching the news coverage on the shooting. The maid made a comment about 'what a pity it was' about Susan. To which Rina replied, 'The pity is that the St. Jacque woman didn't kill the bastard before she died.' Then she started ranting about the way Lucas used women—and how he wasn't going to get away with using her . . . the usual stuff."

"I'm surprised Rina hasn't taken her case to the press."

"She's smarter than that," Riley said, then quoted, "'Anything you say can and will be used against you in a court of law.' Having her own words on tape might be more damning than the hearsay of a witness."

"True." A rueful smile tugged at a corner of her mouth. "You know, the professional side of me wishes she'd give up this obsession with Lucas. And the selfish side of me wishes she'd make another attempt and help prove my case."

"I understand." He lit a cigarette, then cracked his window open to let the smoke trail out.

"Are we picking Bannon up at his office or is he meeting us at the house?"

"He'll meet us at the house." Riley glanced at his watch. "In fact, he's probably there. He wanted to familiarize himself with the scene before we walked through what happened and when." He sent her a quick grin. "Got your memory cap on?"

Delaney nodded. "There have been times when I wished I could take it off. I've replayed the shooting so many times in my head, I think I know it frontwards, backwards, and sideways."

"Good. Just keep the picture sharp and pay attention to the details."

"I will."

A half-dozen photographers lounged outside the driveway's entrance, chatting among themselves, occasionally trading comments with the two uniformed policemen on duty. When they saw Riley driving up, they scrambled into action, crowding close to the car and aiming their lenses at Delaney. She ignored them as best she could.

"How long before that gate's installed?" she muttered out of the corner of her mouth.

"It can't be too soon, can it?"

Vance backed the rental car out of the way and Riley drove through the opening. As they drew level with him, Vance rolled his window down and waved an arm to stop them. "Mr. Bannon said to tell you he'd be in the house."

"Right." Riley nodded and drove on. "He's probably interviewing Lucas, finding out what he remembers about the shooting."

"Probably," Delaney agreed.

They parked alongside Bannon's black pickup, then got out and followed the walk to the front door. Wyatt opened it, the two-way radio in his hand. "They're in the living room."

"Thanks." Her glance strayed to the foyer's antler

chandelier. It had been a mere thirty-six hours since she'd been in this house. Thirty-six hours, yet so much had happened, so much had changed.

Suppressing a sigh, she headed for the snow-white living room. Arthur met her at the archway.

"It's good to see you, Delaney. I won't even ask how you've been. I know it's been hell. Pure hell."

Beyond Arthur, Delaney spotted Tom Bannon sitting in one of the white armchairs, quietly observing their meeting. He was dressed in Levi's and a short-sleeved white shirt. A tan sport jacket lay over the back of the chair.

"I hope you know how terrible I feel about all this, Delaney," Arthur said with unexpected briefness and sincerity.

"I think we all feel that way, Arthur."

"I know," he said with a sudden troubled frown. "But it wasn't supposed to happen like this."

A movement in her side vision caught her eye. She turned as Lucas came striding toward her, a black polo shirt covering his muscled chest and black slacks running their sharp creases down his long legs. With his dark hair and eyes, the effect could have been somber and funereal. Instead it was sexy and virile.

"Delaney." Relief was in his voice, concern in his eyes.

"Hello, Lucas." She moved past Arthur to meet him. "How are you?"

"No, the question is—how are you?" He stopped before her, his hands coming up to curve around her upper arms.

"I'm fine." Yesterday morning, that answer would have been a lie. Today she meant it.

"Are you sure?" His hands slipped up and down the silk sleeves of her blouse, absently rubbing at her arms.

"Very sure."

"God, I can't believe what's happened," he said tightly. "It's my fault. I said it was Rina—"

Arthur broke in, "If it's anybody's fault, it's Rina Cole's. She had us all jumpy after that phone call. Hell, she had us jumpy before it."

"I just told your attorney, Mr. Bannon, about the call from Rina." Lucas released her and partially turned to include the lawyer.

"Bannon," the attorney corrected, rising to his feet and extending a hand toward Delaney. "Glad you could make it, Delaney. Hope you managed to get some rest."

"I did." She went over to shake hands with him.

"Have a seat." He motioned toward the twin of his armchair. "We were just going over what Mr. Wayne remembers about the shooting and the events leading up to it."

When Delaney sat down, Lucas moved a Peruvian-design pillow out of the way and took a seat on the white sofa opposite them. Arthur remained standing. Riley and Wyatt drifted over to stand out of the way.

"All right," Bannon continued, "what happened after the phone call? The one from Rina Cole."

"Nothing. I mean, it shook me up. The woman is crazy. Sick." Leaning forward, Lucas propped his elbows on his knees and combed through his hair in obvious agitation. "Anyway . . . after that we ate dinner, although I don't think anyone had much of an appetite. I know I didn't. Then we came back here, into the living room. I had a drink—I don't remember if I fixed it or Arthur did."

"I did," Arthur volunteered. "It was a brandy."

"Right." Lucas nodded as if remembering. "I know when the phone rang a few minutes later, I dropped the glass. I thought it was Rina calling back, but it was Susan."

"Did you answer the phone?" Bannon questioned.

"No, I did," Delaney said. "It was Susan. I recognized her voice. She asked to talk to Lucas."

"What time was this—approximately?"

"It must have been between eight and eight-thirty," Lucas replied after a short pause. "I remember it was dark outside."

"What did Susan say to you?"

"She was calling from somebody's house. If she told me whose, I don't remember it. I have to be honest, I wasn't paying a lot of attention. My mind was still on Rina." Lucas sat back and nervously rubbed his hands over his thighs. "Susan wanted to drop some papers by for me to look over. It had to do with a painting that she had shown me a couple days earlier. I told her that was okay and hung up. Unfortunately . . ." He sighed and cast a look of regret at Delaney. "I didn't bother to mention she would be stopping by. It didn't seem important, I guess."

Bannon offered him a nod of benign understanding. "Then what happened?"

"Riley and Arthur left right after that—"

The attorney interrupted him to say to Riley, "That's when you went to relieve the man in the drive so he could eat."

"Right."

"And I tagged along to get some fresh air," Arthur put in.

"Which left you and Delaney here alone," Bannon concluded.

"Yes. We talked for a little bit. I remember I apologized—"

"Apologized?" Bannon said.

"I had yelled at her earlier, for no reason other than she was handy and my nerves were shot. Anyway, right after that, I suggested going on the deck for some fresh air."

Turning sideways in the armchair, Bannon looked behind him at the living room's wall of glass and the deck beyond it. "When you say you went out on the deck, I assume that's the one you mean?"

"Yes."

The attorney stood up. "Do you mind going out and showing me approximately where you were standing?"

"If you think it will help." Lucas pushed to his feet.

Delaney followed them out the door, with Riley, Wyatt, and Arthur on her heels. Outside, Lucas hesitated only briefly before crossing to a point along the rail. "I think this is it."

"Delaney, do you concur?"

When she walked over to look, she saw the distinctive yellow tape used by the police to rope off a crime scene. It was strung around a wide area of the brick path, marking the area where Susan had been shot. There was a white outline of a body on the ground. Delaney stared at the spot where Susan had lain, seeing her again in her mind. She felt the sick, cold feeling coming back and mentally shook it off again, detaching herself from her emotions.

She checked the angle from the deck to the walk,

visualizing the way it had been that night. "Another six inches this way, I think." She shifted her position and nodded. "This is it."

"Sorry—" Lucas began.

"Not necessary." Bannon waved off the apology. "It's a moot point anyway. Go on with your story, Mr. Wayne. You came out here and stood at the rail."

"We talked. Or, at least, I talked and Delaney listened—"

"Excuse me," Bannon interrupted. "What about outside lights? Were there any on?"

"The lights along the walk and shrubbery were on. They operate on a timer and come on automatically at eight o'clock," Lucas explained. "But none of the deck lights were on."

"All the living room lights were on full bright," Delaney inserted.

"I see." He glanced from their position to the walkway. "Which means the two of you would have been clearly visible to anyone coming along the path. Sorry. Go on. The two of you were talking, then what?"

"I happened to glance that way. I don't know why. Maybe I saw a movement. Anyway, there she was—"

Bannon held up a hand to stop him again. "Do you have any idea how long you'd been out here talking at that point?"

Lucas frowned and glanced questioningly at Delaney. "What would you guess—five minutes? Ten?"

"In that neighborhood. It wasn't very long, I know that," she agreed.

"How did Susan get here? Did she drive?" Bannon directed his questions at Riley.

"She walked."

"Which explains why they didn't see any headlights or hear a car," he said, nodding his head. "And by then you were at the entrance to the drive."

"Wyatt and I both were."

"I see. And where were you, Mr. Golden?"

"Walking," Arthur replied. "I had gone with Riley down to the road. He and Wyatt started talking and I was too restless to stand around, so I wandered back toward the house."

"Did you see Susan St. Jacque, either when she arrived or when she walked up to the house?"

"No." Arthur shook his head. "I guess I was somewhere around the garage then, or maybe in back of the house. I know that's where I was when I heard the shots."

"You're getting ahead of me, Mr. Golden," Bannon said with a smile, and turned back to Riley. "So tell me what happened when she arrived."

"She said she had some papers she needed to leave with Lucas and I passed her through. I remember thinking at the time that I should have given my radio to Delaney," Riley recalled with a touch of grimness. "Hers wasn't working that night, so I couldn't notify her that Susan was on her way to the house."

"Then you thought Delaney and Mr. Wayne were still inside? You didn't know they were on the deck?"

"No. This area can't be seen from the drive. It's blocked by bushes."

"And vice versa, it seems," Bannon murmured after checking to see if the driveway's entrance could be seen from the deck. "I wonder how Susan knew you were out here—how she knew to come along this path instead of going to the front door. Can this deck be seen from the front walk?"

"Easily," Riley answered.

"Tell me, Riley, how did Susan seem to you? What was her manner?"

"She seemed in a hurry, but other than that, there was nothing to make me suspect there might be trouble."

"All right—now, back to you, Mr. Wayne. You glanced at the path," he said to allow Lucas to pick up where he'd left off.

"I glanced at the path and I saw her—only I thought I was seeing Rina. In my mind, that's still who I see. I don't know why I thought Susan was Rina. Maybe it was the blonde hair or the leather pants. Most of Rina's clothes are made out of leather, suede, or fur, and she never wears anything under them. She has some fetish about wearing animal skins against her flesh." Lucas lifted his head, his look intensely serious. "But if I could make a mistake like that when I've known Susan longer than I've known Rina, then it makes sense that Delaney would mistake her for Rina, especially when she had a gun. And she did have a gun, Bannon. I saw it. I don't know why the police couldn't find it."

"I'll tell you why they couldn't," Arthur spoke up. "Incompetence. Sheer incompetence."

Bannon silenced him with an upraised hand. "Go on, Mr. Wayne. You saw the gun."

"I told Delaney it was Rina and she had a gun."

"Delaney was standing there with you?"

"She was facing me . . . and away from the path. As soon as I said that, Delaney pushed me down to the deck and told me to get in the house. I scrambled for the door on my hands and knees. I heard the shots. By the time I reached the door—"

"How many shots did you hear?" Bannon asked, and Delaney felt herself tensing in anticipation of his answer.

"Four. I think it was four," Lucas replied, and her heart sank.

"It's your turn, Delaney. Pick up the story from your side *after* Mr. Wayne told you he saw Rina and she had a gun."

"I pushed him down and told him to get inside. At the same time I turned, drawing my weapon. Before I was completely around, I saw a gunflash and heard a—"

"Wait a minute," Bannon stopped her. "Riley, would you mind going down on the walk and standing in for Susan? I'd like to do a little reenactment here, establish places and positions."

"Sure." Riley walked over to the steps that led off the deck, then followed the intersecting side path to the main walk. He ducked under the tape and went over to the general area of the body.

"Turn your back to him, Delaney, and show me what you did, when you saw what," he instructed.

She turned her back to the path, closed her eyes and let the images run through her mind, acting them out. "With my left arm, I pushed Lucas down as I turned, pulling my gun. She shouted, 'Bastard' and her voice was hoarse." Delaney stopped in mid-motion. "I was about right here when I saw the flash from her gun."

"Approximately where did the flash come from?" Bannon asked, then added, "I recognize daylight is something of a handicap, but try to remember how it was that night in the dark. Riley," he called to him. "Assume what you think Susan's firing position would have been."

Delaney held her angle while Riley shifted his stance, both arms outstretched, his hands clasping an imaginary gun. "Not there." She closed her eyes, summoning the image again. "The flash came from the outer edge of that bush on the far side of the walk. It was lower, too." She opened her eyes. "I think she must have fired from the hip." Obligingly, Riley lowered his right arm to simulate that position. Delaney frowned. "It was still lower than that."

"Riley is taller than Susan, which probably accounts for the difference. Go on."

"The next instant is when I actually saw her. By then I was firing. After she fell, I kept her covered until Riley got there. Wyatt was with him," she remembered. "I told him to call the police and an ambulance, then bring the emergency kit from the house. Then . . ." Delaney moved from the rail and crossed to the steps leading to the path. "I went down." She stopped. "Do you want me to continue?"

Bannon nodded. "Do exactly as you did that night," he said and went down the steps behind her, followed by the others.

She stopped at the point where the two paths intersected. "I came this far and saw Riley crouching beside the body." Riley assumed his position that night. "Arthur was there, too."

"Mr. Golden." Bannon motioned him toward Riley.

Delaney waited until Arthur had maneuvered under the barrier and joined Riley. "I tried to ask if she was dead, but I couldn't get the words out. Riley told me he couldn't find a pulse, that she was dead. That's when I threw up," she admitted with a trace of chagrin.

"Perfectly natural." Bannon gave her arm an assuring pat.

"Riley said the same thing when he came over. He

also told me it was Susan, not Rina. I didn't believe him and went to look."

With a nod, Bannon indicated that she should continue acting out her role that night, and raised the barrier higher to allow her to slip under it. "Riley, am I correct in assuming you were by the road when you heard the shots?"

"Wyatt and I were both there."

"And, Mr. Golden, you said you were behind the house when you heard them?"

"Right, although at first I didn't realize that's what they were," Arthur said. "There was this pop-pop-popping sound. I thought somebody had set off fire-crackers. It wasn't until I heard someone shouting—I don't know who—that I realized I must have heard gunfire."

"How many shots did you hear?"

"I don't know. I wasn't paying attention to the number. There were several. They came right on top of each other. Three, four, five, maybe more, I don't know."

"What about you, Wyatt? How many did you hear?"

Wyatt stood next to Lucas Wayne. "Five."

Delaney realized that Bannon had deliberately not asked how many shots she had fired, eliminating the possibility they would be influenced by her answer, thereby forcing them to rely on their own memory even if it conflicted with someone else's.

"And you, Riley." He put the same question to him.

"Six, for sure."

She could have kissed him.

"All right, Delaney, you checked the body and saw it was Susan." Bannon made a circling turn with his fingers, prompting her to continue.

"Right after that, I think I asked Riley why Susan would try to kill Lucas. At that point, we looked for her gun. We didn't see it near the body. Then we heard the sirens. The police—"

"Hey!" Toby lumbered up the path toward them, his heavy features drawn in a scowl. "You better get outta there. The policeman's gonna be mad when he catches you. Nobody's supposed to go inside the yellow lines."

"It's all right, Toby." Lucas stepped forward to intercept him. "The police gave them permission to go inside."

"But the policeman told me nobody could go inside, Luke," Toby insisted.

"I know he did." Lucas nodded patiently. "But this is Mr. Bannon and he's helping Delaney, so the police said it was all right." He glanced apologetically at the attorney. "I'm sorry for the interruption. This is Toby Williams. He—he helps the groundskeeper look after the flowers. And he's very conscientious about doing what he's told."

"That's good." Bannon smiled at Toby. "And you were right to tell us we shouldn't be in here. But the policeman did tell me we could—just this one time."

"If you say so." But Toby didn't look entirely convinced. He continued to watch them as if he expected them to do something else wrong.

Ignoring him, Bannon turned back to Delaney. "When you didn't see the gun near the body, then what happened?"

"Nothing. The police were there and I assumed they would find it when they searched the area. I knew she had a gun. If anything, I thought it had been thrown out of her hand and landed farther away in the flowers or the

360 ~ JANET DAILEY

bushes along the walk." She looked around, still half-expecting to see it lying somewhere. "I don't understand why they didn't find it. It makes me wonder how thoroughly they searched."

"They went over the whole area with a metal detector," Wyatt volunteered. "I watched them."

"And I watched them the next morning," Arthur said. "That's when they were looking through all the bushes. I guess they thought the gun might have become lodged in some of the branches. I remember this evergreen bush"—he walked over to a spreading shrub that stood chest-high to him. "Every time they pushed the branches apart, they were jerking their hands back and swearing. I guess the needles were sharp." As if to see for himself, Arthur pushed down one of the thick-growing branches. "Hey, look! There's something in there."

Bannon checked the movement Riley made toward the shrub. "Better let me."

Approaching the shrub, he took a white handkerchief from his hip pocket and wrapped it around his right hand to protect it from the needles. He crouched in a squatting position and pressed down the branch that Arthur held. Delaney watched him, inwardly straining closer as Bannon peered into the shrub's thickness, the seconds crawling by.

"It would seem, Mr. Golden, that you have stumbled across the missing weapon," he announced with a calm Delaney envied.

"Are you sure?" She was almost afraid to believe this incredible piece of luck.

"Very." Still holding the branch down, he said, "Frank Johnson was on duty down by the road. One of you get him and bring him here. We'll need a pair of gloves and something to use for an evidence bag, too."

"I have a pair of driving gloves and there's plastic bags in the kitchen. Will they do?" Lucas asked.

"That'll work fine." Bannon nodded. While Wyatt radioed Vance to send Frank Johnson to the scene and Lucas went up the steps to the deck, Bannon made a closer inspection of the gun's hiding place. "I wonder how it could have gotten so far back in the bush. It would have to have been thrown with considerable force, unless . . ." Experimenting, he moved the branch up and down. "Interesting. Each time the branch moves, it works itself back a little deeper. Which might explain why they missed seeing it."

When the policeman arrived, Bannon showed him the location of the weapon and explained how they had chanced upon it. Using gloves, the officer retrieved the gun and slipped it into the plastic storage bag.

As soon as the policeman left with the new evidence, Arthur rubbed his hands together in satisfaction. "I think this calls for a celebration. With the gun found, they will have to drop the murder charge against Delaney. Let's all go in the house and have a drink. I don't give a care what time of day it is."

Smiling, Bannon took Delaney's arm and guided her out of the cordoned area. "We have every reason to be optimistic that this whole business will have a quick and favorable outcome. The gun definitely supports your claim that she was armed. However, call me superstitious, but I don't believe in celebrating prematurely, so I'll pass on that drink."

"It's still a tremendous relief to know the gun's been found," Delaney said. "Now it's more than just my word and Lucas Wayne's."

"You were sweating that a little, were you?" Bannon asked, his eyes twinkling.

"Yes."

"So was I," he admitted with a faint grin.

"I just realized something." Arthur stopped halfway up the steps to the deck. "Now that the gun has been recovered, what do we do about the funeral on Wednesday?"

Bannon frowned. "What about the funeral, Mr. Golden?"

"Should Lucas send flowers or not? I know the woman tried to kill him—for whatever reason—but she is dead and we have to put the best face on this we can. I don't want Lucas to come off as being hard and callous." He frowned as he tried to figure out what would be best for his client's image. "You're a local, Mr. Bannon. Do you have an opinion?"

The attorney shrugged. "I don't see what harm there would be in sending flowers, although I think it would be inappropriate for Mr. Wayne to attend the funeral."

"Arthur, we have been over this before," Lucas protested. "I'm sending flowers for Susan. The decision is made. There's nothing more to discuss."

"There's a great deal more to discuss." Arthur climbed the rest of the steps to the deck. "What kind of flowers? How lavish should the display be? How should the sentiment read? Should it say—In remembrance? In remembrance of what? That she tried to kill you? I don't think so. No, we need to get the PR people on this."

"Why do you have to make everything so damned complicated, Arthur?" Lucas demanded in irritation, not noticing when Bannon steered Delaney a discreet distance away, the two of them trailed closely by Riley and Toby. Arthur glanced at Wyatt, maintaining a close but respectful distance from his charge.

"Because it's a complicated and awkward situation you're in," Arthur replied.

"I know." Even with nearly half the deck between them, Delaney could hear his heavy sigh.

"Lilies," Arthur decided. "A spray of lilies. That way we could work the forgiveness angle."

Beside her, Toby mumbled a troubled, "I don't understand."

"What don't you understand, Toby?" she asked.

"When you're dead, you can't see or smell flowers. Why does Luke want to send her flowers?"

Delaney found herself groping for an answer. "Because it's . . . customary to put flowers on a person's grave."

"Why?"

Why indeed? she thought. Neither Riley nor Bannon showed an inclination to come to her rescue, so Delaney tried again. "It's a way of showing that you're sorry someone died." Toby listened with fixed concentration, his eyebrows furrowing together as he struggled to grasp the meaning of her words. "You're sorry that Susan died, aren't you?"

"She didn't like me." His lower lip jutted out in a pout.

"Maybe she didn't." Delaney conceded that point, experiencing a surge of sympathy for mothers who had to come up with answers for children's difficult questions. "But you are still sorry she's dead, aren't you?"

"I guess so."

"But you can't tell her that you are sorry, can you?"

"She couldn't hear me. She's dead."

"That's right. But inside, you are sorry and you want to do something to show how you feel, so you put flowers on her grave." She held her breath while he thought about that for a long minute, bracing herself to hear him ask "why" again.

"Does that make you feel better?"

"A little."

She waited for Toby to say something, but apparently her explanation had satisfied him. He wandered off, his head bowed in deep thought.

Bannon said to Riley, "Now you know why God made women the mothers."

"You have that right." Riley smiled at her, his gaze warm and his look quietly approving.

Delaney couldn't help feeling a little proud of herself as she smiled back, chiding, "I could have used some help."

"Not from where I was standing," Bannon replied. "You did fine. All in all, I would have to say this has been a good morning."

Lucas Wayne walked up in time to catch the last. "A *very* good morning."

"But"—Bannon tipped his head at an angle—"like all good things, it too must come to an end, and I have to get back to a stack of work waiting for me at my office." He turned to Delaney. "I'll be in touch with you sometime later today. Let's hope with good news."

"I'll be waiting, anxiously, to hear from you."

"Mr. Wayne, I appreciate the time you gave me this morning." Bannon shook hands with him. "I hope it wasn't too much of an inconvenience."

"Not at all."

"If you'll excuse me, I'll collect my coat and brief-case, then show myself out."

As he walked away, Riley said, "We need to leave, too."

Lucas frowned. "You aren't going already, are you, Delaney?"

Riley didn't give her a chance to answer. "I want to slip her out while I can. My guess is those reporters have found out we located the missing gun. They will be too busy tracking down the story to follow us."

Delaney saw the irritated thinning of Luke's lips and inserted, "Riley is right."

"I know." The annoyance vanished, his mouth crooking. "But that doesn't make me like it any better." His eyes grew serious, seeking an intimacy. "I miss you, Delaney. I'll be glad when this is over and you're back with me where you belong."

"Look on the positive side of this, Lucas." The ex-pression on his face made her want to smile and stroke his hair. "Maybe Rina will be scared off by this and decide it's too dangerous to make another try for you. It wouldn't surprise me. That often happens when someone finds out a victim isn't as vulnerable as they first thought."

"I'd still want you at my side, Delaney. I can't imag-ine my life without you anymore."

"A lot of recovering patients say that to their doc-tors, too," she reminded him as Riley's hand prodded at her back.

"It's not the same thing." A wry smile tugged at his mouth, lightly mocking her.

"If you say so." She chose not to argue the point. "I'll be in touch—if not personally, then through Riley," she promised and let Riley lead her away to the car.

TWENTY-FOUR

SHORTLY AFTER ONE O'CLOCK, Riley dropped Delaney off at the ranch. She waved a goodbye and headed for the house, conscious of the lightness in her step and her spirit. She met the teenaged Laura coming down the porch steps, dressed in a lime green tank top, faded jeans, and old cowboy boots. A cowboy hat hung from a string around her throat.

"Hi, how's everything going?" Laura paused to greet her, a pair of riding gloves clutched in one hand.

"Very well, thanks," Delaney smiled, quickly taking in the girl's attire. "Going horseback riding, are you?"

"Yeah, we got a couple horses in the home pasture that were scraped kinda bad a few weeks ago when they lost their footing in a rocky area. I promised Dad I would check on them today. I was on my way to the barn to saddle up. Would you like to come along?"

"I think I'll pass, but thanks for asking." She glanced toward the house. "Is Kit inside?"

Laura shook her head. "No, she should be outside here somewhere. She just put the boys down for their afternoon nap, and she usually works in the yard while they're sleeping."

"I'll look around."

Delaney found Kit on the west side of the house, pulling weeds from a bed of pink geraniums. A baby monitor sat atop the porch railing near the flowerbed. Catching the sound of Delaney's footsteps, Kit looked up and sat back on her heels.

"You're back earlier than I expected," she said, smiling. "I don't think I have to ask how things went. You look very happy."

"Happy, relieved, satisfied, vindicated—all of the above," Delaney replied, then told her about the discovery of the missing gun. "Hopefully, it will be simply a matter of going through the formalities now."

"Thank God," Kit murmured.

"I second that."

Kit pushed to her feet, eyes twinkling. "I think this news calls for a glass of very tall, very cold iced raspberry tea. Sound good?"

"It does," Delaney agreed.

After retrieving the portable baby monitor from its railing perch, Kit started into the house. "You did have lunch in town, didn't you?" she asked in an afterthought.

"Actually, no. I—"

"Good heavens, you must be starving."

As if on cue, her stomach rumbled, protesting its emptiness, and Delaney laughed. "To be honest, I'm suddenly famished."

"We'll fix that."

An hour later, Delaney wandered back onto the front porch, replete after a meal of crab salad on a croissant, coleslaw with pineapple, and fresh fruit. Her iced tea glass was filled to the top once again. She took another sip of it and glanced at Kit.

"Lunch was delicious, Kit. In case I forgot to say it before, thank you."

"You're welcome." She tipped her glass to Delaney in a gesture of acknowledgment. "I have to admit, it was good to see you finally clean up a plate. You've picked at your food worse than a runway model ever since you came here."

"I've had a lot on my mind." Yet she felt completely untroubled as she surveyed her surroundings. The majestic Rockies dominated the scene, rugged upthrusts of granite bristling with spruce. Here and there, splashes of white marked thick stands of aspen trees, cloaked in summer-green leaves. "This is a beautiful place," Delaney murmured. "So quiet and peaceful."

"Enjoy it now," Kit warned with a twinkle. "There won't be much peace and quiet once the boys wake up from their nap, which should be any time now." She glanced at the monitor as if expecting to hear the sound of them stirring, then lifted her head and turned to look down the long lane to the highway. "Sounds like someone's driving in."

"It could be Riley. He was supposed to pick up my dad at the airport." Delaney looked as well, the sound of an engine growing louder, more distinct. Seconds later a sporty red Camaro roared into view, a German shepherd poking his head out the window, testing the air. Delaney smiled, shaking her head in bemusement. "It's my dad *without* Riley."

She had a brief glimpse of her father behind the wheel as the car swept into the ranch yard and fishtailed to a stop near the log house. Leaving her iced tea glass on the railing, she went to greet him.

Gordon Wescott climbed out of the car one step ahead of the German shepherd. The dog turned to wait for him, then spotted Delaney and took off like a bullet straight for her, whining and yipping his joy. Laughing, Delaney crouched down, bracing herself for the impact of the ninety-pound dog launching himself at her.

"Ollie, you silly old boy, how are you?" She cradled his head in her hands, scratching behind his ears in rough affection and doing her best to elude the dog's attempts to wash her face with kisses as the German shepherd squirmed around her like a puppy. "I missed you, too, Ollie," she whispered and gave his head a final scratching pat, then straightened to meet her father. "I didn't expect you to bring Ollie along."

"I thought you could use your bed partner to keep the bad dreams away." He paused, eyeing her in quick interest. "You haven't gotten yourself a new sleepmate, have you?"

Delaney knew at once that he was referring to Jared. "No, I haven't."

Satisfied, he opened his arms to her, his rich voice saying, "So, how's my girl?"

"Wonderful, Dad. Just wonderful." She started to kiss him hello, then stopped when she saw the white bristle of whiskers on his face. "What's this?" She touched the scratchy beard growth while the German shepherd bounced around them, his tongue hanging out in a silly grin.

"I'm growing it for my new part." He pulled a pair

of clear-lensed glasses from his pocket and slipped them on. "What do you think? When it gets longer and fuller, won't I look like a history professor?"

"A very stern and erudite one," she confirmed, even though to her he would never look like anyone but her father.

"I'm playing a tough old bastard who turns out to have a marshmallow for a heart."

"The writer must have known you." She kissed him, then pulled back, scowling as she rubbed her lips. "Your beard scratches."

"When it gets longer and softer, it will tickle," he promised with a smile and a wink, then paused, his expression softening, his eyes gentling. "Riley told me the news. I'm so glad for you, precious. So relieved."

"Me, too." She hugged him briefly, then turned, keeping an arm around him as she guided him toward the porch. "Come. I want you to meet—"

Delaney never had a chance to complete the introduction to Kit Bannon as her father broke in, amazement lacing his voice, "Well, as I live and breathe, if it isn't the virtuous Marilee from *Winds of Destiny,* alias Kit Masters," he declared, walking forward. "I know you can't possibly remember, but we met once—briefly—at an awards show—"

"You are wrong. I most certainly do remember." Kit reached with both hands to greet him, then threw a smiling look of reproval at Delaney. "You didn't tell me your father was *the* Gordon Wescott, the villainous Stefan in *Bay City.*"

"It didn't occur to me that you two might know each other," she admitted. "Sometimes I forget what a small community Hollywood really is."

"And Stefan was a good many years ago," her father inserted. "I'm flattered you remember."

"How could I forget?" Kit said with a laugh. "Our resident villain on the *Winds of Destiny* soap was green with envy, constantly haranguing the writers to let him do deeds as foul as your character's."

"Stefan was quite monstrous," he said with pride.

"People loved to hate you," she agreed. "So, how was your flight?"

"Long, crowded, and uneventful—the best kind."

"Where is Riley?" Delaney wondered. "I thought he would bring you out here."

"What for? I have my own wheels." He waved a hand at the flashy red Camaro. "All I needed was directions to get here. I knew if I could find my way around Los Angeles, these mountains should be a snap. I was right."

"And I noticed you were driving as though you were still on a freeway. You might want to take it a little slower, Dad," Delaney suggested, aware she was wasting her breath.

"I'll try," he promised, none too sincerely.

"Delaney and I were just having some iced tea. Would you like a glass?"

"I'd love one."

"I'll be right back. Make yourself comfortable." Kit waved a hand at the old wooden rocking chairs on the porch before proceeding into the house.

Delaney climbed the porch steps arm in arm with her father. The dog shadowed both of them and pushed his nose under Delaney's hand the instant she sat down. She rubbed his head and looked at her father, affection welling in her throat.

"You didn't have to come, but I'm glad you did," she told him.

"So am I," he said. "So am I."

With her emotions running a little too close to the surface, she felt herself choking up and sought to dispel it. "So, how were things in L.A. when you left?"

"It was insanity. Absolute insanity," he declared. "The phone rang day and night. Every writer, producer, and studio flunky I know called to find out whether you had sold the movie rights to your story yet, and how they could get hold of you. Glenda told me she had been inundated with the same calls."

"I probably should be flattered, but I'm not."

"Face it, Delaney," her father said. "You have all of Hollywood talking. The other night David Letterman called you 'one pistol-packin' momma that you don't want to mess around with.' And Jay Leno suggested you were a 'female Rambo who shot first and asked questions later.'"

"Great," Delaney grumbled. "That is precisely the kind of publicity I *don't* need."

"You can't complain too much. They *are* spelling your name right," he teased.

"How reassuring," she mocked without rancor.

Kit returned to the porch with a glass of iced tea for Gordon Wescott and a bowl of water for the German shepherd. An uncertain cry came through the monitor's speaker. Kit heard it and glanced sideways at Delaney, a resigned smile touching her lips.

"Sounds like naptime is over," she said and excused herself.

Within minutes she was back, carrying the baby in

her arms and trailed by a still-drowsy Tommy. His eyes snapped open when he saw the German shepherd lying at Delaney's feet. "A dog!" he exclaimed, all excited. "Can I play with him, Mommy? Can I?"

"I don't know—" Kit began.

Delaney cut in, "Do you have a ball, Tommy? Ollie likes to chase balls."

He ran back inside and came out with a threadworn softball. Ollie spied it and bounded to his feet, wagging his tail in eagerness for the game. Tommy hurried to the porch steps and hurled the ball into the yard. The German shepherd raced after it while Tommy clapped in approval and started down the steps. Before he reached the bottom, Ollie was back, dropping the ball at his feet, ready to chase it again.

"Tommy has been begging for a dog," Kit murmured, watching the pair. "Maybe we should get him one."

"They are great companions," Delaney remarked as Ollie broke off the game and trotted toward the lane, barking to announce the approach of a vehicle.

"It's Bannon." Kit recognized her husband's pickup. "He's home early. Maybe he has some news for you."

"Let's hope." Delaney mentally crossed her fingers and pushed out of the rocker to meet him.

The pickup came to a stop next to the red Camaro. In shirtsleeves and jeans, the sport jacket discarded, Bannon climbed out of the truck and lifted a hand in greeting, the gesture accompanied by a somewhat perfunctory and tired smile. "Hello. Beautiful out, isn't it?"

"It is." Delaney smiled back, studying him as he approached the steps, looking for something in his body language that might indicate the nature of his news. Nothing.

When Bannon glanced at her father, noting his presence, she automatically made the introductions, then waited through the customary exchange of pleasantries, an inner tension building, making her impatient. At the first break, she said, "You must have talked to the prosecutor by now. Has he agreed to drop the charges against me?"

Bannon hesitated, his eyes studying her in thoughtful silence. "Why don't we go inside where we can sit down and talk."

Immediately wary, Delaney demanded, "Why do I need to sit down to hear this? What happened? Surely he isn't going to persist—"

"I'm afraid he is. If we could go inside . . ." He gestured with his hand toward the door.

Rather than waste time arguing, Delaney turned and walked into the house, not stopping until she reached the stone fireplace.

"I don't understand," she said in agitation. "We found the gun—"

"We found *a* gun," Bannon corrected her.

She pivoted sharply. "What does that mean?"

"It means a gun was found that had two rounds fired from it." He sat down on the sofa, but he didn't bother to insist that Delaney take a seat. "However, there were no fingerprints on it. It had been wiped clean. And a gunshot residue test on Susan's hands came up negative. She hadn't fired a weapon."

"What?" Delaney frowned, unable to believe what she was hearing. "That's impossible. There were shots. I heard them."

But had they come from Susan? She pressed a hand to her forehead, trying to picture that instant in her mind when she saw the gunflash. Susan had been the only one there. It couldn't have come from anyone else.

"I'm sorry, Delaney, but the evidence indicates otherwise," Bannon stated, tenting his fingers together. "I'm afraid your situation has taken a somewhat serious turn."

"I don't understand." Her father sank into one of the living room chairs, looking as shocked as she felt. "What did you mean—the evidence indicates otherwise?"

"I mean there is no evidence to corroborate your daughter's statement that she was fired on. There were no witnesses to the actual shooting," he said. "It's true that Lucas Wayne told the police he saw a gun in Susan's hand, but he also said he heard only four shots, and Delaney fired four times. Plus, Mr. Wayne thought Susan was Rina Cole. If he could make that mistake, then he could also be mistaken about seeing a gun in her hand."

"But what about the gun that was found?" her father argued.

"Yes, the gun we so conveniently found," Bannon murmured dryly. "The prosecuting attorney hinted—strongly, I might add—that it could have been planted there by someone who wasn't aware a residue test had already proven Susan St. Jacque hadn't fired a weapon, someone who felt that a gun found at the scene would support Delaney's claim of self-defense."

Delaney thought about Wyatt and Vance, both former policemen. It wasn't unheard of for a policeman to carry a second gun, an unregistered weapon—a throwaway, they called it—one that could be "produced" at a scene to prevent an officer from being charged with shooting an unarmed suspect. At one time, carrying a throwaway had been a standard practice, and for some, it still was.

Both men had been at the house since the shooting. Either one of them could have slipped under the police line and planted the gun in the shrub. Riley had also had access to the area. But she was certain he wouldn't have done it, not even to protect her.

Her father frowned. "But Delaney told me that Arthur Golden was the one who found the gun wedged in this bush. Don't tell me the prosecutor thinks Arthur put it there, then 'pretended' to find it?" He openly scoffed at the idea. "Arthur isn't that great as an actor, Mr. Bannon."

"Truthfully, Mr. Wescott, it isn't relevant at this point who put the gun there or why. Unfortunately, finding it has raised more doubts and suspicions in the prosecutor's mind. To make matters worse"—he paused and glanced at Delaney—"Susan's will was filed this afternoon. It seems she never bothered to change her will after she divorced Jared McCallister. Except for some family keepsakes that go to her aunt, Susan left everything to Jared—her bank accounts, her art gallery, everything, including the house in the West End that she received from him in the divorce settlement."

"The house in the West End." Delaney looked at Bannon in surprise. "The one she lived in—it belonged to Jared?"

"It was built by his family—his ancestors—years ago. Susan fixed it up," he explained. "At the time of their divorce, she got the house and Jared kept the ranch and the cash."

"I don't think I like what you're saying," Delaney murmured.

"I don't like saying it. But you have to see how it could look to some people—Susan is dead. One way or another, you are responsible for her death. Jared inherits a house worth close to two million dollars—a house he might rightfully feel should be his anyway. And the two of you have known each other for several years."

"Are you suggesting premeditation?" she challenged.

"I'm suggesting that it raises some questions in the prosecutor's mind."

"This is crazy." She stood up, impatient, angry, confused. "It doesn't make sense. None of this makes sense. Somewhere there has to be an explanation."

"One more thing, Delaney."

She swung around, this time braced for anything. "I'm almost afraid to ask what!"

"The prosecuting attorney indicated that, in the interests of bringing to an end all the adverse publicity this case is creating for both you and Aspen, he would entertain the acceptance of a guilty plea to voluntary manslaughter—"

"No!"

Bannon raised his hand to check her quick and angry refusal. "Hear me out," he insisted. "The prosecutor also mentioned that he would recommend to the judge that any sentence be suspended. Naturally, there is no guarantee that the judge will abide by his recommendation. However—"

"No," she broke in again. "Under no circumstances will I plead guilty to voluntary manslaughter. I am not going to have a felony conviction on my record. In the first place, I know what happened that night. I don't care what the prosecutor thinks, what the evidence may indicate, or what conflicting statements the witnesses may have given—I returned fire. It was self-defense, and there is no question in my mind about that. In the second place, a felony conviction would mean the end of my career, the end of my company. You can't honestly expect me to give that up in return for a suspended sentence when I am not guilty of anything but doing my job. And I don't give a damn how much adverse publicity Aspen gets—or I get. If you disagree, say so now, Bannon, and I will get myself another lawyer with the guts to fight *for* me."

A small, pleased smile touched the corners of his mouth. "That won't be necessary, Delaney." He stood up. "It won't be necessary at all. And if that impassioned speech you gave is anything to go by, you would have made a helluva criminal lawyer. In fact, I might borrow some of it for my summation to the jury."

"My God, was that some sort of a test?" Delaney demanded, still angry and still vibrating with it.

"You could call it that," he admitted without apology. "We could have a tough fight on our hands. I like to know before I go in how much backbone my client has."

"Well, now you know," she said stiffly.

"Now I know." He nodded.

"Have you told Riley any of this?" she asked suddenly.

"No."

"I need to talk to him. We need to put our heads together and find some answers," she said, talking out the jumble of thoughts in her mind. "There has to be something we've overlooked, something we haven't considered." Coming to an instant decision, she turned to her father. "I need you to drive me into town, Dad."

Her statement took him by surprise. It was a full second before he managed to reply, "Of course. I'll be happy to."

"I'll need a few minutes to pack, then we can go."

"Pack?" It was Bannon's turn to look at her in surprise.

"Yes, I'm moving back to the condo."

"But the reporters—" Bannon began.

"That's a problem I'll deal with when it comes. In the meantime, I can't keep hiding out here, isolated from everything. There's an explanation for this mess I'm in, and I won't find it here."

"I don't think it's a good idea, Delaney," he cautioned.

"Don't worry. I'm not going to go off half-cocked. I'll be careful," she assured him. "But I can't sit around anymore doing nothing."

"I can understand that." Bannon nodded in sympathy. "Just be sure you don't step on the wrong toes."

"I will be very careful."

Twenty minutes later, the red Camaro pulled away from the log ranch house with her father behind the wheel and Delaney in the front passenger seat. The German shepherd had the entire back seat to himself. The dog nuzzled the back of her head and whined in happiness. Absently, Delaney reached back to pat Ollie's nose, but her attention never wavered from the road ahead of them.

Somewhere at the end lay the answers to her dilemma, and Delaney was determined to find them.

TWENTY-FIVE

Using her key to the condo, Delaney unlocked the door. The German shepherd pushed his way past her and entered the condo ahead of her. The light above the worktable was on, but the chair behind it was empty.

"It's about time you got back, Gordon." Riley's voice came from the kitchen. "I was about to organize a search party—Delaney." He stopped in the doorway, nearly dropping the cup he held. "What are you doing here?" He saw the suitcase in her hand, and the mate to it in her father's. "What's going on? How come you're here?"

"Is there more coffee in the kitchen?" her father asked before Delaney could answer his questions. "My last cup was cold by the time I got around to drinking it."

"No, this was the last," Riley replied, still looking to Delaney for an explanation.

"I'll make some more." Her father set the suitcase on the floor and went past Riley into the kitchen. Ollie followed, his toenails clicking on the vinyl floor.

By the time her father returned with two steaming cups of freshly brewed coffee, Delaney had told Riley about her meeting with Bannon, the results of the residue test, the lack of fingerprints on the gun, and Susan's will.

He crushed his cigarette in the coffee table's large glass ashtray, then rolled to his feet, taking two quick steps away from the sofa before stopping. "Who would have planted that gun?" He ran a hand through his hair.

"Any number of people had the opportunity." She had given the question considerable thought during the ride from the ranch. "I think we can safely eliminate Toby and the caretaker. Toby is too afraid of a gun to touch one, and the caretaker, Harold Walker—what reason would he have to do it? Wyatt or Vance might have done it, but they're both ex-cops; they would have known a residue test would be done. You can be eliminated for the same reason. Which leaves—Lucas and Arthur. Arthur found the gun, which makes him the obvious choice. In a way, it's almost too obvious," she said and sighed. "Dad pointed out that Arthur is not an actor, and I'm inclined to agree. Arthur is not an actor. I don't think he could have pulled off *pretending* to find it."

"That only leaves Lucas." Riley dug in his shirt pocket for another cigarette.

"It was probably a misguided attempt to help me." She carried the cup to her lips, blowing on the dark surface to cool it before she took that first sip.

Nodding, Riley took a long, deep drag on his cigarette and exhaled the smoke in a quick stream. "Makes sense. He's blamed himself often enough for mistaking Susan for Rina."

"I know." She lowered the cup, holding it with both hands. "Now if we could only get him to admit that to the police, assuming he is the one who planted it."

"You've lost me." Her father frowned in bewilderment. "What would that accomplish?"

"It would take some of the suspicion off Delaney and take away the smell that she acted in a way that needs to be covered up."

"I see." His frown turned thoughtful as he considered Riley's answer. "One thing bothers me, though—if Lucas Wayne planted the gun in that bush, how could he be sure someone would look there? How could he be sure Arthur would find it?"

"You just found the hole in Delaney's theory," Riley admitted. "It's possible Arthur might have made a comment to Lucas about the haphazard way the police searched the bushes. Lucas might have picked up on that and told Arthur he should tell somebody about it. If Arthur hadn't, Lucas might have been forced to come up with something on his own. Unfortunately, we'll never know."

"This gun is sidetracking us from the one truly important thing." Delaney set her coffee cup down. "Who shot at Lucas that night? Somebody did. If it wasn't Susan—and all the evidence seems to prove it wasn't— then who? The prosecutor and the police think I made up the gunshots just like I obviously imagined seeing a gun in her hand—"

"I heard *six* shots that night," Riley stated. "I didn't imagine them, Delaney. I counted them off."

"Unfortunately, you are the only one who did."

"Wyatt was talking. Maybe that's why he missed hearing the first one."

"Maybe. But who fired it?" She came back to her original question. "Everybody on the grounds was accounted for, except Arthur. You were with Wyatt. I was with Lucas. And Toby was with the caretaker. Arthur was the only one alone at the time. He claims he was walking out back, but—what if he wasn't? What if—" Delaney stopped and shook her head, then unconsciously flipped her hair back behind her ears with a comb of her fingers. "It doesn't make sense. Why would he shoot at Lucas?"

"Publicity?" her father suggested. "Maybe he wanted to reinforce all this press about Rina Cole being out to get Lucas."

Delaney dismissed that. "Rina does an excellent job of that without his help."

"Maybe he wanted to keep Lucas scared," her father said.

She frowned. "Why would he want to do that?"

"To keep Lucas needing him, turning to him, not giving him a chance to think about his career. Believe me, as hot as Lucas is right now, Arthur has to be sweating blood that Lucas will dump him for a big-name management company. Why he hasn't already is anybody's guess."

"That reasoning sounds shaky to me, Gordon." Riley squinted at the smoke curling from the cigarette that dangled from the corner of his mouth.

"If we eliminate Arthur, then someone was on the grounds that we don't know about," Delaney said. "And there's only one person I know who wants to see Lucas Wayne dead."

Riley nodded. "Rina Cole."

"All along we have been operating on the assumption that Susan fired the shots—you, me, the police, everyone. No one has checked the hedges along the perimeter to see if anyone came through them, have they?"

"No."

"You and I will. Tomorrow morning."

Her father rubbed his hands together in satisfaction. "We have a plan now. That makes me feel better. In fact, it puts me in the mood for a big dish of Rocky Road. How about you, Delaney?"

"I don't think we have any ice cream, Dad."

"Yes, you do. I had Riley stop and pick some up on our way from the airport. So, how about it?"

She shook her head. "I think I'll pass."

"Riley?"

"None for me. Thanks, Gordon."

"You two don't know what you're missing." He headed off for the kitchen.

Delaney picked up her cup and took a sip of it, then stared into the coffee, its dark surface pulling at her and mirroring her thoughts.

The sun was a yellow ball in the sky above Smuggler Mountain, its rays slanting onto the summer-lush slopes of the Rockies and glancing off the town sandwiched between its ranges. The sounds and voices of workmen busy installing a security gate at the entrance to the drive rang clearly through the crisp morning air.

Delaney watched them for a minute, her glance automatically noting the number on the job and the presence of the uniformed officer lounging against the side of a panel truck. "No reporters," she observed as

Riley tucked his radio into its belt holster.

"The funeral is this morning," he reminded. "They're probably off covering it."

"I forgot." She wondered if Jared was at the funeral, then decided he was. Despite the divorce and their conflicting views, Jared was the kind of man who would feel it was his duty to pay his final respects to the woman who had once been his wife. The thought of not attending Susan's funeral wouldn't occur to him.

"How much longer do you think the police will keep a man stationed here?"

Riley hooked the zipper of his tan windbreaker together, raising it a couple inches. "With the funeral and the gate going up, they'll probably pull out after today."

"At least the gate will make our job easier."

"Too bad gates and fences only keep out honest people."

"True." Delaney buried her hands inside the slash pockets of her vest. "If you're ready, we might as well check the hedge along the front first and work our way around the property."

"Let's go."

Angling away from the workmen, they cut across the lawn and began their search approximately ten feet from the driveway. The bushes had been planted mere inches apart, their dense, interlocking branches forming a seemingly impenetrable barrier along the two hundred feet of road frontage. They walked its length, stopping every few feet to peer under the drooping branches, looking for any gap between the plants wide enough for an intruder to wiggle through, then moving on again, scanning the tangle for broken branches.

At the cornerline, Delaney spotted a small opening

between the plants and got down on her hands and knees to inspect the tunnel-like gap. Behind her, Riley swore suddenly and savagely under his breath.

"What's the matter?" She backed out of the bushes, briefly snagging her tapestry vest on a twig.

"You can kiss goodbye any thought of finding a freshly broken branch. Look."

Delaney stood up, automatically brushing at the knees of her black jeans as she glanced in the direction of his curt nod. At almost the same instant, she saw the gray-haired caretaker and heard the snip-snip-snipping of the pruning shears in his hand.

"Great." She sighed in disgust at the neatly trimmed hedge that stretched behind him, and the long pile of chopped-off branches beside it. "Why did he have to pick today?"

"Who knows? Come on. Let's go talk to him," Riley said. "Maybe he's seen something."

The grizzled caretaker saw them coming and lowered the shears to his side. "Saw you crawling around on the ground," he said. "Did you lose something?"

"No. We were hoping to find something," Riley replied, deliberately sounding cryptic. "These bushes grow pretty thick, don't they?"

"Thick and fast," the man snorted. "Trimmed all this five weeks ago, but you'd never know it by looking at it now."

"Are there any places where a person might be able to crawl through the hedge?" Delaney asked.

"There's a couple, three places," he said, nodding thoughtfully. "A body could probably get through them. The coyotes do."

"Would you show them to us?" Riley lifted his hand,

inviting him to lead the way. The caretaker hesitated, then turned and followed the trail of hedge clippings.

In all there were four gaps in the dense hedge, three on the east property line and one along the north, rear boundary. Riley and Delaney inspected each in turn, looking for scuff marks on the ground, clothing threads on the branches, broken twigs, anything that might indicate recent passage.

Finished with the last one, Riley got to his feet and dusted off his hands. "Anything?" Delaney asked.

He shook his head. "The ground's too hard. The branches are trimmed too close. There is no way to tell whether someone's been through it recently."

"What makes you think somebody would?" the caretaker asked, unable to contain his curiosity any longer.

Delaney answered, "Because we think someone else might have been on the grounds the night of the shooting. You didn't happen to see or hear anything unusual that night, did you, Mr. Walker?"

"Just the commotion in front of the house."

"And you didn't hear or see anything when you went to find out what that noise was all about?" Delaney suggested.

He thought about that a moment, then slowly shook his head. "No."

"What about Toby?" Riley inserted. "Maybe he did."

The caretaker shook his head again. "As scared as that boy is of the dark, he would've said something right then. If there was anybody else out there, we didn't see him."

Delaney briefly met Riley's glance. "I guess that's all, Mr. Walker. We appreciate your time."

"No problem," he said and moved off, armed with his pruning shears.

"No neighbors on either the north or the east side," Riley observed. "All four openings are well away from the road. It's possible someone could have crawled through unseen."

"She would have needed a flashlight to find Lucas, though." Delaney automatically thought in terms of Rina Cole.

"But as dense as these shrubs are, the light wouldn't be seen from this side."

"Probably not." When she started toward the front of the house, Riley fell in step beside her.

"What next?"

She shrugged, not really sure herself. "While we're here, I'd like to take another look at the scene. Whoever fired that shot must have been hiding behind the bush. I'm almost sure the muzzle flash came from the edge of it."

"The police have trampled all over that area looking for the gun."

"I know, but I want to see it just the same." They linked up with one of the brick paths that wound to the front of the house. "It might help me remember something else—a movement, a sound, anything."

The police barrier was down, giving them free access to the area. When Delaney stepped over the pink and white petunias that edged the walk, her foot came down on bark chips. "Cedar mulch," she said to Riley. "We wouldn't have found any footprints even if the police hadn't walked back here."

"You're right, unfortunately."

Delaney turned to face the deck and studied the rail,

trying to determine approximately where she'd been standing that night. Shifting sideways, she moved behind the tall bush, visualizing in her mind the reverse angle.

"I think this is it. You stand here, Riley, while I go up on the deck and see."

"Okay." He took her place and Delaney maneuvered around him back onto the walk. She was halfway to the steps leading to the deck when she heard Riley say, "Bingo," in a soft, discovering voice. "Hey, Delaney," he called immediately. "Come look at this."

She came quickly. "What is it?"

"Come around here and see." He motioned for her to come behind the bush. When she did, he put a hand on her shoulder and forced her to crouch down. "I remember you said the muzzle flash was lower. See that."

"See what?" She stared at the deck rail, scanning the wood face of it for a bullet hole.

"The leaves." He touched the end of a twig. "What does that look like to you?"

She refocused her eyes on the twig's green leaves, barely a foot from her face—green leaves that were peppered with black. "Powder burns," she whispered, then looked at Riley.

He winked at her. "Thank God it hasn't rained." He pulled his radio from its holster and said into the mouthpiece, "Vance, get that cop up here on the double."

She looked at the leaves again to make sure her eyes weren't playing tricks with her, then straightened from her crouched position, and released a long, relieved breath.

"Maybe this will convince the prosecutor someone did shoot at Lucas."

"I don't see how they can accuse us of planting it."

"Me either." She glanced at the deck. "Wonder where the bullet went. With all that glass, I'm surprised it didn't break a window."

"I think the police will have another search on their hands," Riley said.

"And I think it's time we found out where Rina Cole was Saturday night between eight-thirty and nine."

"I think you're right."

At that moment, Lucas Wayne walked out onto the deck. "Delaney." He broke into a smile. "Toby said he saw you outside. When did you get here? Why didn't you let me know?"

"We were busy." She hesitated and threw a quick glance at Riley. "You can finish up here without me, can't you?"

"Sure."

"In that case, I think I'll get a cup of coffee."

He nodded, the light in his eyes letting her know that he guessed she wanted to sound Lucas out on a few things, like the gun. "Save some for me."

"I'll try." She headed for the steps. "You do have some coffee made, don't you, Lucas?"

"Wyatt just made some." He met her at the top of the steps.

"Where is Wyatt?

"Taking a shower. I know—" He held up a hand to stave off any lecture. "I shouldn't have come outside without him. The truth is—I tend to be a bad boy when you're not around." He flashed her another one of his wicked smiles and hooked a hand on her shoulder, steering her toward the glass door to the living room.

"Why am I not surprised?" she countered.

"Maybe because you know me."

"You could be right." She opened the door and waved him through ahead of her, then followed him inside. "Where is Arthur?"

"Still sleeping, I guess." His hand found its former resting place on the ridge of her shoulder, guiding her across the white living room to the foyer and the kitchen beyond. "So—are you back to stay? Have they finally dropped the charges against you?"

"No. And I'm not sure they will anytime soon," she replied, aware that finding the powder burns on the leaves only proved that someone had shot at Lucas.

Startled by her answer, Lucas faltered, his hand loosening on her shoulder. "What? Why? We found the gun—"

"There weren't any fingerprints on it. It was wiped clean." She stepped ahead of him into the kitchen. "More than that, the residue test showed that Susan hadn't fired a gun."

"Residue test. What are you talking about?" Frowning, he followed her to the counter where the coffee maker sat.

"Anytime someone fires a gun, an invisible residue is left on the hand. The police have a chemical test that will reveal whether there is any residue. In Susan's case, there wasn't."

Delaney said it all very matter-of-factly as she took a ceramic mug from the cupboard and filled it with coffee, holding on to that emotional detachment that was so vital to maintain. "Want some coffee?" She held up the glass pot.

He stared at it blankly, then shook his head, his frown deepening. "No. But the gun Arthur found— doesn't that mean something?"

"I think it was probably planted there"—Delaney hesitated deliberately and watched for his reaction—"by someone who thought it would help me."

"Who? Do you know?" he asked. A little too quickly, she thought.

"No. But whoever did it, I wish they would admit it to the police. I'm already in enough trouble and the gun only adds to it."

"My God, what a mess this is." He turned at right angles and slumped against the counter, gripping the edge of it with his hands. "I can't believe any of this is happening. Susan is dead and it's my fault."

"She was trying to blackmail you, wasn't she?" She hadn't meant to say that. It just popped out. She watched his head come up, saw the sudden stiffening of the muscles in his neck, as well as the convincing mask of surprised confusion on his face.

"What makes you think that?"

"I overheard some things she said to you, and read between the lines. I think she knew Toby was your brother. I also think she was threatening to make it public if you didn't buy that painting she showed you."

He stared at her as if she had suddenly grown two heads. "My God," he whispered. "Is that why you killed her? To protect me? To protect Toby?"

Stung by his words, Delaney nearly retaliated by throwing the hot coffee in his face. Somehow she managed to push the mug from her hands onto the counter. "No, I did not. Like you, I thought she was Rina."

"I'm sorry." He shut his eyes and tipped his head toward the ceiling. "I don't know why I said that. Of course you didn't. You wouldn't—you couldn't have."

She couldn't stay angry with him, not when the

same thought had crossed her own mind. But it made her sensitive—and testy. "It's okay—"

"No, it isn't okay," he snapped and pushed away from the counter, taking two quick steps before stopping. "Don't you see, Delaney, I'm the reason you're in trouble. None of this would have happened if it wasn't for me."

"That isn't true."

"Isn't it? Then why the hell do I feel so guilty?" He turned back to her, his eyes dark and tortured. "Isn't there something I can do? I want to help. Let me get you a lawyer."

"I have one."

"That local guy, Bannon? I'm talking about a criminal lawyer, one with a name."

She couldn't resist suggesting, "You mean like Matlock or Perry Mason?"

"Dammit, I'm serious, Delaney!"

"I know you are." She smiled a little ruefully, regretting that she had made light of his offer. "Sometimes I need to find a reason to smile. It's a way of coping, I suppose."

"This whole thing has been rough on you."

"It definitely hasn't been easy," was the most she wanted to admit.

Hearing footsteps, she glanced at the doorway as Riley came into view. "There's still some coffee, I hope."

In answer, Delaney took another mug from the cupboard and filled it with coffee. "All done outside?" she asked when she handed it to him.

"All done, at least for now." He sipped at the coffee, then glanced around the kitchen. "Where's Wyatt?"

"Right here." The tall and lanky John Wyatt walked

into the kitchen, his sandy hair still wet from the shower. "Wouldn't you know, I leave Lucas alone for ten minutes and the boss shows up."

"Consider yourself lucky it wasn't Rina Cole," Riley replied, only half in jest. "By the way, I might as well warn you that you'll have more company out here later today."

"Who?" Lucas frowned.

"The police."

"What for?" Wyatt finished tucking the tail of his blue sportshirt inside his slacks.

"Susan didn't take a shot at you, Lucas, but someone did Saturday night. The police will be going over the deck and the front of the house to see if they can find any bullets."

"What happens if they don't find it?" Lucas wanted to know.

"That's what I like—positive thinking." Wryly, Riley lifted his coffee mug in a mock salute.

"Sorry, but the way Delaney's luck has been running—" Lucas began.

"Then she's due for a change." Riley downed another swallow of his coffee, then glanced at Delaney. "Are you ready? Your dad's probably pacing the floor, wondering why we're not back yet."

"I'm ready whenever you are."

He took another quick drink of his coffee and set the mug on the counter. "Let's go."

"Don't forget what we talked about, Delaney," Lucas said, making no attempt to persuade her to stay longer.

"I won't."

Once they were outside, Riley glanced at her curiously. "What is it you're not supposed to forget?"

"He offered to hire me a big-name criminal lawyer."

"Let's hope you don't have to take him up on the offer." He dug the car keys out of his pocket as they approached the rented Lincoln.

"Amen."

"Did you say anything to him about the gun being planted?"

"I did." Delaney headed for the passenger door as Riley split away from her to walk around to the driver's side.

"And?" he prompted the instant he slid behind the wheel.

"And—I would be willing to bet he knows how the gun got in that bush." She buckled her seatbelt.

"In that case, let's keep our fingers crossed his conscience works on him and he ends up telling the police." He started the car and reversed it to head out the drive, then waited for the workmen to move out of the way.

"In the meantime, I want to find out where Rina Cole was Saturday night. We might as well start at her hotel."

"First we have to stop at the condo." Riley raised a hand in Vance's direction as they drove past him onto the winding street.

"What for?" Delaney frowned in sudden suspicion. "I'm going with you, Riley."

"I didn't think I'd be able to convince you to stay with your father," he said with a faint smile.

"Then why do we have to stop at the condo?"

"To change, so that when we ask our questions, we look official and intimidating." He skimmed her with a quick side glance. "The newspapers have been carrying that photograph of you with your hair down. Better wear it up."

An hour later they were back in the car, Riley in a dark business suit and an ultraconservative tie and Delaney in a crisply tailored navy suit with a shawl collar, her dark hair swept up in a french twist, and a pair of smoke-tinted sunglasses on her nose. They dropped her father off near the Jerome to explore his old haunts, promised to meet up with him later at the J-Bar, then went straight to Rina Cole's hotel at the very base of Aspen Mountain, mere yards from the high-speed gondola that whisked passengers to the top.

Riley walked directly to the registration desk. "We need to speak with your manager." He took a slim leather identification case from his wallet and flipped it open for the clerk. Taken by surprise, Delaney stared at the case, catching only a gleam of a badge and a glimpse of a very official-looking ID complete with a photograph.

The clerk took one look at it and backed away. "He's in his office. I'll get him for you."

"Thank you." He lowered the case, keeping a forefinger between the leather folds.

As soon as the young brunette was out of sight, Delaney murmured softly, not letting her lips move, "It's illegal to impersonate an officer, Riley."

"I'm legal," he assured her, his eyes twinkling as he turned the ID case toward her, opening it slightly and shifting his finger off the line that read Special Deputy, Los Angeles County. A title that was more honorary than official. Delaney nearly choked on a laugh.

"Don't knock it," Riley murmured. "It worked."

"You better hope the manager doesn't take a good look at it."

"He won't. People only get suspicious when you jerk it away," he replied and proceeded to demonstrate the technique when the manager came, flipping it open and holding it chest-high but tilted down, making it difficult to read. "We understand Rina Cole is staying with you. Is that correct?" he asked, at the same instant distracting the manager's attention from the ID.

"She is, yes," he replied somewhat hesitantly.

"How long has she been here?" Riley continued to hold it up.

"Approximately a week. I can look up the exact date of arrival if—"

"That won't be necessary." He waved aside the offer, using the gesture to slip the case back in his pocket. "We're interested in her whereabouts Saturday night."

"Shouldn't you be asking Miss Cole?"

"It's standard procedure to verify all information we receive. I'm sure you can appreciate that."

"Of course. Unfortunately I can't be of much help to you. I'm rarely here in the evenings—"

"Who is your night manager?"

Armed with his name and address, they went to the man's apartment and got him out of bed. Still groggy with sleep, he barely glanced at Riley's badge. Claiming he couldn't remember whether Rina Cole had gone out any night, let alone Saturday night, he directed them to the concierge on duty that evening, Todd Blackwell.

After two hours of chasing around Aspen, they finally tracked Todd Blackwell down at the tennis courts at the Aspen Club. Delaney stood behind the low chain wire fence and watched a sun-bronzed blond in tennis whites poised on the back line of the near court waiting for his opponent's serve. Tobacco smoke from Riley's cigarette drifted to her on the afternoon breeze, warm with summer's heat.

As she turned to ask Riley the score, the yellow ball streaked across the net. An ace. With a smiling shake of his head in defeat, the off-duty concierge, Todd Blackwell, jogged to the net to congratulate his opponent. The game was over.

When he came off the court, Riley and Delaney waited at the gate to intercept him. Riley immediately went through his routine, flashing the useless deputy's badge and asking his question about Rina Cole.

"Saturday night," Blackwell repeated, eyeing both of them curiously while he wiped the perspiration from his mouth with one end of the towel draped around his neck, his golden locks curling onto it in damp ringlets. "Do you think she had something to do with that St. Jacque woman getting killed at Lucas Wayne's place?"

"Should we?" Delaney countered, earning a glance of approval from Riley.

Caught off guard by it, the concierge hedged a little nervously. "Rina Cole hasn't exactly made a secret of the fact she'd like to see Wayne laid out in a satin-lined coffin."

"Have you personally heard Miss Cole make threats against Lucas Wayne or anyone else?"

"Personally—no. Why? Had she threatened somebody else?" he asked, then broke into a wide smile. "I get it now. You're Secret Service, aren't you? I saw you were government something-or-other, but it didn't connect. That rumor about the First Lady attending the literacy thing at the Institute must be true, then."

Riley deliberately didn't comment. "About Saturday, do you know if Miss Cole went out?"

"Yeah, she went out to dinner with this professor type, Dr. . . ." He snapped his fingers, trying to recall his name. "I remember he had two last names. Dr. Collins-something."

"Collins-Jones." Delaney supplied the name of the philosophy professor who had escorted Rina Cole to the cocktail reception on Friday.

"That's it. Dr. Collins-Jones." He nodded. "I remember he had dinner reservations for eight-thirty at Gordon's and I had to change them to nine o'clock because Rina—Miss Cole was late."

Riley picked up on that. "She was late?"

"That's right. The professor came to pick her up . . . it must have been around eight o'clock when he stopped at my desk to ask where the house phones were located. I told him. Then five or ten minutes later, he came back, said he had been trying Miss Cole's suite, but wasn't getting an answer. I had Housekeeping check and confirm she wasn't there. I figured she'd probably stood him up, but she came sailing into the hotel a few minutes late with a ton of packages from Smith's. She'd been shopping and lost track of time, I guess. Anyway, she went up to her suite to change and that's when I called Gordon's to switch their dinner reservations."

"Did the professor go up to the suite with her?" Riley asked.

"No."

"Not at any time?" she inserted.

"No. At least, I don't think so. I remember when I heard the police and ambulance sirens, I stepped outside to see what it was all about and the professor came out, too. About an hour later, I heard about the shooting."

"What time did Miss Cole come down?"

"A few minutes before nine," he said and grinned. "She really had the professor sweating that he might have to change the reservations again."

"You're sure their reservations were at Gordon's?" Riley asked, testing to see if he could get the concierge to doubt his facts.

"I'm positive. I remember thinking at the time that the professor would be happier at Abetone's. I mean, he doesn't exactly look like a scene-maker. More than likely, Miss Cole picked the restaurant."

"Do you remember what she wore to dinner?" Delaney ignored the puzzled look Riley directed at her.

"Are you kidding? Who could forget?" he declared with an exaggerated roll of his eyes. "She had on this black Spandex jumpsuit with a neckline down to her navel and a black-and-white-spotted pony vest with boots to match."

"When they left, did they go in his car, take a cab, or walk?" Riley asked.

"I couldn't say." Blackwell shrugged. "The doorman might know."

But the doorman didn't remember, and the parking attendant had no record of Rina Cole's car leaving the garage at any time on Saturday.

"As far as I'm concerned, we have established motive and opportunity," Delaney said over her shoulder as she pushed through the streetside entrance to the Jerome Bar. "Now all we have to do is figure out how she got from the hotel to the house and back."

"She could have walked," Riley pointed out above the drone of a drink blender.

"True." Greeted by a steady chatter of voices punctuated by laughter and the rattle of ice cubes, Delaney paused to scan the late-afternoon crowd in the bar, then spotted an upraised hand and the silver-white head below it in the old tearoom that adjoined the bar. "There's Dad."

She was nearly to the table before she saw Jared sitting with him. He had on a tie and a brown suit so dark in color it almost looked black. He'd been to Susan's funeral; she knew it without asking.

"Hello." She smiled, but he didn't smile back. When he started to stand up, she laid a hand on his shoulder to keep him in his chair and sat down in the one next to him. "This is nice. I didn't expect to see you here."

"I ran into your father." His eyes had a dark and brooding look, like storm clouds gathering on the horizon.

"I'm glad." She watched him nod to Riley, then lift his glass and take a slow sip of beer. The funeral, the long, silent ride to the cemetery, the graveside service—she could hardly expect him to be cheerful after all that.

Riley lit a cigarette and blew the smoke toward the ceiling. "Did you find some of your old haunts, Gordon?"

"I wish," her father grumbled, a touch of melancholy in his voice. "Aspen has changed as much as Hollywood has in the past forty years. About the only thing they haven't torn down, repainted, or remodeled are the mountains. I'm not sure I would have recognized this place if it wasn't for the tin ceiling and the back bar."

The waiter shoved a wicker basket mounded with popcorn on the table. Riley ordered draft beer and Delaney played it safe with a Virgin Mary.

"So, how was your day?" her father asked. "What were you able to find out about Rina?"

"We found out she was alone, allegedly in her suite changing clothes from approximately ten minutes after eight to a few minutes before nine. That's forty-five minutes, give or take. And our phone call to the police was logged in at eight-thirty-seven." Riley tapped his cigarette on the edge of the ashtray.

"And she was wearing a black Spandex jumpsuit when she came down." Using her finger, Delaney plucked a half-dozen kernels of popcorn from the fluffy white pile and dropped them in her palm. "What could be more ideal for her to wear? Black to blend in with the shadows. Snug-fitting to cut down the risk of a branch snagging it. Yet an outfit so basic, it can be dressed up with a loud vest and some flashy boots."

"Then you really think it's possible she might have snuck up there?" Her father scooted his chair closer to the table.

Riley nodded. "It fits her previous pattern." He was interrupted by the waiter returning with their drinks. When he moved to another table, Riley continued. "In her previous attempt at Lucas, it was at night as well. She managed to slip into a hotel unseen, then had a maid let her into the suite. It wasn't a spur-of-the-moment thing. I think she planned it—just as she possibly planned this one. Only this time, she tried to establish an alibi."

"The problem is"—Delaney nibbled on her popcorn—"we don't know how she got from the hotel to the house. According to the valet, her car never left the garage on Saturday."

"I still say she could have walked." Riley held the frosted beer mug half way to his mouth. "It can't be much more than two miles from the hotel to the house. Three at the outside."

"But look at how much of it is up," Delaney reasoned. "I don't think she would take the chance of getting all hot and sweaty. Besides, it would shorten the amount of time she would have at the house. She couldn't be sure Lucas would be outside."

"The windows aren't bulletproof," Riley reminded her.

"I still think she had some kind of transportation."

"The road up the mountain is too narrow and crooked; there's no place she could have parked a car," Riley argued.

"At the bottom. Then she would only have the walk up."

"But where did she get the car?"

"Maybe while she was doing all that shopping, she rented another one and left it parked a block or two away."

With a nod, Riley conceded that possibility. "We'll check the car rental agencies tomorrow."

"Why couldn't she have taken a cab?" her father asked.

"We'll check the cab company tomorrow."

"What if she wore a disguise like she did in New York?" Delaney chewed on popcorn that had become tasteless.

"We'll just have to check out every fare and every rental." Riley rolled the tip of his cigarette around the bottom of the ashtray.

"Right." Delaney dusted the popcorn salt from her hand, then stirred her drink with the leafy celery stalk sticking out of it. "Wait a minute." She sat up straighter. "What about a racing bike? You see them whizzing along everywhere. It would be easy to park and easy to hide.

The black Spandex jumpsuit, a helmet over her hair."

"Sounds good. We'll check that out first thing."

"No. First I think we should run some times—see how long it takes by car, then by foot to get from the hotel to the house and back." She glanced at Jared, realizing that he had said nothing during all this; instead he had sat moody and silent, studying his beer. "What do you think, Jared?"

He looked up from his beer. "Me? I thought you didn't do investigative work," he said in a flat and hard voice.

Behind the fine lines of tension in his expression, she detected anger and resentment. She felt herself bristle in response. Somehow she managed a calm, if somewhat stiff, "The situation—the circumstances—have changed that."

"All because you had to protect him." His mouth twisted in a humorless smile.

"It was my job." Delaney spoke more curtly than she had intended.

"Your job," Jared murmured and lifted his beer glass as if needing something to rid his mouth of a bad taste.

It was too much. Delaney felt everything start to snap.

A chair leg scraped the floor as Riley pushed back from the table. "I think I need to wash my hands. Which way's the men's room, Gordon?"

"It's downstairs," her father began as Riley stood up. "Hold on a second and I'll go with you."

Delaney barely gave them time to get clear of the table before she turned on Jared. "All right, Jared, out with it. Exactly what is this all about?"

"Isn't it obvious?" he snapped right back at her.

"Susan is dead, and you are being held responsible. And why? Because of some cheap actor. Because you felt you had to protect him." He lifted his glass again, muttering into it, "His life isn't worth one ounce of the hell you're going through."

She noticed a shaggy-haired man staring at them from the next table and carefully lowered her voice. "That isn't for me to judge. Or you."

"Be honest, Delaney. His death wouldn't be any great loss to mankind."

"I see," she murmured tightly and used the celery stalk to stab at the ice cubes in her drink. "Before I take on a client, I'm supposed to check first to see how important he is, what kind of contribution he makes to humanity, is that right? Or maybe I should simply eliminate all actors, singers, and comedians. Who cares if their lives are threatened, right? Or maybe I should quit this kind of work altogether. That's what you'd really like, isn't it?"

"Delaney, I'm worried about you. Dammit, I—"

"You're the Wescott woman, aren't you?" The shaggy-haired man in glasses stood by her chair. "I'm Lee Connors with the *Post*. Have you got a few minutes? I—"

"No." She snatched up her purse and rose to her feet. "I have an appointment."

When she tried to leave, the reporter stepped into her path. "I'll walk with you. That way we can talk—off the record, if you want."

Off the record—that was a laugh, but she didn't dare say it. Polite. She had to be polite and not show her anger or she'd find herself splashed all over the papers again. "I'm sorry. I really don't have time."

"Come on, I think you're getting a raw deal. I just want to get your story out there—"

"Sorry." Riley was there, shouldering the reporter out of the way. "Another time, buddy."

He whisked her out the side door, then straight to the street and the car.

"Thanks," she said when they pulled away from the curb.

"For rescuing you, or the reporter?" he asked with a teasing smile. "You looked like you wanted to haul off and hit him—or someone."

She knew he was referring to Jared. "I was tempted." But she didn't want to talk about her argument with Jared, aware it had been brewing for some time, possibly from the beginning. "Where's Dad?"

"Taking care of the check. He'll be along."

The shiny red Camaro turned into the condo's parking lot as Delaney climbed out of the car. She scanned the street, but there was no black pickup behind him. She should have been glad, but too much had been left unfinished.

The German shepherd was at the door to greet her when she walked in ahead of Riley. She gave the dog an absent pat and turned toward the kitchen. "I'm going to put on some coffee."

"Sounds good. I'll check in with Wyatt and see if the police found anything."

She heard Riley talking on the phone as she rinsed the old coffee from the pot. A key turned in the lock. A second later, her father walked in. He saw her at the sink, hesitated, then simply waved and continued into the living room. She set the glass pot back on its burner and carried the filter with the used coffee grounds to the wastebasket.

Riley stuck his head around the doorway. "Nothing

yet," he reported. "Wyatt said they've only covered about half of the area. They'll finish up tomorrow." There were two quick raps at the door. Ollie growled and Delaney stiffened, conscious of Riley's questioning look. "Are you here?" he asked, his eyes cool and quietly challenging.

Like her, he guessed it was Jared. "I'm here." She turned on her heel and walked back to the coffee maker.

Her hand trembled as she reached for a new filter, all her former tension coming back in a rush. She didn't look at Jared when he walked into the kitchen.

"I was out of line," he began.

"About as far as you can get." She shoved the paper filter into the holder, then started slamming through the cupboards looking for the can of coffee.

"I was worried about you. I was upset and angry. I know that isn't an excuse—"

"It certainly isn't," she snapped, more out of hurt than anger, although the anger was there. She found the coffee and poured two scoops into the filter.

"I'm sorry, Delaney. What else can I say?"

"If you try, maybe you'll think of something." She walked around him to the sink and turned the cold water on full force.

He shut it off. "Dammit, I'm not asking you to give up your work. I would never do that."

She turned on him. "No, but it's what you want me to do."

"I want *you*." He caught her arms, holding her in front of him as if he was afraid she'd walk away. "The things I said . . . it was wrong and I know it. But I'm not perfect, Delaney. That doesn't mean I don't love you."

Had she expected perfection? Had she expected

408 ~ JANET DAILEY

total support and understanding? She wasn't sure; she wasn't sure about anything. "I hate fighting," she murmured finally.

His hand stroked the neatly smoothed twist of her hair. "Then you are in the wrong business."

She jerked away from him. "I am in the *right* business for me."

"That was a joke."

She shook her head, troubled and angry. "I don't care for your sense of humor."

"You don't understand," Jared began. "Today at the funeral—when I saw the lilies Lucas sent—something snapped inside." He sighed. "It's hard to explain."

"That's obvious." But she could easily imagine the rage Jared must have felt—the rage of needless death, needless trouble, the quiet kind that had no ready outlet.

"Do you know that right now I want to hold you, to help you more than anything, but I can't," he challenged, a cynical twist to his mouth. "The news is out about Susan's will—which makes me the last person you should be seen with. And all because of him—her former lover."

"You can't blame everything on Lucas Wayne."

"Can't I?" he countered.

A fiery retort trembled on her lips. Delaney clamped them together for a quick four-count, then managed a curt, "Look, let's agree that we're both upset for different reasons and just leave it at that, shall we?"

"Delaney, I'm sorry—"

"You said that before, and I accept your apology. I can even accept that we have different points of view on this, but don't push for more than that right now, Jared."

He looked at her for a long beat of silence, then

released a heavy sigh. "You're right. I guess it would be bad timing. But I love you, Delaney, and I guess I'm irritated with all these complications that keep getting in the way, that keep me from showing you how very much I do love you. It's as though the fates are conspiring against us."

"I know what you mean." She nodded, her anger slowly dissolving.

Riley strolled into the kitchen, the German shepherd at his heels. "Have you got that coffee made yet?" His glance traveled between them, his sharp eyes gauging the tension.

"Not yet." Delaney turned back to the sink and filled the coffee pot with water, Riley's presence bringing a whole new set of undercurrents into the room.

Riley crossed to a cupboard and opened the door. Cups rattled as he took down a stack of three. He reached back in the shelf for more, then paused and glanced at Jared. "Are you having a cup?" he asked. "I should warn you, though, our coffee maker is notoriously slow. It's the kind that tantalizes you with aroma, then takes forever to deliver."

Jared hesitated, his glance resting on Delaney. Then he shook his head. "I'll pass. It's time I was getting back to the ranch. . . ." He waited a beat, as if to give Delaney a chance to object and urge him to stay. She saw the opening, but the words wouldn't come. They were trapped inside her, caught in a tangle of conflicting emotions. He laid a hand on her shoulder. "I'll talk to you in a day or two," he said and walked away.

"Take care," she said over her shoulder and turned off the water faucet.

The click of the apartment door closing competed

with the panting breaths of the German shepherd. Both sounded loud in the stillness. Delaney nudged the dog out of her way and poured the water into the coffee maker. Riley watched her, a hip leaned against the counter in a pose of nonchalance that didn't match the keenness of his steady gaze.

"Can I guess what you two were arguing about?"

"You mean you weren't listening?" She shot him a doubting look and slipped the glass pot onto the burner.

Riley pressed a hand to his chest, pretending to be shocked. "Do you think I would eavesdrop?"

"In a heartbeat," Delaney muttered, pushing past him to collect the clean cups and carry them over to the counter beside the coffee maker.

"Maybe I did overhear one or two snippets of conversation," he conceded, then paused, his eyes gentling in their inspection of her. "Do you want to talk about it? I can be a very good listener. If you want, you can even use my shoulder."

She turned, her glance drawn to the breadth of his shoulders, the solidity of them. She thought back to all the times she had leaned on him, all the times she had poured out her troubles to him.

"Thanks, but not this time." She didn't feel right about it, and she wasn't sure why.

"Have you fallen back in love with him, 'Laney?" His voice was quiet and very serious.

She had a lump in her throat. She didn't know where that came from either. "About halfway." She tried to smile, make light of her answer.

Riley straightened away from the counter, a look of disgust and irritation flashing in his eyes. "Love isn't a halfway thing, Delaney. It's all or nothing."

She was surprised by the sharpness of his tone and the anger that laced it. "I know that," she replied, bristling a little.

"Then which is it? You are either in love with him or not. There is no in-between."

"Maybe I don't know yet," she countered defensively.

He looked at her long and hard. "And maybe if you don't know by now, that means you're not."

"Maybe." She was suddenly uneasy with this whole subject.

"Sooner or later, you'll have to decide."

Delaney swung around to face the coffee pot. "Then it will have to be later. I have too many other problems to solve right now to spend my time thinking about that."

"Love isn't something you think about, Delaney. It's something you feel." Riley walked out of the kitchen, leaving her alone to think about that.

TWENTY-SIX

THE WORKMEN INSTALLING THE security gate were a welcome sight, almost as welcome as seeing Riley standing there waiting for her. Delaney pulled out of a painful jog and hobbled to meet him, favoring her left leg.

"What happened?"

"Leg cramp," she said and let him help her to the Lincoln parked in the driveway.

She lowered herself onto the front passenger seat, sitting sideways to leave her legs out. Riley squatted on his heels, one knee touching the pavement for balance while he rubbed at the cramped muscle in her calf.

"Rina couldn't have made it, not on foot," she said with a tired shake of her head, her ponytail swinging with the movement. "She would have been too exhausted when she got here. I am, and I'm in better condition than she is." Delaney grabbed a towel off the seat and used it to wipe the sweat from her face. "The bike has got to be the answer."

"You're probably right."

His kneading fingers found the sore area. Delaney winced. "That's it." As he continued to work on it, she glanced at the house and spotted a man perched on a ladder. "No bullets recovered yet," she guessed.

"Not yet." Riley sat back on his heels. "Better?"

She flexed her foot, testing the muscle. It was still tender, but the searing pain was gone. "Much better. Now all I need is a shower."

"Go ahead." Riley dug the car keys out of his pocket and tossed them onto her lap. "They're getting ready to test the remote on the gate. I want to make sure it's working properly. After you get cleaned up, you can come back and pick me up."

"You have a deal." She swung her legs into the car and started to slide across the seat to the driver's side.

"Your dad said something about going to the grocery store today. Ask him to buy me some cigarettes. I'm almost out." He fingered the pack in his shirt pocket.

"Will do."

But when she reached the condo, both her father and her dog were gone. She found a note propped against the telephone that read: "Father Hubbard has gone to the store to fill the cupboard. Ollie wants a bone!" That was it. No signature, no "Love, Dad." Smiling, Delaney headed for the bathroom, peeling off her clothes on the way.

An hour later, she was back in the car, her jogging clothes traded for a white silk blouse and navy slacks and a pair of tortoiseshell combs replacing the ponytail band to hold her freshly washed hair away from her face. The air conditioner was off and the windows down, letting in the breeze that smelled of pine and summer's heat.

As she made the turn onto Red Mountain Road, she spotted a heavyset man coming down the other side, traveling at a familiar head-down, scurrying walk, a ragged bouquet of flowers clutched tightly in his hands. Delaney slowed the car, a quick glance in the rearview mirror verifying there was no traffic behind her.

"Hey, Toby." She leaned her head out the window. "Where are you going?"

He darted a quick look at her, then tipped his head down again and checked his hurried pace. He chewed on his lower lip as if trying to decide what to do, and walked on several more steps before angling toward her car.

"It's okay for me to be out," he told her and ducked his head down again.

"Of course it is." She hadn't meant to imply that she thought he was doing something wrong. "Those are pretty flowers. Have you got a date with a girl?"

"No." He shook his head quickly at that.

Delaney touched a finger to a white daisy, finally putting two and two together. "You're going to put these flowers on her grave, aren't you?" she guessed, remembering the awkward questions he'd asked about flowers for dead people.

He nodded. "I picked them. Mr. Walker said it was okay. He said you didn't have to buy flowers."

"Mr. Walker is right. In fact, I think it's nicer to put flowers on a grave that you picked yourself."

"Yeah, well, I gotta go now." He backed away from the car, plainly anxious and uneasy.

"Do you know the way?"

"Yeah."

"Then climb in. I'll give you a ride."

"You don't have to. I can walk."

"I know I don't *have* to, Toby. I *want* to. It would make me feel good." Delaney added, "Let me give you a ride."

He hesitated, then nodded uncertainly. "Okay."

She watched while he walked around the car and climbed in the passenger side. When he had trouble fastening his seatbelt and holding onto the flowers, Delaney hooked it for him, then checked the mirror again for any cars behind her.

The road was clear in both directions. Taking advantage of it, she made a U-turn to head in the opposite direction. "I don't know the way to the cemetery, so you'll have to tell me where to turn, Toby."

"You gotta take that road." He let go of the flowers long enough to point to the street coming up on their left.

She slowed the car and turned onto the street, then glanced sideways at Toby. He sat forward, intent on the road, his hands tightly gripping the flowers he held between his knees.

"I'm glad you decided to put flowers on her grave even though she didn't like you very well," Delaney said when they crossed over Hunter Creek. "And I'm proud of you for coming up with the idea all on your own."

"I'm sorry she died."

"I know you are."

Farther on, Toby instructed her to turn left again, then almost immediately make another left onto a dirt road. Delaney frowned when she recognized the old mining road they had used for a jogging trail. She didn't remember any cemetery along here, not even an abandoned one. In fact, she didn't recall seeing any cemetery on the east side of town.

"Are you sure this is the right way, Toby?"

"I'm sure." A decisive nod accompanied his answer.

Yet Delaney saw that he was nervous as he leaned close to the dash, the seatbelt taut across his shoulder, his hands twisting at the flower stems, his tongue darting out to lick at his lips. Where was he taking her? All along she had assumed that the flowers were for Susan's grave. Now she realized Toby had never actually said that. But if not hers, then whose?

"Is it much farther?" The road narrowed, the trees closing in. The sunlight came through in broken patches, and the air was resinous and still.

"No."

"Do you come here often?" When he failed to answer, Delaney stole another glance at him. He was watching her out of the corner of his eye, a trapped, nervous look on his face. She knew he'd heard the question, but he was trying to ignore it. "Do you, Toby?"

"No," he said in a very small voice.

"Then it's good you remember so well," she replied a little brightly, trying to put him at ease. "People forget sometimes, but you didn't. I'm glad. I always liked—" She stopped and forced a short laugh. "Isn't that silly? I forgot her first name. What is it? I'll bet you can remember it."

His mouth remained tightly closed, his lips pressed together in a pouting line. He fixed his gaze on the road and refused to look at her.

"Come on, Toby. Tell me her name." Delaney used her best coaxing voice.

"You gotta stop here," he ordered instead.

"Why? Is this it?" She automatically slowed the car and shifted her foot to the brake pedal while she scanned the area.

On the left, almost hidden by undergrowth, a trail branched off the road—the same trail she had noticed when she jogged along this road with Lucas, speculating that it led to an abandoned silver mine. Distracted by it, she was late recognizing the click of the latch. When she turned, Toby was out of the car, scurrying around the back of it.

"Toby, wait." She threw the gearshift into park and switched off the engine, then fought briefly with the catch of her seatbelt. Free, she pushed her door open. "I'll go with you."

"No." He glowered at her, his big hands strangling the flowers, a slight tremor in them.

Delaney stayed by the door. "Please. I'm sorry she's dead, too."

"No, you can't come." Toby shook his head from side to side in agitation. "Nobody can come. Not nobody."

Faced with his adamancy, she hesitated. "All right, I won't go. I'll wait here for you."

"No. You gotta leave."

"But—don't you want a ride back?"

"No. You gotta go." He took a step toward her, angry and frightened, close to tears. "You gotta go now!"

Unable to judge how much she dared to push him, Delaney gave in. "Okay. I'll go." She climbed back into the car and started the engine.

Toby remained where he was, watching as if he didn't believe she would leave as she said. She felt a twinge of guilt, aware he was right not to trust her. She drove slowly away, keeping an eye on Toby's reflection in her rearview mirror. He never budged from his spot near the road's edge.

The old mine road made one of its curving twists, following the uneven contours of the mountains, and Toby was lost from sight. Delaney drove on another twenty yards, then stopped the car. She waited, silently counting off thirty seconds, then switched off the engine and stepped out, easing the door shut.

Moving as quickly and quietly as possible, she went back to the curve, staying close to the tangle of weeds and bushes along the roadside. Toby was nowhere to be seen.

How clever was he? she wondered. Had he taken that old trail? Or had he used it as a diversion and disappeared into the woods at any number of a dozen places? Was this even where he was going? Or had her questions frightened him into insisting she stop and let him out? There was only one way to find out. She broke into an easy run, backtracking to the spot where the old trail joined the dirt road.

The hard-packed ground gave no indication of the direction he had taken. She swept her glance over the forest of trees on both sides of the road on the off-chance she might catch a glimpse of his blue plaid shirt. Nothing. She elected to check the trail, aware that if Toby hadn't taken it, she had no hope of finding him.

The trail was overgrown with wild grasses, bushes, and saplings. Erosion had gouged deep ruts in it, in places washing it out altogether. Delaney hurried along it, running where she could, walking fast where she couldn't, the terrain's roughness forcing her to divide her attention between the ground at her feet and the trail ahead.

As she came around a sharp bend, suddenly there he was—not fifty yards ahead of her—his head down, scurrying along in that quick, leg-rubbing walk of his. Delaney ducked into the trees.

She stayed in the trees, moving deeper into the pines where the going was easier, keeping parallel to the trail and keeping Toby in sight as much as possible. Among the trees, the light was dim, almost holy, the air cool, smelling of damp and mold.

For more than a mile the trail wound its way into the mountains, following its creases and always climbing. Then it abruptly stopped at a ravine strewn with rubble and choked with weeds and brush. Cautiously, Delaney slipped closer.

She spotted the tumbledown ruins of a shack. The wood was rotted and broken, with columbine thrusting up through it. Pieces of machinery, reduced to rusted metal, lay among the rocks. A little farther up the ravine was an entrance to a mine all boarded up. A broken signboard hung drunkenly from a cross timber, its lettering faded. DOLLY-something was all that Delaney could make out.

Toby approached the mine slowly, almost reluctantly, then laid the flowers down in front of it and backed hurriedly away. He turned and immediately took off at a fast run-walk back down the trail, stumbling in his haste to get away.

Scrambling, Delaney managed to make it to the deep cover of the spruce before he saw her. Once there, she didn't slow down, finding her runner's stride and keeping it as she retraced her path and reached the road ahead of Toby.

When she got to the car, she looked in the glove

compartment, under the seats, and in the trunk. As a last resort, she pawed through the contents of her purse, but she had no flashlight. Without one, she would never discover what was in that mine. Frustrated, she started the car and drove back to the condo.

"Dad!" she called out when she let herself in.

When she didn't receive an answer, she went straight to the kitchen and slammed through the cupboards, looking for a flashlight. She found one in a bottom drawer. She flipped it on, making sure it worked, then snatched up two spare batteries. She headed for the door, then hesitated. Giving in to an innate sense of caution, Delaney went over to the worktable and scratched out a quick message: "Gone to explore the Dolly mine. If not back in two hours, come look for me.—D." She set it on top of the note her father had left.

A faint wind stirred through the brush, the sound a ghostly whisper in the mountain stillness. The sun was warm on her face as Delaney paused to survey the old mining site that the rugged land was fast reclaiming as its own. She lifted her gaze to the rock faces of the craggy peaks, sharply outlined against the backdrop of a flawlessly blue sky. They looked back at her indifferently.

She picked her way carefully over the loose rock of an old tailing and skirted the rusted wheels of an old ore cart, then climbed the slope to the entrance of the abandoned mine. The flowers waited for her, their petals drooping and curling, their stems crushed and mangled, their fragrance strong. Bending down, Delaney touched a wilted daisy.

"Who are they for, Toby?" she murmured absently. The answer had to be behind the sheet of corrugated tin that blocked the tunnel's entrance. A sign read DANGER—DO NOT ENTER. Ignoring it, Delaney located a broken tree branch and used it to pry back the stiff metal sheet and create an opening wide enough for her to pass through.

She flashed her light inside, running it over the jagged sides of the narrow tunnel and the scattering of loose rock on its floor, the beam showing her the endless blackness beyond. She took one last look at the sun and the sky, then ducked through the opening and hit her head on the low ceiling when she tried to stand up. She rubbed at the sore spot, recalling too late that people were a lot shorter 100 years ago when this tunnel was dug. It was only on movie sets that they were wide and high.

Crouching to avoid hitting her head again, Delaney took a cautious step forward, aiming her flashlight into the eerie darkness. Twin ribbons of rusted iron trailed back into the tunnel, the track used by ore carts. She stepped sideways to walk between the rails, then ventured forward into the primal damp of the tunnel and away from the sunlight and fresh air.

Moving slowly and cautiously, she followed the rusted tracks, using them to guide her, occasionally flashing her light over a rotting timber and trying not to think about the tons of rock above it. Beyond the reach of her flashlight came sounds of something scurrying to safety. A mouse? A rat? She ignored it. The association from rats to cats was too easy to make, and from cats to what killed them.

"What are you doing here, Delaney?" she murmured to herself. "This is crazy. What do you care why Toby put flowers at the entrance?" The jagged walls gleamed with reflected light from her flashlight, here and there the gouge left by a pickax clearly visible. "If you *had* to do this, why didn't you get Riley? That would have been the smart thing to do."

She stopped and flashed her light back toward the entrance, a rectangle of bright light that seemed very far away. By now, Riley would be wondering what had happened to her. Maybe he had called and found out from her father about the note she left. If she were really smart, she would go back and wait for him.

She aimed the beam back into the narrow tunnel and used its light to search what was ahead. She would go just a little farther, then go back and wait for Riley.

Ducking her head to avoid a sagging beam, Delaney moved on. She heard the faint, slow drip of water coming from somewhere ahead of her. She paused a moment to listen, recalling the things Jared had told her about the silver mines, the tunnels, shafts, drifts, air shafts, cave-ins, and floodings. She picked up a rock and lobbed it into the darkness beyond her flashlight. It clattered noisily over more rock. She pressed on. The powerful beam of her flashlight made a puny dent in the blackness.

Three steps farther along, Delaney saw a tumble of rocks blocking the tunnel. Stopping, she used the flashlight to inspect the cave-in from a safe distance. The wall on the right had collapsed. Not completely, though. Darkness gaped beyond the sloping pile of rock on the right. The ore-cart tracks were covered, but a foot of room remained on the left.

Cautiously, she inched closer and ran the light over the cross-timber supporting the ceiling. It looked solid. She tried to see what was beyond the rubble. The shaft to the mine's various levels had to be somewhere. Was it on the other side of the small cave-in? She couldn't tell.

Delaney crouched beside the pile of rock and pushed aside the larger ones, searching for a small one to throw. She saw something white and froze.

For a long second, she didn't move. Then, slowly, she laid the flashlight on the tunnel's cold floor, keeping the beam aimed at that fragment of white. She started lifting aside the larger chunks of rock, careful not to dislodge the rest of the pile. As she moved the last one, the full skeletal bones of a hand were revealed.

She turned her head from the sight, fighting back a wave of nausea, simultaneously realizing how much she had wanted to be wrong about the reason Toby had left flowers outside. She dragged in a deep breath and steeled herself to turn back. Resting her weight on her knees, Delaney moved more of the rock, exposing part of the right arm's radius and ulna bones. When she rolled aside another rock, there was the left hand.

A gold ring circled the bone of the ring finger. Delaney picked up the flashlight and shined it on the ring. It was a class ring. She bent closer. The initials on the side read K.M. Stunned, Delaney sat back on her heels, never hearing the soft, protesting cry that came from her throat.

Behind her a stone clanked against the rusted rail of the track. She swiveled around and immediately threw up a hand to block the blinding light aimed directly at her eyes, protesting instantly, "Don't. I can't see."

The light was directed away from her face, but she continued to see the white glare of it that had burned itself onto her retina. She blinked in a vain attempt to get rid of the white spots.

"You found her." That voice—it didn't belong to

Riley. "Why, Delaney? Why did you have to come look? Why couldn't you have left well enough alone?"

"Lucas." She breathed his name in shock as her eyes gradually began to work again, allowing her to make out the shape of him, his tall body hunched by the low ceiling. He came closer, the backglow of his flashlight reflecting on the planes and hollows of his face, showing its tortured look of regret. She felt a sudden, low sweep of anger. "It's Kelly McCallister buried under these rocks, isn't it?"

"It was an accident. You have to believe that, Delaney. Toby didn't mean to kill her—"

"Toby," she repeated in surprise, then saw the gun Lucas carried, and experienced the first sense of danger. She knew she had to keep her head. She had to keep him talking. "What kind of accident? What happened?"

"It was her fault," Lucas insisted. "If she hadn't come charging into the house—Susan and I were upstairs, you see. Toby was in the old parlor watching television. She started yelling at Toby. When I came down to find out what was going on, she grabbed a fireplace shovel and started hitting me with it, screaming at me to get out of her house, accusing me of ruining her brother's marriage. Somewhere, Toby found the gun Susan kept for protection."

In town. The old Victorian house on the West End, the one Susan had gotten from Jared in their divorce settlement, the one she lived in—and the one Toby had run from in terror the evening they walked back from the concert at the Music Tent. Now it was easy to guess the reason. Toby had been afraid of it.

"Toby wanted her to stop hitting me. That's why he shot her. To protect me." His voice wavered. "He didn't mean to kill her. He didn't even know what he'd done. A week before, I had taken him to the dress rehearsal for a play I was in. It was a small part. My character was killed in the opening scene. Toby got upset and rushed on stage thinking I was really dead. I showed him the prop gun, the fake blood. That night . . . he couldn't understand why Kelly didn't get up." His hand tightened its grip on the gun, his knuckles showing white in the light of the flashlight. "Don't you see? It was all a horrible mistake. An accident. She was ·dead. There wasn't anything I could do. I couldn't call the police. They would have taken one look at Toby and put him back in an institution. I couldn't let that happen to him. It wouldn't have been right. It wouldn't have been fair."

"That's when you decided to hide her body in this abandoned silver mine?" Delaney remembered the night of the shooting, the way Toby had stared at Susan's body and asked Lucas if he had to touch her—and other times when he had expressed his abhorrence of dead things.

"The mine was Susan's idea. I wanted to dump the body in the woods, but she was afraid some hunter or cross-country skier might find it and the police would start asking questions." He stopped, expelling a harsh laugh. "God, she had a devious mind. She had plans for herself, and she didn't want any murder scandal ruining them. She came up with the idea of making it look like Kelly had run away. She went out to the ranch and got all of Kelly's clothes and things, then met us on the old mining road. After that, we hauled everything back here."

Delaney altered her position slightly, angling her body more directly toward him, trying to be casual about it, covering the movement by asking, "What about the locket? How did it end up in that pawnshop in L.A.?"

"Luck," Lucas replied with a smile. "I stayed around Aspen only a couple weeks after Kelly 'ran away,' then split for L.A. When I was unloading my things from the car, I found the locket in the trunk. I took the pictures out and burned them, then paid a girl five dollars to hock it for me. When the investigator Jared hired finally located it, everybody was convinced she was another runaway. It worked. It all worked."

"Until Susan started blackmailing you over this."

"She was never satisfied, no matter how much she got. She was bleeding me dry," he said angrily. "We had to stop her."

"We?"

He hesitated, as if regretting his words. "I had to tell Arthur. She was making demands I couldn't meet. I didn't know where else to turn. I couldn't go to the police. Arthur thought of you."

"And Rina?" She had to grit her teeth to hold back the rage she felt.

"Rina turned out to be a godsend. Suddenly we didn't have to invent an imaginary stalking fan." He paused and looked genuinely contrite. "I'm truly sorry we used you like that, Delaney. You have to believe that."

"You knew all along it was Susan, didn't you? You knew she was coming over. That's why you wanted to go out on the deck, isn't it? It was all a setup to get me to shoot her. And I fell for it." She felt raw, every nerve screaming. "I suppose it was Arthur who fired that first shot. The gun you have—is that the one he used?"

"No. His was loaded with blanks." His mouth twisted in a rueful line. "We had it all worked out, even to the point of sabotaging your radio. Then it all started going wrong. Arthur was supposed to get there first so he could put the gun near Susan's body, but your men reacted too fast. He had to hide again before they saw him. When he got there, it was too late."

"So you waited until the next day to plant the gun?"

"You weren't supposed to get arrested. It was supposed to look like self-defense."

"What happens now, Lucas?" She shifted more of her weight to her feet, aware that she had to get that gun away from him before he used it on her.

"I wish I could believe you would walk away from here and forget what you've seen. For Toby's sake, not mine. But you won't, will you? Dammit, why did you have to tell Toby about putting flowers on people's graves? Why did you have to give him a ride? Why couldn't you have stayed out of this?"

"It's no use, Lucas—" She heard the screeching protest of the corrugated tin at the mine's entrance.

"Delaney! Are you in there?"

Distracted by Jared's shouts, Lucas turned toward the entrance, giving Delaney the opening she had been waiting for. She lunged for his gun hand. As her hands closed on his wrist, his fingers automatically tightened their grip on the weapon, squeezing the trigger. The tunnel reverberated with the loud clap of the shot, the bullet ricocheting off the rocks in an angry whine.

Using her forced impetus, Delaney slammed his hand against the rough wall, knocking the gun loose. As it went clattering off into the darkness, she rammed an elbow into his face. He staggered sideways from the blow. With a quick twist, she jerked his arm behind his back and forced him against the wall, face-first. Only then did the sound of Jared's running footsteps finally register.

"Delaney, are you all right?"

"Yes." She was breathing hard, partly from exertion and partly from the swift flow of adrenaline. She saw the flashlight on the floor and gave it a kick toward Jared. "His gun is over there somewhere. Get it for me."

He picked up the flashlight and shined the beam over the floor. "I found it."

"Thanks." She held out her hand for it, not taking her eyes from Lucas. Jared pressed the gun into it. "How did you know I was here?"

"I stopped by the condo to see you. Your dad showed me the note you left." He raised the light to Lucas's face. "What's going on? What's he doing here?"

She hesitated, then stalled. "It's a long story." She loosened her grip on Lucas. "Don't move until I tell you, Lucas," she warned. "I think by now I've proved I not only can use this, but I will." She released him and stepped back. "Okay, turn around. Slowly."

Lucas did as he was told, cautiously flexing the arm she had wrenched behind his back. "I wouldn't have hurt you, Delaney. I swear."

"Save it," she snapped. "We're going to walk out of here, and you are going first."

Jared pushed the flashlight into her left hand. "Take this," he said as her fingers automatically closed around it. "I'll get the other one."

A second later it hit her that he meant the one she had left next to Kelly's remains. "Jared, no, don't go over there!"

"Why—somebody's buried under these rocks."

"I know." There was no gentle way to tell him, so she said it bluntly. "It's Kelly."

He was behind her, making it impossible for Delaney to see his face, but the silence from him was deafening.

She moved sideways a foot to bring him into her side vision, keeping the gun trained on Lucas.

Jared was kneeling beside his sister's bones, his hat shadowing his face and the grief that contorted it. She wanted to go to him, comfort him. But she couldn't leave Lucas unguarded. She moaned in her throat, wishing it had been Riley or her father who had come to find her—anyone but Jared.

He lifted his head. "You killed her. You bastard, you killed her!" He sprang at Lucas, shooting past her before she could react to stop him. The two men tumbled to the floor, Jared's hands seeking and finding his throat.

"Jared, no." Delaney made one futile attempt to pull him off, then swung the flashlight, clipping him alongside the head, stunning him just enough to enable Lucas to throw him. Immediately she stepped from between them, ignoring choking coughs for air from Lucas.

Dazed, Jared pressed a hand to his head and looked at her, the rage that came from intense grief still in his eyes. "How the hell can you protect him? He killed Kelly. He killed my sister!"

"No—"

Lucas broke in before she could say more. "It was an accident." There was a hoarse edge to his voice. "She found out I was seeing your wife. She came over—she had a gun. I tried to get it away from her. We struggled and . . . it went off."

Delaney stared at him, then realized what he was doing. The actor was rehearsing a confession scene, perfecting his delivery, adding the emotional touches where they would be the most convincing. He had to get it right before he performed it for the police. His life depended on it. And more important to Lucas, Toby's life depended on it.

Something blocked the light at the entrance. Then Riley's voice called out, "Delaney, is that you?"

"Yes. I need help."

Riley wasn't alone. Wyatt was with him. When they reached her, Riley glanced at Wyatt. "I guess we can stop looking for Lucas," he said, then explained to Delaney, "I called the condo to let you know he had pulled a disappearing act on us. Your father told me where to find you." He arced his flashlight at Jared sitting next to the pile of rock, his hat dangling from his hands. Then he saw the remains. "Better get the police, Wyatt."

"Right." He headed back to the entrance at a crouching run.

"What happened?"

Delaney gave Riley the gun. "It's Jared's sister."

He swore a soft and succinct, "Damn," then waved Lucas toward the entrance.

She turned to Jared. "Are you coming?"

He shook his head, the sheen of tears on his cheeks. "I'm staying with Kelly. I can't leave her here by herself."

"I'll stay with you."

"No." His voice became thick. "I want to be alone with her."

She hesitated, then reluctantly gave him his private time to grieve, and turned to follow Riley.

Twenty minutes later, the police drove up in a four-wheel-drive vehicle and the questioning began. Delaney kept her answers brief and left the elaboration to Lucas Wayne. It wasn't a conscious decision; it was merely the way it happened.

From a distance, she watched an officer take a Miranda card from his pocket and read Lucas his rights. Then he fastened handcuffs to his wrists.

She knew Lucas had given a convincing performance. She wasn't surprised. She remembered how completely he had convinced her that the threat from Rina Cole had him living on the edge of his nerves—convinced her to the extent that she had lived that way, too.

"It looks like we're out of a job," Riley commented when Lucas was led to the patrol vehicle.

"He manipulated me into killing Susan. He used me, Riley," she murmured. "He turned me into a weapon. He had me primed, loaded, and cocked. In a way, he even pulled the trigger."

"It hurts, doesn't it?" he said quietly. "But pain is usually the source of wisdom. I don't know why."

A stir of activity at the mine's entrance had Delaney turning to identify the cause. They were bringing Kelly's remains out. Jared stepped into the mountain's shadow, emerging from the mine for the first time since he went in. He paused and pushed his hat back on his head, then started down the slope.

Delaney hesitated, then went to meet him. He saw her coming and stopped. His eyes were red-rimmed but dry, the pain washed into them instead of out of them. He faced her, not so much looking at her as through her.

"Jared, I want you to know I wasn't protecting Lucas. I was protecting you," she said. "I couldn't let you kill him."

He considered her words for a long second, then nodded and walked away.

TWENTY-SEVEN

$\mathcal{D}$ENSE CLOUDS HUNG LOW, concealing the peaks of the Elk Mountain range. Delaney stood at a window in the airport terminal and watched the fall of a gentle rain. A tank truck loaded with jet fuel lumbered past, its windshield wiper rhythmically sweeping back and forth, its tires splashing through the shallow puddles on the airport's tarmac.

A newspaper was pushed in front of her face, jolting her into noticing that Riley had joined her. "I thought you might be interested in this little item."

She took the Entertainment section of *USA Today* from him. It was folded open to a celebrities-in-brief kind of gossip column. She glanced at the paragraph he had indicated, half-expecting to see a mention of the charge against her being dropped. Instead she read that Rina Cole had married Dr. Timothy Collins-Jones the previous day at a wedding chapel in Las Vegas.

"Interesting," she murmured and gave it back to him.

Riley glanced at it again, shaking his head. "The sexpot and the scholar—talk about a marriage made in Hollywood."

Unable to smile at his wry observation, Delaney leaned down and picked up her overnight bag. "Are you ready to go through security?"

Riley checked his watch. "Our flight won't be boarding for another twenty minutes yet."

"I know, but we can find a seat in the gate area."

"You seem to be in an awfully big hurry to leave Aspen. It's almost as though you're trying to run away from something."

"That's nonsense."

"Is it?" he countered dryly, annoyingly sure of himself. "Have you talked to Jared since his sister's body was found?"

"No." She lifted her chin a little higher.

"Why not?" He arched an eyebrow in silent challenge.

"There never seemed to be a good time."

"Then everything is still hanging between you? Nothing has been settled?"

"Like I said, there was never a good time."

"So you're just going to walk away, with none of your ghosts from the past put to rest?" A thinning patience showed around his mouth, narrowing its line.

"That's precisely what I'm going to do." Pivoting, Delaney headed toward the security screen.

Riley fell in step with her, murmuring out of the corner of his mouth, "I gave you credit for being smarter than that, Delaney."

"Let's drop the subject, Riley," she said, curt with him as she dumped her purse and overnight bag on the X-ray machine's conveyor belt.

In silence, they went through security and proceeded to the gate. Few other passengers were in the waiting area, leaving plenty of empty seats available. Delaney chose the closest one. Riley snapped the newspaper open to an article on lung cancer while Delaney flipped open her notebook to begin making a list of the things she needed to do when she got back to Los Angeles. But she couldn't seem to make her mind focus on the task.

Riley touched her arm and nodded. "A good time or not, there's no time like the present."

She looked up and saw Jared enter the gate area, his hands shoved deep inside the pockets of his denim jacket. He looked tired and drawn—and angry. Delaney put her notebook away and rose to meet him, tightly clutching the shoulder strap of her purse.

"I stopped by your condo." Jared's gaze bored into her. "They told me you had left for the airport. You were going to leave without saying goodbye, weren't you?"

"It seemed best."

"Why? Do you think I'm still upset because you pulled me off Lucas Wayne?"

"No."

"Then why are you leaving like this?"

"Because I don't see how it could ever work between us," she said in all candor and heard the rustling of a newspaper as Riley turned a page.

"Just like that?" Jared argued. "You decided it won't work without ever talking to me?"

The boarding call for her flight came over the public

address system. Riley stood up, folded the newspaper, and tucked it under his arm before he walked over to them and handed Delaney her flight coupon and boarding pass. "I'll be on the plane," he told her and nodded to Jared, then joined the line of passengers at the door.

"How can you leave like this?" Jared demanded again. "I love you and I thought you loved me."

"Be honest, Jared." Delaney struggled against the heaviness she felt. "You hate my work. More specifically, you despise the people I am paid to protect. Even if I moved my offices to Aspen and worked out of here, that wouldn't change."

His expression hardened. "What you are really saying is that your work is more important."

"No, it isn't more important. But it is a part of me— a part of who and what I am. I enjoy it. I enjoy the satisfaction it gives me. But I can't talk to you about it. I can't complain about the bad days or brag about the good ones. Every time I try, I end up defending what I do or the clients my company protects."

"I could learn to accept it," Jared insisted, his eyes pained.

"You would try," she said gently, aware that the prejudices of a lifetime weren't so easily discarded. Especially not for Jared when the circumstances surrounding Kelly's death were still so fresh in his mind. Delaney realized that even if she told Jared about Toby's role in it, he would still regard Lucas Wayne as being ultimately responsible.

"Dammit, I love you, Delaney," he declared, his voice thick with emotion.

In that instant, everything crystallized. Suddenly she saw the truth.

"Do you, Jared?" she wondered. "I don't think so. I think you are in love with who you want me to be."

"That isn't true."

"Isn't it? If you were really in love with me, my work wouldn't come between us the way it does. I'm not saying you would love it, but you would take pride in my accomplishments, celebrate my victories, and stand beside me when things go wrong. But you can't do that."

"You're wrong. I love you—"

"You *want* to love me," Delaney said, and recognized a second truth. "And I wanted to love you. For a while, I even convinced myself I did. I was wrong. We were both wrong." She lifted a hand, wanting to touch him, then let it fall back. "I'm sorry, Jared."

She turned and walked to the passenger door. When she stopped to hand the flight attendant her boarding pass, she glanced back and saw Jared striding angrily away. As she walked onto the plane, Delaney felt incredibly free, and incredibly alive for the first time in years.

Riley sat in a window seat, his head turned to look out. When she swung her overnight bag onto the floor in front of the aisle seat, he turned with a startled look. Then a slow smile spread across his face.

"You dumped him," he guessed, his eyes glinting with satisfaction.

"No, I finally recognized it was all an illusion. Smoke and mirrors with no substance." She sat down and buckled her seatbelt, using her feet to shove the overnight bag under the seat in front of her.

"I'm glad to hear it," Riley said. "That means you're free to marry me."

"Right," she mocked, certain he was joking.

"Don't laugh. I'm serious," he informed her calmly.

"In case you don't know it, there are two kinds of love. The most popular is the instant, fire-and-flames kind, with rockets going off and bells ringing. But there's another kind of love, one that sneaks up on you. One day you turn around and there it is—strong and deep and true."

Delaney stared at him. "You're crazy."

Riley smiled. "Crazy in love with you. I have been for years."

His gaze locked with hers, a warm steady light shining from the depths of his eyes. To Delaney's absolute and utter amazement, she felt her pulse quicken.

Dear Readers,

It has been more than fifteen years since I last wrote
about the Calder family. When I finished *Calder Born,
Calder Bred*, I felt that the saga was complete, that the
story had been told. It made me a little sad, because, after
having written four books, I loved the characters so
much. Then I started getting letters from readers, all asking the same question: "Why don't you write a fifth
Calder novel?" When readers ask you to write about
something, you have to consider it seriously, and I did. I
found myself excited by the prospect—why *not* revisit the
family, find out what happens to the next generation?

The Calders hold a special place in my heart. As soon as I
picked up my pen, I was back in Montana, back at the
Triple C Ranch, and it was if I had never left. I hope you
enjoy reading this chapter from my upcoming novel
Calder Pride. I enjoyed writing it.

> With love,
> Janet Dailey

Here is an excerpt from
New York Times bestselling author
JANET DAILEY'S next novel,

Calder Pride

Coming soon from HarperCollins*Publishers*

PART ONE

*Living is never easy
When someone you love has died,
And you have nothing to fall back on
But that iron Calder pride.*

$\mathcal{A}$ north breeze swept across the private airstrip and rustled through the grass at its edges. It was Calder grass, growing on Calder land and stretching in all directions farther than the living eye could see.

Directly southwest of the airstrip stood the head-quarters of Montana's famed Triple C Ranch, the home of the Calder Cattle Company. For well over a hundred years, the land had tasted the sweat, the blood, and the tears of the Calders.

Too many tears, Chase Calder decided and leaned heavily on his cane. For a moment, his big shoulders bowed under the weight of the thing that hung so heavily on him. But there was no one around to see this brief display of weakness by the Calder family patriarch. He stood alone outside the airstrip's metal hangar.

The drone of a twin-engine aircraft had Chase Calder squaring his shoulders and lifting his gaze to the immense blue sky overhead. His sharp eyes quickly spotted the plane making a straight-in approach to the landing strip. His son Ty was at the controls, and his daughter Cathleen was the plane's only other occupant.

The plane touched down and rolled toward him. Chase

glanced at the heavens, the ache intensifying in his chest.

"Where am I going to find the words, Maggie?" he murmured, talking as he so often did to his late wife.

But there were no words that could dull the pain of the news he carried. Just as there had been none to blunt the knife-stabbing pain he'd felt five years ago when he learned his wife Maggie had died in the plane crash that had so severely injured him.

Chase shifted more of his weight onto the cane, his expression grim as he watched the twin-engine plane taxi to a stop near the hangar. Within seconds of the engines' being shut down, the plane's rear door opened and out stepped his twenty-year-old daughter, Cathleen.

His eyes softened at the sight of her. In many ways, Cat, as the family called her, was the image of his late wife, with her glistening black hair and eyes that were as green as the Calder grass in spring. It was a striking combination, made even more stunning by the mingling of fineness and strength in her face.

Simply dressed in navy slacks and a white silk blouse, Cat came toward him with quick, confident strides. Chase glanced briefly at his son when Ty emerged from the plane, experiencing a familiar surge of pride for this tall and broad-shouldered man of thirty-five who bore the unmistakable stamp of a Calder in every hard-boned line.

But it was Cat who concerned him now, this full-grown woman who was his little girl. Chase straightened to stand squarely on both feet, abandoning his reliance on the cane, needing to be strong for her.

With a smile on her lips that was positively radiant, Cat ran the last few steps and wrapped her arms around him, hugging him tightly. He held her close, reminded again of his daughter's tremendous capacity for emotion, a capacity that could swing to the extremes of laughter, softness, and anger.

"It is so good to be home again, Dad," she declared on a fervent note, then pulled back to arm's length, her green eyes sparkling with happiness. "Where's Jessy?" She glanced beyond him, then tossed a teasing smile over her shoulder when Ty walked up. "Don't tell me Ty's bride-to-be is off somewhere chasing cattle?"

"She's at the house." Chase saw the startled lift of Ty's head and the sudden sharpening of his gaze as he caught the faint scent of trouble in the air.

Cat was oblivious to it. "Wait until you see the sexy nightgown I bought Jessy for her wedding night, Dad. On second thought, maybe you shouldn't." She stepped closer and studiously straightened the collar of his shirt, slanting him a look packed with feminine wiles. "At least, not until I talk you into making this a double wedding. It's ridiculous that Repp and I should wait to get married until after I finish college. That's—"

"Cat." He gripped her wrists to still the movement of her hands, his cane hooked over his arm. She looked up, surprised by the hard tone of his voice. "I have bad news."

"Bad news?" Her eyes made a quick search of his face. "Don't tell me Tara decided to contest the divorce from Ty at the last minute? It's supposed to be final—"

"No, it isn't that. The divorce is final," Chase said. "It's Repp. There was an accident late last night—"

"Dear God, no," she murmured, her eyes widening in alarm. "Is he badly hurt? Where is he? I have to go to him."

She tried to pull free of his hands, but Chase tightened his hold even as Ty gripped her shoulders from behind, bracing her for the rest.

"It's too late, Cat," Chase stated in a firm voice. "Repp was killed instantly."

She stared at him for a long, brittle second, her expression awash with shock, pain, and denial. "It can't be true," she said, in the thinnest of whispers. "It can't be."

"I'm sorry." There were no other words Chase could say.

"No." She said it over and over, her voice growing in strength and volume until she was screaming it. Chase gathered her rigid body into his arms and silently absorbed the pounding of her fists on his chest, waiting through the rage until she finally sagged against him and broke into wild, body-wrenching sobs.

"I'll bring the truck around," Ty said quietly, and Chase nodded.

By the time the luggage was transferred from the plane to the ranch pickup, that first violent shock of grief had subsided, leaving Cat numb with pain. She felt wooden, unable to move on her own, and offered no protest when two pairs of hands helped her into the cab.

She sat between the two men, her head lolling against the seat back, her eyes closed against the horrible ache that moaned through her. Some part of her knew that all the tears in the world wouldn't lessen it. But she didn't bother to wipe away the ones on her pale cheeks.

"How did it happen?" Ty asked.

At his question, her impulse was to cover her ears and shut out her father's reply. A few years ago, a younger Cat would have done that. But she was older now, and wise enough to know that denial was foolish. It changed nothing. So she opened her eyes and listened to her father's answer.

"Neil Anderson's youngest boy Rollie was driving

on the wrong side of the road. The tire tracks indicate Repp swerved to avoid a head-on, but Anderson's pickup plowed into the driver's side."

"And Rollie?" Ty asked.

"He had a gash to his forehead." The grimness in her father's voice was tangible.

"He'd been drinking, then," Ty muttered in a tone that matched her father's.

"His blood alcohol level was way over the limit. He passed out at the scene."

With a strangled sound of protest, Cat swallowed back a sob. It lodged in her throat until it hurt to breathe. Beside her, Ty muttered a choice expletive and fell silent.

A breeze tunneled through the pickup's opened window, carrying the bawl of a young calf and the fresh scents of spring to her, of life reborn. She wanted to scream at the sounds and the smells, at the sunshine that washed the land, but no sound came from her.

The warmth and roughness of her father's hand settled over hers. In his touch there was both comfort and strength. The urge was strong to turn into his arms and cry more tears. But it wasn't what he would have done. Calder men never made a display of their grief; it was something they held inside. Only the very discerning saw the pain that lurked in their eyes.

Never once had she seen her father break down after her mother died, Cat recalled. For the longest time she believed that he had resisted it because to do otherwise would have been a sign of weakness. Now she understood that the pain and grief were too personal, too intimate, reaching beyond anyone else's understanding.

So she wrapped her own pain deep inside and remained motionless, accepting the comforting weight of her father's hand but seeking nothing more.

The pickup truck pulled up in front of the massive two-story house that four generations of Calders had called home. Long known as simply The Homestead, it stood on a knoll overlooking the cluster of buildings that made up the Triple C headquarters. It was built on a large scale, a silent statement of dominion over the vast, rolling plains that sprawled in all directions.

Through tear-blurred eyes, Cat saw her brother's soon-to-be bride, Jessy Niles, waiting on the front porch. Slim-hipped and long-legged in her typical dress of boots, blue jeans, and white cotton shirt, she had been raised on the Triple C. Her roots went deep into the soil. From the first day the ranch had come into existence, a Niles had worked on it. It was a claim that could be made by several other families, including Repp Taylor and his parents.

Repp. A fresh wave of anguish ripped through Cat at the thought of never seeing him again, of never feeling his arms around her. He had been her first love, her only love. Now he was gone forever, leaving Cat with a gaping emptiness in her life she didn't think she could endure. But of course she would. That's what made it so painful.

"Cat." There was a tug on her hand, followed by her father's gently insistent voice. "Come on. Let's go in the house now."

His hand was at her elbow when Cat stepped from the cab. Jessy came to greet them, her attention centering on Cat, but not before her glance had run to Ty in a quick, warm look of love and relief that he had safely returned to her. Then her hazel eyes were on Cat, direct as always and full of compassion.

Jessy offered no trite words of comfort, but simply curved a hand on Cat's shoulder. "The Taylors send you their sympathies."

"You have seen his parents?" she asked, only now giving a thought to the enormity of their loss.

"I stayed with them for a while this morning."

Cat looked in the direction of their house. "I need to go see them."

"Later," her father stated.

Some distant part of her acknowledged that she was in no fit state to see them now. Without protest, Cat submitted to the guiding pressure of the hand that directed her toward the house. She never noticed when Jessy swung in behind to walk with Ty, each slipping an arm around the other, needing the reassurance of contact, with death striking so close.

It was a quiet group that entered the big house and walked directly to the sprawling living room. Chase paused beside his favorite armchair, his hand falling away from Cat's arm.

"I think we could all use some coffee." He leaned his cane against the chair.

"I'll get it." Jessy took a step toward the kitchen, then hesitated when Cat continued toward the oak staircase.

Chase noticed her movement as well. "Cat?" A look of concern darkened his eyes.

"I'm going to my room." Her voice was flat, drained of all emotion.

As one they watched as she climbed the stairs, holding herself stiffly erect. Her pale cheeks glistened with the wetness of earlier tears, but her eyes were dry now.

When she was nearly to the top, Ty murmured to Jessy, "Maybe you should go with her."

Jessy shook her head. "No. I think she would rather be alone right now."

Jessy sensed Ty's disagreement and understood its cause. For too long he had regarded his sister as head-strong and impetuous, on the irresponsible side, and more than a little spoiled by an adoring and indulgent father. He didn't realize that in addition to his mother's beauty and capacity for sudden fury, Cat had also inher-ited a good deal of Calder steel and that unbendable iron pride of a Calder. And—like a Calder—she wanted to grieve in private.

"I'll check on her later," Chase said firmly, settling the matter.

The sound of an upstairs door closing broke the stillness that had held all three of them motionless. Chase lowered himself into the armchair while Jessy left to bring coffee. Sweeping off his hat, Ty dropped it on an end table and sank onto the couch.

"What about Rollie Anderson?" he asked. "Has he been arrested?"

"I was told charges would be filed as soon as he is sober enough to understand them." A thread of anger edged the clipped reply. It was still there when his father continued, "I understand he has three previous drunk-driving convictions. With a manslaughter charge, it's vir-tually guaranteed he'll serve time."

"That will make things rough on Neil Anderson and his wife," Ty remarked idly. "Anderson is too old and too crippled with arthritis to keep the place going without help. And they can't afford to pay a hired hand."

The Andersons owned a small farm along the eastern

boundary of the Triple C. Most of the time they had barely eked out a living. Rollie Anderson was the youngest of three sons, and the only one still living at home.

"If Anderson is smart, he'll sell the place and retire," Chase stated as Jessy returned to the living room with the coffee.

"Who should retire?" She set a mug of steaming coffee on the table next to Chase.

"Neil Anderson," Ty answered. "We were just saying it would be best if he sold his farm."

"I wouldn't count on that happening any time soon. That farm means as much to Neil Anderson as the Triple C does to you." As always, Jessy spoke with a man's directness. "He will hang onto it until his last dying breath."

"I have no doubt he will try," Chase agreed as Jessy handed a mug to Ty, then sat on the couch next to him, their legs touching.

"Which brings me to something else I wanted to talk to you about, Ty." Her hand slid onto his knee in easy possession. "Under the circumstances, I think we should postpone our wedding until next week."

"What do you mean—postpone it? Why?" Ty challenged her.

"Because I don't think it would be right for us to get married so soon after Repp's funeral."

"It wouldn't be right if we were having some lavish wedding with acres of guests, but it's only going to be your family and mi—" Ty broke off in midword. "Cat," he said in understanding. "From the moment I picked her up at the airport in Helena, she was full of plans to turn our wedding into a double ceremony." He covered Jessy's hand with his. "You're right. We'll wait a week, but no longer than that."

452 ~ JANET DAILEY

"No longer." Her slow smile of agreement tunneled into him, touching all the soft places. Ty never ceased to be amazed by the warm ease he felt with Jessy, an ease that produced its own kind of heady glow. This was love, strong, steady, and certain.

Looking back, he knew now that he had never truly loved Tara, his first wife. He had been so dazzled by her dark beauty, he had mistaken infatuation for love and completely ignored the fact that they shared neither the same values nor the same loyalties—until Jessy opened his eyes.

"Later, I want to run into Blue Moon and take a look at the pickup," Chase said. "According to the highway patrol, it was totaled."

"I'll go with you," Ty said, then something—some movement, some whisper of sound, pulled his glance to the side hall that ultimately led to the rear of the house.

A lanky, dark-eyed man with metal-gray hair stood in the hall's shadows two steps back from the arched opening to the living room. Culley O'Rourke had a coyote's stealth, always somewhere around but rarely showing himself. And when he did, he was always silent, like now.

"Hello, Culley." Although the man was his mother's brother, Ty had never felt comfortable enough with Culley to address him as his uncle. He still remembered when Culley's hatred toward the Calders had been all-consuming. Even now, after twenty years, it made him wary of trusting Culley too much.

"I heard the plane." Culley fingered the brim of the battered hat in his hands, his sharp gaze darting between the two men. "Where is Cat? Didn't she come home with you?"

"Yes. She's upstairs in her room." Whatever personal doubts he had about Culley O'Rourke, Ty never doubted that he adored Cat as much as he had once adored Ty's mother.

"I'd like to see her." He looked directly at Chase.

"I don't know if you heard that Repp was—"

Culley cut in before the sentence was finished. "I heard about the boy dying. I'd like to see Cat," he repeated.

"Go ahead." Chase granted the request.

Without another word, Culley crossed the room on silent feet, skirting the area where they sat and heading straight for the oak staircase. No one had to tell him the location of Cat's room, even though he'd been in the house no more than a dozen times in his life.

He had long ago figured out which of the bedrooms belonged to Cat, and spent many a night watching for a light to shine from its window. He didn't take lightly the vow he had made at the foot of Maggie's grave to look after her daughter and keep her safe from harm.

Unerringly he stopped outside her bedroom, hesitated, then rapped lightly on it and waited. But no sound came from inside. Concern for the girl who was his sister's image overrode any further hesitation. He gave the doorknob a turn, found it wasn't locked and opened it far enough to slip inside.

The bedroom was bright and young-girl feminine with floral-patterned wallpaper in tones of mauve, pink, and green. But Culley didn't notice it or the wide ruffles that ringed its old-fashioned vanity table. His gaze went straight to the dark-haired woman standing at the window. She was motionless, her arms hugging her elbows and her face in profile, her gaze fixed in a sightless stare at the world outside.

He studied her for a long minute, seeing again the strong resemblance to his sister and recalling the time their father had been killed. Maggie's face had been just as deathly pale as Cat's was now, and her green eyes had burned with the same bottomless pain that no amount of tears could ease.

Culley had thought she was unaware of his presence. Then Cat spoke. "Repp is dead. Did they tell you?" she asked in a voice completely devoid of emotion.

"I knew." Culley walked over to her. He longed to hold her and ease some of her suffering. But he had lived too many years without that kind of contact. Made self-conscious by the sudden wish to offer it now, he kept his hands at his side. "You're hurtin' bad, but in time, it'll get better. I swear it will, Cat."

Time. Cat almost laughed at him, but she didn't. There would have been too much bitterness in the sound, and she knew her uncle had offered the empty platitude out of a sincere desire to console her. She nodded and kept silent.

"I wish there was something I could do," he said after a moment.

She caught the note of anguish in his voice. "Thank you, but there is nothing anyone can do."

As she continued to gaze out the window, she noticed a movement below. Focusing on it, she saw her father and Ty walking to the ranch pickup. They climbed into the cab, with Ty sliding behind the wheel. A moment later, the vehicle reversed away from the house. Cat half expected to see the truck head either toward the barns or toward the Taylor house. Instead it swung onto the road that led to the east gate.

"I wonder where they're going." She frowned.

"Who?" Culley stepped closer to the window.

"Dad and Ty."

He spotted the pickup traveling down the east road. "Probably headed for town. They were talking about seeing how bad the truck was wrecked."

Culley had already seen it. Knowing that Cat was coming home, he had slipped into town early that morning to pick up some chocolate doughnuts and brownies to have on hand in case she came to see him. He had just pulled up to Fedderson's convenience store when the tow truck arrived with the wrecked pickup. His sharp eyes had instantly spotted the Triple C brand stenciled on the vehicle's passenger door. One look at the rest of the smashed and mangled cab told him no one could have survived the crash.

For a fleeting moment, he had thought Chase Calder might finally be dead. Although he was no longer gripped by hatred for the man, Culley would have felt no regret at his passing, only sorrow for the grief it would have caused Cat. But he had quickly learned Repp Taylor had been behind the wheel, the man Cat loved—something Culley had never quite understood, believing as he did that she deserved better.

"The pickup was totaled," he told Cat. "Ain't nothin' left of the cab but a bunch of twisted steel and crumpled metal." A low, horrible moan came from her as she wheeled from the window, eyes tightly closed against the grisly image. Culley realized what he'd done and hurried to rectify it. "It had to have killed him outright, Cat, without ever feeling nothing, without even knowing what hit him. You've got to think of it that way."

"I wish I couldn't think at all." Her voice was little more than a thready whisper.

He lifted a hand to comfort her, then let it fall back to his side, uncertain what to do or what to say. He turned and looked out the window at the dust plume left in the wake of the departing ranch pickup.